THE 23RD HERO

REBECCA ANNE NGUYEN

CASTLE BRIDGE MEDIA
DENVER, COLORADO, USA

CASTLE BRIDGE MEDIA
Denver, Colorado

Cover photo by Rayyân/Unsplash
This photo has been modified.

This book is a work of fiction. Names, characters, business, events, and incidents are the products of the author's imagination. Any resemblance to actual persons, living or dead or actual events is purely coincidental.

THE 23rd HERO
©2024 Rebecca Anne Nguyen
All rights reserved.

ISBN: 979-8-9895934-1-5

Praise for *The 23rd Hero*

Praise for *The 23rd Hero*

"A love story that transcends time with a hero the reader will never forget. This compulsively-readable debut will transport you from a dystopian future to the idyll of 16th century France, all on the wings of a love story for the ages. Nguyen's razor-sharp humor, gorgeous prose, and lush world-building had me turning the pages late into the night. A writer to watch."
— Jessica Pearce Rotondi, author of *What We Inherit: A Secret War and a Family's Search for Answers*

"*The 23rd Hero* is a thrilling, escapist ride through time, an old-fashioned romance, a modern parable about climate change, and, most importantly, the story of a woman finding her purpose. This is a delightful page-turner by an exciting new voice in fiction. Do yourself a favor and get lost in this story; you'll return feeling a little more hopeful about everything."
— Mandy Berman, author of *The Learning Curve* and *Perennials*

"The passion Rebecca Anne Nguyen captures between the two [lovers] is equaled by the challenge to their psyches…as the story evolves. Readers who look for intriguing time travel settings will find the tale steeped in unusual connections. The result will appeal to both romance readers and time-travel enthusiasts…with satisfyingly original dilemmas and outcomes."
— D. Donovan, *Midwest Book Review*

For Julia Cameron and Diana Gabaldon

"O here love, O love right here.
Find your happiness, dear wayfarer,
With your beautiful lips and body
So sweetly opened,
Yielding their vital gifts upon
This magnificent
Earth."
— Daniel Ladinsky
The Subject Tonight Is Love: 60 Wild and Sweet Poems of Hafiz

"We are born of love; Love is our mother."
— Jalal ad-Din Muhammad Rumi

PART 1

SLOANE BURROWS WAS CYCLING UP traffic-clogged New Street, swerving around electric cars and self-driving trams as she followed the GPS inside her filtration mask. The sky was tinged a concerning shade of umber, the air tinny and sour through her mask, and the frequent rain showers in this part of town always carried the faint zest of nitrates. Still, she felt relieved to have gotten a gig on the south side of the harbor. Especially when she took a hard right and pedaled away from Stanley Park, turning her back to the depressing view of the Lions Gate bridge. She remembered how she used to look for the bridge through a screen of towering hemlocks, and how the hue of the sweeping green arch so closely matched the color of the trees that the city's two most iconic fixtures seemed to become one; it was as if humanity was in perfect harmony with nature. Twenty years later, Sloane was no longer a child, and the bridge was no longer hidden. Painfully visible against the yellow-brown sky, it was the only thing in Vancouver that was still green.

When she reached Application Booth 439, Sloane hopped off her government-issued bicycle, inserted it into the nearest docking station, and pushed her way through the masked crowd, holding her Boothie badge above her head. Her boss, Brody, was always talking about the link between crowd control and confidence, but Sloane kept her eyes on the ground, overcome with the feeling of making her way down a gauntlet. If only she could fix the Program application booths without having to interact with the people who used them. The booths were quiet. The booths never complained. They'd always reminded Sloane of old-fashioned phone booths, except they were bright blue and just about everywhere—next to the self-checkout in vegan groceries, inside the terminals of high-speed train stations, and on pretty much every street corner throughout every inhabited area in the world. The Program had recently used a drone to deliver an application booth to a village in Far Western Nepal, which up until last week had been the last remaining area of human habitation without a booth within twenty kilometers. Some people thought it was overkill, all the booths, but Sloane thought it showed how committed the Program was to finding the planet's next Hero no matter where they came from, whether they were a yogi living in a remote Himalayan cave or an environmental engineer from San Francisco. (Okay, so most Heroes were environmental engineers from San Francisco, or Copenhagen, or Tokyo. But the 2nd Hero had been an organic farmer from Wisconsin who prevented the discovery of DDT. And the 7th Hero was an auto mechanic from Ireland who convinced Henry Ford to invent an electric Model-T. So technically, the Program could choose anyone to be a Hero, as long as that person could effectively carry out their Mission once they traveled back in time.)

As Sloane moved through the crowd, most people rolled their identical bicycles to the side to let her pass, but a few told Sloane exactly how long they'd been waiting, and one guy reminded her that his tax dollars paid her salary.

"How long's it gonna be?"

Sloane looked up to find the man at the front of the line frowning at her through his Full Face filtration mask. She resisted the urge to roll her eyes— those Full Face masks were three times the price of the government-issued masks, and the built-in VR wasn't any better. The only difference was the Full Face mask was made of clear, recycled polycarbonate so other people could see your entire face instead of just your eyes. Not that this guy's entire face was bad to look at, but still. If Sloane had that kind of money, she'd spend it on one of those $10,000 Bernese Mountain dogs. She couldn't fit a mountain dog inside her studio apartment, but every time she saw one, it reminded her of her childhood timeline. There had been lots of dogs back then. Dogs and seagulls. Babies, even. But who was she kidding. If Sloane ever had extra money, she'd have to give it straight to her father, Harry; no matter how many times a Hero made the timeline change, the debt she owed Harry stayed the same.

"Last time this happened, the Boothie said he'd be done in three minutes," said the man in the Full Face mask. "And when I rode past three hours later, he was still there."

Sloane swallowed a sigh of exasperation and used her handheld to calculate how long the fix would take her. Usually, she was in and out of the booths in less than five minutes, completing the same rote tasks at every booth she serviced: run diagnostics on the software, empty the DNA samples from their respective compartments (blood and hair samples only—absolutely no semen!), secure the samples in her temperature-controlled cooler, and deliver the DNA to the nearest Program drop site. From there, drones would pick up the samples and deliver them to Basecamp, the Program's headquarters, for processing. But this booth did not require routine maintenance. It appeared to have something wrong with its operating system, which might actually be an interesting problem to solve—the kind of problem Sloane could be solving every day at some sexy Hidden Valley tech company, if only she'd been born into one of those families where the parents actually wanted their children to succeed. Full Face was actually right—something complex like troubleshooting a buggy OS would take the average Boothie hours to complete. But the average Boothie did not remember every word of every book she'd ever read, including the thick tomes she'd consumed at-a-glance while earning her Bachelors in TechnoEngineering. The average Boothie couldn't summon any moment from her training and play it back like a movie in her mind. The average Boothie couldn't recall with perfect clarity every character she'd ever read in the programming language of every operating system she'd ever encountered, and the average Boothie couldn't troubleshoot an error 98.3% faster than any of her peers.

"Give me seven minutes," said Sloane, scanning her badge to open the door to the booth.

"Can you make it three?" asked Full Face.

Sloane turned to him, grateful the look on her face was hidden behind her mask. "I'll see what I can do."

"It's just that I have to get across the Lions Gate before they close it," he said.

"Who said they're closing the bridge?"

Harry's sixtieth birthday was tonight, and it was impossible to reach Sloane's childhood home without crossing that bridge. If Harry would just move to the south side of the harbor, closer to Sloane and her twin brother, Simon, she could avoid the panic attacks that threatened every time she cycled over the bridge and reached the sixty-meter-high crest. She'd picture herself flying off the bridge into the churning, toxic waters of the Burrard Inlet, her body floating among the corpses of Chinook salmon, the City fishing her out with a giant net to be converted to zero-carbon fuel, a fate only slightly less distressing than missing her dad's party. There was no avoiding it, though. If she wanted to reach Harry, there was always some sort of toll.

"The seawall's closing, too," said Full Face. "They're forecasting a king tide."

"The 17th Hero fixed that," said Sloane. "There haven't been king tides in the Burrard Inlet in over five years."

"I thought the 19th Hero stopped the king tides."

"Seventeenth," she said. "The last king tide was during the storm surge that happened five years ago. It was Wednesday, March 16, at 4:57 p.m." Full Face's eyes widened behind his mask. His look of surprise, along with the way her stomach just turned, were both warning signs that she had gone too far, said too much. "I just mean once a Hero fixes something, it stays fixed," she said.

"They make Boothies memorize the outcomes of the Hero Missions?"

"Sure," said Sloane. "I mean, no. No, not every outcome—"

"My cousin's a Boothie, and he never had to memorize—"

"Hey, everyone?" said Sloane, clapping her hands. "Everyone! If you're in a hurry, the booth two blocks down is fully functioning."

The crowd began to disperse. Relieved, Sloane stepped inside the booth, slung her cooler onto the cushioned bench beneath the touchscreen, and rummaged for the half-eaten baguette she kept to quell her frequent nausea. Whenever she failed to hide what Harry liked to call her "freak memory," (wherever someone noticed, and in noticing, felt obliged to make some comment, which was always some version of 'Who the hell remembers something like that?'), the sickness would surge, only growing in intensity the more they probed, the closer they got to the truth: Boothies didn't have to memorize anything except their username and password. It was Sloane who had everything memorized because Sloane remembered everything. Sloane remembered the precise moment of the last king tide the same way she remembered every moment of her entire life—in crystalline detail, from where she'd been and what she'd been doing to what she'd been thinking and remembering at the time, her mind like a funhouse mirror, memories within memories without end. If she focused hard, she could keep the memories contained in the back of her mind. But if she was especially tired or got a little too drunk, every past reality could converge on the present moment like too many holograms projected onto the same spot—a dizzying phenomenon for which sleep was the only respite. Her memory made her sick. Her memory made her avoid application booths she had serviced in the past because the memories of past fixes would distract her from the present problem, muddying her focus. Her memory made her feel different from everyone around her, as if she were an alien. Or a robot. Or someone with a disease so rare, she'd never met anyone else who had it. It was better for everyone, but especially for Sloane's stomach, if she ignored her freak memory as best she could and pretended it didn't exist.

She heard a *thwack*, and she flinched. Full Face's hand was splayed against the booth wall to block the door from closing. Sloane lifted the front of her filtration mask and stuffed the baguette into her mouth before he could say something else about her memory and send the contents of her stomach spilling onto her sneakers; she knew from experience that vomiting in an application booth was the most humiliating place a person could vomit, except maybe an airplane. But hardly anyone was flying on those anymore.

Full Face hesitated, watching Sloane chew. Something about her face seemed to surprise him, as if he'd only seen her eyes through her mask and was now stunned to learn she had a nose and mouth, too. "I can't go to the booth down the street," said Full Face. "By the time I cycle two blocks, wait for the trams to stop, cross the street, and wait in the lineup, the bridge will be closed.

Plus you'll be long gone, and I'll have no way of getting your number."

"My Boothie number?"

"Your personal number."

Sloane swallowed the bread, her cheeks darkening. "Seven minutes," she said, scanning her badge to force the door shut. "Watch your hand."

Sloane pulled her mask all the way off and set it on the cooler. She closed her eyes and took slow, deep breaths, filling her lungs with the purified air as it passed through the booth's filtration system. With each exhale, her nausea dissolved, along with the impulse to give Full Face her number. She knew he wasn't actually interested in her—he was just flirting so she'd fix the booth faster. But it was tempting to give him what he wanted just to see the look on his face, because technically, she *could* fix the booth in under three minutes. If she wanted to. If she wasn't convinced that she'd give him her number and he'd never call, or that he'd call, but she'd find a way to ruin things. Besides, placating a Program applicant—even a handsome Program applicant like Full Face—was nowhere near as satisfying as playing out the fantasy of becoming an applicant herself.

Sloane set the booth timer to seven minutes—three minutes to fix the booth, four minutes to indulge in the guilty pleasure no one else knew about. Instead of keying in her Boothie number, she entered an old passcode she remembered from training. The passcode opened a test environment that simulated a civilian's experience in an application booth. In her seven years of service, her boss, Brody, had never bothered changing it.

"Ready to get started?" asked the AI.

"Ready," said Sloane.

The booth flashed and went dark. Pop. Snap. Whooooosh. The flickering images of a burning forest grew brighter. Sloane watched the fires spread across Europe until the continent was swallowed by flame. The footage of the fires gave way to rising seas and catastrophic flooding across Asia, followed by Alaskan heat waves, North American famine, and global infertility. "Ten years ago, the climate crises facing our planet were so extreme, the scientific community considered them insurmountable," said a female voice. "For some, our situation led to hopelessness and despair. For others, it revealed untapped reserves of human ingenuity." The disaster footage dissolved, and two life-sized figures materialized in the booth. Sloane recognized Matt Williams, the planet's 1st Hero, standing next to then-President Winfrey during the first-ever Hero ceremony a decade ago. "Today, our progress in reversing climate change has exceeded our wildest expectations." Sloane turned in a slow circle, watching the holograms diverge and converge in hyper-lapse speed—rising ocean levels receding to reveal forgotten Florida beaches; a thick mass of smog dissolving over Beijing; Brazilian cattle ranches overgrown with reforested rubber trees. "Eighty-nine percent of North Americans support the continued funding of the Program. Seventy-nine percent of the global population has applied to the Program at least once. Sixty-seven percent of worldwide job growth over the past decade can be attributed to the Program. Since the first Hero went back in time, there's been a forty-nine percent increase in reforestation in the Amazon, a thirty-seven percent reduction in air pollution worldwide, and a twenty-seven percent increase in global birth rates."

The Program updated this video whenever a new Hero went back in time. During her career as a Boothie, Sloane had watched some version of the video 597 times. She knew it was dumb. Brody would say she was driving down his efficiency metrics, and it's not like she needed to re-watch footage that was already lodged in her memory for all time. But watching in the booth while standing inside the holograms thrilled Sloane in a way her memories couldn't; inside the booth, it was easier to pretend that the Hero on the podium next to the president was her.

As the holograms morphed into weepy parents holding their miracle babies, the voiceover touted the Program's patented advances in Climate Reversal Technology, which had contributed to ten thousand births globally over the past twelve months. "While these numbers do not guarantee the future of our species, we exist at the crossroads of possibility. Climate Reversal Technology has prolonged the survival of the human race and Planet Earth, one Hero and one Mission at a time. The Program is working tirelessly to build a more robust solution capable of sending teams of Heroes back in time to accomplish more complex Missions more frequently. Until we reach that urgent goal, we rely on individuals like you who are willing to sacrifice everything for the good of us all. Now, more than ever, humanity needs you—"

"To be a Hero," said Sloane.

The holograms dissolved and the touchscreen blinked blue, inviting Sloane to START A NEW APPLICATION. She took a deep breath, pushed all the indomitable reasons not to apply from her mind, and imagined what it would feel like to be a civilian applying to be a Hero for the twenty-third time.

Name: Sloane Sophea Burrows. Age: 29. Address: 1 Crappy Studio Apartment Way, Vancouver, British Colombia, the United Nations of North America (UNNA). Occupation: Boothie. Also, night and weekend barista at a hipster analog coffee shop on West Cordova. (actual coffee beans, very expensive). Also, indentured servant to the student loan debt she owed Harry for covering her university tuition, a cost that had skyrocketed after Canada merged with the United States and tuition assistance and scholarships were universally abolished, and which she expected to pay off sometime in the 23rd century. Race/Ethnicity: Mixed race white and Southeast Asian, Cambodian Khmer on her mother's side. Biological sex: Female. Gender: Cisgender woman. Sexual orientation: (select one).

Sloane hesitated over the list of choices. She opened the Frequently Asked Questions, of which she had many when it came to sexual orientation, not to mention sex. Like if you're a woman attracted to men, but it's been 913 days since you've had sex with one, are you still considered heterosexual? Or, if you're a woman attracted to a man you've never actually met in real life, which option should you select from the dropdown?

Marital status: Never married. Children: You have to have sex to have children, and even then, getting pregnant would be a hair shy of impossible given the current toxicity levels. Immediate family: Twin sister to Simon Burrows. Daughter of Harry Burrows (yes, that Harry Burrows, AKA Dr. Harry Burrows, AKA Harry Burrows, Ph.D., Ph.D., Ph.D., the world's preeminent scholar on Cambodian history). Mother: Deceased. Number of previous applications to the Program: Zero.

Oops, responded the system. *Are you sure that's right?*

Sloane confirmed her response. From the moment the 1st Hero had accomplished his Mission to eighteenth century England, Sloane had felt a sharp, insistent yearning to follow in his footsteps. And yet besides her

Boothie colleagues, she was one of the only people she knew who had never applied to become a Hero herself. Not once. Not even when the urge to apply was really strong. Boothies were subcontractors for the Program and were barred from applying because it was a conflict of interest, which was precisely why Sloane had taken the job. During her senior year of university, she'd been recruited by half a dozen Hidden Valley tech companies, but she'd turned them all down to take an entry-level Boothie position that didn't even require a degree. Far from a dream job, it was a dream-prevention job; a job that made becoming a Hero impossible, which was the only kind of job Harry would approve of. She'd learned to shove the yearning to be a Hero into the back of her mind where she stuffed her least favorite memories. It was only during stolen moments alone in a booth that she dared admit the desire was still there. Only then could she bear to take it out, to look at it, to marvel at the way it continued to flourish in the face of her neglect, how it had the audacity to exist without caring what anyone thought, not even Harry.

"How we coming in there, Boothie?" asked Full Face, rapping on the door.

Sloane glanced at the booth timer—04:47 left. "Be out soon," she said.

Terms and conditions came next. Did Sloane understand that by applying to the Program, she'd be competing against millions of applicants per cycle and the chances of being selected were less than .0000167%? Y/N. Did she understand that if selected to become a Candidate, she would undergo a Candidate Assessment, competing against four other Candidates for the chance to become the world's next Hero? Y/N. Did she agree that if she was selected as a Candidate but not chosen as the Hero, she would be compensated with a one-time payment of $10 million NASD, payable by lump sum or installment? Y/N. Did she understand and agree that, upon being selected as the next Hero, she would relocate to Basecamp, the Program's secret headquarters, to train for her Mission? Did she agree that, if selected as the next Hero, she would give up her life in the present and travel to the past, unaccompanied by family, friends, personal possessions, or pets, never to return to this timeline? Did she understand that if she was chosen to be a Hero, a beneficiary of her choice would receive financial compensation for the remainder of their natural life as restitution for her sacrifice? Who would she like to designate as the beneficiary on her life insurance policy should she be chosen as Hero? Sloane entered her dad's name on the policy and imagined paying him back for her university tuition in one fell swoop. Even better (and even more fantastical), she imagined Harry graciously accepting the money even though he didn't approve of the way she'd gotten it.

Now the system wanted her DNA. Sloane moved the selector from "blood" to "hair." She reached up and twirled a single strand around her finger, plucked it out, winced. Simon had been aghast when she'd copped to pulling out a strand at every booth she fixed, as if going through the motions might trick the universe into letting her apply to the Program for real. Simon was just jealous because his hair was already thinning on top while Sloane had plenty to spare, her waves and spirals only growing wilder as she reached her late twenties. They'd always reminded Sloane of a brain, as if her head couldn't contain all the memories it was carrying around and they'd spilled out of her scalp as hair. She stuffed the rogue strand into her sweatshirt pocket as a precaution. You never knew if the Program had developed some secret technology to identify the DNA in strands of hair left in the wastebasket or something. It was a gazillion-to-one chance, but if they found her hair and chose her as a Candidate, Harry would never speak to her again.

Sloane confirmed her DNA submission on the touchscreen, triggering the final step in the simulated application process: an optional personal statement that the applicant could submit by recording themselves in 4K, syncing pre-recorded audio, or typing into a text field. The prompt consisted of a single question: WHY DO YOU WANT TO BE A HERO?

Sloane closed her eyes. The booth's platinum silicone walls dulled the sounds of the humming trams and thumping car stereos from outside, enveloping her in near-perfect silence. She inhaled the purified air, holding it in her lungs as long as she dared. Her memory stirred, looking for correlations between the present and past, latching onto the last time Sloane had experienced silence in the foreground, traffic in the background, fresh air in her lungs. A memory rushed forth from the deep recesses of her mind, taking shape in her mind's eye the way every memory did—as if it were happening again right now.

She is seven years old, and her grandmother, her *Yeay*, is taking Sloane and Simon on a picnic in Stanley Park, which isn't a park so much as an urban rainforest on a verdant peninsula edged with sandy beaches and steep, wet rockface. They head north into the center of the park, where downtown traffic and the churn of the sea are almost entirely muted. There, Yeay and the twins stand absolutely still, imitating the trees that surround them. Yeay says the trees are kindred spirits to Sloane because they remember everything, too. If the trees remember, reasons Sloane, why not everything in the natural world? Trees remember, rocks remember, sand remembers, water remembers. Just like her, the Earth remembers everything.

The memory faded from Sloane's mind just as the trees had faded from the city. But she and the Earth were still kindred spirits; they were the ones who remembered how things used to be before everything fell apart.

I want to be a Hero so I can bring back Stanley Park.

The booth timer dinged thirty seconds. Shit. She ran a script to wipe all her personal data from the simulated application flow, which felt a lot like scratching off the winning lottery number then ripping up the ticket. When she tried to code a fix for the issue with the OS, she found Brody had blocked her access to the system. A notification from him blinked on her handheld. "Why u in test mode 6+ minutes – do ur job maybe?" She submitted a request for five more minutes, but Brody subtracted four minutes before approving it, and Sloane cursed under her breath. She started writing a script to speed up the debugging process, trying to think up an excuse for logging in to the test environment and declining so many service requests. Brody didn't know she was avoiding repeat booths because of her memory. He didn't know she secretly wanted to be a Hero. He just knew that when Sloane Burrows worked, she usually worked fast, driving up service speed averages for the whole department. Maybe if she reminded him of that, he'd let this tiny hiccup slide.

Fifty seconds later, the OS was operational again. With her mask in place and her cooler full of other people's DNA, Sloane opened the door to find Full Face with his fist in the air, about to knock again. Behind him, pale evening sunlight had broken through the smog, altering the color of the water from a disturbing cerulean to a subtler slate gray, a shade that stopped Sloane's breath. She knew that color. She was intimately familiar with a certain someone whose eyes were that exact shade of gray. Calling him her boyfriend seemed too casual, but it was hard to convince herself he was her lover or her partner when they'd never met in real life. They'd never talked about what they were, either, but it didn't matter. She knew he was hers. And it was a quick mental leap from the color of his eyes to the way he looked at her, as if there were no one else in the world he'd rather see.

"Earth to Boothie," said Full Face, snapping his fingers.

Sloane mumbled an apology, and when she glanced his way, his expression softened. "That's okay," he said. "What are you doing in there, applying yourself?"

Sloane blushed and pushed past him, heading for the bicycle docking station.

"Hey!" he called after her. "Hold up. The screen's still frozen."

Sloane spun around, frowning.

"It took you eight minutes," he said when she joined him in the booth. "And it looks like you just made things worse."

"It's not frozen," she said, peering at the touchscreen. "That's an alert state. It only happens when they're about to—"

A siren started wailing in the street, and an artificial voice blasted through the speakers that were embedded into streetlights, storefronts, and trams. "Citizens!" it said. "Proceed to the nearest SafeSpot® immediately."

"It happens when they're about to make a Program announcement," said Sloane.

"Jesus," said Full Face. "There's been, like, ten announcements in the past three weeks."

"There's been seven in the past three weeks," said Sloane. "And a hundred and sixty-seven announcements since the last Hero...never mind."

Full Face stared at her, and a geyser of stomach acid shot up Sloane's esophagus. Why couldn't she keep her stupid mouth shut?

"Seriously, how do you remember this stuff, like how many announcements there's been?"

"I don't..."

"I thought Boothies were just contractors for the Program," he said. "But you must actually work for them. Special Booth Ops or something."

"Nope," she said. "I just…um…"

"Citizens!" said the voice. Two trams stopped abruptly on the street in front of them, air brakes squeaking and puffing. Groups of pedestrians scattered onto the sidewalks and gathered around booths, leaving their bicycles in the street. "Proceed to the nearest SafeSpot®. Be sure your masks are powered on, charged, and connected to the network." Traffic had come to a standstill. Floating timers hovered in the air beneath stoplights and streetlights, counting down from thirty seconds. Sloane's handheld buzzed in her pocket.

BRODY NOAH: *Be ready for overtime depending k*

SIMON BURROWS: *Where u at? U safe? $50 we're going under.*

Sloane typed *yep* and sent it to both of them.

"You gonna watch it here?" asked Full Face, as if there were some alternative. "Wanna watch it together?"

The President of the United Nations of North America flickered and materialized in the middle of the intersection, but most people didn't even notice. Everyone stood clustered in groups, facing odd angles, waiting for the president to appear inside their darkened masks and speak directly to them. In reality, President Nanda was being projected into everyone's mask, not to mention every train car, living room, and public toilet across the country. Sloane had disabled her own VR because she preferred to watch these announcements live, especially if she was outside when they happened. Up and down the street, she could see holographic copies of the president, who appeared to be standing in the open air with no mask or water tank. The sight of her uncovered face was an unspoken promise that such a thing might be possible again for all of them.

"My fellow North Americans," said President Nanda, "thank you for your attention and your time. As I'm sure you know, the World Health Organization has reported ten thousand births in the past twelve months, an accomplishment that would not have been possible if it weren't for the Program. I know we are all unspeakably grateful to the Program's world-class crew for their tireless service, and to the Program's founder for giving us the gift of time travel. Fred, I've said it before, and I'll say it again—if you're willing to come forward and take credit for your work, I'm not the only one who'd like to thank you in person."

No one knew who had invented Climate Reversal Technology and started the Program. They didn't even know if it was one person, let alone a man, let alone a man named Fred. But the media had branded Fred a tech genius-cum-playboy in an attempt, Sloane supposed, to make saving the planet sexy.

"However," Nanda continued, "it has now been 337 days since the 22nd Hero traveled to the eighteenth century to stop the invention of coal-burning steam engines. Since the Program's inception, we've never gone so long without sending a Hero back in time. Every day that goes by without a Hero leaves our planet—and the great United Nations of North America—vulnerable to climate regression. If we don't find the 23rd Hero in the next three weeks, I will be forced to initiate Operation Underground, evacuating all coastal and high-risk zones to the underground bunkers we've prepared for the day we hoped would never come."

Sloane took long, deep breaths, trying to circumvent the humiliating way her wristband dinged whenever her blood pressure increased, which was often. It wasn't the thought of going underground that scared her so much as knowing she could have helped fix things but didn't. If the world ended and humanity with it, Sloane couldn't shake the feeling that she would be responsible, somehow. Stupid, she knew. And even if she could make a difference, it's not like she had a choice. Boothies couldn't apply to be Heroes. And it was too late to find a different job just so she could apply—no one would be hiring during a Hero shortage. And even if she could find a new job, apply, and beat the zillion-to-one odds of getting chosen, she'd still be saving the world only to lose her dad.

"But even now, it is my fervent hope that the 23rd Hero will be found," said Nanda. "Effective immediately, the Program is opening applications to everyone in the world, with the exception of current Program agents and Basecamp crew. Past agents, Program subcontractors, and past Candidates are now eligible to apply. Minors aged 16 and up are also eligible with parental consent. Additionally, the Program will now cover the cost of life insurance for every applicant, removing any remaining financial barriers to apply. If you've already applied this cycle, visit the nearest application booth for a full refund. And whether you apply every cycle, or you've never applied before, I beg you—for the survival of our species and our beautiful Planet Earth—to volunteer for the Program. Humanity needs you to be a Hero. Thank you, God bless you, and God bless the United Nations of North America." The president flickered and dissolved. In her place appeared the Program's logo—a glowing blue sphere calmly spinning on its axis as if the world wasn't about to end. Beneath it, the Program's slogan promised to repay "service for a lifetime" with "the adventure of a lifetime."

Sloane's underarms were damp. She powered down her wristband to stop the beeping and squatted with her head between her legs, the president's words echoing in her mind.

Past agents, Program subcontractors, and past Candidates are now eligible to apply.

Program subcontractors were now eligible to apply.

Sloane was now eligible to apply.

"CITIZENS! PLEASE HOLD AS YOU are transitioned into your family environments for emotional debriefing."

With shaking hands, Sloane switched her VR back on and forced herself to stand up. As the viewing pane on her mask darkened, she wondered if she might hyperventilate the second she saw Harry. The pixels in her viewing pane reversed course, growing brighter, then spinning themselves into a floor, a ceiling, a chair. The static on Sloane's audio feed turned crisp, and she found herself standing in the virtual dining room of her childhood home. Simon was already there, his life-sized avatar leaning against the doorjamb in the front entryway, arms crossed, his gaze fixed on the virtual dining room table, where Harry's usual spot was occupied by a blonde woman Sloane had never seen before.

"Hey," said Simon to Sloane, his avatar reflecting the expression inside his mask—eyebrows high, dark eyes wide, the look alone sufficient to transmit his thoughts to his twin: Who the fuck is this and what's she doing in our dining room?

"Looks like they got some wires crossed?" said Sloane.

"Sorry," said Simon to the woman. "You're probably like, 'Where the hell am I right now?'"

"I'm actually sitting at the dining room table," said the woman, gesturing to said table. "The real one."

"Sorry?" said Simon.

"Sai, I think it's our bad," said Sloane. "Look—the pictures of Mom aren't there." Harry's dining room shrine to his late wife, Thida, consisted of dozens of framed photographs of the twins' mother, plus pictures of their Yeay and their extended family back in Cambodia. The rest of the house was maintained by hired cleaners, but Harry dusted the photograph collection himself every day when he was home. He'd even asked Sloane to add the photos to their virtual environment, insisting on replicas so precise that the project had taken her months to complete. With the photographs absent from the mantel and sideboard, it was clear Sloane and Simon had been ported into the wrong place.

"These older North Van homes all look the same," said Sloane. "Sorry about that! We'll log out and log back in."

"It's fine!" said the woman. "We're all in the right place. Burrows family debrief, right?"

The twins blinked at her, then each other.

"Is your last name Burrows, too?" Simon asked.

"Not yet," she said brightly.

The twins stared.

"I'm Chastity," she said, as if that explained everything. "You two should see the looks on your faces right now. Harry's going to die."

"Oh?" Simon managed.

"You're Simon, and you're Sloanie, and I am—drum roll—Chastity!"

"You're…"

"Chastity!" said Chastity, splaying her fingers into jazz hands.

"Oh!" said Simon. "Yeah."

"You're Harry's…," said Sloane.

"…new TA?" finished Simon.

Chastity's virtual cheeks flushed. "His fiancée."

Sloane's mouth went dry, and Simon tried, but failed, to conceal his surprise. "Of course," he said. "Will…Harry…be joining his family for the family debrief?"

"Absolutely," said Chastity. "Just as soon as he gets off the line with the Mayor. And makes his way through the swarm of adoring fans in the living room. Ha, ha!"

"The Mayor?" said Simon.

"Swarm?" said Sloane. "Are you talking about his birthday party? Because that's not supposed to start until—"

"We started the party early so we can end early and get down to the docks in time to welcome the refugee ships from Cambodia," said Chastity. "The house is filled with student volunteers right now. Who better to welcome the orphans of Cambodia than the person who understands their plight better than anyone in UNNA?"

Simon threw Sloane a look—did the Mayor know that Harry hadn't been to Cambodia since before the Program started and spoke Khmer about as well as a three-year-old?

"Our civic leaders and those refugees need Harry more than we do right now," said Chastity solemnly. "That's why he sent me into the debrief as his proxy."

"A proxy," said Simon. "For a family meeting."

"Well," said Chastity, smiling bravely, "I'm going to be part of the family."

"You look young enough to be his granddaughter."

"I'm thirty-four," said Chastity.

"Like I said," said Simon.

"Wow," said Chastity. "Ha, ha! I can see why Harry suggested keeping the family debriefs to just him and me from now on. Lucky for you, I insisted we include the children."

"The Cambodian orphans?" said Sloane.

"She means us," said Simon.

"I told Harry it was important to stay connected with both of you during the Hero shortage, especially since neither of you has anyone," said Chastity.

"Excuse me?" said Simon.

"I just mean you haven't found your soul mates yet," said Chastity, pressing one hand to her chest. "But that's only because you don't love yourselves. Yet. Harry and I love ourselves more than we love each other. That's why we work as a couple. Your love relationship with yourself is the most important relationship in your life. Wow. First speech as Stepmom. How'd I do?"

It had been a while since Sloane's nausea had been caused by something other than her memory. Simon took one look at his sister and told her to take off her mask before she puked.

"Where are you?" he asked Sloane. "You off work? I'm two blocks from Raffi's Place."

Before Sloane could respond, there was a break in the ambient audio, and the room was momentarily flooded with the sounds of laughter and clinking glasses—the familiar discord of grad students and other groupies who followed their dad around like he was a Hollywood celebrity. Harry's signature houndstooth scarf materialized above the table. His disembodied head was a fast follow, and Chastity clicked her tongue. "Baby," she said, "your settings." She fluttered around the floating head for a few moments, making adjustments to Harry's mask. The noise from the party faded, and the rest of Harry appeared, untying his scarf so he could tie it again.

"Alright, Carmella," he said, still mid-conversation with the Mayor. Switching to Khmer, which the Mayor neither spoke nor understood, he thanked her ("*saum arkoun*") and said goodbye ("*leahaey!*").

Harry ended the call and promptly reached for Chastity, taking her virtual face in his virtual hands. He pressed his forehead to hers and murmured something the twins couldn't hear, then released her, spun around to face his children, and fixed them with his most formidable glare. "How do I feel about disruptions in the middle of dinner?" he asked, the question already containing its answer. It was the way he used to admonish them for checking their handhelds on the rare nights they were all together for the evening meal.

"We'll be sure to let the president know she needs to accommodate your schedule," said Simon, and Harry laughed appreciatively.

"What did I tell you?" Harry said to Chastity. "Fast as lightning, that one."

"Happy Birthday, Harry," said Sloane. "And, um, engagement? Wow, that's just...Congratulations!"

"Thank you, Sloanie," said Harry.

"So, Operation Underground," said Sloane.

"Never gonna happen," said Harry, taking the seat next to Chastity.

"They always find a Hero."

"Right!" said Sloane. "Exactly what I think, too."

"I don't think, Sloanie," said Harry. "I know."

"Right," said Sloane. "It's definitely gonna happen in time. They always find a Hero. It's like…one more reason to celebrate."

"Too bad you guys couldn't make the little celebration over here," said Harry. "Just your old man's sixtieth. No big deal."

"It was supposed to start at seven," said Sloane.

"How could it start at seven?" said Harry. "The ship gets in at seven."

"The ship we heard about for the first time thirty seconds ago?" said Simon.

"Ha, ha!" said Harry.

"I was on my way to your place from work," said Sloane. "Or I was about to be, before the announcement, but—"

"They closed the bridge, anyway," said Simon. "King tide."

"There hasn't been a king tide under that bridge since the 19th Hero," said Harry.

"Actually," said Sloane.

"Actually?"

"Oh! Um. Actually I thought that even if we can't come in person, we could hang out virtually. After you welcome the Cambodian orphans and I service about seventy-five application booths. It's still your birthday until midnight, right? So we should at least have cake. Virtual cake. Or…"

"Or?" said Harry.

"Or…trivia?"

Harry turned to Chastity. "Told you she'd come to trivia."

"No trivia," said Simon.

"Trivia time!" said Harry, scraping his chair back from the table. "Plenty of time for a round or two before we head to the docks."

"Am I muted or something?" asked Simon. "NO. TRIVIA."

"One round?" asked Sloane.

"Do I seriously need to remind everyone how this is going to go?" said Simon. "Harry invites you to play because he's trying to beat you. You let him win so he doesn't get mad. He senses you're letting him win and gets mad anyway. You get nauseous. He 'accidentally' throws something, you throw up on the carpeting, he sends you his carpet cleaning bill."

"Why should I have to pay for someone else's vomit?" asked Harry.

"Technically, he didn't throw something last time," said Sloane. "He pounded the table, and the green Buddha fell off and shattered."

"Speaking of missing relics," said Simon, "where are the photos of Mom?"

The twins waited for Harry to finish tying his scarf for the third time, but his avatar froze mid-tug.

"He had another call," said Chastity. "But I'm happy to respond to your question about the photos."

"Madame President," said Simon.

"Ha, ha!" said Chastity. "It's just that Harry is so in tune with my needs, such a natural empath. I never said anything, cross my heart, but he sensed that the pictures of your mother were making me uncomfortable, so he took them down. Of his own accord."

"Just in the virtual dining room, I hope," said Sloane.

Chastity grimaced. "Sorry."

"Let's go, Sloane," said Simon. "Film production is on pause because of the announcement. I'm furloughed for the next three weeks. So, since I'm basically unemployed, the human race is doomed to live underground forever, and I'll never get to go hang gliding again, we should go to Raffi's. Drown our sorrows in a mountain of hummus and stuffed grape leaves."

"It's Harry's birthday," said Sloane. "Not ours."

"You're worried about the *nom ko* you made," said Simon, "but they won't go to waste. I'll eat all sixty myself, right after you buy me dinner."

Outside the booth, Sloane slapped her hands against her mask in exasperation. Her brother had the enviable superpower of not caring what their only living parent thought of him. Sloane, on the other hand, had been searching her whole life for that magic bullet that would finally win Harry's approval. She'd gotten it right once when she was twelve and won the Regional Gymnastics championship. Unlike winning the national spelling bee, which "didn't count" because her memory gave her an "unfair advantage," Harry had not only attended the gymnastics competition but had given her a pat on the shoulder afterward. "Not bad out there," he'd said. Ever since, she'd been striving for another "not bad." For the past year, she'd been practicing her mother's *nom ko* recipe, and she'd finally gotten it just right—sixty sweet, sticky coconut- and mung-bean cakes, one for each year of Harry's life. He would be so surprised, so moved by her effort, that it wouldn't matter that she'd "cheated" to get the recipe. It wouldn't matter that there was no recipe (nothing written down, anyway). Just a memory of a rainy Wednesday night twenty-two years ago, when Sloane's Yeay had showed her how to add palm sugar and salt to a large pot of rice flour, coconut milk, and mung beans. It was the same recipe Yeay shared with Sloane's mother, Thida, when she was a girl. The same recipe Thida made for her husband, Harry. The same recipe Thida would have passed down to her daughter, had Sloane not stolen her first breath of life just as her mother, in the final throes of labor, had drawn her last. Harry wouldn't mind that Sloane had used her memory to make the *nom ko*—it would be obvious she wasn't using her memory to give herself some kind of "unfair advantage." It would be so clear she was using it for him.

Harry's avatar came to life, but his head had dissolved, leaving a pair of reading glasses floating in the air above his scarf. The glasses and scarf rotated in Sloane's direction and asked her if, given the announcement and all the uncertainty around the Hero shortage, she was still going to be able to make her student loan payment this month.

"Baby," said Chastity. "Your settings."

"Sloane is working sixty hours a week at two different jobs just to pay you back, and you don't even need the money," said Simon.

"Do you want to hear how many hours your mother used to work back in Cambodia?" asked Harry.

"No," said Simon.

"Yes," said Sloane.

"She had one day off per month," he said. "Fourteen-hour days, making the equivalent of two dollars an hour. You do the math."

"Here's some math," said Simon, pulling a text message from his handheld into the environment so everyone could read it. "Three weeks furlough without pay is now a furlough until further notice."

"Don't look at me," said Harry. "I'm still out sixty-five grand from your sister's college."

"Maybe I can get you some hours at the coffee shop," said Sloane.

"Maybe you can finally apply to the Program and become the next Hero and we can get the platinum suite in the underground bunker," said Simon.

Sloane shot Simon a look of death. Her brother was the only person who knew what she wanted more than anything, and he had this infuriating habit of threatening to reveal the truth without *actually* revealing the truth so she would *admit* the truth and finally apply, already.

"The Program," said Harry, his gaze trained on his scarf. "Gonna apply, now that you can?"

Sloane's stomach dropped, and her heart started thumping so loudly she feared he would hear it inside the environment. Harry had never asked her point blank about applying before. The only time they'd come close to discussing it was during the 1st Hero ceremony a decade ago, when Sloane had been so inspired by the earth-shattering revelation of Climate Reversal Technology that as soon as the broadcast finished, she'd leaped up to find one of these new 'application booths' and apply. She was good at fixing things. Why should fixing the planet be any different? It even seemed easier than fixing whatever had always been broken between her and her dad. But when he'd clocked her excited expression, Harry had scoffed, and she'd frozen mid-step.

"I wonder how your mother would feel to know you'd blow off your chance to finish college because of something you saw on TV."

Sloane had dropped her keys on the antique Khmer rug and vowed then and there never to apply to the Program. Harry was right. Her mom had quit school when she'd married her dad, planning to finish her degree after they moved to Canada. But then she'd gotten pregnant with the twins, and Canada wasn't Canada anymore, and she'd died before she could realize her dream of being the first woman in her family with a college degree. Applying to the Program was a symbolic act. It meant Sloane was willing to give up her life in the present to travel to the past; a life Mom would have given anything to live, a life she would have lived if it hadn't been for Sloane. To apply would be to dishonor her mother's memory. So, Sloane didn't apply to the Program, and she didn't quit school, and after she graduated, she still didn't apply to the Program, the link between applying, dishonoring Mom, and disappointing Harry calcified in her mind. Harry reinforced the link by falling into stony silence whenever Sloane mentioned the Program or waxed poetic about the achievements of a particular Hero, and she learned never to bring up the topic in his presence. And yet if Simon talked about his lust for a particularly handsome Hero, or how long he'd waited in line to apply, Harry would respond with a resounding, "Ha, ha!"

The twins swapped theories to explain the inconsistencies in their father's demeanor toward his children, psychoanalyzing the professor over cocktails or Persian food. Sloane thought Harry hated anyone accomplishing anything they hadn't earned. Since becoming a Hero was the ultimate accomplishment, it was an honor that should only be bestowed on people who had toiled for decades, people who had worked hard enough to deserve that status, people like him. A designation like Hero shouldn't be handed out to just anyone—especially not people born with freak memories who hadn't strived or studied a day in their lives.

Simon, on the other hand, was convinced Harry was threatened by Sloane's memory, a theory Sloane found preposterous, what with her father's world renown, umpteen degrees, and countless awards. "He knows that if you wanted to, you could accomplish everything he's accomplished and then some in a fifth of the time, probably less." Harry needed her to stay small, Simon reasoned, so he could feel big. If Sloane used her memory professionally, let alone to become a Hero, Harry would no longer be the most successful person in the family. He'd lose his entire identity. Sloane's memory, and therefore Sloane herself, was a threat to Harry's very existence, according to Simon.

Whatever the reasons that fueled Harry's disapproval of Sloane, his disapproval was palpable, and she modified her life, her words, even her thoughts to minimize that disapproval; as long as she didn't dishonor Mom or threaten Harry, as long as she kept herself small, there was a chance that someday, Harry might start relating to her the way he related to Simon, or Chastity, or the Cambodian orphans he'd never met before. If she snuffed out her burning desire to become a Hero and hid the ashes in the same dark corners of her heart where she stuffed her worst memories, there was still a chance her dad might find a way to love her someday.

"Of course I'm not going to apply," said Sloane, her voice breaking like a teenage boy's. "Whoa, something's wrong with my audio! I should go. People are lining up for their refunds at every single booth in the city. Brody's spamming me. It's pretty much all Boothies on deck."

"You're too good for that job," said Harry.

"Thanks, Harry," said Sloane, her cheeks flushing. His compliments, which usually doubled as insults, were her reward for keeping herself small, and yet somehow, they always made her feel smaller.

"If the bridge is closed and we have to go virtual tonight, we should still make plans to see each other in person. Soon."

"Didn't I say the bridge is closed?" said Harry. "I just said that."

"We can come over Sunday, maybe, if the tide goes down by then? I made *nom ko* for your party, but it won't keep very long, and you should at least try one."

Harry laughed. "Do you know *how* to make *nom ko*?"

Sloane stared at the virtual floor. Chastity coughed. Simon started to say something, but Harry cut him off.

"No sweets, anyway. Chastity has me on a diet."

"Then we'll just bring ourselves," said Sloane, glancing at Simon. "And maybe talk about the quarters request for Operation Underground? Simon and I requested you for our bunker, but I think you have to request us back, otherwise they won't honor the—"

"Just stop," said Simon, gesturing to the table. Chastity was nothing but the wisp of a blonde ponytail, and Harry's avatar had dissolved to just a scarf. A farewell text from Chastity floated in the air above Harry's chair— Ping me!—the Xs and Os mingling with the digits of her personal voiceline.

"Damn it," said Sloane, her heart pounding, her breath coming short inside her mask.

"It's fine," said Simon.

"What the actual fuck, Sai?" she said. "'Maybe you can finally apply to the Program and become the next Hero—?'"

"It's what you want, is it not? And now you're finally eligible to apply. Your adolescent obsession with Harry's approval is the only thing standing in your way now."

"I shouldn't have mentioned the *nom ko*," said Sloane, wringing her hands. "I shouldn't have even made the *nom ko*."

"Sloane. It's impossible to please Harry because Harry is impossible to please."

"He seems pretty pleased with you. The 'funny one,'" she said. "He seems pretty pleased with Chastity. And with the Cambodian refugees and the student volunteers and the freaking Mayor. Everyone but me."

"Will you just give up on him, already?" said Simon. "Seriously, Sloane. My heart. Let it go."

'My heart' was shorthand for 'My heart is your heart,' a secret phrase the twins had made up as kids to comfort each other after Sloane had asked Harry if he loved them, and Harry's answer, after several moments of silent contemplation, had been, "Sure."

#   #   #

Outside the booth, Sloane pulled off her mask, sucking metallic air. The trams had been rendered immobile by the unclaimed bicycles blocking their sensors, and their bells dinged on repeat like quiet sirens. Actual sirens wailed in the distance. All around her, throngs of irritated people were still suffering through their own family debriefings or scattering at their completion. Within seconds, the scattering mutated into a crowd converging on the booth to get their life insurance refunds from the Program. Someone grabbed Sloane's arm and pulled her out of the way before she got trampled.

"Not that I don't like the view," said Full Face, drawing Sloane to the side. "But you should really put your mask back on." He took it from her, placed it over her head, and told her she could take it off when they were at dinner.

Sloane felt her cheeks go hot. Her handheld was buzzing with incoming service requests, and she realized it had been buzzing nonstop for the past two minutes.

"Pretty sure I have to work."

"After work, then," said Full Face.

"I can't."

Full Face studied her for a moment. Sloane blushed deeper. "There are just things about me that you probably wouldn't…" she said. He waited, smiling at her. "Okay, first off, I'm always working. I really don't have time for…And even if I did, I'm not like other people. I tend to make things… hard." Full Face raised an eyebrow, and Sloane couldn't help it. She laughed. "What I mean is, I'm not easy." Full Face raised the other eyebrow, and she laughed again. "I'm not easy to *be* with because it's not easy being me." She considered explaining how her memory worked, how divisive it was, how it had separated her from her own father. But just the thought of talking about her memory out loud made her stomach swim, so she told Full Face she had an "issue" with her "brain," which must have sounded like she had a brain injury, which must have been even more confusing when she said she'd give her condition "zero out of five stars."

But Full Face just smiled wider, a knowing look in his eyes. "Is this your awkward-but-charming way of turning me down because you're already seeing someone?"

Sloane glanced over at the water. It was purplish now, but it was easy to conjure the memory of perfect slate gray and picture the someone else she'd been seeing. She wondered if she'd see him tonight. Most nights, he was there.

"Maybe?" she said. "It's something like that. Sort of."

"Is he good to you?"

"Yeah."

"I mean in bed."

"Oh."

Sloane remembered last night—how he'd looked naked, the way he'd said her name. "Yeah," she said. "Especially in bed."

IN THE SWEET, SACRED NOTHINGNESS of the blue place, there is nothing to see, nothing to do. There is nothing to think about because the memories wrangle themselves, and all she sees and feels is the immediacy of now—a blank, blue sky that permeates her mind with peace. But then, in all this nothing, she sees something. A spot in her vision that spins toward her, growing bigger, taking shape. She moves toward it, floating through the nothingness, wanting it desperately even before she realizes it's him.

He is floating on his back as if he's been laid out for a funeral. Is he dead? But how could a dead man be so beautiful? She remembers that all that matters is him. She can move closer to him simply by thinking the thought, and then she's there, hovering over him, aching to touch him, yearning for him to wake. But his eyes remain closed, and he is so still, he doesn't even seem to be breathing. *Please don't be dead*, she thinks. His skin is pale peach, but a soft blue sheen pulses from inside him as if he's swallowed a spotlight. He has a sharp, straight nose, traceable cheekbones, and gibbous, pink lips that pout above his cleft chin. The man is naked, and she lets her gaze fall over his broad shoulders, down the flat planes of his chest, past the bumpy range of his abdomen to his groin. He is flaccid in a way that strikes her as sacred, innocent, and for a split second, she feels safe. And then the safe feeling unfurls into hot, urgent desire, and she wants his hair in her mouth, the scent of him. But when she leans in, her head merges with his, blurring the lines between them. She pulls back, trying to cup his face, but her fingers pass through his skin. She calls out for him to wake up. She calls and calls, but no sound comes out of her mouth. She starts to weep, and her tears roll across his cheeks.

His eyes flutter open and lock on hers—gray charcoal and slate sea, drawing her in, deeper and deeper, until she knows she could dive inside and gladly drown. A rush of warmth overcomes her, and a sense of deep knowing rises up from somewhere forgotten inside. She remembers everything, but she had forgotten this; when she is with him, she is home.

Sloane, he says.

She feels the memories surging before she can get control of them. She panics, trying to hide them, but trillions of memories—every moment of her life—explode into sparkling points of light, surrounding them in a glimmering halo, and there is no hiding. She watches him watch the lights, and she knows he knows everything—what her memory is, what it means, what it would mean for him to be with someone like her. When he looks at her again, her fear dissolves. He is not frightened of her memory. He is not ashamed of her, or for her. It is the opposite. Her memory makes him love her more. She understands that here in the blue place, with him, is the only place she will ever be loved and accepted for who she is, and she is grateful. It is more than enough.

This is the part of the dream where she always wakes up. Only she doesn't wake up. She stays in the blue place, and the man is reaching out to take her face in his hands. *Don't*, she thinks. *It isn't going to work.* But he keeps reaching for her, and this time, when she leans into him, his touch is solid. She weeps with relief, pressing her face into his hands, his touch drawing her toward the edge of an abyss she never wants to return from.

#   #   #

Sloane came to in that place between awake and asleep, caressing her own face. When she realized the hands were hers and not his, she sprang up in bed, blinking in the dim light of her apartment, her heart racing. She untangled herself from the blankets and collapsed back on the bed, her head hitting the pillow with a breathless, agonized *tha-rump*.

When the dreams had first started, she and Simon had sifted through every possible explanation for their recurrence. Simon thought the man in the dream was Sloane's soul mate, or maybe her "spirit guide." Sloane thought the man in the dream was a metaphor for the love she would never experience in real life. She was resigned to the obvious fact that her only chance of being loved, freak memory and all, was in her dreams. But she cherished the dreams just the same. Every night, she relished the moments just before sleep when she knew she'd see the man in the dream again. Every day, she replayed the memory of the dream over and over, like one of Simon's mantras, to the point where she felt the man in the dream was always with her, a secret security blanket no one could take away. What Sloane couldn't understand—and what unsettled her so much she couldn't fall back to sleep—was why, after nearly a decade of the same exact story, the dream had changed.

WITH OPERATION UNDERGROUND TWO WEEKS away and no Hero in sight, Brody told Sloane he was letting her go.

Wait.

That couldn't be right.

Maybe he said *I'm lying low*, or *I'm putting on a show*. Or was he saying Sloane *had some room to grow*? It was hard to tell because Brody was mouthing the words from inside his Brain Bubble®, a conspicuous but legal alternative to filtration masks. Sloane was standing outside Application Booth 007, trying to read Brody's lips as he chugged toward her on his StreetStrider, pantomiming that he was on the phone. As he closed in, his bodysuit-encrusted limbs skiing through the smog, Sloane saw several miniature, holographic heads floating inside his Brain Bubble®. He must be on a conference call. She tried scanning her badge again to open the booth, but no dice—she'd attempted to answer three different service requests this morning, but her access had been denied each time. None of her regular hacks could resolve the issue, so she'd been forced to initiate contact with Bubble boy, who could have restored her access remotely but insisted on meeting her in person instead. Impatient, Sloane waved her badge at Brody, trying to get his attention. He maneuvered the StreetStrider onto the sidewalk in front of the booth, hovering a few inches above the ground as he continued his conversation with the people floating around in his Bubble.

"The Program's failure to select a Hero is nothing but an unethical publicity stunt," Brody was saying. "Even with the rapidly dwindling population, where people have a point-five percent chance of getting pregnant, they'll wait. Then, right when we're about to get on the elevators to the underground bunkers, wham! They'll choose a Hero to swoop in and save the day. They're manipulating the global population into an even deeper obsession with 'Fred' and with the Program."

Sloane tipped her head to the greenish sky, mentally parroting Brody's rant, which she'd heard seventy-three times over the past seven years. The Program paid Brody's salary, but in his free time, he volunteered for the Anti-Program Program ("A-ProPros" to Brody)—a group of (mostly) white (mostly) cisgender men who wanted to outlaw masks, eat "real" meat again, and bring back "real" cars, "because freedom."

"We don't even know who runs the Program," Brody continued. "We don't know who built the technology that allows us to travel through time. We don't even know *who Fred is*. I know…I know. They even keep Fred's identity a secret from the governments that fund the Program. Uh-huh…Right. Two secs, guys."

Brody muted the call and lifted his Bubble off his head, peering down at Sloane with a bemused expression.

"Hey, is there an outage or something?" she asked. "You should probably keep your Bubble on, the ground-level ozone is super high today."

"So they say," he said, rolling his eyes. "No outage. I just wanted an excuse to see you."

Sloane blushed, fumbling with her badge. "That's weird because my badge hasn't been working all morning. The network looks fine on my handheld, but if other Boothies are having access issues, I can come up with a fix. Unless it's the sensor in the badge itself, in which case—"

"Your badge isn't working because I deactivated it," Brody said. "Like I just said, I'm letting you go."

Sloane flashed on the memory of his mouth forming words through his Bubble, then slowed it down to study the movements of his lips. He had said, "I'm letting you go." But maybe "I'm letting you go," in the context of their current conversation, meant "I'm letting you off the hook." Or "I'm letting you go away from this booth."

"Sloane," repeated Brody, and she realized he'd been talking for a while. "Do you understand what I'm saying?"

"Sorry?"

He sighed, pressing his thumbs into the sockets above his unprotected eyeballs, which had to be burning by now. "We invested so much in your development," he said, "so it's definitely a loss." Sloane frowned, remembering how she'd spent the majority of her Boothie training *training other Boothies* using skills she'd 'developed' long before she'd started working for Brody. "But when we consider your performance over the past few months, the team feels you can offer the most value in an alternative environment."

An alternative environment. Like on a different team?

"I'm excited for you, Sloane," said Brody, sounding genuinely excited. "We hope you appreciate this opportunity to add value in a role that holds more potential for you and your career." She stared at him, trying to make the words mean he was promoting her. "And it's not because you're a woman," he continued, suddenly defensive. "Or because you're Cambodian or half-Cambodian or whatever. So don't bother going to HR with that."

"I wasn't going to," she said.

Brody scrutinized her, his eyes turning pinkish in the open air. "Good, because like I said, this isn't a race or gender thing. My executive assistant is a woman, and I think it's bullshit that the Program has never chosen a woman as a Hero. And you know that A-ProPros constantly sues them for that, or at least tries to. And I have lots of Black friends."

"Um. I'm not—"

"It's just that we need Boothies who are 110% committed 110% of the time."

"I'm always asking you for more hours—"

"Do you have any idea how many resumes I get? I have a hundred people chomping at the bit for your job." His handheld dinged. "Make that a hundred and one." After asking the floating heads to hold for another "two secs," Brody tapped his handheld and began to read. "Average Boothie task acceptance rate: 89%. Sloane Burrows task acceptance rate: 57%. Average number of booths per hour: 2.75. Sloane Burrows booths per hour: 0.67.

Average number of serviced booths per week: 110. Sloane Burrows booths per week: 26.8."

Sloane's stomach turned, her brain scrambling for a reason that a normal person would avoid going back to the same booth. She could say she had OCD and couldn't touch the same surface twice. She could say she had mysophobia, except instead of other people's germs, she was afraid of her own. She could tell Brody pretty much anything except the truth about her memory, and not just because of her nausea, but because telling the truth put her at risk. From the earliest age, Harry had taken a historical perspective on her memory, lecturing on how certain "gifts" could be considered "curses" or "disabilities" depending on the time period, and how certain disabilities could get you put on a train, depending on the government. It was safer to keep it to herself.

It started to rain, the droplets bouncing off Brody's head in little puffs of toxic smoke, making it look like his hair had caught fire. "I'm committed to my professional development," she heard herself say. "If you check the logs, you'll see I've only declined booths I've already serviced in the past in the hopes of getting new booths so I can fix something new. Because I'm constantly on the lookout for new challenges."

Brody blinked repeatedly. "All the booths are identical, Sloane."

"Yes, but the problems differ from booth to booth, right? On the rare occasions I passed up on a routine service call, it was in the hopes of fixing something more complex, like a complete system shutdown."

"Boothies don't get to pick and choose. I've got 101 resumes of people who'd be happy to just run the diagnostics, get the DNA from point A to point B. During a Hero shortage, I can pay them half what I pay you."

"What about speed to resolution?" she asked. "The other Boothies take twenty minutes just to service a booth. Ninety if there's a problem, and new people will take even longer. I'm five to seven minutes per booth, no matter what's wrong. Doesn't that count for something?"

"Not when six of those five-to-seven minutes are spent wasting time in the test environment."

Sloane gulped. So this was about last Friday.

"Last Friday," said Brody, scanning his handheld. "Last Tuesday.

December 9th, December 3rd, December—"

"A few times."

"A hundred and nineteen times, according to my review of your activity logs. And that's just this year."

"I was logging in to the test environment to gain a deeper understanding of the applicant experience."

"Why do you need a deeper understanding of the applicant experience to collect blood and hair samples?"

"Because…" She broke off, her stupid memory trying to be helpful by opening all the browser tabs of her brain at once, pulling up thousands of images of the blood and hair samples she'd collected over the years. Sloane swallowed back the excess saliva that coated her throat right before she vomited.

"You okay?" asked Brody. "You look a little green."

"Just the reflection from the sky."

This couldn't be happening. She couldn't be fired. Harry was going to kill her if she got behind on her student loan payments again. He'd used the life insurance money from Thida's death to pay for Sloane's university. If Sloane didn't pay him back every cent, he'd once said, it was like profiting off her own mother's death.

"No one will be hiring during a Hero shortage," she said.

"Don't make this harder on me than it already is," said Brody. "Anyway, the shortage won't last much longer. They'll find someone—two secs, guys!—they always do."

"Can I at least keep working until they announce the next group of Candidates? I'll accept every request. I'll do five booths an hour, more if they're close to each other."

"Sloanie," said Brody. "Don't you know me at all?"

She did. Slow to hire. Quick to fire. Quick to replace a Lead Boothie of seven years with someone who didn't have a freak memory that made people think she was a lazy, incompetent, ungrateful, entitled slacker.

"If I know you at all, I'd say my desk is being packed up as we speak."

Brody laughed. "Give me a little credit," he said. "Your desk is already packed up. You can pick up your personal items when you return your equipment to the office."

She was seriously thinking about telling Brody, once and for all, that *irregardless* was a double negative and not a real word.

"Think positive," he said, hopping off his StreetStrider with outstretched arms. "You get the rest of the day off, and I won't even dock your pay." With his eyes watering profusely, he pulled her into an artless hug. "Mmmmm," he said. "Don't be a stranger, okay?" Brody released her, replaced his head gear, and unmuted his call. Sloane watched him pump down the street, his smoking scalp fogging up the Bubble.

At the office, it took precisely ninety seconds to walk from Security to her desk. In those ninety seconds, when it was clear from the absolute silence that everyone else already knew she'd been fired, Sloane thought of the man in the dream. When she saw her vitamin D light, succulent, and water tanks neatly boxed and awaiting her departure, she pictured his eyes filled with longing. When she struggled to return her equipment while answering an incoming call to her voiceline, she remembered the euphoric sensation of his touch. When she realized it was Brody on the line and that he was asking her to dinner (and if not dinner, just sex, now that they no longer worked together), she remembered how the man in the dream made her feel loved and accepted for who she really was. It was the memory of that feeling that kept her from bursting into tears when she realized she had no way to transport a box of stuff on her bike and she could no longer afford to take the tram.

Sloane put the Vitamin D light and the plant inside her bike basket, but the planter was too heavy, the basket straps snapped, and everything fell to the ground, the glass base of the light smashing into a thousand shards on the sidewalk. As she was gaping at the mess in disbelief, a pedestrian attendant wrote out a $2,000 citation for littering. Sloane placed as many shards as she could into the nearest receptacle, put the plant back in the box, and set the box inside the nearest application booth. She'd miss her vitamin D light. She hoped someone would give her plant a good home.

A WET, HEAVY SMOG CLUNG to downtown Vancouver that night, the blueish mist so thick that Sloane and Simon needed the flashlights on their handhelds to maneuver the dimly lit streets in the direction of Raffi's Place. Instead of their usual feast of hummus, pita, and soy chicken kababs, they planned to pool their money for a single order of stuffed grape leaves, the cheapest thing on the menu, and split it.

"I'll meet Harry at the bar for trivia," Sloane was saying, "and help his team win. Then I'll casually mention losing my job and needing an extension on my student loan payments."

"That's the worst idea you've had all night," said Simon.

"What, then? Just say nothing and hope twelve hundred dollars magically falls from the sky by the time the next payment's due?"

"My heart," said Simon, "you don't have to deal with this tonight."

"I have to tell him. My coffee shop hours don't even cover my rent."

"You got fired today," he said. "Now we're both unemployed. During a Hero shortage. If you're gonna throw up tonight, it should at least be for a good reason. Let's go to Good Co. and get smashed."

"With what money?"

"Sometimes the hot bartender gives me free drinks."

"Is he the hot bartender who bought you illegal beef jerky from the underground meat market? Or the hot bartender you took on your signature first date?"

"None of the above," said Simon with a sigh. "But he's definitely signature-first-date material. Or he would be if the air quality wasn't too shitty to go hang gliding and this stupid furlough was over. I can't even afford to take myself right now, let alone someone else. Like, 'Hi, want to go hang gliding with me? I'm unemployed and you're paying.'"

"Take him to coffee. It's 98% cheaper and 100% less likely to result in your untimely death."

"How many times have I been hang gliding?"

"Just thinking of you up there makes me—"

"How many times? I'm not asking rhetorically; I'm asking the memory machine."

"Sixty-seven times, including the time you went with the straight guy who wouldn't hold your hand in public."

"And have I died? Are you talking to the ghost of your dead brother right now?" Sloane slugged him in the gut, and Simon groaned dramatically. "The best way to get over your fear of heights is to face it."

"You mean fall on my face from ten thousand feet in the air."

"Don't you want to see the Earth from above before we descend into her bowels for all eternity?"

"Thank God they always find a Hero so we can avoid both of those scenarios."

"They're cutting it kinda close," he said.

"They'll find someone."

They approached a lineup of Program hopefuls waiting to enter an application booth. Simon slung an arm around Sloane's shoulder and steered her toward the end of the line as if they were queuing for a food tram. Sloane shrugged him off and hurried past the booth until hers were the only footsteps beating on the wet pavement. She turned back to see her brother stopped in the middle of the sidewalk, the look on his face indecipherable through the dark haze. She moved closer, asking him what was wrong, but he simply repeated her words in a faraway voice: "They'll find someone."

"You're being weird," she said. "Come on, it's about to pour out here."

Simon snapped his fingers as if snapping himself out of his trance; dinner—yes! How could he have forgotten that he'd never gotten his insurance refund after they'd made the announcement the other week? The Program owed him $58.37! That was enough for two orders of grape leaves, maybe even half a kebab. He grabbed Sloane's hand, ignored her groans of protest, and dragged her back in the direction of the application booth.

#   #   #

The panels inside the booth glowed blue as Simon tapped the touchscreen. Sloane leaned against the wall with her eyes closed, listening to the sudden downpour pummeling the roof. She wished she was home and asleep so she could forget today ever happened and lose herself in the electric embrace of the man in the dream. If only she could find a way to stay in the dream with him forever. If she never woke up, she'd never have to start frantically applying for jobs that didn't exist.

When it seemed Simon's tapping would never end, she sighed and cracked an eyelid, squinting at the familiar glow of the touchscreen, where a cursor blinked to the right of her father's name. Sloane peered over Simon's shoulder and saw that he wasn't on an insurance refund screen like she'd thought. He wasn't even in a refund flow. He was on the insurance screen of the application flow, and he had inputted Harry as his insurance beneficiary instead of Sloane.

"Thanks a lot," she said, scoffing. "Since when do you want the millions to go to Harry instead of me?"

Simon startled, and quickly tapped through to the next screen.

"Hold on," said Sloane. "You must have already applied this cycle. Otherwise how could you get a refund?"

"Well…," said Simon. He tap, tap, tapped to the next screen, a summary screen, which was filled with familiar data points. She knew the address, the postal code, the birthdate. She recognized the National ID number, the height and weight, and each digit of the personal voiceline. She also knew that none of those data points save their shared birthdate belonged to Simon.

A big, blue button blinked at the bottom of the screen: SUBMIT YOUR APPLICATION.

"Wait," she said. "What are you—?"

Tap.

Congratulations, Sloane Burrows! Your application to the Program has been received. Submit your DNA sample NOW to complete the process.

"No!"

Simon made a sound like a soldier sprinting into battle and lunged for her, wrestling her into a headlock to pluck a hair from her scalp. Sloane howled in pain, pummeling him with her fists, but Simon managed to not only extract a hair but press the hair inside an envelope, seal the envelope, and slide it through the slot in the wall before Sloane could stop him.

The twins faced each other, out of breath, Sloane's mouth hanging open in shock.

"About freaking time," said Simon with a smirk. "Let's eat."

Sloane stood there sputtering, her mind racing with ways she might undo, cancel, delete, exit, escape! Could she call a former Boothie colleague to come fish out the envelope and destroy it? Or maybe just destroy her brother instead?

"Relax," he said. "You have a better chance of getting pregnant than getting chosen."

"If you tell Harry about this, so help me—"

"My lips are as sealed as that envelope."

"If you so much as hint—"

"No more hinting now that it's done."

"If anyone finds out about this, I'll…"

Simon raised his eyebrows. "You'll what?"

"I…will…find your Grade 7 crush Tommy Sanchez and tell him how you spent an entire winter break building a gaming environment just so you could superimpose his and your faces onto the bodies of male models to make them make out."

"You wouldn't," he said.

"Try me," she said, pulling out her handheld. "Chippie Ngo is still friends with him on Augment. I'll just send her a quick DM—"

Simon snatched the handheld, opened the booth door, and took off running through the rain and smog. Sloane shrieked, tearing after him, the two of them hurtling threats and insults that grew more and more outrageous until they both dissolved into laughter, doubled over in the street with their clothing soaked, rain and mud smeared across their masks.

"Truce?" said Simon, wheezing. She nodded, and he surrendered her device. He slung a soggy arm around her neck and guided her back onto the sidewalk in the direction of the restaurant, and when she rested her head on his soaked shoulder instead of pushing him away, he didn't ask why. She didn't have to explain how she'd always imagined this moment, the moment after she had finally gone through with it and applied. She'd pictured herself being seized by guilt, dread, and a terror of Harry so potent it would snatch her breath the second she finished tapping the Submit button. She didn't have to tell Simon she felt none of those things now; that maybe it hadn't even been the fear of Harry's disapproval that had kept her small, forced her into a dream-prevention job, and stopped her from applying all along. She didn't have to share the realization as it dawned on her: even more than Harry's silent disdain, what scared her most was applying to the Program, letting herself admit how much she wanted to be chosen, then not getting it, which was only slightly less terrifying than getting it but not being good enough, not being big enough, and ruining everything. She didn't have to tell Simon there was a big difference between trying and failing and not failing because you never tried, and that one of the core tenants of staying small, and therefore safe, was to not even attempt the thing that might make you unsafe. She didn't have to say any of that, though, because the second her head hit his shoulder, he just knew.

AT THE COFFEE SHOP THE next morning, Sloane's coworker, Lucas, was heating oat milk for a latte when the steam wand came loose from the espresso machine and started rotating in lightning-fast circles, sending clumps of boiling hot milk ricocheting off the pastry cases. Lucas leaped back with a yelp and dropped the steel pitcher on the grate. Sloane rushed toward the contraption, shielding her eyes from the hot liquid, and grappled with the electrical cords until she found the right plug and pulled. They watched the steam wand lose momentum until it hung, limp and swinging, from the broken machine. The floor was soaked, the entire barista station covered in a fine mist. With milk dripping down her neck and back, Sloane set about collecting rags to clean up. A line had formed behind a tall, white man waiting at the register. She started to explain she'd be with him in just a minute, but he pushed back his mask, and the words caught in her throat.

He peered at Sloane as if he were waiting for her to remember him, but that was the thing—she didn't remember him. She had never seen this man before in her life. At the same time, his face was more familiar to her than her own. His name? She didn't even know *her* name, or what city she lived in, or what year it was. She felt as if every memory she'd ever made had dissolved in his presence. Besides, how could anyone—even her—remember anything when faced with such a face? His eyes were gray moonstone, a color that should have struck her as phenomenal, and yet the most phenomenal thing was that she knew those eyes, somehow. She knew the statuesque bone structure, too—the straight nose, square jaw, the slight cleft in the chin. She knew the mouth, so full and pink she wanted to suck his top lip between her teeth in broad daylight. She knew the careless nature of his hair, the way it stuck out from beneath his mask in shades of amber and chestnut. She knew if she rested her head on his shoulder, his essence would be an elixir of pear and cedar and salt. Just a whisper of the sea. She knew if she tore off his windbreaker, she'd find the body of a lesser god, lean and broad-shouldered, hard in all the places she was soft. Where had she seen this body before? But she had never seen *him* before. She would have remembered.

Immobilized, she watched him watching her, his eyes growing wider the longer he looked. He started to say something, but all that came out was a little puff of air from the back of his throat. They both smiled, and she felt as if she were standing on a beach, watching a tsunami surge toward the coastline. If she didn't move, she knew she would be swept away. But she didn't move. And neither did he.

The customers in the lineup behind the man coughed and tried to catch Sloane's eye. She became peripherally aware that Lucas had joined her by the register to take the man's order. The man had to clear his throat several times before he managed to order a coffee. The rich timbre of his voice made something inside Sloane unfurl like a rose opening to the sun. Her cheeks burned with blush. The man smiled again—a heart-stopping flash of light— and she looked down, sure her face had turned purple as an eggplant.

Lucas pulled her away from the register, her Converse skidding over the slick floor. "You okay?" he asked. She nodded. "I'll clean up," he said. "You get the coffee?" Coffee. Right. She made her way to a stack of bamboo to-go cups, gripping the countertop to steady herself. Was he watching her? Every cell in her body tingled with excitement. Which made sense—anyone with a pulse would be excited by him. But it wasn't just that. His nearness made her feel relieved, somehow, as if she'd been waiting for something her whole life but she never knew what it was and now he was here, and it was him. This stranger.

She placed the to-go cup beneath the retro coffee carafe and began to pump, dying to catch another glimpse of him but willing herself not to look. She secured a lid on top of the cup, shimmied back to the register, and slid the coffee across the counter, noticing, for the first time, the Program-issued sustainable travel mug in his hand. "Sorry," she said, flustered. She reached for the travel mug just as he reached for the to-go cup. When their hands touched, a spark visibly crackled in the air. She gasped and pulled her hand away, knocking over the coffee, which splattered across the counter.

"Oh!" said the man. Sloane scrambled after both cups, but her feet slipped out from under her, and she landed on the floor with her butt in the air, cups rolling in a sea of dirty milk and coffee. Mortified, she glanced up at the man. He cringed, squeezing his eyes shut as if he felt responsible for her fall. And there, with his eyes closed, her memory stirred, resurrecting itself like a booth restarting after an OS upgrade, and she realized exactly where she'd seen him before.

He stepped back from the register, bumping into the women in line behind him. Mumbling an apology, he replaced his mask and made a beeline for the exit. Sloane rushed after him, but by the time she reached the dining room, he was outside, standing on the sidewalk with his back to her as if deliberating his next move. She continued to the window, praying he'd turn around and look at her. And then he did, spinning to face her through the glass, just his eyes visible behind his mask. He shook his head disappointedly, as if there was something crucial he'd meant to say to her but hadn't because he *couldn't*. Then he tore his gaze away and was gone.

"Sloane!" said Lucas. "A little help, here?"

She stood frozen in the middle of the dining room thinking of Harry. Losing her job wasn't an excuse to stop making student loan payments—he'd just tell her to find a new job. But he couldn't expect her to make payments if she checked herself into a psychiatric hospital, which she was absolutely going to do because she was certain she'd lost her mind.

The man who'd just left without his coffee or travel mug was, without question, the man in the dream.

SOMETIME AROUND 10 P.M., SLOANE made her way home from the coffee shop, riding her bike down deserted Cardero Street through the smog. A block away from her apartment building, she noticed two figures standing inside the glass vestibule off the main entrance, a place to wait for trams and taxis without having to mask. Hundreds of people lived in this building. They could be anyone. But Sloane's heart skipped a beat anyway, hoping that one of them was the man in the dream, and that he was there somehow, waiting for her.

All day and into the night, she'd willed him to come back to the coffee shop, even convincing Lucas to give her his evening shift. He had to come back for his travel mug, right? Whenever the bell on the door had rung with the entrance of a new customer, she'd dashed to the register to see if it was him. By 9 p.m., she'd started to lose hope. She'd closed the shop down and mopped the dining room thrice, replaying every precious moment of their interaction on an endless loop inside her mind.

The most rational explanation was that the stranger just looked like the man in the dream, and she'd made a mental leap fueled by longing; ever since he'd touched her in the dream, she'd wanted nothing more than his touch in real life. But if he was just a random stranger, that didn't explain the relief she'd felt when he was near, or the way her uterus turned inside out when she heard his voice, or why he'd looked at her like the man in the dream looked at her—as if he saw all of her, all at once, and there was no one else in the world he'd rather see. She'd always thought her only chance to feel loved and accepted was in her dreams. But if the man in the dream was incredibly, inexplicably real, maybe other parts of the dream were real, too. Maybe it was possible to be loved and accepted by another person when she was awake.

Now, as she rode closer to her building, she did not see a figment of her subconscious made flesh, but a Black woman in a tailored suit waiting with an East Asian man in flowing orange robes. They eyed her as she rolled to a stop, and she looked away, self-conscious. When she docked her bicycle and approached the entrance, they were still watching her, and when she opened the door and moved through the vestibule toward the lobby, they followed her inside.

"Sloane Burrows?" said the woman.

Sloane took off her mask. "Um. Yeah?"

"Don't worry, Sloane," said the woman. "Everything's okay. I'm Eleanor. This is Enkh. Let's go upstairs so we can talk."

Eleanor wore her sophistication like a skin. Sloane would have bet her life the woman did not own sweatpants, never stress-ate, and would feel painfully out of place in Sloane's shabby apartment. Enkh seemed from another world entirely. His skin was lighter than hers, and he had a narrow face and nose, which gave him a Slavic appearance. But his dark, deep-set eyes were teardrop-shaped, like hers, and she wondered if he was mixed, too. As if he'd read her thoughts, the monk smiled as brightly as if he'd swallowed the sun. He pressed his hands together in front of his chest and bowed deeply from the waist, a movement that, for reasons she couldn't fathom, made Sloane choke with emotion.

"Are you from the FBI?" she asked, mostly joking. "I knew Brody didn't own the copyright to those sloth videos, but I never thought he'd stream them in every application booth in Metro Vancouver."

"We're not from the FBI," said Eleanor.

"Are you from some pro-Program NGO sent to kill me because I worked for the organizer of an A-ProPros? Because I don't even work for him anymore."

"We're not concerned with the anti-Program orgs," Eleanor said. "They can't touch us."

Sloane's feet felt like they'd hardened into blocks of cement. "Who's 'us'?"

"Enkh and I work for the Program," Eleanor said. "Let's go upstairs so we can talk." She took Sloane by the elbow and guided her toward the stairs. Enkh silently keyed in the access code to the stairwell that led to Sloane's apartment, his shiny bald head reflected in the glass door.

Sloane stammered through the beginnings of sentences without finishing one. Eleanor said it was normal to feel shocked, and that it happened to nearly every Candidate they notified.

Candidate.

Candidate.

Candidate.

"We'll take the stairs so you can burn off some adrenaline. Ready to climb?"

Sloane nodded and did as she was told, following the representatives of the Program up twelve flights of stairs to her apartment. When they reached the twelfth floor, she was still so stunned that she turned left down the hallway when she should have gone right.

"We're going to your apartment, Sloane," said Eleanor.

"How do you know where my—?"

"We know everything about you."

Sloane's stomach dropped into her groin. She wondered if they knew how long she'd wanted to apply to the Program, and why, before last night, she never had. She wondered if they knew about the man in the dream.

With his robes swishing against the worn carpeting, Enkh guided Sloane back down the hallway to the threshold of her apartment, where the door, which she remembered locking before she left, was wide open.

#   #   #

This couldn't be her apartment. It smelled of incense and citrus and was cleaner than it had been when she'd moved in. Bouquets of bright, fragrant roses filled the kitchen countertop, and the Mom Chair—an ancient recliner that once belonged to Thida—was adorned with a shimmering sapphire Ikat quilt, just like the ones woven by hand in Thida's village.

Sloane stood there gawking as Eleanor searched the pockets of her blazer. "Take a seat," she said, patting herself down. Sloane remained frozen, but Enkh sat down in the middle of the floor, closed his eyes, and within seconds, seemed to have slipped into a state of transcendental bliss. Sloane blinked, squinting from him to Eleanor and back, convinced she must be hallucinating.

"Apologies about the time," Eleanor said. "We didn't realize you worked a double shift."

"How did you know I—?"

"All we need tonight is a signature on your NDA," she said, patting her pants pockets now. "Tomorrow you can arrange to be away for a few days, get Lucas to cover your shifts, that sort of thing. You can also see family and friends if you want, just as long as you don't disclose what's happening."

"What is happening?" asked Sloane.

"For the love of god. Where in the world is my—?" Eleanor plunged her hand inside Enkh's robes, fished around a bit, and withdrew a small projection device. "Ah ha! Sorry, it's been a while since I did a house call. Usually it's the Notifications team, but my boss insisted Enkh and I gave you the good news tonight. We'll get through it together, okay?" Sloane sank to the floor where she stood, practically plopping into Enkh's lap. Eleanor sighed, grabbed Sloane under the arms, and hoisted her into the Mom Chair with a grunt. "This is where you sit, right?" Sloane nodded dumbly, her mouth suddenly bone dry.

Eleanor tapped the projection device, and two life-sized figures materialized in the apartment. Sloane recognized Matt Williams, the planet's 1st Hero, standing next to then-President Winfrey during the first-ever Hero ceremony a decade ago. It was footage from the booths.

"It'll just take me a second to pull up your stuff," said Eleanor, swiping Matt Williams away. "Oh—and I am obligated to tell you that for the next twenty-four hours, we can access your location and everything you say and do in real time. Not that we will, but know that we can."

"It sounds like you already have," said Sloane.

"Skip ahead," said Eleanor.

"Is this…some kind of twisted joke? Like Brody's way of testing my loyalty so I can get my job back? Are you guys professional actors?"

"You're not getting your job back," said Eleanor, swiping through a series of menus. "Ah! Here we go. Display candidate." Another life-sized avatar appeared, spinning slowly in 360 degrees. This figure had glossy, spiraling hair that framed her high cheekbones, and voluptuous, heart-shaped lips that popped against her tawny skin. Her deep-set eyes were golden-brown, her physique strong and muscular, her white, high-top Converse radiating the perfect mix of irreverence and confidence. Sloane scoffed, glancing at the four pairs of used Converse lined up by her door. Given the other visual proof that this far-too-gorgeous Candidate was clearly not her, she could write off the shoes as coincidence. But the personal information that appeared next to her avatar—National ID number, DNA design, the fact that her Hemoglobin E trait came from her mother, not her father—was slightly harder to overlook.

"I can't go."

Eleanor paused mid-swipe. "I'm sorry?"

Sloane collapsed against the Mom Chair with a sigh. "Just remove me, okay? Pick someone else."

"But why?"

"I just have some unfinished family business. That I couldn't leave undone."

"Family business that can't wait a few days?"

Sloane rubbed her eyes, groaning. "I couldn't risk—"

"You only have a one-in-five chance of getting chosen. And we've never picked a woman as a Hero before. The odds are not in your favor."

"Yeah, why is that anyway?" asked Sloane. "Is the Program sexist, or is it that history is sexist, and powerful men in the past would never listen to a woman? And how does the Program manage to keep operating with the constant lawsuits from gender equality groups?"

Eleanor grinned at Enkh as if his eyes were open. "Looks like Sloane Burrows has given this a lot of thought."

Enkh smiled wider, and Sloane blushed. "No, I haven't. I mean, I don't care, 'cuz like I said, I can't go. I was just curious."

"If I told you why we've never chosen a woman," said Eleanor, "I'd have to kill you." She waited a full five seconds before cracking a grin. "Look, Burrows, you can pretty much assume you won't get chosen. But come, have some fun. At the very least, get the money."

"He'd kill me," said Sloane. The thought of Harry finding out she'd been chosen as a Candidate filled her with a sickening dread. Her *nom ko* had been a bust. She'd missed his birthday dinner, and she wouldn't be able to make her student loan payment. It would be hard enough to fix things as they were without adding the mother of all offenses to the list.

Eleanor projected a grid of contracts in need of Sloane's signature. "Your dad will come around," she said. "You're one of five people selected from thirty-three million applicants. I'm sure he'll be proud."

Sloane laughed out loud at the thought. Eleanor narrowed her eyes in confusion, and Sloane curled up in the Mom Chair with her head in her hands, focusing on all the reasons she couldn't, couldn't, couldn't, and trying to ignore the wave of yearning that threatened to wash all those reasons away.

"You look tired," Eleanor said. "We just have a few documents for you to sign, and we'll be out of your hair. They basically say you can't inform anyone of your status as a Candidate until the President of the United Nations of North America has announced it publicly." She paused, but Sloane didn't budge from the chair. "That means Simon and Harry find out you're a Candidate when the rest of the world does. Sign here."

Sloane eyed Eleanor through her fingers. "I said I'm not going."

Eleanor regarded her for a moment. Then she tapped the device and the documents disappeared. Enkh was already at the door. "Get some rest," Eleanor said. "You'll think about it." Enkh smiled at Sloane, pressed his palms together, and brushed past Eleanor into the hallway.

"Oh! I almost forgot—we owe you an apology for the coffee shop incident this morning. Believe me when I say that's the last time we send an intern out on a prep assignment. He was supposed to prepare you so tonight didn't come as such a shock, but apparently, he choked. Know who I'm talking about? The awkward guy in the coffee shop who stared at you but didn't say anything?"

A tingling sensation spread from Sloane's face to her feet, her heart threatening to beat through her ribcage. She managed a nod.

"It was his first time," said Eleanor. "He must have been nervous. Anyway, we'll be in touch in twenty-four hours. Just to see if you've changed your mind."

Eleanor shut the door. Sloane heard a key she had never given them turn in the lock.

#   #   #

Sloane awoke with a gasp. She'd fallen asleep in the Mom Chair and her eyes burned. Blinking in the early morning light, she dared a look around the room and found the roses still there. They seemed to have bloomed overnight. Which meant last night couldn't have been just a dream. Which meant people from the freaking Program had been standing in Sloane's apartment, and that Sloane now knew someone who knew the man in the dream. Eleanor had said he was an intern. Eleanor probably knew his name. And if Sloane wanted to know it too—if she wanted a chance of ever seeing him again—she had to go with Eleanor wherever Candidates went and pray that the man in the dream would be there, too.

She slid on her Converse and bolted down the stairs, not thinking to grab a coat, not caring if it rained. She had to arrange to be away for a few days. She had to get Lucas to cover her shifts. And she had some unfinished family business that she couldn't leave undone.

Sloane found her bike in the docking station outside the building, another bouquet of roses bursting from the basket. The flowers upstairs were pink and fuchsia and coral. Not these.

These roses were red.

ALL WAS QUIET WHEN SLOANE slipped through the front door of her childhood home. She listened for the sounds of Harry puttering in the kitchen, but there was only the ticking of the clock over the ancient wooden sideboard. She tiptoed over the creaking floorboards toward the stairs, realizing she had no clue what she was going to say to him. Somehow, she had to prep him for the moment she'd be projected into his living room with all the other Candidates, convince him she somehow deserved this honor despite her memory, and wrench the truth from him so if she never saw him again, she didn't spend the rest of her life regretting this. The truth was that deep down, he did approve of her. Deeper still, he accepted her memory, even if he thought it gave her an unfair advantage he'd never have. And even deeper than that—so deep he'd never been able to say the words—he loved her. Maybe, if she used the Candidate money to pay him back for the student loans all at once, he would finally realize it.

Outside Harry's bedroom door, Sloane heard the snore she'd hated so much as a child. Now it made her feel relieved because it meant she had time to think. She was headed back downstairs to practice what she was going to say when she saw the attic door open a crack. Shit. Harry did this sometimes, rummaging through Mom's old trunk, sniffling over ancient photographs. Sloane slipped past the door, stepping around the twelfth-century Angkor figurines that lined the staircase to find the trunk open, her mother's wedding crown and jewelry strewn about the attic floor. While she was replacing the items in the trunk, Sloane found a book she'd never noticed before—a leatherbound journal with page after page of her mother's elegant script. Every third or fourth Khmer symbol jumped out at her, and she flashed on the lessons Yeay had given her and Simon before she died. There were thirty-three consonants and twenty-four vowels in the Khmer alphabet, the symbols strapped together to form words, the words smushed together to form sentences. As a child, Sloane had loved how the swirly, curling characters insisted on so much togetherness, like a family that couldn't bear to be apart. She'd learned nearly half the consonant characters and their corresponding sounds, but Harry had stopped the lessons before she could finish the alphabet, claiming it was too painful a reminder of Thida.

Sloane turned another page and a loose sheet of paper floated toward the floor. She caught it, flipped it over, and saw her name and Simon's name written in English at the top of the page. Beneath it, more Khmer. It was a letter to her and Simon from their mom, she was sure of it! She figured Harry couldn't have seen this; he would have hidden it from her or thrown it away, not wanting memories of Thida to belong to someone other than him. Sloane decided to take it and not tell him. She would transcribe every character she could or find someone at the university to translate it for her. She tucked the letter into her pocket, replaced the journal, and closed the heavy lid of the trunk with a *thunk* just as the sound of footsteps floated up from the bedroom below. She thought of what the letter might say and felt a surge of courage. If her mom could reach her from beyond the grave, surely she could reach someone standing right in front of her.

Sloane flew down the attic stairs just as Harry stepped into the hall in his old nightshirt and houndstooth scarf. He jumped, startled at the sight of her, and shut the door to his bedroom.

"Hey!" Sloane said. "Sorry, I was just—"

"Breaking and entering?" said Harry. He clomped down the stairs and into the kitchen, grumbling about her practically giving him a heart attack.

"Sorry, it's just that I'm going out of town for a little while."

"Oh?"

He pressed the right combination of buttons on the coffee machine and slid a mug beneath the spout.

"For work," she said as he rummaged in the refrigerator. "So I just wanted to see you before I left."

He poured cream into the bottom of a second mug. Sloane waited, hoping he'd stop putzing and look at her. "I might be away for a while, so I was just hoping—"

"I heard they're looking for Boothies to work in the Northwest Territories. Pays good. Dangerous work, though. Those people are as anti-Program as you can get, which is pretty convenient if you ask me since they've been the least affected by all this."

Harry took a loud slurp of his coffee, then started brewing the second cup.

"I actually don't work for Brody Noah anymore," Sloane said. "This is a new—"

"Still going to be able to make your payments?"

"Of course," she said, fighting the urge to tell him she'd be able to pay him back all at once.

"Including the foreign transaction fees? They'll charge you more to send money from overseas."

Sloane's palms went damp. "What makes you think I'm going overseas?"

"Fatherly intuition."

"Just Seattle. For a few days. But then maybe, you know, working remotely for a while. Maybe check out one of the high-speed trains, try and get to Florida before it sinks. If Operation Underground doesn't happen, of course."

"Operation Underground won't happen. They always find a Hero."

"Right. Exactly what I think, too."

"I don't think, Sloanie," he said. "I know. And isn't travel kind of frivolous for someone in so much debt?"

Harry grabbed both coffees and pushed through the kitchen door into the dining room.

"Can we talk?" Sloane asked, following him.

"We are."

"It's just with Operation Underground, and now with me going away, I've been thinking about what really matters."

He paused at the bottom of the stairs, coffee cups suspended in his hands. His bedroom door creaked open, and Chastity called his name.

"Coming, baby," he said, starting up the stairs.

"You matter to me, which is why I've always wished I knew how to make you happy."

"I am happy, Sloane."

"I know that. I guess I meant happy with me. With who I am. Because sometimes I get the feeling you're not."

Harry retreated down the stairs, sat the coffee cups down on the table, and made a 'let's have it' gesture.

"Maybe it's because we don't really say things…to each other? 'I love you,' 'I accept you for who you are,' that sort of thing. And if you never say things, people might not know how you feel. And what if we went underground forever, not that we're going to, but what if? Or, what if one of us got run over by a tram tomorrow and we'd never said…If there's anything you want to say to me, you can say it. Good or bad, I can take it."

Chastity coughed.

"And if there's nothing to say, then I'll just be the one to say that you're my dad and I love you. And I hope that if there's anything I've done, or anything I do that you might not love, you could maybe separate that from who I am and maybe still love…me."

"'I wuv you, Daddy,'" he said, doing his best impression of a three-year-old.

"Harry, come on."

"Fine, fine," he said, palms up in surrender. "I appreciate it, okay? I gather you mean well most of the time."

"I mean well all of the time."

Harry laughed, a solitary blat he made when he found something ironic.

"What's funny?"

"That you always mean well. The intention is just so different from the outcome."

"What does that mean?"

"Nothing. It's just that I've always thought of you as sort of a…Well. You know."

"I don't know," she said. "I don't know how you've always thought of me."

"It's early, Sloane. At least let me—"

"How have you always thought of me?"

Harry sighed. "I've always thought of you as this walking tornado that destroys everything in its path. Happy?"

She stared at him.

"Don't be dramatic, Sloane."

"What have I…?"

"I take it back, okay? You're not a walking tornado, you're a well-meaning tornado."

"I'm not trying to destroy anything. I'm trying to fix things, to do something that's actually good enough for you for once. That's all I'm ever trying to do. And no matter how hard I try, nothing's ever good enough, is it?"

"It doesn't matter if you're trying or not," he said, unwrapping his scarf so he could wrap it again. "It's not even what you do. It's just how you are. It's who you are."

"So it *is* my memory," she said. "Simon's always saying that's why you don't—"

"Is it your *memory*?" he said, incredulous.

"I know you don't like me using it as a crutch, that you think it's cheating, but it's not like I chose to be born—"

"Surely, with such an incredible memory, you can recall a time or two when you managed to ruin things for me without even trying?"

In her stunned silence, Sloane was besieged by a dozen memories and the accompanying nausea of Harry mentioning her memory. There were the trivia nights Harry lived for, which she'd ruined countless times by getting more answers right than him and making him look bad in front of his students. There was the time in junior high when he'd had to cut his book tour short because she'd been hospitalized from dehydration from vomiting because of her memory. There was the time she'd sat in on one of his lectures and used her memory to correct a date he'd gotten wrong, only it happened to be the day the Department Chair was evaluating him, and after the lecture, the Chair conducted a fact-checking review of all Harry's lesson plans and materials, and upon finding additional errors, denied his application for tenure.

"You're right," Sloane said. "The well-meaning tornado. I don't mean to ruin things, but I always find a way."

Harry tugged his scarf. "And the saddest part is you don't even know when you're doing it. It's a Sunday morning and you barge in here at the crack of dawn, uninvited, and demand I make you feel better about the way you are. You don't even think about my plans, what I'm doing, how I want to be spending my time."

"You're right," she said. "I didn't think. I'm sorry."

"It's not my fault you are the way you are. I'm a victim of it."

She wiped her eyes, trying and failing to suppress the tears she knew he'd hate.

"And this, right here, is exactly what I'm talking about. I've often wondered if the memory thing has affected your mind. Mental illness runs in your bloodline, you know. Thida's father. One day, he climbed up on the roof and he never came down. Her family said he was possessed by the spirit of Hanuman, the monkey god. I always thought it was schizophrenia, but maybe he had the freak memory, too, and it drove him insane. You should get evaluated to see if there's anything they can do to help you. At least take preventive measures or some such. Or medication for the…crying. I don't know."

Harry grabbed the coffees and headed up the stairs. "Good luck on your quest to the Motherland," he called. "I assume by 'train to Florida,' you mean 'boat to Cambodia.'"

Sloane said nothing.

"Right. Not that I would know anything about the topic, but I'm sure you're aware the rainy season has extended into December with all the climate change Sort of pointless going this time of year if you ask me, but what do I know?"

As he climbed the last few stairs, Sloane maintained the tiniest speck of hope that Harry would stop and say something, anything, to make it okay. But he disappeared over the landing and shut the bedroom door, shutting out all hope of ever being good enough for him, of ever being anything other than she was—a freak. A walking tornado that destroyed everything in its path.

If her own father didn't love her, how could anyone? How could she love herself?

She ran out of the house and got on her bike and pedaled as if it were possible to pedal away from herself.

SLOANE SAT ON A LOW, flat rock at English Bay tossing pebbles into the waves, conjuring a time before the water there was toxic. She let the memory overtake her, and soon she was looking out over the expanse of water through a seven-year-old's eyes. The shadowy bodies of the islands across the bay made her heart ache; she wanted to jump in the water and swim until she reached them. She watched the fat, gray gulls circle the water in a smog-less sky, their cries as comforting to her as Yeay's hand around hers. She made inukshuks along the waterline, stacking flat rocks into little towers and squishing her toes in the wet sand. She was building up, not knocking down. Nothing around her was ruined. Nothing destroyed. It was the opposite—she could feel the sky and water and trees converging within her as if she was a hub for all the elements of the Earth; her blood like rushing water, her growing limbs like tree branches, the sweat on her skin like the salt of the sea, her heart soaring like a gull, her soul as infinite as the sky. She believed with absolute certitude that she could fly just like those gulls; she was not yet afraid of heights.

Now, the skies were empty, the gulls long gone. Now, there were no more trees, no more kindred spirits to remember everything just like she did, to make her feel less like a freak. Her connection to the natural world had been severed, but the yearning for connection had never left her, and she longed to find it again. As she watched the way the polluted sea received the pouring rain, Sloane thought restoring the world of her childhood would be impossible, just like getting chosen as a Candidate was impossible, just like a dream appearing in real life was impossible. And yet all these things seemed more possible than earning her dad's love.

#   #   #

At 10:13 p.m. that night, Sloane was sitting in the back of an unmarked electric car with Enkh by her side and Eleanor in the driver's seat. It had been difficult to pack for an unknown destination, so she'd stuck to the basics: her white Converse, utility jacket, and her favorite orange maxi dress with Thida's letter from the attic snapped inside the hidden pocket. To this ensemble she added a black ski mask, which she pulled over her head and into place with Enkh's help. Eleanor sped away from her apartment, tires squealing, and Sloane's pulse thudded in her ears as they drove. It couldn't have been more than five minutes when she felt the car stop, the door open, and Enkh's fingers thread through hers as he guided her from the vehicle. They started to walk. She listened to Eleanor's boots tapping on the pavement, Eleanor murmuring into her satellite phone. Sloane strained to hear, but the wind howled, and she could only make out snippets of the one-sided conversation.

"…arriving now…coffee shop…Site 1032a."

There was a sound like rushing water, a sharp temperature drop, and a sudden gust of wind that blew the mask tight around her neck. Sloane coughed, her throat constricting, and Enkh gripped her hand more tightly.

"Sloane!" said Eleanor, shouting over the roar.

"Yeah!"

"You're going to feel a slight change in altitude. Nothing to be worried about, okay?"

Someone was pulling at the sleeve of Sloane's jacket. She gasped as a needle pierced her skin and cool liquid entered her veins. Shortly after she felt like she was losing air, she realized she was about to lose consciousness.

PART 2

SLOANE BURROWS WAS STANDING ONSTAGE in a spacious auditorium alongside four other Candidates for the Program. An entourage of hair and makeup people surrounded her, fussing and worrying over every miniscule detail of her appearance, especially Kofi, her lead stylist, who was busy cinching the waist of her sky-blue column dress with a crop of stealthily placed clothespins. Dozens of crew surrounded them, shouting and moving equipment with such swift precision it looked like choreography.

"House going dark!"

"Speakers flying in stage left!"

In the narrow strip of space that momentarily appeared between a subwoofer and a rack of floodlights stepped Poppy, a Swedish psycho-neuroscientist with a medical kit strapped to her chest. She moved with purpose toward Sloane, who shuddered at her approach.

"Another small prick, Sloane," said Poppy, opening her kit to reveal the vials of liquid and rows of syringes contained within.

"What's this one for?" Sloane asked, cringing as Poppy selected a syringe from her collection.

"A nutrition shot," said Poppy, who wiped the crook of Sloane's arm with an alcohol pad before sliding the needle into her vein. "It will satiate you until there is time for a proper meal."

Kofi had turned his attention from Sloane's dress to her lipstick, which he pecked with a little foam wand. "It'll protect my work until you ruin it with a proper meal," he said with a smirk.

"Five minutes to worldwide broadcast," said a sleek, artificial voice over a loudspeaker.

As the crew refined the stage lighting and Kofi refined her makeup, Sloane snuck glances at the other Candidates. Surrounded by their own stylists, they all looked enviably at ease, as if this was their fifth Candidate announcement instead of their first.

"Sloane?"

She snapped to attention to find Kofi, Poppy, and half a dozen crew peering at her expectantly.

"Anything else you need?"

"Um," she said.

"Do you feel satiated from the injection?"

"Any nerves?"

"What about the shoes? Any discomfort?"

Sloane lifted the hem of her dress to admire the stiletto pumps they'd made from a pair of deconstructed white Converse. "The shoes are so great," she said. "Maybe just a little wobbly, but that's—"

Eight hands shot out before she could finish her thought. Without a word of discussion, two crew members helped her balance while a third removed her shoes and a fourth inserted cushioned gels into the heels before sliding them back onto her feet; the sequence complete and all wobbles vanished in less than ten seconds.

"Three minutes to worldwide broadcast," said the artificial voice.

The crew wished her luck, then jumped off the stage to choose seats in the auditorium. Sloane tugged at Kofi's jacket before he could follow them, asking if it was too late to use the restroom. Kofi rolled his eyes, touched a finger to his ear and, turning to face the stage right wing, murmured something she couldn't hear.

Sloane felt as if she had arrived on another planet—a planet populated with mysterious yet superior customs, technology, and human beings. She knew she was at Basecamp, the Program's secret headquarters, but she'd been unconscious when Eleanor and Enkh had brought her here, and she had no idea where in the world she was right now. All she knew was that she was surrounded by fellow freaks; intellectual anomalies who would not be here if they weren't superlative at something important. They were so brilliant, it seemed to Sloane, that they had developed defense mechanisms against any condition that might threaten that brilliance; they didn't get tired, uncomfortable, or hungry because they had developed injections for every possible ailment or complaint. They had answers to every question, instantaneous solutions to every problem. They didn't even carry handhelds or wear wristbands but communicated with each other the way Kofi just had—by tapping their ears and murmuring quietly into the air, as if whispering their wishes to an invisible entity who always provided.

Seconds after Kofi performed this mysterious ear-touching ritual, Poppy rushed toward them carrying a vial of blue liquid and a cloth napkin.

"Whoa, Poppy," said Kofi. "Easy, now."

"Here, Sloane," said Poppy. "Drink this."

"Sorry. I meant I need to use the toilet."

"You won't have to after you drink this," said Poppy.

"Open your mouth and she'll pour it in," said Kofi. "Your lipstick is a work of art, and we don't want any water damage."

"Sixty seconds to worldwide broadcast."

Sloane's bladder was starting to burn, so she tilted her head back and swallowed the tasteless drops. Kofi pecked at her lipstick again, scrutinizing her with a professional frown.

"Feel better?" he asked.

Sloane nodded, astounded to find she no longer had to pee.

A holographic rendering of the Oval Office in Washington DC materialized downstage from the Candidates, and Sloane watched in wonder as the President of the United Nations of North America took her seat behind her holographic desk. To the viewers at home, the Oval Office and the Basecamp auditorium would be projected as a single location, with the dutiful Candidates standing behind the president with their backs to the South Lawn. To enhance this optical illusion, the technology enabled people in both locations to see and interact with each other in real time as if physically sharing the space. Not only could the Candidates see the president—the president could see them. As Sloane watched Nanda smooth a strand of dark hair back into place, the president shifted her focus to look directly at Sloane. "Congratulations," she said with a wink. Before Sloane could thank her, Nanda spun around to face the broadcast cameras, and the artificial voice counted down from three, two…

"Citizens of Earth," said the president. "It is with incredible gratitude and relief that I appear before you today to announce the next cohort of Program Candidates, our planet's potential saviors. Chosen from tens of millions of applicants, these five Candidates are willing to sacrifice everything for the good of us all. By this time tomorrow, it is my hope that the Program will have selected its 23rd Hero. In three weeks, that Hero will be sent back in time to accomplish their Mission, delaying and possibly eliminating the need to activate Operation Underground."

Paolo Oliveira. Debbie Allen. Dara Chanthavong. Khalil Lloyd. Sloane Burrows.

When the holo-cam materialized in front of Sloane for her close-up, she smiled for the camera like they'd asked her to, trying to forget that she was being projected into the homes of billions of people around the world, and that one of those people was probably smashing his most valuable Angkor relics against the wall. She couldn't let herself worry about Harry right now. Simon was somewhere in Vancouver jumping for joy, and for the first time in her life, everyone was smiling at her. President Nanda was smiling at her. Maybe the man in the dream was out there in the audience somewhere, smiling too.

SLOANE STOOD IN THE CENTER of a windowless, gymnasium-like training room, rubbing her sweaty palms over the bio-sensitive wicking fabric of the tracksuit Kofi had designed just for her. The imposing space was empty save a small, square table in the center of the room. Enkh sat on the floor with his eyes closed, and Eleanor paced between the monk and the table with a finger pressed to her ear, issuing commands, demanding answers, and intermittently yelling at whoever she was speaking to. After several startling exclamations that involved the Chancellor of Germany and something about "designated safety zones," Sloane threw a pleading glance to Enkh—was this a bad time? Should she come back later?—but the monk remained still as stone, never stirring from his meditation.

Sloane tried to slow her pounding heart. She clasped her hands behind her back, put her hands on her hips, forced her hands to dangle at her sides. She snuck glances at the objects on the table as if she might glean some insight as to their purpose and in doing so, secure some kind of advantage for herself, some head start. There was a Rubix cube, a partially disassembled laptop, and a circular device no bigger than a blueberry the likes of which she'd never seen. Intrigued, she reached out to pick it up just as Eleanor ended her transmission.

"Burrows!" she said.

Sloane flinched and withdrew her hand. Eleanor marched toward her, producing a razor-thin, rectangular piece of glass from her jacket pocket, which she consulted continuously but which appeared to Sloane to be completely blank.

"You are here for your Candidate Assessment. First thing's first. Whatever you've heard about Candidate Assessments, it's wrong."

Eleanor looked at her pointedly, and Sloane nodded.

"There are two rounds. In the first round, I'll give you three tasks to complete. If you're like 99% of Candidates, you'll fail, we'll do some paperwork, you'll go home."

"And if I pass?"

Eleanor's eyebrows shot up. "In the unlikely event that you pass the first round, you'll move on to the second round, which I can almost guarantee you will fail. Got it?"

Without waiting for a reply, Eleanor swiped her palm over the glass and projected a menu into the air next to Sloane. "Go ahead and choose a work environment, and we'll get started."

In the left column of the floating menu was a list of places Sloane knew: her West End apartment, Application Booth 439, the coffee shop. In the right column was a list of places she didn't: Koh Phi Phi beach bungalow, Montmartre café, Ittoqqortoormiit fishing hut.

"Does it matter what I—?"

"Choose an environment where you'll feel the most comfortable. And focused."

Sloane selected the item marked "Coffee shop." Her finger pierced the hologram, and all around her, the room began to transform. A 360-degree virtual view of the coffee shop overtook the training room, which disappeared behind a shroud of spinning pixels and shifting light. Enkh no longer appeared to be sitting on the floor in an empty training room, but beneath windows that opened onto West Cordova Street. The Rubix cube, laptop, and blueberry device now appeared on the same table where Sloane and Lucas rolled silverware, and an avatar that looked just like Lucas passed behind the virtual register carrying a tray of drinks.

As Sloane marveled at the transformation, Eleanor scanned the objects on the table, deliberating. "For your first task, let's go with…this one." She picked up the Rubix cube and tossed it to Sloane.

"Seriously?" said Sloane, flushing. "That's kid's stuff."

"So what?" said Eleanor. "Let's play. And if it's so easy, go ahead and solve it."

Within thirty seconds, Sloane had tossed the cube back to her, each side a solid color. Eleanor examined it for a few seconds before flinging it over her shoulder, the cube soaring in a perfect arc against a backdrop of quivering pixels. With his eyes still very much closed, Enkh reached up and silently caught the cube in his hand, sending a thrill of excitement shooting up Sloane's spine. She felt she had been abducted by an advanced race of alien beings and she never wanted to be sent home. Not only was she finally a freak among freaks; she might just be the least freaky out of anyone here.

"She's right," said Eleanor. "That was too easy. Let's try the laptop."

Sloane peered at the open device, eyeing the processor and graphics chip. "What do you want me to do?"

Eleanor touched a finger to her ear, glancing at Sloane and away as she listened to whoever was speaking on the other end of the line. "I want you to fix it, of course."

"Oh!" said Sloane. "But it's not broken."

"Oh, it's broken," said Eleanor. "I did the honors myself."

"Hm," said Sloane. "Well…is the battery charged?"

"There is no battery. It's solar powered."

Sloane bit her lip. She replaced the keyboard without touching any of the machine's internal components and pressed the power button until a glorious, dinging startup chord rang out in the room. The screen came to life, and she spun the laptop around to face Eleanor.

"If you broke this, you did a terrible job. There's not a part out of place. And you must be thinking of a more recent model because these older versions weren't solar powered. They still ran on lithium-ion, and you've got seventy-nine percent battery life left."

Eleanor lifted a finger to her ear and listened. She nodded once and glanced at Sloane with a twinkle in her eye. Sloane pumped a fist in the air, feeling the same victory high she felt in those fleeting interims between beating Harry at trivia and remembering she wasn't supposed to beat Harry at trivia. The difference now was that it was actually okay to win.

"Final task for this round," said Eleanor, pinching the tiny blueberry device between her thumb and forefinger. "Seen one of these before? Just a military-grade wireless earpiece. It's how we communicate with each other throughout Basecamp. Quieter than walkie-talkies. Less cumbersome than handhelds." With that, Eleanor dropped the earpiece on the ground and smashed it with her foot. "Fix it," she said. "You've got two minutes."

In the window of the coffee shop, a countdown timer materialized already in a rapid freefall toward zero. Sloane chased after the tiny parts of the earpiece as they rolled across the floor in every direction, her heartbeat pounding in her ears. Each part was no bigger than a necklace bead, and when she examined them closely, she could make out the delicate, perforated edges where the parts snapped back together. Eleanor had applied just enough pressure to break the earpiece apart without completely smashing it—the big stomp was just for show.

Sloane set the parts on the table in a neat pile and dislodged one of the ten thousand Bobbie pins Kofi had used to restrain her hair earlier that day. Working the pin like a tiny crowbar, she opened the laptop again, detached the network card, and broke off the thin metal separator from the card's edge, using it to reassemble the earpiece and lock each part into place. With a glance at the clock, she placed the device inside her ear and disappeared behind the virtual counter of the coffee shop to test out her fix in private, concerned with the optics of a failed first attempt.

"Hello?" she said.

"Hi," said a voice.

Sloane flashed on the previous morning in the actual coffee shop, when the man in the dream had sputtered and cleared his throat, managing a single word—"coffee." Now, she compared the timbre of "coffee" with the warm, hushed sound of "hi," and realized that a person who was not supposed to exist had spoken to her in real life. Twice now.

"I knew you could do it," he said, using the same intimate tone he used in her recurring dream—as if there were no one else in the world he'd rather be talking to.

Sloane was peripherally aware of the rapidly descending clock, but she held a frozen vigil behind the virtual counter, bewitched by the silence that followed his words. He inhaled as if to speak again, but the breath caught in his throat. What was he going to say? Say it! She didn't dare open her own mouth for fear she'd say too much, and say it wrong, and he'd retreat into the dream like a touch-me-not snapping its petals shut. Thirty seconds on the clock. Twenty-five seconds. Sloane peeked around the counter to see Eleanor looking impatient, but she couldn't break away—not when she might hear his voice again. "Can I talk to Eleanor, please?" he said. Sloane's body responded before her mind could catch up, and she soared across the space toward Eleanor, plucking the earpiece from her ear and presenting it to her like a precious jewel. It was only when she watched Eleanor examining her work that Sloane realized she had just given away the thing she longed to keep.

"Does it work?" asked Eleanor, holding the earpiece up to the light. Sloane shrugged, waiting for the feeling to return to her face. Eleanor placed the earpiece inside her ear and tapped it. "Ohhh," she said, sounding dismayed. "It's you." Sloane's chest constricted with envy. Not only did Eleanor know the man in the dream—she knew him well enough to tease him. Maybe Sloane could ask for the earpiece back. She could think of no better souvenir from her time at Basecamp than the voice of the man in the dream in her ear all day and night, until there was no one on earth who knew him better than she did.

"Color me surprised," said Eleanor. "Sloane Burrows is moving on to Round Two."

Sloane laughed out loud, a momentary joy humming in her chest for half a second before she managed to tamp it down. She told herself she shouldn't get her hopes up, not recognizing the sound of Harry's voice in her head—a voice so deeply embedded it often sounded like her own.

Swiping a hand over her glass, Eleanor dissolved the simulated coffee shop, and within seconds, they were back in the assessment room. When she projected again, it was a grid of enormous tiles that filled the air from floor to ceiling. Each tile was as tall as a person, and each contained a unique image. Sloane immediately began ingesting the details of every tile. There were portraits of kings, paintings by Leonardo Da Vinci, and sketches of Galileo's inventions. A sixteenth-century history test, she thought, flashing on her high school history textbook. She wasn't special. She wasn't better than anyone else. But she could do this.

After a few moments, Eleanor asked Sloane if she'd had a chance to look at the tiles, and when Sloane said yes, the tiles disappeared. They weren't representative of topics she would be tested on. Eleanor explained she would be tested on the tiles themselves—on her memory of their exact order and position. Round Two of Sloane's assessment for the Program was to play her least favorite game in the world: the Game of Memory.

Her nausea surged, and a memory overcame her with such force that the training room disappeared. She was no longer a twenty-nine-year-old woman in the assessment room at Basecamp, but a four-year-old girl in her childhood bedroom. She was sitting up in bed in her rosebud nightgown, the sheets damp with sweat, a cherry-flavored electrolyte drink in a sippy cup on the nightstand. Home sick from preschool, Sloane was playing the Game of Memory with Harry, who was flipping the game cards over and back, over and back, his face growing redder as they played. Slap, slap, slap. He slammed the plastic cards on the floral bedsheet. Little Sloane threw up into the mixing bowl next to the bed. She wiped her mouth. Harry said nothing. She found the matching rocking horse and added another match to her stack. She knew her dad was furious with her. He was furious that she remembered. It wasn't normal to remember. It wasn't supposed to be this easy, and if it was this easy, it was because there was something wrong with her. She was ashamed. She was ashamed and nauseous and about to vomit again because of her memory. And from then on, that's how she'd always be.

Sloane shook her head, batting the memory away. She scanned the training room for a sink or trash bin, but there was nowhere to be sick.

Eleanor displayed the projected tiles again and instructed Sloane to arrange them into their original configuration. Sloane forced herself to look up. There were forty-eight tiles in total, and she could see with a quick scan that they'd made twenty-three changes to what they'd initially displayed. They'd switched Galileo's *Drawings of the Moon* with an image of the Mona Lisa. They'd swapped da Vinci's *Vitruvian Man* with a portrait of a Ming Dynasty Emperor. She could see all twenty-three changes, all at once, and they all made her want to puke.

"I'm sorry," said Sloane. "I can't."

Eleanor waved her glass in apology. "You don't need to move the tiles yourself. Just verbally tell me where each should go, and I'll move them to the right spot with my iGlass."

"No, I mean, I don't remember the original configuration."

Her need to flee the room was becoming urgent. Eleanor said no worries, no one gets them all, she should just try her best, no pressure. Desperate to take attention away from her memory, Sloane responded how she imagined someone with a normal memory might respond. The Mona Lisa had appeared bottom row-center in the original configuration, but Sloane told Eleanor it belonged in the upper-right corner. The portrait from the Ming Dynasty had appeared in the lower left-hand corner, but Sloane said it should be in the center. She was grateful when Eleanor did not correct her obvious mistakes.

"Can I be done now?"

Enkh guiced Sloane from the space. His hand was cool and comforting in hers, but it wasn't enough to suppress the tsunami of nausea that crested just as they reached the exit. The training room wall parted to reveal the other four Candidates sitting in the waiting area, their heads snapping toward her expectantly. Debbie Allen, the blonde Southerner Sloane had been paired with to give interviews—answering questions like "Who are you wearing?" and "Do you think you'll fall in love in the past?" while the media asked the men what they hoped to accomplish—rushed toward her now, her arms outstretched.

Sloane retched. She got most of it in the fiddleleaf fig planter, but the spray ricocheted, and a little bit of vomit got on Debbie Allen's sneakers.

THE SECOND SLOANE SAT DOWN in the waiting area the next morning, the wall parted, and Debbie Allen burst from the assessment room. "Sloane!" said Debbie, embracing her so tightly Sloane worried about throwing up on her again. "Omigod, are you done? Did you already have your follow-up? Tell me everything."

"I'm done," said Sloane, eyeing Debbie's shoes. "Did they, um, replace your…?"

Debbie lifted her freshly sneakered foot. "Oh, yeah—these are new! I am so sorry I freaked out. I've just never been thrown up on before. But I don't even care, do you? I mean, what does it even matter at a moment like this?"

"Right."

"I didn't even know you were still here," Debbie said, plopping onto the cushion beside her. "I mean, I knew someone was still here. At least one other person, because there has to be two of us, right? But they sent three people home already. I just didn't know it was you who got to stay!"

"Wait," said Sloane. "Wait, what?"

"It's down to us!" Debbie said, grabbing her by the shoulders. "You and me, girl! And just girls, just women, first time in history, can you believe it?"

"I'm not still in the running for Hero. Not after the way I choked during my assessment last night." They stared at each other for a moment, Debbie's huge, blue eyes growing wider. "If everyone else is gone," said Sloane, "and

I'm out, then that must mean you're…"

Debbie squealed with delight. "Do you really think I'm the Hero?" she asked. "My assessment could not have gone better. And then this morning, just now, the follow-up was ah-may-zing. I know we're not supposed to tell each other anything, but I just feel so blessed. And to have you as my alternate!"

"Your alternate?"

"Didn't they tell you about alternates?"

"Um…"

"They pick one person as the Hero and one person as the alternate," said Debbie. "If the Hero gets hurt during training or has a nervous breakdown or something, the alternate steps in and takes their place." The alternate. Like being an understudy in a Broadway play. It was more than she could have hoped for given her performance last night, but Sloane's chest still felt heavy with disappointment. "I asked if I'd get to meet Fred," Debbie said, "and they were like—get this—'We'll see.'" Debbie slapped Sloane's forearm, her pink lips parting in wonder. "I mean, can you believe that? Can you fathom what it would be like to meet Fred in the flesh?" She beat the palms of her hands on her legs in an excited little drum roll. Then, she tugged her tank top down, exposing her left breast.

"It is so fuckin' hot in here," said Debbie. "Are you hot?" She picked at her areola and asked if Sloane could 'borrow her' a pair of tweezers. Before Sloane could reply, Debbie told her the Hero didn't get to choose the time and place of their Mission. They didn't even know what year they were going to until they'd accepted the position, could she believe it? Sloane stared at Debbie's perfectly round breast, convinced they'd made the right decision when they'd chosen her; only a true Hero would be confident enough to pick her nipple hairs in public.

"Did they tell you they design the Mission for the Hero? They create the Mission based on what the Hero's good at. There's eighteen days to train, and you only sleep for four hours at a time. They give you a shit-ton of drugs, though, so you don't even feel it. Omigod, and they don't even let you say goodbye to your family in person! You can talk to them virtually, but only at scheduled intervals, and only for five minutes at a time. You know that once you go through the portal, you never come back, right?"

"You mean once *you* go through the portal, *you'll* never come back."

"OH MY GOD," said Debbie, squishing her breast against Sloane's nylon jacket as they hugged. She pulled back, her face inches from Sloane's, her breath perfumed with strawberry toothpaste. "Did they tell you the worst part?"

"They didn't tell me the worst part. They didn't tell me any parts. I know nothing."

"Okay," said Debbie brightly. "When the Hero goes through the portal, the changes they made in the past show up in the present almost instantly. Because in the present, the past has already happened. The world reaps the benefits of the Hero's Mission right away, but the Hero has to work hard for the rest of their life. And then, after a lifetime of service, they die in the past without ever knowing the outcome of their Mission. They die not knowing if any of it was even worth it!"

"Burrows."

Eleanor was standing between the parted wall of the assessment room, frowning at Sloane as if she were the one responsible for Debbie's naked breast. Sloane peeled herself away from Debbie and stood up to follow Eleanor into the room as Debbie encouraged her to go, girl, because "you got this!" As the wall began to close, Sloane glanced back to see Debbie with her arms in the air, raising the proverbial roof, her heroic breast bouncing as if it might fly back in time before she did.

Inside the room, Enkh stood next to the center table, where five holy texts were propped up on stands as if they were on display in a museum. "What's with the books?" asked Sloane. As usual, Enkh smiled his silent smile, but Eleanor pointed out the Buddhist Tipitaka, the Quran, the Tanakh, the Holy Bible, and the Hindu Bhagavad Gita in turn, telling Sloane she could 'pick her poison.'

Sloane stared at the books, wondering if she was supposed to solemnly swear she wouldn't reveal anything she'd seen during her time at Basecamp.

"Sloane Burrows, congratulations," said Eleanor. "You have been chosen as the world's 23rd Hero and the planet's first-ever female time traveler."

The silence in the room was impossibly loud. Sloane waited for the punchline. Perhaps there'd be a playback of her puking her guts out the night before, and everyone would have a good laugh.

"Which text would you like to use for your swearing-in ceremony?"

Sloane stared at Eleanor, open-mouthed. Time seemed to stop. It was as if Eleanor and Enkh were simulations, as if Sloane herself was a simulation and some mighty gamer controlling the game had just pressed pause. The vast room was so quiet Sloane could hear herself swallow, and she gulped back the hope that what Eleanor had just said was somehow possible when it was so obviously impossible.

"It's true," Eleanor said. "You're the one."

"No, no, no," said Sloane, backing away. "Debbie said—"

"Don't worry about what Debbie said."

"But I failed," said Sloane. "You can't pick me if I failed."

Eleanor's eyebrows knit in confusion. "You didn't fail."

"Did so," said Sloane. "I ruined it. I got the answers wrong."

"No, you didn't."

"Yes, I did!" she said, the memory of last night rushing forth. "I said Mona Lisa should be in the upper-righthand corner instead of the bottom row center. I said the Ming Dynasty portrait should go in the center instead of the lower left-hand corner!" She paused to catch her breath, her stomach swimming. Eleanor tapped her iGlass and the playback of Sloane's voice from seconds before echoed through the room. The three of them stood there listening to Sloane admit she'd known exactly where she should have moved each tile. Sloane's hand flew to her mouth, willing back the surge of nausea and the humiliation of accidentally outing herself and the panic that the Program people knew about her memory—that somehow, they'd always known about her memory. *We know everything about you.*

Eleanor asked if Sloane would like to finish her assessment now.

"I don't feel so good," said Sloane.

Enkh reached beneath the table and produced a wastebasket.

"You have to throw up, so throw up," said Eleanor. "You can be yourself here, Sloane. Maybe it wasn't safe back home. But Basecamp is a safe place to make full use of your abilities. Your memory—"

"Maybe just don't say that word right now?" Sloane whispered, fanning herself.

"Maybe just finish your assessment right now."

Eleanor handed Sloane her iGlass. A crop of miniature tiles was hovering above the device as if waiting for Sloane to rearrange them. The iGlass didn't register her first few swipes because Sloane's fingers were wet from wiping away tears, but she managed to restore the original forty-eight tiles to the correct order without losing the contents of her stomach. When she finished, the tiles dissolved, and in their place, the president of the United Nations of North America materialized in the room.

Sloane tried her best not to stare at the president's life-sized hologram, especially since the perfect angles of the cameras and lenses meant the women could look directly into each other's eyes.

"Congratulations, Sloane," said the leader of the free world. "How do you feel?"

"Um," said Sloane.

"She's just been informed," said Eleanor.

"A little surreal?" said the president. Sloane nodded. "Just follow my lead, and this will all go very quickly, okay?" Sloane nodded again, no clue what Nanda was talking about. Eleanor gestured, once more, to the books on the table. Stammering about how not religious she was, Sloane pointed to one of the volumes at random. Eleanor guided Sloane's left hand on top of the Holy Bible while the president raised her right hand and gestured for Sloane to mirror her.

"Sloane Burrows, repeat after me," she said. "I do solemnly swear…"

"I do solemnly swear…"

"That I will faithfully execute the position of the 23rd Hero."

"That I…that I will faithfully execute the position of the 23rd Hero."

"And will, to the best of my ability…"

"And will, to the best of my ability…"

"Preserve, protect, defend, and accomplish my Mission to save Planet Earth."

The weight of the words struck Sloane in the chest, and her hand began to tremble on the Bible. This was what she'd always wanted. But being offered the object of her desire was a lot different from merely pining for it. She was really good at *wanting* to be a Hero. But she didn't *feel* like a Hero.

A Hero should believe she can accomplish her Mission, even if she has no clue what that Mission might be. A Hero should be brave enough to protect the world, not afraid she'll ruin everything if she tries. A Hero should believe in herself. Love herself, even. She should never think of herself as a walking tornado that destroys everything in its path. It was obvious to Sloane that *that* was the kind of Hero the world needed, and that she merely wanted to be that, and that wanting something was an obvious sign that she didn't have it already. What the hell was she thinking? She couldn't do this. She couldn't even keep her crappy job as a Boothie; how was she supposed to take on the hardest job in the world? She couldn't even manage to save her relationship with her own father; how was she supposed save the lives of billions of people? This was insane. She would have to tell the president no.

"Preserve, protect, defend…" repeated the president.

Sloane started to protest, but a memory swept in to stop her, her inner vision suddenly filled with the most beautiful face in the world—a face that was no longer just a fantasy. She could hear his holy voice saying hi for the first time, his voice telling her he knew she could do it. The man in the dream was somewhere in the Basecamp compound, in the flesh. If she said yes to this, she'd have eighteen days of training to try and find him. She knew she was supposed to say yes to being a Hero for the world, and if not for the world, then for herself. But if she was too afraid to say yes for the world or for herself, she would say yes for him—and never tell a soul that for a moment, the fate of humanity had hung in the balance and was only saved because of something as stupid as love.

Except him. If she found him, she just might tell him.

"Preserve, protect, defend, and accomplish…my Mission…to save Planet Earth."

The president congratulated Sloane again before her hologram fizzled and dissolved. The wall parted and in strutted Kofi, who made a beeline for the makeup station that was rising into the room from an opening in the floor. The station locked into place with a soft click, and Kofi began unpacking his gear, whistling as if Sloane had come into his salon to get her bangs trimmed.

"I need her for thirty seconds," said Eleanor, pulling Sloane toward the exit.

"I don't have an extra thirty seconds," said Kofi.

Eleanor ignored him and guided Sloane out into the hallway, where the excited chatter of the congregated crew stopped the second they saw Sloane. They began to clap, and soon their applause was thundering through the corridors. Sloane stood there and took it, surprised she could look dozens of strangers in the eyes without dissolving into a blubbering mess.

Eleanor shouted over the applause the second it began to wane. "I need a skeleton crew for this announcement, people. C Team, we're broadcasting live with President Nanda in one hour." Dozens of people scattered in the direction of the auditorium. Eleanor tapped her earpiece, and seventy-five hands flew to their ears. "A and B teams, go straight to Mission Briefing. We're about to get the countdown timer up. New people—once that clock starts ticking, the training schedule starts, and there's no pausing, no rewinding, no going back. The schedule gives you three hours to figure out how Sloane Burrows is gonna save the world." A collective groan swept across the crew, who bemoaned the tight timeline in Arabic, Mandarin, and Ukrainian. "Don't shoot the messenger," said Eleanor. "I know we're used to six hours, but three is all they're giving us, so we'll work with what we've got. Talk to your team leads if you need extra injections as we adjust to the schedule. Let's move!"

As Eleanor pulled Sloane back into the room, Sloane caught a glimpse of Debbie Allen across the corridor, shirt on, chatting on a satellite phone as the crew swirled around her. Debbie caught Sloane's eye and pumped her fist in the air, beaming at her without a trace of jealousy or animosity. She looked so happy, in fact, that it made Sloane wonder if they'd doubled up and made Debbie a Hero, too.

Kofi clocked Sloane's expression as she sat down in front of the makeup mirror. "Don't worry about Debbie," he said, running his fingers through her hair.

"She looks too happy."

"She's just an alternate," said Kofi. "Just here for optics."

"She's here in case I ruin it," said Sloane.

"I don't think an alternate has ever replaced a Hero," said Kofi.

Sloane nodded, unsure if that made her feel better or worse. "Do I have to give a speech?" she asked. The 17th Hero had given a speech.

"No, baby," said Kofi, pinning her hair away from her face. "Just a ten-second shot. Stand there and look pretty, just like last time."

In the air to the left of the mirror materialized a digital clockface, which made a buzzy, chiming sound as it tracked the descent of each second.

18:19:23:37.

Eighteen days. Nineteen hours. Twenty-three minutes. Thirty-seven seconds.

18:19:23:36.

18:19:23:35.

18:19:23:34.

Sloane looked at Kofi, alarmed.

"That's just the countdown timer."

"Right. Eleanor mentioned it. Countdown to…?"

"P-Day."

"Pee day?"

"Portal Opening Day. The day you get transported through the time travel portal to the past."

Sloane's body tingled with a cocktail of shock and adrenaline and elation and terror. But as she sat still in the chair, letting Kofi primp and preen and the rest of the crew rush around her, she became aware of a growing sense of serenity underlying the panic she'd felt in front of the President, like the undisturbed depths of the ocean beneath a surface storm. For the first time in ten years, the yearning she'd always felt to become a Hero had been replaced with the realization that she just had. It felt different to be on the other side of yearning. She felt as if she'd been pulled, and pulled, and pulled, and was now suspended at the edge of a harbor, bobbing between the docked ships and the open sea, finally ready to set sail. Minor problem: she didn't know how to sail. She wondered if eighteen days, nineteen hours, twenty-three minutes, no, twenty-*two* minutes, would be enough time to learn.

18:17:21:43 to P-Day

"THIS WILL HELP US SEE inside your mind," said Poppy, uncurling her index finger to reveal the circular, black sticker that was stuck to the tip.

"See inside my mind," said Sloane, staring at the sticker. "Like brain waves?"

"Brain waves, thoughts, emotions—"

"You can read my thoughts?"

"Oh, yes," Poppy said. "May I place the sticker now?"

Sloane and Poppy were in the Mind Mapping room, a low-ceilinged space with a tiki lounge vibe that served as Poppy's office. Eleanor sat in the corner, conversing incessantly with whoever was on the other end of her earpiece, and Enkh sat beside Sloane on a chic rattan cushion, his eyes closed above his serene smile.

"What if you don't like what you find?" asked Sloane. "Am I going to be sent home for un-Hero-like thoughts?"

"We monitor thoughts and emotions to make sure nothing is holding you back from performing at your peak. But your actions during training are what counts."

"What about…private things?"

"In Standard Mode, we only see the quality and frequency of your thoughts—never the content," said Poppy. "Your private thoughts stay private."

90

Sloane nodded her consent, and Poppy placed the black sticker behind Sloane's ear. "Waterproof, sweatproof, training-proof. You can remove the Mind Mapping sticker on P-Day, but otherwise, please do not touch."

With a few swipes of her iGlass, Poppy projected what appeared to be some sort of artwork into the room. The projection looked like one of those abstract splatter paintings with nests of intersecting lines and shapes, except these lines and shapes were moving—simmering and popping like the lines of a heart monitor. Behind them, Sloane could see the wrinkly, compressed curls of her brain.

"This is your Mind Map," Poppy said. "It shows us your brain and its structures, the patterns of your thoughts and emotions, whether they are fleeting or constant, whether they move freely or become stuck. This visual will help us coach you throughout your training so you can overcome thoughts that hold you back. By the time you pass through the portal, you'll have greater control over your mind so you can remain focused throughout your Mission."

Using her hands to move and modify parts of the Mind Map, Poppy amplified the layer of the projection that showed Sloane's brain in three dimensions, enlarging a swollen area shaped like a kidney. "Here, you can see your amygdala, hippocampus, and neocortex, the parts of the brain associated with memory. Both your amygdala and hippocampus are unusually shaped and extremely large. This distortion is what gives you your extraordinary abilities."

Sloane stood up, marveling at the image of her brain: visual proof of her freak memory in all its freakiness. If the Program people had only hypothesized about Sloane's memory before, now they had proof. There was no denying who she was, what she was, even if the surging feeling in her stomach made her want to rip off the little black sticker so no one could ever look at her memory again.

"Fascinating," said Poppy, gesturing for Eleanor's attention. "See these static shapes surrounding the amygdala? We can see precisely where Sloane has attempted to block her gift, almost as if she has willed herself to have a normal memory instead of an extraordinary memory. The blockages begin to bleed together, forming the shape of a normal amygdala."

"Having a freak memory is not a gift," said Sloane weakly.

Eleanor looked surprised, but Poppy tipped her head to the side, as if scrutinizing the behavior of a test subject in a research lab.

"Do you experience memories so vividly it feels as if the events are happening again in real time?" asked Poppy.

Sloane sat back down. If she took shallow breaths that went no deeper than her clavicle, the movement wouldn't make the nausea even worse. "Yes," she told Poppy. "Sometimes."

"Sometimes, or all the time?"

Sloane gave Poppy a mournful look.

"If your memories are painful and you are forced to relive them again and again, then no wonder your gift feels more like a curse than a blessing."

That's right. Her memory was a curse, so Poppy and Eleanor should stop talking about it and looking at it and asking her questions about it already.

"Eleanor, we can consider the initial assessment and interview complete," said Poppy. "Ready when you are with the analysis."

Touching her finger to her ear, Eleanor nodded. "They're logged in and listening," she told Poppy. "Go ahead."

Sloane massaged her forehead, shuddering to think who "they" might be. Probably a bunch of Program bigwigs who were listening in, watching her, and talking about her memory like it was a gift they could leverage for her Mission. What if the only reason they'd chosen her as Hero was because of her memory? If they discovered she couldn't use her "gift" publicly without puking, they would send her home. Away from the man in the dream. She looked at Poppy pleadingly, praying she understood Sloane's memory was a curse, and praying she carried enough clout to convince everyone they should never mention it again.

"There is perhaps no type of brain better suited to time travel than Sloane's," said Poppy. "Because of the physical composition of her brain, and the astonishing faculties of her memory, Sloane already knows what it's like to exist in the present and past, often simultaneously. But in order to make the most of her gift in the context of her Mission, we must remove these blockages around her amygdala so she can explore the full potential of her powers. We must also strengthen her control, so she can choose how she wants to experience each memory—by reliving it, or by watching it from an emotional distance."

Eleanor listened to whoever was on the other end of the line, then asked Poppy the likelihood of Sloane's success if the blockages remained.

"Even with the blockages, Sloane's brain is unlike anything I have ever seen," said Poppy. "But if I am understanding Sloane correctly, there seems to be an inherent risk of deep suffering every time she uses her memory."

"That could explain her struggles during her assessment," said Eleanor.

"Indeed," said Poppy, turning to Sloane. "Did the tasks you were asked to complete during your assessment bring up painful memories for you, Sloane?"

Sloane coughed, swallowing back a fountain of regurgitated stomach acid. She pressed her face into her hands, coughing longer than necessary so she had time to concoct a believable lie.

"The assessment didn't bring up bad memories," she said finally. "I mean, that does happen sometimes, the way you say. Sometimes it does feel like I'm reliving past memories again in the present. But that's not what happened during my assessment."

"What did happen?"

"Just nerves, I guess."

Eleanor and Poppy looked unconvinced, and Sloane knew they weren't just going to let this go. They were going to keep poking and prodding her memory—talking about it, looking at it, making her use it—until she'd been sick all over Basecamp. She'd probably find the man in the dream just so she could puke on his shoes, too.

The second she thought about him, a blue starburst exploded across her Mind Map.

"*Wou!*" said Poppy, pointing out the movement. She began tapping furiously on her iGlass, charting the course of the blast.

"Did my memory explode or something?" asked Sloane.

"This is not memory," said Poppy. "This is most strange. That particular shade of blue indicates a deep sense of…"

"Of what?" asked Eleanor.

Poppy's pale cheeks flushed pink. "Of…longing," said Poppy, peering at Sloane curiously. "Longing and desire."

They all watched as the remnants of the blue starburst moved toward Sloane's amygdala and pierced through one of the blockages like a laser. The shape exploded, the blockage faded from the Mind Map, and the amygdala looked a bit more like the shape Sloane had been born with.

"Fascinating," said Poppy. "The blue lines of longing appear to be dissolving the blockages around her amygdala." She zoomed in even closer, extracting a single blue line from the Mind Map and pulling it out to examine it. Sloane was terrified she would unwrap it like a fortune cookie and pull out a headshot of the man in the dream.

"This particular shade of blue is—eh, what is the word in English? It is like longing that leads to love."

Another blue firework burst across the Mind Map, the shrapnel blasting through several more of the blockages. Poppy and Eleanor yelped with excitement.

"This is most unusual," said Poppy, beaming at Sloane. "Whatever it is you long for, Sloane, you should just keep focusing on that. The more unblocked you become, the more your true abilities will shine through, and the more control you'll gain so your gift does not cause you sorrow."

Sloane happily did as she was told, conjuring memories of the blue place, the coffee shop, and the few precious moments of his voice through the earpiece, reveling in them as long as they'd let her. By the time Poppy stopped projecting the Mind Map, the wild blue lines of longing had multiplied to form a pulsating, protective nest around Sloane's amygdala, needling and nosing and bumping against the blockages, looking for a way through. If just the memories of the man in the dream were powerful enough to alter her brain, Sloane couldn't fathom what would happen when she saw him again in real life.

"SO, SIXTEENTH-CENTURY FRANCE, HUH?"

Simon's voice crackled over the satellite phone, but whether it was because of a bad connection or because he was hoarse from squealing with delight and uttering more *omigod*s in quick succession than she'd ever heard, Sloane couldn't tell. Either way, Simon sounded like he was on the other side of the world, which for all she knew, he might be. She still had no idea where in the world she was, and she wouldn't find out until moments before she went through the portal on P-Day, the crew taking running bets on whether she'd guess their location and how close she'd come to getting it right.

"Sixteenth-century freaking France," she said between bites of macrobiotic enchilada. Sloane was in her Basecamp bedroom, a large, windowless space that felt light and airy thanks to the virtual picture window that stretched the length of her bed. It was set to an ocean view now, the virtual sunlight sparkling over the virtual water and pouring into her room at the perfect angle for the time of day. The vision was accompanied by a soundtrack of lapping waves and a gentle, artificial breeze that billowed through the room, drying the nervous beads of sweat that kept pooling at the base of her throat. She had exactly seventeen minutes to dress, eat lunch, and talk to her brother before her first official training session as Hero.

"Do they know your French accent is abysmal?"

"It's not modern French," she said, fumbling with the clunky phone as she pulled a fresh T-shirt over her head. "They actually spoke Middle French in the sixteenth century."

"I can't tell if that's better or worse."

"They have this AI language assistant called LORI. They inject it straight into your bloodstream."

"What."

"Language Open Receptor Injection. They give me a shot of LORI, and the medicine increases neural connections in my brain so I can learn the language faster. Shit, I don't know if I was supposed to tell you that." She waited to see if the connection would be cut or if Poppy would barge in and confiscate the phone. "Any Program special ops swarming your apartment?"

"Not yet?" said Simon. "So, hurry up and tell me everything before they get here."

"So, LORI is like having a personal translator inside your head. She translates what you hear in real time, tells you what to say in response, that sort of thing. They'll give me a few injections during training and a longer-lasting one right before I go through the portal. By the time LORI wears off, I'll have had enough time to learn the language naturally, like a native speaker."

The bedroom's AI apologized for interrupting them. "Four minutes remaining for your call, Ms. Burrows."

"Sorry, Sai. Did you hear that? I don't have much time."

"It's fine," he said. "I'm just glad I get to hear your actual voice instead of the recordings of your Candidate interviews. They're playing them on an endless loop—"

"Oh, God, please don't—"

"Stop it. You looked great and you didn't sound stupid at all, and my heart is your heart, and I am so fucking proud of you. People all over the world are superimposing your face over Catherine de Medici's!"

"Please don't tell me what people all over the world are doing. And Catherine de Medici became Queen Regent of France in 1559. I'm going back to 1521."

"Right! Omigod omigod omigod, 1521. Do you know where you're going, exactly? They haven't announced any details yet."

"The Renaissance Château at Fontainebleau. I think I can tell you that. It's the primary residence of King Francis I. The Mission officially begins at his palace southeast of Paris."

"Omigod, omigod, oh my *God*, Sloane. Renaissance Paris at a king's freaking palace."

"Mmph," she said, chewing.

"I'm suddenly afraid someone's going to poison your mutton or something."

"Day One: Mutton poisoning. Day Two: Bubonic plague."

"But aren't you gonna stand out? Or were there lots of Eurasians among the French aristocracy?"

"They actually want King Francis to notice me," she said. "I'll be posing as a royal concubine from the Ottoman Empire, and they think my foreignness will spark the king's interest and he'll be more willing to meet with me privately."

"Privately?" said Simon, affronted. "They're whoring you out? The first-ever female Hero, and the best they can come up with is a concubine who sleeps with a sultan becoming a courtesan who sleeps with a king. Total waste of your abilities. And I looked up King Francis. The dude was bald, and his nose looked like a sausage."

"Simon, with you, everything is sausages."

"Omigod omigod omigod YOU'RE THE HERO. YOU ARE THE FREAKING 23ᴿᴰ HERO, SLOANE."

"And I'm not going to sleep with him. I'm going to be his fortune teller."

"WHAT."

"Three minutes remaining for your call, Ms. Burrows."

"Apparently it's a thing," she said, tying her sneakers. "Royal astrologers."

"Astrologers? But weren't the royalty super Catholic back then?"

"They were, but back then, the two weren't mutually exclusive. Even the pope had his own astrologers."

"You're gonna be a female Nostradamus."

"Pretty much."

"And just make shit up?"

"Worse," she said. "They want me to predict the future by memorizing the past."

The line went silent.

"Hello?" she said.

"The Program people know about your memory?" he said.

"They definitely know."

"Shit," said Simon. "Shit, shit, shit, I should have known. They know everything, don't they? They chose you so they could build a Mission around your memory."

"Unfortunately. Yeah."

"But on the news, they're saying your Mission is to stop France from colonizing the Americas, so I thought maybe—"

"The Mission is to stop King Francis from investing in the first French expedition to the Americas. The longer I can delay French colonization in the New World, the fewer indigenous people will perish over the centuries. Imagine if the Mi'kmaq people had retained control of Nova Scotia and New Brunswick. The more indigenous people survive, the more they'll be able to maintain their zero-carbon footprint way of life for future generations."

"But what does that have to do with predicting the future?"

"When my predictions always come true, King Francis will start to trust me. The idea is that the more accurate I am, the more he'll start to rely on me, especially with political and economic stuff. And by the time Verrazzano—"

"The Italian guy?"

"The Italian explorer, Giovanni da Verrazzano. By the time Verrazzano asks King Francis to invest in his expedition to the New World, the king won't make a move without consulting me first."

"So where does the memory machine come in?"

"They want me to memorize sixteenth-century European history. Like, all of it. Then, I'll be able to accurately 'predict' where the plague will strike next, who will win the next battle, that sort of thing. But I'll also predict who's coming to court that day, how much game King Francis will kill on his hunt, who's secretly sleeping together…"

"Two minutes remaining for your call, Ms. Burrows."

"The history, I get," said Simon. "But how could you possibly know how many quails this guy's gonna shoot or whatever?"

How, indeed.

Sloane eyed the antique leatherbound journal open on her bed, required reading from her Mission Reveal ceremony earlier that day. The first journal entry was dated 1517, and the entries continued through 1533, each one composed by a man who had been dead for centuries and yet had only left this century six years ago—the journal's author had been the 12th Hero. The designers of his Mission had sent him on several trips to France during his lifetime in England so he could gather intelligence that might be useful for future Missions. Missions like hers. The 12th Hero's secret reports in this journal would allow Sloane to make more nuanced, personalized predictions for King Francis. Personalized—and personal. She was under strict orders not to speak about the journal or reveal any of its content, but she was tempted to read Simon her favorite entry so far:

5 June 1518. After months of failed attempts, Francis has finally managed to get Françoise de Foix to join him in his bedchamber. Not sure how husband Jean will react when word gets around court, but I smell a duel. Also, let the record show that I don't miss my handheld, I definitely miss tacos, and the absence of bikini waxing has required me to do some serious recalibration on what I do and do not find sexually attractive.

The journal was Sloane's first indication of just how complex a Hero's Mission could be, and she had quickly grown overwhelmed—with her own Mission, with what could be asked of her beyond her Mission, with all the future Missions she, herself, might end up influencing. At the same time, the mental gymnastics required to create an interlocking web of Missions reassured her she was surrounded by the brightest minds on the planet, and that at Basecamp, having a freak memory was perhaps one of the least freaky things a person could have. For the first time in her life, she was among people just like her. But that also meant that for the first time in her life, she was separated from Simon, and not just physically.

"I can't tell you how I'll be able to predict the personal stuff for King Francis," she told him. "But I will. I'm sorry. I hate not being able to—"

"I'm asking because unless there's some patented Program technology to actually turn you psychic, I'm assuming you're going to memorize the personal stuff the way you memorize the history, and I'm also assuming there are going to be people around asking you to use your memory and witnessing you use your memory. Yes?"

"Lots of people. Hundreds of people."

"Haaaave you thought about how you're going to manage that without puking all over everyone?"

Sloane eyed the journal. She'd already memorized half the book, a feat as effortless as turning the pages if she was alone. Using her memory in front of the crew, on the other hand, was likely to create a biohazard situation for everyone. Eleanor had said it was safe to be herself here. Even if she could believe that, Sloane doubted it would be enough to undo the shame reflex that seemed part of her DNA. But she didn't know how to tell the most brilliant minds in the world that crafting a Mission reliant on her memory was a really bad idea.

She told Simon she was hoping to convince them to change her Mission. Every Mission had A- and B-objectives, right? Take the 6th Hero. His A-objective was to give Brazilian cattle ranchers a more profitable alternative to ranching so they'd abandon it and let the Amazon rainforest grow back. His B-objective was to convince beef-consuming populations that eating beef caused disease to lower the demand for meat. Sloane's A-objective was delaying French colonization of the Americas by becoming King Francis's Royal Astrologer—for now. She was sort of hoping she could make her B-objective the whole Mission instead because her B-objective was all about inventions. The first compound microscope, the first graphite pencil, and the first water thermometer were all invented in the mid-fifteen-hundreds. If Sloane helped King Francis invent them earlier in the century, the French Crown would be able to sell the inventions all over Europe, making inventions more profitable for France than colonization. Sloane would make sure everything was manufactured with sustainable, eco-friendly materials and processes, so that in the new timeline, France's Industrial Revolution will have wreaked far less havoc on the planet. Plus, inventions were cool. Inventions meant she got to fix stuff, make stuff, work with her hands.

Inventions wouldn't make Sloane sick.

"I like it," said Simon. "Less fortune telling, more inventions—"

"—less puking," said the twins.

"One minute remaining for your call, Ms. Burrows."

"Can you hear this?" asked Simon. "There's someone from the Program on this talk show, but I don't think they got the memo about the inventions."

What happens if Verrazzano never sets sail for the New World? asked an interviewer.

With French colonization delayed, indigenous people will survive European invasion in greater numbers. They'll be able to preserve their way of life, and that zero-carbon lifestyle will ripple across the centuries, impacting our present-day timeline.

Where will we see the greatest impacts?

We're predicting a huge improvement in air quality in UNNA's North Atlantic, a seven percent reversal of Arctic ice melt around Greenland, and a one-point-five percent sea level-decrease in the Atlantic.

So, Sloane Burrows can solve the sinking Florida problem from sixteenth-century France?

Exactly.

Exactly. As if it would be as easy as saying the words.

"Simon?"

"I'm here."

"Can you turn that off? I can't—"

"It's off. Sorry. Too much pressure?"

"It's just that…right now, all I can handle is *what*. If I think too much about *how*, I'm going to completely lose it."

"Talk about something else. Any hot guys there?"

"Your call is ending," said the AI.

"Oh my God! I didn't get to tell you about the man in the—"

"Goodbye."

"—dream."

DEEP IN THE BELLY OF Basecamp, a string of expletives echoed through the corridors. Someone was not happy, and the someone sounded a lot like Eleanor. Sloane threw Enkh a questioning glance, but the monk merely smiled and glided confidently forward, escorting her, with Poppy's aide, through the underground matrix to her first training session.

"Five minutes to session," announced an artificial voice. Again Sloane heard Eleanor's exasperated voice, which sounded closer this time. When they reached the next intersection, Poppy steered the group to the right while Enkh pulled left. After a brief tug-of-war, the monk won the battle, the group made a left turn, and Eleanor's agitated speech grew louder still.

"—elevator at the end of Corridor *B*," she was saying, followed by something Sloane couldn't make out, followed by Enkh's name and more cursing. Enkh steered Sloane toward another turn, but Poppy hung back, hissing at Enkh to stop. He didn't, until they rounded one more corner and came to a sudden halt. Sloane looked up to see Eleanor standing in the middle of the corridor. Behind her, a member of the crew was leaning against the wall, pinching the bridge of his nose as if he had a headache. Or a nosebleed? Sloane did a double take.

The crew member with the headache or nosebleed was the awkward guy from the coffee shop. The intern. The man in the dream.

"Oh, *hey*, Burrows!" said Eleanor. "I was just on my way to your first training session. Shall we?" Before Sloane could respond, Eleanor tried to shoo Enkh back the way he'd come, but the monk smiled his innocent smile and planted his feet next to Sloane's, refusing to budge. Eleanor's nostrils flared in annoyance, and when still Enkh did not move, her eyes darted to the man in the dream, giving Sloane an excuse to look at him.

Him. But not even a him or a man so much as a black hole summoning her beyond the event horizon, until she had no way of ever getting back to herself, no hope of avoiding annihilation and no desire to. She felt her whole body leaning toward him and wondered if Eleanor would catch her when she inevitably fell. Without a bulky windbreaker or filtration mask pushed back on his head, his resemblance to the man in the dream was uncanny. His careless hair fell in the same soft, chestnut waves. The slope of his nose and the angles of his jawline made his profile just as Athenian. His lips were just as pink and pillowy, and in a thin T-shirt, linen trousers, and slim white sneakers, his swimmer's build seemed immune to gravity. Looking at him, Sloane was besieged by every memory of the dream, by his face in the coffee shop, his voice during her assessment, the exploding blue bursts on her Mind Map. Her longing grew so palpable, she couldn't fathom being satiated, not ever. She did not know it was possible to want another person as much as she wanted this person and she thought she might never breathe again.

"Four minutes to session."

The man in the dream sighed as if resigned to his headache, pushed himself off the wall, and made his way toward them. Sloane didn't want him to catch her staring, so she kept her gaze trained on his hands; the long, thick fingers; the clean, square nails; the koa-wood wedding band wrapped around his left ring finger.

He was married.

She felt an avalanche inside her; the years of reality she'd constructed around him crumbling and toppling from an impossible height to drill a deep crater in her heart. She flashed on his eyes in the coffee shop, the eyes that had looked at her as if there were no one else he'd rather see. She tried to hold onto the look while mentally adding a third party to the mix, but when she did, his look became a lie—if there was no one else he'd rather see, there could be no one else, and certainly not a spouse.

She'd forget him, then. Shut it all down.

She stood there waiting for her longing to dissolve, for the faceless partner to obliterate it. But as the man in the dream moved closer and the vision of the wedding ring grew sharper, her longing remained, even leveraging the depths of the crater to take deeper root in her heart.

Eleanor smiled politely at the man in the dream as if he were a regular human and not an Adonis. A married Adonis. She asked if the two of them had met.

"Not exactly," he said, inviting Sloane to look into his eyes. They sparkled, more of a bluish silver than slate gray in this light. His expression was cautious, but even if he'd been scowling at her, it wouldn't have dispelled the peculiar relief she felt to be near him again.

"Sebastian," he said, extending his hand, and Sloane slipped hers inside his dry, warm grasp. A shock passed between them when their fingers touched, but neither of them flinched, as if they'd both been expecting it. "And you must be Sloane. Congratulations on making history." His grip was firm, and her hand molded to his so perfectly, it felt like it had disappeared inside his grasp. They were touching. He was touching her. *Omigod omigod omigod.*

When he let go, she had to remind herself to place her arm back at her side and force herself not to weep over the empty space where his hand used to be.

"Thank you," she said.

"Sorry about the coffee shop."

"Last time we send an intern on a prep assignment," said Eleanor with a snort. "Was he as embarrassing as he says he was?"

Sloane opened her mouth to speak, but after several seconds, no sound had come out.

"Three minutes to session."

"Anyway," said Eleanor, corralling Enkh and Sloane back in the direction they'd come from, "you might see Bastian in your training sessions from time to time, observing the process."

"If that's okay with you," he said. Enkh and Eleanor were guiding her forward, so Sloane had to crane her neck for another glimpse of Sebastian as he followed behind. Sebastian. Or was it Bastian? He was keeping pace with the group until their eyes met, upon which he slowed, his gaze softening. And then he stopped walking altogether and she was walking away from him. They were taking her away from him!

"It's totally okay," she said. "I mean, that's fine with me, Sebastian. Or is it Bastian?"

"My friends call me Bastian," he said, and for a split second, she could have sworn he looked at her with *that look*—the exact way he looked at her in the dream.

"Okay, okay, now that everyone's *friends*," said Eleanor, practically dragging Sloane down the corridor. When Sloane risked a final glance over her shoulder, Bastian was standing in the middle of the hallway, watching her go.

SLOANE GRABBED HER ASSAILANT'S WRISTS before he could wrap his arms around her neck. He grunted with surprise as she dug her nails into his skin and pulled down hard, snapping her head to the side to prevent the chokehold. Fast as lightning, she slipped a leg behind his, grabbed him behind the knees, and lifted up at the pressure points. He toppled over, landing on his back with a groan.

And then he looked up at her and smiled.

"Brilliant," said Johnny over applause from the crew. Tall, tan, and excruciatingly fit, Johnny was her movement, weapons, and self-defense trainer. In his charming Australian accent, Johnny explained his job as "keeping Heroes alive—because a dead Hero is a useless Hero." While Sloane would be relatively safe at King Francis's palace, she had to get there first. Johnny said most Heroes were dropped within a few hundred kilometers of their Mission start, but that Sloane was slightly fucked because Program intelligence suggested an initial drop point of Toulon, France, a southern port city that lay some 700 kilometers south of Paris, and by the way, the roads between the two towns were overrun with murderous thieves. Not to worry, though, because drop points were great for obtaining intel she could use later in her Mission. When she landed in Toulon, Sloane would be able to buy a horse and hire a *valet de chambre* to serve as her bodyguard on her journey to the palace. The valet was more for optics than anything; in the company of a male chaperone, she would be less likely to raise eyebrows as a woman traveling alone. Johnny's goal for training was six-on-one: Sloane Burrows would pass through the portal confident she could not only defend an attack but fight and defeat six grown men at a time while wielding the weapon of her choice. Sloane figured herself more of a run-and-hide than a stay-and-fight type, but she would have learned how to manipulate a medieval war scythe if it meant getting to be close to Bastian.

Sloane helped Johnny up from the floor, her gaze darting to the corner of the training room, where Bastian had been standing all afternoon with a finger perpetually pressed to his ear. Whenever she looked at him, he looked at her, his eyes like magnets every time she snuck a glance. But just now when she looked, his expression was tense, and when their eyes met, he looked away.

Johnny tapped his earpiece and frowned. "Let's take five," he said. "You can check in with Poppy, and I can get yelled at." Johnny got yelled at a lot, mostly by Eleanor, mostly in the hallway. Sloane couldn't fathom what the problem was. Wasn't this going well?

"It's not you, it's me," Johnny said with a grin. "Promise." Sloane watched him jog toward the training room exit, where the wall split open to reveal a perturbed-looking Eleanor waiting for him.

"How are you feeling?" asked Poppy, rushing to Sloane's side like a boxing coach to the ring. Her iGlass had projection software and an attachment that connected to the Mind Mapping room, allowing her to display a miniature version of Sloane's Mind Map from anywhere in Basecamp. After injecting Sloane with her fourth "small prick" of the day, Poppy scrutinized the moving lines and shapes on the map.

"Johnny has asked you to remember five complex moves in the past fifty minutes, but we haven't seen any new blockages form," said Poppy. "I assume recalling the moves is not bringing up bad memories?"

Sloane shook her head. No bad memories. No sour stomach. With Bastian nearby, the threat of nausea was about as threatening as a water balloon through a brick wall. Besides, no one could tell she was using her memory to instantly retain each move Johnny taught her—they probably just thought she'd taken self-defense before. And even if they did know, maybe that was okay. Maybe Bastian's presence had cured her nausea reflex and she'd never have to worry about vomiting in public again.

"The blue lines of desire have increased significantly in the past hour," said Poppy. "Perhaps your desire to perform is neutralizing the anxiety around using your memory."

Desire to perform. Sure.

"But there is new movement," said Poppy, pointing to a crop of spinning blue spirals on the Mind Map.

"Blue is a good color, right?"

"Well, yes. But this shape could be problematic. It is a type of distraction."

"Ready to rock?" asked Johnny, jogging toward them.

"She's good to go," Poppy said. "We'll keep an eye on the distraction. From what you've learned so far today, I can't imagine it's going to be a problem."

Sloane smiled and thanked her, her eyes darting straight to the source of the distraction, who was standing with his hands on his hips, watching her. She was so mesmerized by his eyes that when they darted to her left, it was almost too late—she ducked out of the way just as Johnny lunged for her in a surprise attack. She dodged him and jogged away, her body surging with cortisol and adrenaline, and the crew broke into applause.

"There's that Spidey Sense!" Johnny said, clapping for her along with the crew. "Now, in addition to core skills and intuition, you're going to need strength. A strong body can better withstand those gnarly sixteenth-century plagues. May I?" He nodded to her upper arms. She consented, and Johnny wrapped his hand around her puny bicep, clicking his tongue.

"Go on and make a muscle, then," he said.

"I am," she said.

Johnny tutted, shaking his head. "Down you go, love."

Sloane hit the floor to the sounds of hooting and applause, which were quickly replaced by Johnny's painfully slow counting of one endless push-up after another. When Sloane glanced up to look for Bastian, she saw everyone in the room down on the floor in plank position, pushing up and down with her in solidarity. Her heart swelled with gratitude and the choked-up feeling that for the first time ever, she didn't just have Simon; she had *people*. Her people. Bastian was part of that. He was not only down on the floor but doing his push-ups one-handed, as if he might earn extra credit with Johnny on her behalf. His eyes darted her way at the top of a push-up, and when he caught her watching him, he quickly looked down again. She couldn't help but notice him speed up his efforts, pumping at a slightly faster pace than the rest of the group.

THE NEXT DAY, SLOANE WAS being held captive in the Mind Mapping room until she told Eleanor and Poppy the truth about why she couldn't stop puking. They'd had the Mom Chair shipped from her apartment to Basecamp for the occasion, and she sat in it now, sulking and plotting ways to get herself the hell out of this pointless 'therapy session' or whatever it was and back into the training room. Back to Bastian.

During her first history lesson, Sloane had memorized decades of recorded history in minutes without incident. But when her trainers had quizzed her on the material in front of everyone, she'd vomited four times. No matter how much she told herself it was safe to be herself, and that everyone wanted her to use her memory because the Mission depended on it, her stomach would not listen to reason. Desperate to end the public mortification, Sloane had suggested a few minor tweaks to her Mission, such as more inventions! And less fortune telling! And maybe no fortune telling at all! But Eleanor squashed her hopes, fast: they'd chosen her as Hero precisely because of her memory, and they considered her technical skills a nice bonus. If she couldn't use her memory, Sloane just knew they'd send her home, away from Bastian, and make Debbie Allen the new Hero. So, she'd hidden the real cause of her nausea, telling Eleanor she must have food poisoning from yesterday's enchiladas, and come to think of it, she was allergic to hot sauce, and on top of that, she had the stomach flu. She stuck to her story, too, even when the Program physician ran test after test and could not find any viruses or harmful bacteria in Sloane's system.

"I'm not seeing major activity between your amygdala and neocortex," Poppy said now, moving the shapes around on Sloane's Mind Map. "You're not reliving old, painful memories as you memorize the new content, are you?"

She wasn't reliving old memories. Not exactly.

Poppy threw Eleanor a look. "It's what I thought, then." She pointed to a reddish, tornado-like shape that had first appeared on Sloane's Mind Map in the training room and had grown tenfold in the hours since, spinning faster and faster as the day wore on. The tornado covered the entire Mind Map now, blotting out the blue lines of desire and overtaking everything in its path.

"But her amygdala was looking more and more unblocked," Eleanor said, mystified. "The blue longing lines that destroy the blockages—those have been increasing by the hour, right? Her speed, receptivity, and retention rates are rapidly improving."

Poppy set down her iGlass and looked at Sloane, tapping her stylus against her chin. "All true. But your sickness today has nothing to do with any of that, does it, Sloane?" Sloane regarded her sourly, not sure how much more scrutiny she could take. "Having attention placed on your gift makes you feel sick, but you're used to that feeling. Sometimes, you relive bad memories, but you're used to that, too. You can bear it. But what you cannot bear, at least not without becoming ill, and certainly not in large doses, is the feeling of shame."

Sloane stared at Poppy, stunned. Exposed.

Eleanor's face twisted in confusion. "What does she have to be ashamed of? She's been getting all the answers *right*." Sloane felt her stomach turn, but thanks to the industrial strength nausea medication they'd given her, it felt like nothing more than a muscle spasm.

Poppy whispered to Eleanor that getting all the answers right was precisely the problem.

She extracted the red-orange tornado of shame, swept the other lines and shapes away, and enlarged the tornado until its movement was clearly visible. The tornado's every ring looked like a snake eating its own tail. With each rotation, a spinning ring was destroyed and replaced by the spinning ring beneath it. And so the tornado was not destroying everything in its path; it was destroying itself, over and over again, its very existence dependent on this act of destruction.

"What is the origin of your shame, Sloane?"

Sloane couldn't help rolling her eyes. "Look, I took the medication, okay? I'm not throwing up anymore. Can I please go back to the training room?"

"Answer the question, Burrows."

"It's not that big of a deal," she said, exasperated. "It's just that my memory tends to cause problems. I tend to cause problems. For other people, and for myself."

"Interesting," Poppy said, eyeing the movement of the tornado. The spinning rings had slowed ever-so-slightly, each ring replacing the next with a newfound sense of hesitation. "Have you always felt this way?"

"Since I was a kid, I guess."

"And how far back into childhood can you remember?"

Sloane's stomach lurched; apart from Simon, she had never told anybody the answer to that question for fear they'd think she was a freak, but also because nobody had ever asked. "Um. To my birthday."

"Which birthday?"

"The original. Day of birth."

Poppy let out a little sigh of awe. "So, if I asked you to recall a particular moment from your first week of infancy—"

Eleanor said they didn't have time for this.

"My apologies, Sloane," said Poppy. "Professional curiosity. Please recall the first time you felt ashamed of your memory."

Sloane looked down. Remembered. In her mind's eye, she was no longer sitting in the Mind Mapping room but sitting up in her toddler bed in her rosebud nightgown, the sheets damp with sweat, the sippy cup on the nightstand. "Who are you with in this moment, during this first experience of shame?"

"With my dad," she said, picturing his face growing redder and redder as she beat him at the Game of Memory.

"And why does your dad shame you?"

"I'm ruining a game that's supposed to be fun. I'm not supposed to be able to beat him. He's a grownup and I'm just a kid. It's not normal. I'm not normal because there's something wrong with me, and I'm ruining the game like I ruin everything because I'm a walking tornado that destroys everything in its path."

"According to your dad."

"He's right. No matter how hard I try to be normal, my freak memory just…ruins things."

"People with normal memories ruin things every day," said Poppy.

"Not at the same rate," said Sloane.

"Please name something you have ruined."

"Um, my relationship with my dad, every romantic relationship I've ever had, my job of seven years, the Program—"

"The Program?" said Poppy.

"I've only been here three days, and I've already failed my assessment, puked all over everyone, delayed training, completely screwed up the schedule, and freaked out the whole crew."

Poppy and Eleanor burst out laughing, and even Enkh opened his eyes to join them. Sloane's cheeks burned, and for the first time since coming here, she wished she were back in Vancouver.

Eleanor was quick to apologize and compose herself, but Sloane couldn't tell if the apology was meant for her or the person Eleanor was always talking to through her earpiece. She said governments tried to dismantle them every day. They had M16 and the MSS and Mossad trying to pinpoint their location at all times, and that not a day went by when someone, somewhere, wasn't trying to sue them or pass legislation to shut them down.

"What she means is it would take a lot more than a little vomit to destroy the Program," said Poppy, "and that nothing has been ruined. So, perhaps Harry is mistaken. Perhaps your memory is not a mechanism for tearing down, but a tool for building up. You would not be here now if we did not believe you and your memory can be a powerful force for good in the world. Perhaps it is a gift to be grateful for."

"I know all that," said Sloane. "I know you all think my memory is some kind of superpower you want to leverage for the good of the planet. And I want that, too. But it's not just a tool I can pick up and use like anything else. Not after a lifetime of trying to hide it or not use it in the first place. And I'm sorry, but how can I be grateful for my memory when it's the reason my own father doesn't…" She broke off, swallowing the lump in her throat. "It's what makes me who I am," she said quietly. "And he hates who I am."

Poppy squatted in front of the Mom Chair, taking Sloane's hand. "Does it really matter what one man thinks of you when the entire planet is wishing you well and cheering you on?"

"God, you sound like my brother," she said. "Look, I wish I didn't care what Harry thinks, but how can I not? He's the only parent I have."

"Good work, team," said Eleanor, swiping her iGlass. "We're making progress. Let's shift focus for a minute and take care of some admin. Sloane, we just need your eyes on a couple of legal docs authorizing our attorneys to take care of these lawsuits."

"Lawsuits?" she asked. "Against…me?"

"It's not unusual for a Hero to—"

"Wait, law*suits*? As in, multiple? How many are there?"

"Two," Eleanor said.

"Two?!" said Sloane. "Do you see what I'm saying? Only I could turn the greatest opportunity on earth into a legal problem. I bet none of the other Heroes got sued."

Eleanor waited, fighting a smile. She said the average number of lawsuits per Hero was fifteen.

Oh.

"The first suit is a complaint from your former employer."

"Why would Brody want to sue me?"

Eleanor frowned at her iGlass. "He's basically arguing that you used knowledge gained during employment with him to help you beat out the other Candidates." Sloane's nostrils flared, and Eleanor laughed. "About what I thought."

"What's the second lawsuit?"

"The second lawsuit…was filed in Vancouver yesterday. By Harry Burrows."

Sloane's stomach dropped.

"He didn't qualify to be a beneficiary on the insurance policy you took out when you applied, so now he's trying to get money by suing you. Looks like he's asking us to cover your student loan debt, but he's also asking for additional damages for emotional distress."

"Emotional...?" she said, sputtering. "Wait, why couldn't he get the insurance money?"

Eleanor glanced at Enkh. The monk's eyes were open and fixed on Sloane, his gaze like burning obsidian. When Eleanor continued, Sloane listened to her words but found she couldn't look away from Enkh.

"The beneficiary on the policy has to be a blood relative of the Hero, or the spouse, domestic partner, or legally adoptive parent or child of the Hero." Something had just happened, and while she couldn't immediately deduce what it was, Sloane felt a mix of mourning and relief, like finding out a terrible president had just been assassinated. "The insurance company we work with requested the DNA from your application, which is pretty typical for these types of policies. They required a paternity test for Harry before he got the payout. He failed."

"He...failed," said Sloane.

"He failed," said Eleanor.

"He failed because..."

"Because Harry Burrows is not your biological father."

Enkh was at her side, holding her hand, letting her crush his fingers without complaint. Sloane waited for the memories to wash over her—everything she'd ruined, every way she'd disappointed him, every ounce of effort she'd made to win Harry's love over the course of three decades. But all that came was a vague feeling of relief she wasn't ready to feel, and the desire to see her brother.

"Does Simon know?"

"You have a family phone call scheduled between your morning training sessions tomorrow," Eleanor said, peering at her iGlass. "You can call him then."

"Did he...I mean, is *that* why Harry's always been so...?" She practically choked on the question, but Eleanor seemed to read her mind, and she didn't have to finish it.

"We can't be sure what Harry knew or when he knew it," she said. "But our data scientists have analyzed everything we have on him for the past twenty-nine years, and we're eighty-nine percent confident that he believed he was your biological father."

She nodded, her thoughts knocking into each other like mismatched puzzle pieces. "And our...our real...?"

"That's enough for today," said Eleanor. Sloane was so exhausted she didn't protest and let Eleanor guide her from the room. When the wall split open, she glanced back to see that Poppy had pulled up her Mind Map again. The shame tornado had faded and moved to the background layer of the map. When Poppy pulled it out to examine it, Sloane saw that the circular rings were no longer destroying themselves. They hovered in the shape of the tornado as if the door to a cage had been opened but they weren't quite sure how to move through or what might be on the other side.

MINUTES AFTER ELEANOR BID HER goodnight, Sloane's bedroom wall split open again and Enkh glided into the room. The monk seemed intrigued by the virtual picture window over her bed. It was set to a mountain view, and they watched in silence as the first virtual stars blinked on above the virtual, snow-capped peaks.

"Um, Enkh? Is there something you needed? Because I'm pretty sure I'm supposed to be sleeping now."

But Enkh just could not get enough of that window. He moved closer to it, and then he started touching the screen, swiping his palms along the window's edges. He touched a spot in the corner of the window, and the virtual mountains disappeared to reveal a very real, very solid concrete wall. In the center of the wall, there was a door. Enkh moved to a scanner next to the door and stood still while a beam of light scanned his retinas. He waited for a soft click, and when it came, he pushed the door open. A rush of cool wind tussled Sloane's hair. It was real wind, the air so fresh it conjured an autumn afternoon in Grade 5—the last day she'd been allowed to walk home from school without a mask.

Enkh stepped aside, and Sloane flew through the opening to find herself on the first step of a spiraling wooden staircase. It twisted around and around, stretching up toward a canopy of ancient evergreens whose tops disappeared into the black night sky above. She took the first curving spiral of stairs in a rush before glancing back to see if Enkh was behind her, but the monk was still on the ground floor outside her bedroom, and he gestured for her to continue on her own.

She raced up the staircase, trying to outpace the thoughts of *Harry*, step, step, *Simon*, step, step, *my birth father*, step, step, step. The staircase led to an enormous viewing platform that emerged above the canopy, where she stepped out onto a tower that had been built on top of the highest mountain peak in a sea of mountain peaks; a vast, rugged tapestry of limestone karsts that stretched across the land like frozen waves. Sloane gasped for breath, sucking in the thin, sweet air and the fragrance of lush vegetation all around her. She couldn't stop touching her face, marveling at having the air in direct contact with her skin for so long. All was silent, save the soft whoosh of the breeze and the chirping of crickets in the trees. The bright, iridescent light of the waxing moon painted each peak in a thousand subtle shades of black-purple-gray, drawing the news of Harry from her mind until it seemed the earth had swallowed the thought of him. Who could think of anything when there was a visible moon in the sky, and real stars? She counted five, ten, twelve of them, more stars than she had seen since childhood. Down the mountain, scattered lights cascaded over the steep hills, and beyond them, the lights of a sprawling city shimmered and twinkled as if its inhabitants had strung every street with lanterns. Her body pulsed with electricity, and she felt as if this was the only moment of her life that mattered.

In the darkness, someone cleared his throat. Sloane spun around, startled to see the silhouette of a figure sitting on a bench behind her. At first, she thought Enkh had glided up the tower stairs in her wake after all, but the figure shifted on the bench, and the moonlight illuminated a tendril of careless hair. Enkh, she reminded herself, did not have any hair.

"Hi," said Bastian, tucking his earpiece into the pocket of his trousers. She stood there, staring at him in stunned silence. His earpiece was in his pocket, Enkh was far below, and Poppy had shut off Sloane's Mind Map for the night.

They were completely alone.

Every thought she'd ever thought about him, every word she'd imagined speaking to him, every question she'd wanted to ask him assaulted her at once. The onslaught of memories brought with them the intensity of that day's session, the fact that her dad was not her dad, the mystery of the father she'd never met, and the devastating realization that she was going to blow this chance to say the perfect thing to Bastian. All of that, juxtaposed against the elation she felt that he was there and the vision of his figure in the darkness rushed through her at once, demanding to be released. Her eyes filled, and soon the tears wouldn't stop.

Bastian jumped up from the bench and held out a hand, beckoning her. She crossed to him, and he wrapped his arms around her waist, sat back down on the bench, and pulled her into his lap as if it were the most natural thing in the world. She felt safe in his arms, but inside she had leaped off the tower and was free-falling with nothing to latch onto, her mind unable to keep pace with their bodies. She pressed her wet cheek to his, suddenly enveloped in warm skin and hard muscle and his essence, oh God, the exact cocktail she had imagined—pear and cedar and salt. A whiff of the sea. As if the sea she was meant to sail upon had always been him, and he was finally rocking her gently upon his waves. They fit together. Her body melted in his arms as easily as her hand had disappeared inside his, and she threaded her fingers through the thicket of his hair until she heard his breath catch. He buried her in his full embrace, which only fueled her longing, and at the same time, there was no hope of sating her longing save his touch. There in his arms, her tears subsided, and the moment alone with him in the darkness materialized as the miracle it was. She found enough purchase within herself to realize this was her chance, that she should say something, anything. Maybe not something about how good he smelled, but anything else.

Sloane pulled back to look into his eyes just as she heard footsteps clomping up the tower stairs from below. Without a word, Bastian lifted her up, set her down on the far side of the bench, and leaped back to his seat, tucking his legs beneath him as if he'd been meditating in that exact spot for hours. When the sounds of footsteps neared the top of the platform, he tore his gaze from hers and stared out over the dark mountains.

Eleanor was relieved, then furious, then relieved again to find Sloane sitting on top of the tower. Poppy scolded Sloane, insisting she'd arrived on time to give Sloane her bedtime injection but that Sloane was nowhere to be found. Eleanor reminded Sloane of the massive security protocols she had just breeched and the massive importance of security throughout Basecamp. She could be spotted by an anti-Program spy. She could fall off the tower. She could get eaten by the world's last remaining mountain lion. The list went on, but nothing Eleanor said could dampen the elation Sloane felt at having been in Bastian's arms; it was inconceivable to her that she had been crying just moments before.

Neither Eleanor nor Poppy said a word to Bastian, nor he to them, as they escorted Sloane toward the stairs. She stole a final glance at the man who'd just rocked her in his arms like a child, wondering if he'd been careful to hide their embrace because of the ring on his finger or because a lowly intern would get in big trouble for holding a Hero in his arms. Especially the first-ever female Hero. Especially if she was crying. Through the darkness, she found his eyes, which were glistening like ocean-covered moons. The scent of him, the warm dewiness of his skin, the thickness of his damp hair, the way she'd melted in his arms all ignited and sated her longing, and she suddenly felt brave. He made her feel brave.

As Sloane listened to Eleanor's reprimands, which continued all the way down the stairs, she even felt brave enough to reflect on the man who'd always been her dad. Her mind didn't quite believe it, but her heart entertained the possibility that Harry's disapproval need not weigh on her as heavily as it always had, and that his opinions need not be regarded as fact— especially his opinions about her. Maybe what she'd come to think of as her tornado-like destructive nature was nothing more than one man's myth, and a man who wanted nothing to do with her at that. It was absurd to think she ruined *everything*. It was irrational to believe she couldn't make things better if she tried. It was too late to repair things with Harry, but she could still fix things for Simon. Three flights from the ground, Sloane told Eleanor that Simon should replace Harry as her new beneficiary on the insurance policy and that her brother must always be taken care of.

Eleanor's eyes widened in surprise. "Of course he'll be taken care of," she assured Sloane. "It's too late to deal with insurance, but we don't need it. Whatever you want Simon to have, he'll have. Unless it's billions of dollars or his own island or something. I'd probably have to get approval for that."

Eleanor leaned into the retina scanner to reenter the building as Poppy withdrew a syringe from her jacket pocket.

"I want to talk to him," said Sloane. "Get Simon on the phone right now. Please."

Eleanor reminded Sloane, not without a tinge of exasperation, that she had a call scheduled with Simon in the morning and that right now, she needed her sleep. When Eleanor pushed the door open, Sloane stood her ground outside, charged and a little woozy with the foreign, unexpected feeling of asserting herself. She felt as if she were floating between two selves—behind her was Harry Burrows' slumped-shouldered, disaster-prone daughter with the freak memory; before her was the 23rd Hero, chosen out of millions of applicants precisely because of her memory. And here she was, existing in some sort of limbo between them, unsure how she'd respond if Eleanor refused her request. It seemed equally likely that Sloane would shrivel and back down as insist on speaking to Simon until she heard her brother's voice on the line.

Eleanor started to protest, and in a quivering voice, Sloane insisted she would speak with her brother *now*. The look of consternation on Eleanor's face softened. "Our Comms team will need five minutes to get you set up via satellite," she said. "You can take the call in your room."

Sloane turned back toward the tower and peered upward into the darkness, where the man she never stopped thinking of had made her feel brave enough to think of other things.

"THIRTY SECONDS!" SAID KOFI, HIS voice ringing out from the other side of the dressing screen.

Sloane didn't need thirty seconds. She had already finished fixing a golden caul and French hood over her hair and sliding a pendant necklace between her breasts. She'd already adjusted the embroidered, elaborately puffed sleeves of her plum-colored gown, folding the cuffs up to her shoulders to reveal the satin lining encrusted with pearls. She'd already breathed a sigh of relief that she wouldn't have to don a whalebone corset for at least another twenty years. She didn't need the time, but she'd take it. Standing alone behind the dressing screen, she closed her eyes and debated how she might spend it.

She could rehash the details of her identity as Mahidevran, a royal concubine of Suleiman the Magnificent, Sultan of the Ottoman Empire. According to her backstory, Mahidevran was traveling in France because the sultan's chief consort, Hürrem, had grown jealous of his affections for Mahidevran and insisted he send her away.

But she didn't think about what it was going to be like to be Mahidevran.

She could practice her Ottoman Turkish accent. It was important that Mahidevran sound like she hailed from sixteenth-century Constantinople, so in addition to teaching her basic Turkish, Arabic, and Persian, Sloane's language trainer was schooling her in accented versions of the languages she'd speak in France: the Provençal dialect of Occitan, which she'd need when she first landed in Toulon, and Middle French, which she'd speak at the king's court. Layering on a foreign accent to two new languages was a complex, nuanced undertaking that would have been impossible without the Language Open Receptor Injection. A dose of LORI increased the neural connections in her brain, making Sloane as receptive to new languages as a young child. Her memories of foreign languages—particularly French—became sharper and even faster to retrieve. When she listened to her instructors speak Provençal or Middle French, LORI not only translated their words into English; she served up ready-made responses for Sloane to repeat, 'speaking' to Sloane in an inner voice that sounded like her own. Poppy showed Sloane how to control LORI with her mind, tweaking the amount and type of assistance LORI provided. At the Learner level, LORI offered a word-by-word translation into English, which was helpful for memorizing vocabulary. At the Native Speaker level, Sloane could understand both languages instantly upon hearing them. She could just as easily open her mouth and let LORI's words pour from it, only grasping the meaning of what she was saying as she said it. Using the Native Speaker level was exhilarating and terrifying, like the trust exercises Brody used to make them do at Boothie bonding retreats. And in Dormant Mode, Sloane could relegate LORI to the background using the same control she was developing to corral her memories.

But she didn't spend her thirty seconds practicing her accent, either.

She could perfect the daily prayers she'd learned in Arabic to further enhance her cover story. Mahidevran would arrive in France as a practicing Muslim, then publicly convert to Catholicism within her first few years at court. In 1521, King Francis was still tolerant of other religions, but if Sloane waited too long to convert, she'd risk a similar fate to the thousands of Huguenot Protestants who were burned as heretics during King Francis's reign.

But she didn't practice her prayers, either.

In those few delicious seconds, Sloane did not rehash, practice, or perfect anything except the memory of Bastian's embrace.

She'd arrived at her training session the following morning feeling brave enough to ask him what, exactly, had happened between them up there.

She wanted to know if he felt as relieved as she did when they were close. She wanted to know if he felt the same sense of longing, and if it ached in his chest the way it did in hers. She wanted to know if it was possible that *he'd* been having recurring dreams about *her*. And she especially wanted to know about his wedding ring and how he could look at her the way he looked at her when he was committed to someone else. But when the session had started, Bastian was nowhere to be found, and a thicket of blue spirals—the distraction kind—had grown like weeds across Sloane's Mind Map. As the afternoon wore on and he was still nowhere in sight, she concluded that Bastian regretted holding her, which devolved into him never wanting to see her again. Poppy was baffled by the blue spirals of distraction, but the sudden appearance of depression mystified her more. Sloane told her it was residual pain from discovering Harry Burrows was not her biological father, and Poppy refrained from calling her bluff—for now.

The longer Sloane went without the real thing, the harder she clung to the memory. In the brief breaks between training sessions, she'd use every ounce of her memory control to conjure Bastian's arms around her waist, her fingers in his hair, his hands on her back as he pressed her to his chest, as close as they could get without—

"Five! Four! Three! Two!"

Sloane emerged from behind the screen into a simulation of the ballroom at Fontainebleau. Her trainers and all the crew were outfitted in sixteenth-century attire as if they'd all been swept through the time travel portal together. Kofi looked dashing in a golden, long-skirted doublet and velvet cape; Debbie Allen was beautiful in an indigo gown trimmed with jewels and fur. Satisfied with the folds of her bombard sleeves and the position of her French hood, Kofi ushered Sloane into the center of the room. Johnny, still in cotton cut-off shorts and a T-shirt, increased the volume of the Renaissance polyphonic music and clapped for everyone to take their positions in two parallel lines on the dance floor. Johnny stood in position across from Sloane with a finger to his ear, calling for a stand-in so he could observe the dance. A tall figure jogged toward the line to take Johnny's place, and after some shuffling, Bastian stood across from Sloane in a leather jerkin and dramatic fur robe, looking just like a king. Kofi made a joke about the robe, and Bastian razzed Kofi about his hosen, taking great care, it seemed to Sloane, not to look in her direction.

"It is 152 France, people!" said the French trainer. "That is France before it was France. The king's French is Middle French—I do not want to hear a word of Modern French, English, or any other language, for that matter. And do not let me catch you speaking Middle French with a modern French accent! If you need more LORI, tap out this round and ping Medical with an injection request."

"And remember, the Volta is a scandalous country dance," said Johnny. "Gentlemen, don't be shy about having a squiz at the ladies. Talk and flirt as you go, yeah?"

The crew played their parts with abandoned glee. Two trainers tittered in Sloane's ear in fluent Middle French, gossiping about the king's new lover. The men slapped each other's backs and made eyes at the ladies, bragging about that day's hunt as they stepped down the line to the beat of the music. They peppered their speech with the idioms her French trainer had been drilling into her for the past five days, and Sloane understood everything, except why her dance partner refused to look into her eyes.

"*Monsieur*," she said, taking great care with the foreign accent. "Is it not customary in your country to look into a lady's eyes when dancing with her?" They parted, the pattern of the dance moving Bastian to the line in front of her, but she felt him hesitate as he pulled his hand from hers. When she bowed to her new partner, he launched into a bawdy monologue about how lucky her husband was to have acquired such a luscious peach of a bride, and Bastian's shoulders stiffened in front of her. "I would give him your compliments," said Sloane, "but I have yet to meet my husband."

She glided from one partner to the next, conversing flawlessly, until she was passed back to Bastian for the dance's peak move. He grasped the hard busk of her bodice and used his thigh to lift her off the floor as if she weighed nothing, turning her in an elegant, effortless circle. When he set her down, his hands lingered at her waist, and finally he looked into her eyes. "*Demoiselle*," he said, his pronunciation breathtakingly perfect. "In my country, it is customary to prevent oneself from coming utterly undone. It is for this reason that I now find it necessary to avoid your eyes at all costs."

He released her and turned away, stepping in time with the music, but Sloane stood frozen, her heart ringing like a bell in her chest. Her new partner attempted to pull her back into the line, but her dress caught on her shoe, her ankle snapped to the side, and she gasped in pain, falling to the floor in a heap of skirts. The men rushed to her side while the ladies hung back, still in character, until Johnny cut the simulation. Bastian took two steps toward her, stopped himself, and let the others sweep her from the room.

"SMALL PRICK, SLOANE."

Poppy woke her up in the middle of another dreamless sleep cycle. She brought Sloane her robe, and they waited in silence until the injection had kicked in, Sloane blinking away the dreary nothingness that now ruled her sleep. She couldn't be sure if it was all the injections, but the man in the dream had not appeared once since Sloane had arrived at Basecamp, the blue place as inexplicably absent and unreachable as Bastian had become in real life. The cruel irony of meeting the man in the dream for real seemed to be losing him in both places, and she wondered if she would have come here if she'd known it would mean the end of her dreams, and the disappearance of the blue place—the only place where there was never any question of how he felt about her.

Poppy led Sloane down the darkened corridor to the Mind Mapping room and ushered her through the parted wall. Eleanor and Enkh were already there waiting for her, the purpose of the midnight meeting made immediately clear to Sloane: they were going to fire her. Debbie Allen was already in the training room, and Sloane was being packed up and shipped out.

"Just a talk," said Poppy, reaching behind Sloane's ear to make sure the Mind Mapping sticker was secure. "About why you have been feeling distracted."

127

Sloane rolled her ankle around in her slipper, remembering the price she'd paid for that distraction. The doctor had pronounced the injury an acute fracture, numbed the pain with an injection, and administered several mystery liquids for Sloane to drink. She'd escorted Sloane to a surgical suite, and in the twenty seconds between being given the anesthetic and passing out, Sloane had babbled about how long it had taken Simon to heal when he'd fractured his ankle hang-gliding. At least six weeks, she'd said, hoping, in her delirium, that her training time, and her time with Bastian, could be extended by at least that much. When she came to, her X-Rays were clear, and her ankle felt completely fine. The real damage, she realized now, was in the hours of wasted training time. And it was not lost on Sloane that, should she have gotten injured in such a manner in the sixteenth century, she could have put the entire Mission at risk. She deserved to be fired. Even with the nausea medication, even with the news that Harry Burrows wasn't her father, even with the possibility that he'd been wrong when he'd said she always destroyed everything, she'd still managed to ruin this—the thing she had always wanted.

"Hey, Burrows," said Eleanor. She was holding Poppy's iGlass, frowning at Sloane's Mind Map, which was lit up with the red-orange glow of anxiety.

"Sloane, we want you to know that you have been doing great overall," Poppy said. "The nausea medication is working well, and you've removed fifty-six percent of the blockages around your amygdala."

"But...?"

"But when we look at your Mind Map," said Eleanor, "it seems like you're not making use of your full potential. Almost like your mind is somewhere else." They both looked at her expectantly. Sloane looked at the floor. "Burrows. We really don't want to invade your privacy, but this Mission is too important to continue like this. If you're not able to pinpoint the source of the distraction, we're going to have to switch your Mind Map into Visual Mode to find it."

Sloane gulped, unsure what Eleanor meant by 'Visual Mode' and worried she was about to find out. "You said my thoughts and emotions cannot be used against me," she said. "You said my actions during training are what matters.”

“Your actions are why we’re concerned,” Eleanor said, projecting a video clip from that afternoon’s simulation in the ballroom. Sloane watched herself spin away from Bastian and stop dead in her tracks. Seconds ticked by, but still she remained frozen, as if she had no idea where she was or what she was supposed to be doing. Eleanor swiped the video clip away. She said if Sloane blew her cover, no one was going to accuse her of being from the future. They were going to think she was crazy. Lock her up. Burn her alive.

Sloane considered telling them the truth—that their intern just happened to be the star of her decade-long recurring dream. They’d think she was bonkers. Too lovesick to be a Hero. They’d send her back to Vancouver, away from him. She said nothing.

“You’re probably aware that UNNA is hesitant to continue supporting the Program in light of our recent delays in selecting a Hero, and that we’re under an enormous amount of pressure to succeed. If you fail, they’ll shut us down. But more importantly, you got hurt today. That can’t happen again. Not just because we care about your wellbeing, but because we were already delayed by eight hours at the start of your training. We don’t have this much recovery time built into the schedule.”

Sloane curled her chin into her chest and made a half-hearted attempt to blame her continued distraction on Harry’s paternity reveal, but even she didn’t believe it.

“Fine,” said Eleanor, slapping her thighs. “Let’s do it.”

Sloane watched helplessly as Poppy projected her Mind Map, toggled to a different setting on her iGlass, and switched Sloane’s Mind Map to Visual Mode. All the swirling lines and shapes across the map began to reconfigure themselves, the color and light pulling apart and rejoining to form hundreds, and then thousands of images. Some of the images were still, like photographs. Others were moving vignettes, like film. The common theme across all the various forms of visual media was Bastian.

He wasn’t everywhere, of course. She could also see President Nanda and Simon, King Francis and Enkh. But between every image not of Bastian was an image of Bastian—his eyes seeking hers across the training room, his mouth breaking into a heart-stopping smile, his arms around Sloane on the tower. Oh, Christ, there were even close-ups of his painfully perfect ass.

Just when she thought it couldn't get any worse, Sloane noticed the familiar but unsettling sight of her own bare breasts. In the vignette, her head was tossed back in ecstasy and Bastian's face was buried between her legs—her fantasy of how she hoped he'd respond if she ever worked up the nerve to tell him he was the man in the dream. The scene triggered memories of all the times she had played out the fantasy—five, to be exact—and the memories duplicated themselves and floated around the original on her Mind Map like lights around a marquee: in case anyone hadn't noticed yet, LOOK HERE! Behold how Visual Mode makes absolutely no distinction between the actual and the fantastical, the mildly pornographic and the mortifyingly personal! The technology had even rendered a snapshot of the one time—one!—that Sloane had wondered what it would be like to suck his toes. She gasped, and the image seemed to respond to her attention, enlarging itself and moving into the foreground of the map as if to say, "Is *this* the one you *really* don't want anyone to see?"

Poppy shut off the projection, but Sloane's mortification was complete. They all sat in painful silence, the seconds passing like hours. At one point, Eleanor moved to the corner of the room and started whispering to the person in her ear. Whisper, whisper, "conflict of interest." Whisper, whisper, "distraction." Whisper, whisper, "off-site monitoring." Sloane hung her head in her hands and found her forehead drenched. She didn't know whether to be grateful or more humiliated when Poppy squeezed her shoulder and Enkh gave a few pitying pats on her back.

Sloane had only ever wanted two things with all her heart. It was just her luck that they'd both showed up in her life at once, and now she couldn't have one without losing the other. If she wanted Bastian—and they had plenty of proof that she did—then she couldn't be a Hero. Not when trillions of dollars were being poured into the cultivation of a very different-looking Mind Map: a chaste, focused, organized Mind Map filled with King Francis, Verrazzano the explorer, and all the historical knowledge that would help Mahidevran the Royal Astrologer make accurate predictions for the French king. If she wanted to be the Hero the world needed, she couldn't have Bastian—not even for a few precious weeks before being together would never be possible again. They could fire Sloane and replace her with Debbie or one of the other Candidates. Or they could fire Bastian and send him away so he wouldn't distract her; they could, she thought with renewed sorrow, send him home to his wife. She didn't know which of them would have to go (did Heroes trump crew? Or were crew higher in the Program pecking order because they worked with multiple Heroes?). All she knew was that she'd found the man in the dream only to lose him forever.

When the whispering ended, Sloane braced herself for their decision, but Eleanor had nothing to share except an order for her to go back to bed. Poppy and Enkh helped Sloane to her feet and escorted her to her bedroom, where she collapsed into bed and welcomed Poppy's cool, painful prick of oblivion.

DEBBIE ALLEN SUCKED AT WILDERNESS survival. She was building the outdoor shelter all wrong. The sapling poles kept springing from their holes because Debbie was not applying enough pressure when she drove the stakes into the synthetic soil with her hammer. And the holes were supposed to be six inches deep—any idiot could see that.

It was infuriating to try and direct Debbie from a hospital bed, but the doctor wouldn't let Sloane back on her feet until her stupid heart stopped skipping its stupid beats, which was never going to happen because Bastian was gone.

In the Program pecking order, it turned out that Heroes trumped everyone, but they especially trumped interns, so Sloane had gotten to stay, and Bastian had to go. And not just to another department or team; they'd sent him to the other side of the world—wherever that was—so the 23rd Hero could continue to train without distraction. When Eleanor had broken the news, Sloane had considered quitting, leaving Basecamp, trying to find him, but Eleanor had convinced her that even if such a thing weren't impossible, that Bastian did not want to be found. Sloane wondered how much he hated her. She wondered if working for the Program had been his dream job. What if she'd stolen the dream of the man in the dream? Her misery was unbearable, so at Poppy's urging, she decided to use her growing control of her memory to repress all memories and thoughts of Bastian, even at night in her room when she was alone; only total suppression would allow her to keep training with a broken heart.

Sloane told herself she was on board with this plan, but thirty-six hours into Bastian's departure, her Mind Map remained as red as a crime scene, and her body continued to betray her. Her blood pressure kept dropping, and when she lay down, it felt like there was an anvil on her chest. The minutes stretched out like years, and every breath was agony, especially because the only cure for her condition was a person who was never coming back.

Eleanor hurried in and out of the training room, fielding satellite phone calls from UNNA and other governing bodies around the world. Because their Hero was strapped to a hospital bed, the Program had not released its' projections about the likely outcome of her Mission. And because they had not released their projections, they couldn't deploy their international agents to help communities in France and North America transition to the new timeline after Sloane went back in time. These abnormal delays in Program protocol were causing speculations about the outcome of Sloane's Mission, none of which were good. Her health was getting worse, not better, and everyone on the crew knew it—it was only a matter of time before the world knew it, too. Even an encouraging phone call from President Nanda, followed by a threatening-to-shut-the-whole-Program-down phone call from President Nanda, did nothing to regulate Sloane's heartbeat or restore her Mind Map to brilliant blue. But for some reason that no one could understand (least of all Sloane), Eleanor refused to officially make Debbie Allen the 23rd Hero.

"Another call for you," said Eleanor, handing Sloane her satellite phone. Sloane groaned, weary of the president hounding her, as if a rightly executed pep talk could bring about instantaneous recovery.

"Madame President," said Sloane.

"Hi," said a familiar voice.

She bolted upright in the bed, but the doctor insisted she lie back down.

"Hey," she said. "Hi."

"I heard you're not feeling well."

"I've been better," she said. She wanted to say she was already better—just the sound of his voice made her whole body feel warm. Especially because it didn't sound like he hated her at all.

The line went quiet. She grappled for the right thing to say, the two or three or five words to pick out of the thousands she wanted to say to him. For the first time, she wondered if he might be hesitating for the same reason.

"What do you think would help?" he asked.

Behind her bed, Poppy and Eleanor began whispering.

"I think I'd feel better if I knew that everyone on the team was…safe."

"You don't have to worry about that, Sloane," he said. "Everyone is fine."

"What I mean is, I'd feel better if everyone was…together again."

The pause on the other end of the line was so long she feared the countdown timer would run out and she'd be whisked through the open portal, hospital bed and all.

"When everyone is together, I'm told you become…distracted." He said the word quietly, and with great care, as if he didn't want to embarrass her. For all she did not know about him, now she knew that he was kind. Her heart swelled with hope, blotting out self-consciousness like the moon eclipsing the sun. She grew bolder.

"When everyone is *not* together, I become incapacitated."

He laughed. Sweet Jesus, that sound, that holy sound, like bells in a temple—and she had been the one to ring the bell. She thought of other things she might say to make him laugh. She would take a class. She would memorize stand-up comedy routines just to hear him laugh again.

"So, better distracted than incapacitated?" he said.

"Definitely."

She waited.

"Can I talk to Eleanor?"

"Okay," she said, unable to mask the hurt in her voice. And then the phone was gone, and him with it.

"This is from ninety seconds ago," said Poppy, shoving her iGlass in Sloane's face. The Mind Map was a fiery sea of red anxiety. "And this is from thirty seconds ago." Poppy toggled forward in the version history, replacing the first map with Sloane's current state of mind—a sparkling galaxy of wild blue bursts and swirling light. Poppy glanced back at Eleanor, who was speaking low and fast into the satellite phone. "I am not supposed to ask you this, but was it your sweetheart on the line just now?"

Before Sloane could answer, Eleanor was shouting, the crew was moving, and Sloane and the hospital bed were surrounded by privacy screens. Eleanor and Poppy stepped inside, and Eleanor handed Sloane the phone again.

"Hello?"

"Me again."

He said they were supposed to talk. She said okay. Asked what he wanted to talk about. Tell me something stupid, he said. Eleanor and Poppy were watching the Mind Map, which was blossoming bluer by the second. Sloane told him she was an okay baker but a terrible cook. People say if you can read a recipe, you can cook, but she said it wasn't true and she was living proof. He said she was so good at everything she tried in training, she couldn't possibly be that bad at cooking, and she said she was, and he said he'd have to taste it to believe it, and Eleanor took the phone away, watching the Mind Map devolve from blue to purple to red when she did. Eleanor ordered them to talk again. This time Sloane asked Bastian to tell her something stupid. He said he used to love parasailing but that he hadn't been in years and that he missed it. She said he would get along great with her brother. He said he'd rather get along great with—but Eleanor took the phone away before he could finish. Poppy tapped her iGlass, recording the rate at which the map was overrun with anxiety when Sloane was denied Bastian, and the rate at which the map glowed with longing when Bastian was given back. They conducted the experiment five times, which Poppy said was the minimum for statistical significance, and it was only when the Mind Map glowed blue five out of five times that a crack appeared in Eleanor's resolve to keep them apart.

IN THE KITCHENETTE OF JOHNNY'S living quarters, Sloane took her third shot of the evening. Johnny poured her another, then topped off Debbie's glass. "If you squint your brain hard enough, it almost tastes like whiskey." Everyone clinked, touched the bottoms of their shot glasses to the Formica, and tossed 'em back.

"Last round," said Sloane, "or I'll be wiped in the morning, even with an injection."

Johnny cut the deck and dealt the cards. For the fourth time that night, Debbie asked Sloane which card was high, Ace or King.

"Debbie, you're never gonna win if you keep showing people your hand," said Johnny.

"As if I could beat Sloane at anything," said Debbie. Sloane cringed, but Debbie smiled. "You know I'm fine with that, right? Seriously, Sloane. After seeing what you can do, I really, really don't want to go back in time. So please don't make me, okay? I mean, you were sick with that weird illness for a few days, but now you're back."

"She's back and kicking ass," said Johnny, arranging his poker chips in neat stacks on the table. "Did you see the flying machine she built today? In seventeen minutes using sixteenth-century tools."

"Are you kidding me? They hated it." Sloane shuddered, recalling

Eleanor's stony evaluation of her practice invention for King Francis. "'Da Vinci *drew* a flying machine—he never actually built one,'" said Sloane, repeating Eleanor's criticism verbatim. "'You know who flies in sixteenth-century France? Mother Mary ascending into Heaven. You know who invents magic flying machines? Goddamn *witches*. Start over.'"

Johnny and Debbie laughed and clapped. Sloane beamed. She'd stopped the nausea medication a few days ago to find she could use her memory publicly with only the occasional whisper of sickness. After having heart palpitations and scarily low blood pressure when Bastian was gone, she realized there were fates far worse than public puking and grew less concerned with people witnessing her freakishness and its foibles. Besides, the more time she spent around the multilingual uber-geniuses on the crew, the less freakish she felt. It was so exhilarating to flex her memory muscles without fear of the consequences that she'd gone from one extreme to the other, flaunting her memory every chance she got simply for the rush of it; she talked and talked like she imagined Enkh would talk if he ever decided to start talking—as if she were making up for lost time.

"But they liked the pencil you invented," said Debbie. Pah. The pencil. If only Debbie knew that during her first training session on sixteenth-century inventions, Sloane had hacked a piece of graphite, slid it inside a hollow rivet of wood, and perfectly mimicked the world's first graphite pencil because she'd been fantasizing about poking Debbie in the eye. Which wasn't Debbie's fault, exactly. Sloane would have had no reason to resent Debbie if it weren't for Bastian.

He'd returned to Basecamp the previous morning, sauntering into her training session with the air of someone who'd never left, and yet everything about him was different. He was wearing a heather gray tracksuit she'd never seen before. He was sporting several days' stubble when she'd only ever seen him clean-shaven. His careless hair was hidden beneath a baseball cap, a look that seemed purposeful in its understatement, like a celebrity dressing down to evade the paparazzi. The cumulative effect of these micro changes was Bastian 2.0, like a new-and-improved piece of software that had already been flawless to begin with. The knowledge he was coming back had improved Sloane's condition, but the vision of him in the flesh was like a lightning bolt. Within thirty minutes, her heartbeat had returned to normal, and the doctor had cleared her to train.

Her orders from Eleanor had been strict: don't look at him, don't think of him, just know he's here so you don't get sick again. Perhaps Bastian had gotten a similar lecture because Bastian 2.0 did not look at Sloane at all. She, on the other hand, snuck frequent glances at him, which was a terrible idea because every time she did, she saw Bastian standing next to Debbie freaking Allen. Sometimes they were just standing side by side, listening to the history trainers quiz Sloane on the significance of Mother Mary in the sixteenth-century Catholic Church. But sometimes, when she looked over, Bastian was touching Debbie's arms or—agony—her hips, correcting her form as they practiced sparring. And once, when Sloane's eyes darted to him and away, he'd been practicing the Volta dance with her. *Their* dance. It was as if he'd been explicitly told he could not have Sloane, so he'd set his sights on someone else. Playing cards with Debbie and Johnny was supposed to distract Sloane from thoughts of Bastian—now that he was back, it was even more impossible not to think about him—but instead, the card game had proven a comforting way to ensure Debbie was not *with* Bastian right now. Sloane had half a mind to follow Debbie to her room after the card game was over to make sure it stayed that way.

The wall opposite the kitchenette split open, startling Sloane from her jealous angst. They all turned to see who it was, but the corridor was dark, and no one entered.

Johnny commanded the AI to shut the wall and eyed the women over his cards.

"Fold," said Sloane. As she set her cards down, she saw movement in her peripheral vision. A pair of feet darted past the open wall, which had not closed on Johnny's command.

"Coupla dags from Engineering were gonna join," Johnny said, giving Debbie a death stare over his cards. "See ya and raise you three." He pushed his chips into the middle, and someone coughed in the hallway.

"Thurza, that you?"

"Fold," said Debbie.

"Debbie, you have a full house. Don't fold," said Sloane.

"Unfold," said Debbie. Everyone laughed so loudly that it was several moments before they noticed the banging coming from the parted wall.

"Little late, isn't it, guys?"

Bastian stood in half shadow in the corridor, his arms crossed, his fingers tapping impatiently against his bicep. Johnny squinted at him for a few seconds, as if he didn't know what he was looking at, then returned his attention to the game.

"You want in, man?" asked Johnny. "Sloane's kicking my ass here."

"Our next session is in four hours," Bastian said. Sloane kept her gaze on the table as all the blood rushed to her face. She wasn't sure if Bastian was there to scold her in particular, or if he was there to invite Debbie back to his room. She shuddered to think it might be both.

Johnny removed the floating P-Day timer from its place above the table and flung it across the room so the hologram landed in Bastian's face. "We're all very aware of the time, Sebastian." They all waited to see what his response would be, but Bastian let the wall slide shut without another word.

"Fucking intern," said Johnny.

"Come on," said Debbie. "He's, like, literally the nicest guy I've ever met."

"Hmm, I wonder why he's nice to *you*," said Johnny.

"He just wants us to get enough sleep."

"That guy only talks to me to tell me I'm doing something wrong. Not that I should be surprised, I guess."

"What do you mean?"

"Apparently, someone high up on the food chain is his uncle or something. Some people even say he knows who Fred is."

Sloane's heart began to pound.

"Is that true?" asked Debbie.

"Like dog's balls," said Johnny. "He used to train with us during recruiting season, help out with the equipment and stuff. But now, he doesn't even take meals with the rest of us. And he just got leave to travel offsite for two days. During training. Nobody is supposed to leave Basecamp during training."

"Why did he leave?" asked Sloane.

"Funeral, apparently. His great aunt or something. Poppy's mom passed during the 21st Hero's training, and she didn't get to go home until after P-Day. But this wanker gets off for his great aunt? There shouldn't be different rules for interns—it's not fair."

Sloane's stomach did a flip-flop. They'd created a cover story to hide the real reason Bastian had left Basecamp, and the real reason he'd returned, both of which were her. She toyed with the idea that he was protecting her, keeping her secret. Or was it *their* secret? She flashed on the memories of the past twelve hours, freeze-framing and replaying them in slow motion, looking for some proof she was right—a sideways glance, his body subconsciously angled toward hers, something. But the few times Bastian had glanced at anyone or interacted with anyone it had been Debbie, which made no sense. He wasn't keeping Debbie's secret. He didn't have to leave Basecamp because of Debbie. But maybe that was why the Bastian she'd known had sent an indifferent twin back to Basecamp in his place—Sloane was too much of a hassle. Her Hero status complicated things. Debbie was nothing if not easy.

"I couldn't believe they accepted him in the first place," Johnny was saying. "The guy only speaks four languages."

"Well, that's four more languages than I speak," said Debbie.

Johnny and Sloane waited for Debbie to realize that she did, in fact, speak at least one language.

"What?" said Debbie. "He's been really nice to me since I got here."

"Debbie, when a guy like that is nice to you, it's because he's trying to sleep with you," said Johnny.

Debbie's face lit up. "Do you really think that's why?"

Johnny threw his cards down in mock exasperation.

"Sloane, do you think Christian's been hitting on me?"

"Bastian."

"He is pretty hot now that I think about it. I've been so stressed thinking I might have to replace you, I hadn't even noticed how hard he's been trying, the poor guy!"

Before Sloane could think of a response that didn't involve her hands and Debbie's neck, the lights cut off, enveloping the suite in darkness. Johnny commanded the AI to turn the lights back on. "Request denied," said the AI. "Nighty night." Muttering a few choice Australian expletives, Johnny lit a path to the exit with his iGlass. When Sloane and Debbie reached it, the wall split open to reveal a smiling Enkh, who was there to escort the 23rd Hero straight to her room and stand watch outside until morning.

SLOANE WAS ALONE IN THE corridor outside her bedroom the next morning when she was attacked. At first, she thought the sound of onrushing footsteps belonged to Debbie. It'd be just like Debbie to be twenty minutes late for their Basecamp spa date, then run up behind Sloane in her matching bathrobe, cover her eyes, and shout, "Guess who?!" But the arms that caught Sloane from behind were gloved, and male, and reaching for her neck. There was an intentionality to his movements, a precision that communicated the specific outcome he was after and the skill he had to obtain it: he wanted her dead.

Sloane's training took over. As the assailant's arms tightened around her, she grabbed his wrists. She snapped her head to the side to prevent the chokehold, slipped a leg behind his, and grabbed him behind the knees. He struggled, fighting her, but she lifted up at the pressure points behind his legs, and he toppled over. She heard his skull connect with the ground, and then she sprinted down the corridor, shouting Eleanor's name.

Sloane flailed around corners, not knowing where she was running, calling for help. Where were Eleanor and Enkh when she needed them? Someone had infiltrated Basecamp. Someone had just tried to kill her! She found Eleanor outside the training room and barreled toward her, near hysterical with fear, babbling about an attack, my attacker, he *attacked*. She pulled Eleanor back through the matrix of the camp until they found him. The man was unconscious, his body splayed across the floor, his face hidden behind a black ski mask. Sloane balked and hid behind Eleanor, who marched straight up to him and tore the mask away, slamming his head on the floor in the process. When he didn't stir, Eleanor kicked him in the ribs. He groaned, but he didn't wake, so she crouched over him and started slapping his face. Sloane stepped closer to get a look at him just as he opened his eyes. The masked man who had just attacked her was Bastian.

#   #   #

Sloane was outside the medical examination room, ear pressed to the wall, eavesdropping on Eleanor and Bastian as they argued. "We couldn't be sure she was truly ready to defend herself unless she was actually attacked," Bastian was saying. "It's one thing to fight when she's in a room with a trainer and she knows it's coming. It's completely different in the real world when it actually happens."

"The real world being you, ambushing her in the hallway like a goddamn psychopath?" said Eleanor.

Sloane's body heat must have activated some kind of sensor in the wall because it parted abruptly and deposited her into the room. She stumbled and came to a stop in front of Bastian's hospital bed, where he was sitting with an icepack strapped to the side of his head.

"Jesus, Burrows," said Eleanor, her hand darting out to break Sloane's fall. "You scared me."

Sloane straightened up, tightening the belt of her bathrobe, and found there was nowhere to stand without feeling like she was standing in the middle of the room. "Sorry," she said, backing into the wall. "I thought that was, like, a thing we were doing today. Bastian jumps out and scares me, I barge in and scare you…"

Bastian laughed, then winced, holding his head.

"He has a concussion," said Eleanor. "Twenty minutes left until he's healed."

Sloane locked from Eleanor to Bastian, but nobody said more.

"I'll just wait, then."

Eleanor looked at Bastian. Bastian looked at the floor. "For an explanation," Sloane added. Still, they said nothing.

"Interesting," said Sloane to the silence. "Because the way I see it, there are three possible explanations." Once more she waited, but Eleanor and Bastian merely glared at each other. "Explanation one," said Sloane. "Super-twisted Hero hazing ritual. Any takers? No? Okay. Explanation two: Johnny put you up to this as some sort of self-defense pop quiz, which seems unlikely because he's not the type of trainer to send a proxy. He's very hands-on, and I think he'd want to do it himself."

Bastian clenched his jaw but said nothing.

"Explanation three: Poppy screwed up my medication, I just hallucinated getting jumped in the hallway, and I'm still hallucinating now."

"Burrows, look. What you have to understand about Bastian—"

"It's what she has to understand about *Johnny*," said Bastian. "I tried, Sloane. Really, I tried, but I couldn't just sit back and watch him go easy on you and not adequately prepare you in the way you need to be prepared. He refuses to follow my—" Eleanor cleared her throat, and Bastian broke off, scowling at the floor. "It's just that you haven't been here for the others, Sloane. He's completely different with guys. It's not fair to you. Just because you're a woman, and you're small, and he wants to get in your pants—"

"I'm not wearing pants."

Bastian glanced at her legs, which were bare beneath her bathrobe. "And Johnny doesn't want…he's been completely professional. And I don't know if you're gunning for his job or something, but if you think he's been going too easy on me, you might want to look in a mirror."

"Exactly. Now we can be sure you can protect yourself if you need to. Because you actually needed to protect yourself."

"From you."

"Yeah. Well."

"Well, I can protect myself, and I did, so now you know."

"Okay, then."

"Okay."

"Fan-fucking-tastic," said Eleanor. "Bastian, stay put—I'm not done with you. Burrows, let's go."

But Sloane wouldn't budge. Not until Bastian said he was sorry. Not just for attacking her, ignoring her, and dancing with Debbie, but for altering the dream of his embrace into an unrecognizable shape, the memory of his arms around her on the tower forever tainted by the memory of his arms around her neck. She wanted to know if he had anything else to say. Bastian looked sad. He said they were talking about her life. That her life was the Mission, that it was serious stuff, and it was no time to be "fucking around." A sizzling heat flushed Sloane's cheeks and throat. She wasn't intimately familiar with the Program's org chart, but she was pretty sure interns didn't get to tell the Hero what she should or shouldn't do.

"Thanks for the feedback, but aren't you just supposed to be observing?"

"That's right," he said, his gaze piercing now. "And what I've observed is that instead of focusing on your Mission, you're taking shots with Johnny after hours."

"*That's* why you…? I don't…They were shots of *wheatgrass*."

"You two have got to be kidding me," said Eleanor. "How Sloane spends her time after training is not the issue here—"

"The issue here is that she's not taking her training seriously."

"So, attack me in a ski mask and scare the shit out of me?"

"I didn't mean to scare the shit out of you."

"What did you think it would do?"

"It wasn't exactly my best thought-out plan—"

"I can take care of myself, okay?" said Sloane. "Haven't I proven that? You people are testing me every day, and I pass every goddamn test you give me. So I really don't see where this sudden concern about my abilities is coming from. Vomiting and broken ankles aside, the only time I've had problems is when you're not here. So, now that you're back, can you please just *be* here, without…all this, whatever this is? Without being all over me?"

"Sure," said Bastian. "I get the feeling Johnny's got that covered, anyway."

Sloane's jaw dropped. "You are such a hypocrite. Giving me hell for playing cards with Johnny *one time*, when you and Debbie Allen are—"

"I'm not the one who's days away from stepping into another time—"

"—suddenly joined at the hip, a fact I'm sure your *wife* would be very interested to know."

She watched her words land, and a mask of surprise overtake Bastian's face. His cheeks turned beet red, and a vein pulsed in his forehead.

"Don't you ever talk about my wife," he said. The wall parted, and he was gone.

Sloane watched the wall close, her memory surging with every word, every touch, every look that had ever passed between them. She turned to Eleanor, feeling like she'd just crushed a baby bird in its shell. She and Bastian hadn't even had a real conversation yet—she wasn't equipped to handle a *fight*. And of all the ways she'd imagined their first real conversation going, she'd never imagined ruining it like this.

"He's coming right back," said Eleanor.

Sloane went after him anyway. When she reached the wall, it parted again, and Bastian was standing there, his eyes filled with such a heartbreaking mix of tenderness and regret that all her longing rushed to the surface to wash the past hour away. He was sorry. He didn't need to say it—she could see it in his eyes, and the look alone made her want to crawl inside him. She knew what it would be like to be with him, now. Not just here, at Basecamp, but out in the world, in real life, as a couple. She would spot the signs of the oncoming storm, track its peak, await its passing. She would know whether he wanted to be left alone or listened to. She would open for him and let him empty all his anger into her until there was none left. She loved learning that Bastian wasn't a dream; that someone so strong and beautiful and larger than life had a small, jealous, petty side, and that he'd let her see it. The intimacy of it intoxicated her, especially because she didn't even know him. Not really, not like she wanted to. All she really knew about this kind, sad, angry, jealous, ambitious, protective man was that she loved him.

"Cut the feeds," said Bastian. The AI made a clicking sound, and the lights flickered.

"Feeds up," said Eleanor. The lights flickered again.

"Cut the feeds until further notice, passcode 724647383, command PERM."

Eleanor cursed under her breath. She told Sloane to give her and Bastian a minute alone.

"We don't need a minute alone," said Bastian. He made his way back to the hospital bed and sat down, gesturing for Sloane to stay.

Eleanor looked like she might burst an appendix. "Seattle," she said. Bastian told her it wouldn't be like that. Eleanor told him that's exactly what he'd said in Seattle.

"Will somebody please tell me what's going on?" said Sloane.

"Eleanor is going to share some confidential information, and everything is going to make sense."

"The hell I am," said Eleanor.

"Tell Sloane who you report to," said Bastian.

"That is Mount Everest above her security clearance."

"She deserves to know."

Eleanor glared at Bastian. "I report to a member of the Program's senior leadership team. Burrows, let's go."

"Tell her who you report to, E."

Eleanor rubbed her eyes, muttering a list of curse words so varied and rich, it sounded like she was reciting a poem. "I am so sorry this happened, Burrows. It is unacceptable, and it's not part of our regular protocol. But if Bastian wants to try an alternative training method, or if he wants me to disclose who I report to, there's honestly not much I can do about it." Eleanor threw Sloane a pleading look, as if willing her to understand something she'd rather not say out loud.

"Why not?"

"Because Bastian is my boss."

The word buzzed in Sloane's ears as if Eleanor had spoken a language where Sloane only understood every third word, and the word 'boss' was not one of the words she understood. "So, the rumors are true?" she asked Bastian. "You have connections high up in the Program. Your uncle or something?"

Bastian grinned, then winced in pain, touching his bandage. "Is that the latest? God, that's boring. I liked it better when everyone thought I was Eleanor's boy toy." Eleanor couldn't help but laugh at that, and soon she was laughing so hard she was crying, which made Bastian laugh, too, but he couldn't laugh without making his concussion hurt worse, which made

Eleanor laugh harder, which made Bastian beg her to stop laughing, because she was making *him* laugh, and laughing hurt his head.

That was it. Sloane moved to the exit, furious that deceiving her was so hilarious to them. She tried swiping and quickly realized she'd never opened one of the sliding walls herself, not on purpose, and she had no idea how they worked, so she stood there, fuming, cursing the day she came to this stupid place with this stupid technology, and it should be illegal to behave in a way that makes someone want to slam a door without providing a proper door to slam.

"Sloane."

"What."

"I'm sorry," said Bastian. "What I meant to say…what I've been meaning to tell you is that it's all mine."

When she turned to face him, it felt as if her body was moving through taffy, like it could take a thousand years to find his eyes. When she finally did, they contained multitudes. He looked hopeful, contrite, as vulnerable as if he were naked. He looked as if he was hoping for her blessing and if she didn't give it all would be lost. Of all the ways he looked when he looked at her, of all the nuance and subtext that was not yet clear to her, there was one thing she could be certain of: he was dead serious.

"B," said Eleanor sharply. "This doesn't have to be an all or nothing—"

"The Program. Basecamp. I'm the one who—"

"Bastian, *stop*."

"Sloane deserves to know the truth. All of it."

His voice sounded sure, but when he looked at Sloane again, she saw fear in his eyes. "It was me who discovered the time travel technology ten years ago. Twelve years ago, technically. That's when I kind of invented it." Sloane looked from him, to Eleanor, to him, to Eleanor as his words repeated themselves in her mind. "And so, you can probably understand why I am very invested, perhaps more than anyone else, in the Program's success. In your success."

Sloane remembered that she had a brain, and that she had a mouth, but it was so difficult to make one work with the other.

"You're not an intern," she said.

"I'm not an intern."

"You're…" She tried to stop herself, but the words found their way into the ether anyway. "You're Fred."

Bastian looked into her eyes. He smiled. "I've always hated that name."

Sloane realized her mouth was open, but she couldn't make it close. Bastian—her Bastian—was the most powerful, most infamous, most wanted man in the world.

"The others don't know?"

"Just Enkh," said Eleanor.

"And the people in this room," said Bastian.

The doors weren't as difficult to open as she'd thought. When Sloane pressed the right spot with both hands, they parted, allowing her to flee from every sorry excuse she'd made to leave the room. She got halfway down the corridor before she heard Bastian calling her name. She didn't stop.

SLOANE SAT IN HER BEDROOM in the Mom Chair, dressed in her orange maxi dress from home, hugging her hastily packed backpack. It hadn't taken long to filter every memory of Bastian through his new identity as Fred. *The* Fred. The most brilliant human being who had ever lived. The man who had saved the planet from imminent destruction and had continued to save it, year after year, Hero after Hero. He was such a god in the eyes of the world that she'd never really believed he existed. He was a fable, a children's fairy tale, a recycled bobblehead for the dashboard of your electric car. She couldn't decide which was more unbearably embarrassing—that she'd told him he was just supposed to be observing the training sessions *he'd invented*, or the fact that she'd harbored hopes that he was interested in her. Her! She laughed out loud at her audacity. He'd been staring at her during training because she was a business investment. He didn't want her. He wanted the Program to succeed. His wife was probably some exquisite, tall, insanely famous white woman with butt implants, and she probably didn't mind if he cheated on her with droves of supermodels and gorgeous actresses because she was the one who got to be married to him. Him, being freaking Fred.

Sloane was too mortified to ever see Bastian again. She'd find Enkh. She'd convince him to open her bedroom door with the eye scanner, and she'd escape. She'd make her way down the mountain until she starved, got eaten by the last remaining mountain lion, or found the nearest village—whichever came first. The Program had chosen her, but they didn't really need her. If they wanted a Hero with a superpower memory, they had data on practically everyone on the planet. They could find someone else. Or they could make Debbie Allen the 23rd Hero. Debbie could just fuck King Francis to convince him not to colonize the Americas. It was a much simpler Mission than memorizing the past to predict the future, anyway.

Sloane grabbed her backpack and moved to the exit to find Enkh, but the wall split open, and she jumped back, startled to see Eleanor standing there with her hands on her hips.

"Burrows," she said. She looked impossibly tired.

"Hey."

"What's with the backpack?" When Sloane didn't answer, Eleanor sat in the chair across from her bed. Sloane hovered at the exit, glaring at her.

"You're mad I kept you in the dark about Bastian."

"You lied."

"I lie to everyone, every day, Sloane."

"Your parents must be proud."

"I had to lie to them too, when they were alive." Sloane winced. Apologized. Eleanor told the AI to close the wall. "I've been with him since the beginning, you know. And since the beginning, he never wanted credit for any of it. But he also kept a low profile because he knew what a dangerous game we were playing." Eleanor nodded to the Mom Chair. Sloane hesitated, then sat down on the arm. "Did you know we used to have Basecamps in UNNA?" Sloane shook her head. "Of course you didn't—we worked really hard to make sure no one did. The last one we had was in Seattle, but after the 6th Hero went back and cattle ranching took a hit, some of the factory farming folks were not too happy. Even with all the precautions we took, they found us. If Enkh hadn't seen them coming and warned us, Bastian wouldn't be here right now. And neither would we."

Sloane loosened her death grip on her backpack, but just a little bit.

"So please don't think we enjoy lying to you or to anyone. Hiding drives him crazy. Not because he wants the glory or the fame, but because he'd like nothing more than to get in there, in the training room, and work with you directly. Especially on the history stuff. He's such a geek."

Sloane set the backpack on the floor and collapsed into the Mom Chair. She'd left the hospital room like a petulant child—shocked and embarrassed, yes, but also angry they'd left her out of a loop she was never supposed to be in. As if she knew how the Program should be run better than them, the people governments trusted to save the world. She wondered if she could use the portal to travel thirty minutes into the past so she could redo the whole sorry scene.

"And he's driving me crazy lately," said Eleanor. "I've got the Prime Minister of India in one ear, and I've got him in the other ear, and all damn day, it's 'tell her this, tell her that, ask her this, ask her that, let me talk to her, don't let me talk to her.' It's exhausting."

"So, he's a control freak?"

"Just with you. He never put on a ski mask for the other Heroes."

"Because he knew they could do it, and he doesn't think I can."

Eleanor raised an eyebrow. "For someone so brilliant, you're really pretty dense."

Sloane frowned.

"Burrows. You're worse than a guy."

"What are you talking about?"

Eleanor looked at the ceiling for a moment as if it, or some deity above it, might offer the patience she needed to answer such a stupid question. "I know how you felt about Bastian before this morning. But the alternative training was…a lot. And finding out he's Fred is a lot. And he understands if you no longer…"

"If I no longer…what?"

Eleanor sighed and rubbed her forehead, muttering that she did not get paid enough to deal with this shit.

"Hypothetically," she said. "After everything that's happened. If I were to tell you that Bastian happened to return your…interest. Your romantic interest. Would it be welcome or unwelcome?"

Sloane stared at Eleanor.

Stroke.

She was having a stroke.

"I find myself in the extremely awkward position of being both our HR department in this scenario and Bastian's best friend."

Sloane didn't realize it was possible that a heart could beat this fast without bursting. Or that she had so many sweat glands.

"Burrows," Eleanor said, snapping her fingers. "Earth to Burrows. I cannot believe this isn't completely obvious to you, but he didn't just attack you in a ski mask because he's an idiot. He attacked you in a ski mask because he likes you."

"No, he doesn't."

"And you gave him a concussion because you like him, too."

"No, I don't!"

"Okay," said Eleanor, standing to leave. "I will let him know." And then, to herself, "I told him not to get his hopes up after that bullshit stunt—"

"It's not because of...I didn't know that he...but he's Fred!"

"He's Bastian," said Eleanor. "And I tried to keep you apart because I don't like this one bit. It's distracting for you, it's agonizing for him, and it's a pain in the ass for me. But what can I do? He's not gonna shut up about it unless he's a hundred percent convinced that he blew it and you don't want him anymore."

Sloane leaped to her feet, her heart soaring to the stratosphere only to fall right back to earth. "But he's married."

Eleanor touched a finger to her ear. (Was it him on the other end? Oh, my God. It had always been him on the other end.)

"Uh-huh," she said. "Great. Okay, I just need ninety seconds." She tapped her earpiece and moved to the exit. "Maybe you should ask him about the married thing yourself."

"I'm not going to *ask* him about that. Why would I ask him about that, especially after how angry he got when I—"

"And for what it's worth, if you took a look at his Mind Map, I'd bet you all the money in the bank it looks a lot like yours. Not sure about the toes thing, but you never know."

"That's... I'm not... he's in charge of the Program. He literally invented the Program! He's thinking about saving humanity from destruction and how not to get himself murdered in the process. I highly doubt he has time to think about *me*. I mean, not like that."

"Ohhh," Eleanor said. "The *Program*. For a minute there, I'd forgotten about that minor detail. Well, you're probably right, then. My mistake." She tapped her earpiece and said that Sloane was ready now. "Go ahead and send them in."

The wall parted, and Eleanor walked out, leaving Sloane standing in the middle of her bedroom, churning with adrenaline.

"Burrows," she called. "You coming or what?"

Somehow, she managed to follow Eleanor out into the corridor, her mind a complete blank for what she might say if she found Bastian waiting for her there.

But it wasn't Bastian she spied hustling in her direction from down the hallway. It was Enkh. The monk was beaming as he moved toward her, hand in hand with the smiling young man at his side.

"Sloane!"

It took several seconds for Simon's face to make sense in her brain, and then they were squealing and colliding and jumping up and down with their arms around each other's necks.

"How did you do this?" Sloane asked, hugging Simon, then Eleanor, then Simon again.

"I didn't," said Eleanor. Her phone rang, and after asking the office of the Chancellor of Germany to please hold, Eleanor leaned in. "But you're right, Burrows," she said in Sloane's ear. "He's not thinking about you at all."

IT WAS CHRISTMAS, AND THE auditorium had been transformed into a tropical winter wonderland to commemorate the one-week countdown to P-Day. The crew had removed half the seats and deconstructed the stage to make room for a white sand beach, bamboo dance floor, and dozens of palm trees wrapped in thousands of twinkling Christmas lights. A virtual sunset exploded above a virtual sea, and they'd altered the airflow to blow a gentle ocean breeze. The upper part of the auditorium was hidden behind a simulated volcano, and plush, red carpeting spilled over the staircase so guests descending to the party appeared to be walking on a river of molten lava. The sounds of lapping waves competed with the music of live musicians, who'd been teleported in from Sydney for the event, their holograms floating above the dance floor like an orchestra of angels.

Sloane and Simon stepped onto the red carpet, marveling at the scene below. "You look stunning," Simon said, his eyes shining with excitement. Sloane snuck another peek at the dress Kofi had designed just for tonight; it was silk-white and flowing, cut down the front to the waist, with bands of chiffon covering her breasts. When she walked, a glorious train cascaded behind her like silk sails.

"We look stunning," she said, admiring the black tuxedo Kofi had insisted on the second he'd laid eyes on Simon. Simon had also laid eyes on

Kofi, the air had buzzed with electricity, and Sloane's heart soared to think of the two of them getting together.

Beaming like proud parents, Eleanor and Enkh were waiting to greet the twins at the bottom of the stairs. "Congratulations, Burrows," said Eleanor. "Welcome again, Simon." Enkh bowed to each of the twins in turn, bending deeply from the waist. Sloane was used to Enkh making smaller, shallow bows all over Basecamp, but something about the deeper bow made her choke up every time. She could have been breaking some kind of monk contact code, but she threw her arms around Enkh and hugged him anyway. To her surprise, Enkh not only hugged her back—he pulled Simon into the embrace, too. The hug lasted so long that Simon started making 'help-me' eyes at Sloane over Enkh's shoulder. Eleanor finally had to peel the trio apart, sending the twins off to the dance floor so Enkh could compose himself.

"Is the monk always teary-eyed like that?" asked Simon.

"No," said Sloane, mystified. "Usually, his eyes are closed."

Sloane made it through three full songs before broaching the topic of Harry, then immediately wished she hadn't. "Never mind, don't tell me. I don't want to ruin our night."

"Who even cares about him," said Simon. "I have bodyguards thanks to you, and I'm just…"

"Bodyguards?"

"After we talked that night, this guy from the Program called me. He said I was your family and that they'd take care of me. Whatever I wanted. And I'll be able to start my own casting agency, Sloane. I'll be able to produce films if I want. Good films. I can literally go hang gliding every day for the rest of my life if I want to."

"If I accomplish my Mission and it's still possible to go hang gliding, you mean."

"Well, yes. If there's still life to be lived above ground, I'm set."

"You don't think Harry will try to come after you for it? He's *suing* me."

"I know," said Simon. "He asked me if I would be a character witness for him."

She pulled away from her brother, fanning her face.

"Don't," said Simon, pointing at her. "Do not mess up Kofi's masterpiece."

"He won't even talk to me, Sai. He had Chastity talk to me to tell me we couldn't have any contact because of the lawsuit."

"The lawsuit is bullshit. The guy on the phone said they'll pay Harry back for your tuition, but otherwise, he's not getting a dime. From the Program or from me. The guy said he was sure."

"He's not even going to say goodbye to me."

"Are you surprised? Because of you, he'll never be Dr. Harry Burrows again. For a few days, he was nothing but the 23rd Hero's father, and now, he's not even that. He is *so* pissed. It's awesome."

Sloane bit the inside of her cheek, fighting back tears, and berating herself for retaining so much as a shred of hope that Harry would have had the opposite reaction to her becoming a Hero than the reaction she'd always anticipated. She realized now that she'd even hoped Harry failing the paternity test would somehow make him see how much she meant to him, and him to her; even though they didn't share blood, they had shared a life, and she had spent most of that life fighting for his acceptance, if not his love. Now she saw that she had been fighting for something he was never going to give her. Not when she already had the memory he would kill for, and now a fame that dwarfed his fame, and a name that would go down in history when his would be lost to it. She had everything he'd ever wanted for himself. She didn't get to have his acceptance, too. It was the one thing he had left that he could withhold from her, so withhold it he would. Forever.

"He's showing you who he is, my heart," said Simon. "Who he's always been. A stone-cold narcissist. No wonder mom went outside the marriage. I say, good for her. Whoever the guy was, I hope she felt loved."

"They can tell us who it is," she said, sniffling. "I wanted to ask you first, to see if you wanted to know. They have it in their database, I'm sure. Oh, and Mom wrote us a letter! It's in Khmer, and I couldn't make it out. I should go get it for you—"

"We'll have time for that later."

"But that's just it. We won't. Because I'm leaving."

"Not tonight."

"But soon," she said. "Really soon, and I know you said you're not mad, but you must be at least a little bit mad at me for—"

"Never."

"I'll write you. So at least you'll have that. They have a way to get it to you. As soon as I go, you'll be able to know all about my life back then, and I'm just…slightly terrified, is all."

"What are you, human? Of course you're terrified."

"But what if I ruin everything, Sai? What if I completely and utterly blow it?"

"You won't. Sure, you mess things up sometimes. But that's why you're so good at fixing stuff. You have a lot of practice correcting your own mistakes."

She smacked him, laughing through her tears.

"No one's better at fixing things that can't be fixed. And the planet definitely falls into that category. You're the most brilliant person I've ever met, Sloane. If anyone can do this, you can. If you can just find a way to believe that, I know you'll be fine."

"Sai," she said. "I just…"

"My heart is your heart," he said.

Sloane held onto Simon for dear life as he sang along to *Have Yourself a Merry Little Christmas*, serenading her. When the song ended, the twins made a beeline for the bar, but the wall on the far side of the auditorium split open, and Bastian stepped into the room.

The wall closed behind him, the dark backdrop accentuating the stark white tuxedo perfectly cut around his athletic frame. His careless hair was smooth and coiffed, his injuries from earlier that day undetectable. How foolish to have thought a man like that could ever be an intern anywhere. He was the sun.

Sloane pulled Simon back onto the dance floor and rotated their bodies until Simon had a perfect view of Bastian.

"Is the most beautiful man you've ever seen looking at us?"

Simon looked.

"Don't look."

"If you're talking about White Tuxedo at twelve o'clock, then yes, he's looking at us."

"Did he see you look?"

"Yes, and now he's walking toward us."

"Don't *look*!"

"I'm not looking. Is it him?"

"Yes. Is it who?"

"The dream guy."

"Oh! Yeah. Sorry, for a second, I thought you were asking if it was F…"

"What?"

"Nothing. Never mind. I just—"

Someone cleared his throat. Simon spun her around, and the twins stood side by side, staring up at Bastian in awe.

"Sloane," said Bastian, nodding politely. "And you must be Simon." He offered his hand and Simon shook it, managing an awkward "hey" in response, not that Sloane could blame him. Bastian introduced himself as "part of the crew" and thanked Simon, on behalf of everyone, for the sacrifice he was making in losing a loved one to the Program. He said Sloane was doing an incredible thing for humanity and for the planet, and that they were so grateful, and that they would always be there to support Simon in whatever way he needed.

"You have the number I gave you over the phone?"

"Oh!" Simon said. "That was—yes, yes I do."

"Use it," said Bastian. "Any time."

The band transitioned to a slow dance; sparse piano, crying strings, the love theme from an old film version of *Romeo and Juliet*. Kofi emerged from the crowd, grabbed Simon's hand, and winked at Sloane before twirling her brother into a tight embrace. Sloane stood there self-consciously as everyone around her paired off and started to dance. Well. Not everyone. In her peripheral vision, she saw a hand extended, palm up, the ring finger naked without its wedding band. She grabbed it as if it were a mirage that could dissolve at any moment, and then she was in Bastian's arms, enveloped in a bouquet of cedar and soap and pear, his ring-less fingers pressed to the small of her back. He led her in slow circles to the beat, moving her where he wanted her to move, lifting her arm to turn her, watching her dress shimmer beneath the lights. When the bridge of the song swelled, he pulled her in close, slowing their bodies to the faintest sway.

"I'm sorry I attacked you wearing a ski mask," he said.

"I'm sorry I gave you a concussion when you did."

He pulled back to look at her, his eyes darting between hers. "Do you want to go somewhere we can talk?" Never in her life had she wanted something so much, but all she could manage was a nervous little exhale, which made Bastian smile. "You don't have to, you know," he said. "It's not a…requirement."

"Um, no. I mean yes. We probably should. Talk."

Bastian pulled Sloane through the crowd past Kofi and Simon, who were locked in a tender kiss. He threw Sloane a curious look—are we happy about this or not happy about this?—and when Sloane gave a thumb's up, Bastian squeezed her hand. "There must be something in the air tonight."

When they reached the edge of the dance floor, Eleanor was waiting for them. "For the love of God, Sebastian. How long are we talking for this talk? We spent way too much money on this party, and Sloane's family is here, and—"

Bastian handed Eleanor his earpiece, fighting a smile.

Eleanor sighed. "You at least have the cell?"

"I have the cell."

"And you're okay with this, Burrows? Because it's not a requirement."

"She knows."

"Maybe she doesn't feel comfortable saying no, now that she knows what she knows about you-know-who."

"It's okay," said Sloane. "I want to talk."

Eleanor let them go, and when Sloane and Bastian reached the auditorium exit, Bastian pulled out an ancient-looking flip phone and speed-dialed her. Across the room, Eleanor answered on the first ring.

"For the love of God, E. Put down the damn phone and go get her already."

Sloane followed Bastian's eye line. Poppy was sitting in a cabana by the infinity pool, gazing at Eleanor with a look in her eyes Sloane had never noticed before. When Eleanor looked over at Poppy, Poppy straightened up, then looked behind her to see who Eleanor was looking at. Finding no one except herself, Poppy blushed and beckoned Eleanor to join her. Bastian watched the two women like he was witnessing a comet shoot across the sky. "I think I just bought us a little time," he said. "You and I haven't had much of that, have we?"

"We haven't had any."

"Hmm," he said.

"What?"

"You noticed."

07:08:50:12 to P-Day

THEY CLIMBED THE WINDING STEPS of the tower together, pausing at each landing to wrangle Sloane's dress or watch the first blushes of sunset. Sloane's heart was pounding, and she kept fighting the temptation to pinch herself. She knew Eleanor wouldn't let Bastian play hooky for long. They probably only had a few minutes to talk, and who knew if they'd ever be alone together again. But she was so nervous, she couldn't even manage to make small talk about how beautiful the mountains were, let alone say something from the heart. Bastian seemed to be in a similar predicament because he cleared his throat several times, but otherwise they climbed step after step in silence.

When they reached the top of the tower, Sloane realized it was not the top at all. Across the viewing platform, the stairs continued, winding their way into a little blue treehouse built around a nest of gargantuan branches, each thicker than she was several times over. The treehouse had a transparent, dome-shaped roof that sparkled in the setting sun, which made the structure look half-ancient, half alien. She knew the little house must be his, but she couldn't tell what it was for. Maybe he held meetings here with Eleanor and Enkh away from the rest of the crew. Maybe he used the treehouse as his personal office. Maybe he'd just always wanted a treehouse as a boy, and when you're Fred, you can have whatever you want. It broke her heart a little, the treehouse. She wondered what else she didn't know about him, and how many treehouses there might be, and whether he'd ever invite her inside. She wondered if she'd ever know him the way she longed to, or if his job title would prove a barrier between them, and she'd always be on the outside, nose pressed to the dome, looking for a way in.

Bastian crossed to the bench and sat where Sloane had found him the first night she'd climbed the tower. Unsure, she resumed her spot on the opposite end of the bench where he'd left her that night, when their first moments alone had been shattered by footsteps. Now the only sounds were those of insects and birds and Bastian intermittently clearing his throat. His gaze was fixed on the sunset, where a violet sky had exploded to the west. The clouds were tinged electric pink, and the limestone karsts trembled with an energy that made the Earth itself seem a living, breathing thing. Sloane remembered how alive she'd felt when she first saw this view at night, and how brave she'd felt afterward—brave enough to say something. Anything.

"How's your head?" she asked.

He laughed. "Still hurts. A lot."

"Good."

They sat in silence for another eternal minute until they both spoke at once.

"I am *so* sorry—" he said.

"But I understand why you—"

"But what a stupid thing to—"

"It's okay," she said. "I'm fine. You're fine. Let's just let it go."

More silence.

"And I never wanted to mislead you about anything," he said. "Not about my relationship to the Program—"

"Your Program."

"Yeah. And not about who I really am."

"Eleanor explained everything," said Sloane. "It all makes sense now."

Bastian glanced at her out of the corner of his eye, looking skeptical. "Please don't think we lied because we don't trust you. Obviously, I trust you, or I wouldn't have told you, and that's saying something because we don't even tell the crew. And we especially don't tell the Heroes because having to keep a secret like that is a burden, and the last thing you need at this point in your training is one more thing on your mind. Plus, every person who knows the truth increases the risk to me and my teams. My cover's only been blown a couple of times over the years, but it's a huge pain in the ass when it happens. We have to pay people off so they don't rat me out to the media. It takes forever to recruit new talent, and it's such a hassle to move Basecamp with all the netting."

"The netting?"

"It's how we avoid satellite detection," he said, gesturing to the space above the treehouse roof. "You can't see it with the naked eye, but without it, this place would be swarming with Mossad special ops the second we got our servers up and running."

Sloane stared at him, blown away by his obvious brilliance. She was a techie, but he was a tech genius. She couldn't convince her boss of seven years not to fire her, while Bastian could convince 87,000 employees he'd never met to do exactly what he said as soon as he said it—and through a proxy, at that. Sloane had spent the past decade steaming 6,968 oat milk cappuccinos and servicing as many application booths, while Bastian had spent the past decade inventing time travel and building a Program to save the world. If her memory made her a freak of nature, then his nature made him a freaking phenom, and she wasn't afraid to say so.

"You were a phenomenal Boothie, Sloane."

She laughed. "Not sure my former boss would agree with you. And I'd rather be doing what I'm doing now. Especially if I get to learn all the trade secrets. And secret identities."

"You're not…mad? About the secret identity?"

"No," she said. "I'm grateful you told me. But if you think it's a burden, why did you?"

He started to speak, then looked down at his hands. The ensuing silence reminded Sloane of the times they'd talked on the phone, or over an earpiece, and how Bastian would wait so long to speak that she'd start to think he'd hung up.

"I'm selfish," he said. "I wanted you to know the real me before you left."

She would have lived on those words if she could have. She would have traded all the macrobiotic enchiladas in the world for a few more of those words.

"That's not selfish," she said.

"It's not?"

"Not when I want to know."

"Oh…you do? Want to know?"

"The real you. Like, why did the real you take off your wedding ring tonight?"

Bastian looked up, surprised, and Sloane's brain was flooded with a dozen other questions she could have asked first. He splayed out his fingers, inspecting the empty spot where the ring used to be. That was the other thing he hadn't meant to mislead her about.

"I am so sorry about that," she said. "It's so completely none of my business."

"It *is* your business, and you should know that—"

"You really don't have to explain."

"Please," he said, turning to face her on the bench. "I want to explain about Ashleigh."

"Ashleigh," she said, the name catching in her throat.

"My wife," he said. Their eyes met, and Sloane felt a pang of sorrow flicker across her face, and there was nothing she could do to hide it.

"She was, I mean," Bastian said. "She passed away a long time ago."

"Oh!"

"We were very young, and she got sick. It was before all of this."

"I'm so sorry."

"I'm sorry," he said, massaging the knuckle of his ring finger. "You mentioned her today, and it caught me off guard, and I just—well. I shouldn't have spoken to you that way. You didn't deserve it." He paused, chuckling to himself. He hadn't even realized she'd noticed the ring.

"Oh, I noticed."

"And, of course, you would have assumed that I was still…"

"I mean, I did think you were married, but I had no idea she was gone, and it's really none of my business, and I didn't mean to accuse you of…

anything, really. My dad, who's not actually my dad, lost my mom, so I know what it's like to…well, not that *I* know what it's like, but…" She blew all the air out of her mouth. "God, you must think I'm such a—"

"I think you're wonderful," he said, rendering her speechless.

"The year Ashleigh passed was the same year I lost my parents in a car crash. The accident was in February, and then, when Ashleigh got sick that fall, we found out she was pregnant. But she was too sick, and they had to… and we lost the baby, too."

"Oh, Bastian."

He threw her a sad smile, but she regretted the intimate way she'd just said his name—as if she could possibly understand what he had suffered. She felt impotent and overcome with regret, as if a piece of her heart had broken off the rest of the organ; she couldn't bear carrying around an intact heart when Bastian was missing valves and ventricles that would never grow back.

"I wore the ring for a long time after she died because I was still in love with her. And then, when everything started with the Program, a wedding ring became part of my cover. Just one detail out of many we've concocted over the years. So anyone who meets me is less likely to make that mental leap."

"Because no one thinks of Fred as a married man."

"Exactly," he said. "We've worked hard on Fred's playboy persona. Personally, I find it kind of gross, but it drives a lot of applications for us."

"Wait, are you saying you created Fred? On purpose?"

"Not at first. But our PR team wanted to get control of the narrative. And now—yes—it's mostly us shrouding me in mystique."

"They've done a very good job."

"Smoke and mirrors," he shrugged. "He's the international man of mystery. I'm an open book. Or I prefer to be when I can be."

"Does that mean you'll answer any question I ask?"

Bastian gestured to the space between them. She nodded, and he scooted closer until she couldn't look down without catching a glimpse of his thigh in her peripheral vision. Sloane's heart raced at his nearness. She caught another whiff of his cologne, which smelled like his essence, only amplified, as if he'd had his own pheromones bottled. Maybe he'd give her a bottle to take with her to France.

"I will answer any question I can without endangering someone's life," he said.

Bastian's cell phone could ring any second and their conversation would be over. As exhilarating as it was to learn more about Fred and the innerworkings of the Program, the only questions that seemed worth asking now were questions about Bastian and Sloane.

"Okay. Um. How about answering the question you didn't answer?"

"Which question was that?"

"Why did you take off your wedding ring tonight, especially since it's part of your cover?"

Bastian sucked in his breath through his teeth. "Can we start with an easier one?" he asked, sheepish. "I might need a warm-up."

"Okay." Beads of sweat had broken out between her breasts, and she ran two fingers down her sternum to wipe them away. Bastian's eyes darted to her chest, tracking the movement, and she lowered her hand, blushing.

"Um, you left Basecamp," she said.

"You noticed."

"My heart rate noticed."

Bastian blushed. She had never seen it before. Pale, pink color dappled his cheeks, and she could almost taste the blood as it rushed beneath his skin. She imagined trailing her lips across his cheek to his mouth, discovering some way to never let go.

"Well," he said, "the mountain air is pretty thin up here."

"That must be it," she said. "My body's not used to the altitude."

He flushed a deeper shade of crimson, and she thought she might kiss him then and there.

"So, where did you go when you were gone?" she asked.

"Ittoqqortoormiit."

"Ittoqqortoormiit, Greenland. One of the choices for a work environment during my assessment."

"Right," he said. "Of course you'd remember that. Sorry. It takes some getting used to. Your memory."

"You're telling me," she said. "Twenty-nine years, and I'm just now getting used to it."

Bastian laughed, nudging her thigh with his. She pictured the heat in his cheeks flushing his whole body and enveloping her, the invisible charge surrounding them like an electric field. If they sat here long enough, the electricity would grow so strong that Basecamp might not even need the special netting anymore.

"I went to Greenland because it's quiet. I have a house there."

"How long did it take you to get there from here?"

"If you're fishing for where in the world we are, it won't work—it took me about ten minutes."

"If we were ten minutes from Greenland, I wouldn't be wearing a dress like this in December."

He looked at her dress. "Now that would be a tragedy."

It was her turn to blush.

"The fact is, we're about ten minutes from most major cities on the planet. One of the side effects of hiring the most brilliant minds in the world is that they invent a lot of cool shit accidentally. The kids who work on the Time Travel Innovation team—Nanda's proteges, the twelve-year-olds? They found a way to travel between various points on Earth by accessing energy tunnels that exist along latitude and longitude lines and cut through the interior of the planet. The project was something of a failure because the tunnels kept the traveler in *this* exact time, but the tunnels have been an awesome way to get around. We're saving billions a year on travel costs. There's no tunnel in Toulon, but if there was, you'd be able to get to Paris in minutes instead of months."

He touched her shoulder, the brush of his hand warm against her skin. "Freaked out?"

She shrugged. "No freakier than time travel, I guess."

He laughed. "It's too bad."

"What is?"

"I would have loved to have taken you to Paris tonight. The tunnel lets out near Montmartre, and we could take a car down to the palace at Fontainebleau. Show you where you'll be living, give or take a few centuries."

Sloane's eyes lit up. "Could we?"

Bastian smiled at her. "Sorry, twenty-three. You're the most recognizable woman in the world. And far too important to risk taking outside. You're precious cargo."

"If I'm so precious, why have you been so hard on me since you came back?"

Bastian's face fell. "You mean the…alternative training?"

"The attack," she said. "And turning the lights out during poker. And you hated my flying machine—"

"What did I say about the flying machine?"

"Now that I know the truth, it's easy to tell the difference between Eleanor talking for Eleanor and Eleanor talking for you."

"The flying machine was awesome," Bastian said. "But if I'd told you it was awesome, you wouldn't have made the pencil, and the pencil was the smartest thing you made given the constraints of the Mission."

He was playing with her. When she said so, Bastian's nervous laughter made him seem more like a large, bashful child than a world leader. He said he was hard on her because they were desperate, that they needed this Mission to succeed or they'd get shut down. She said she understood. She said it probably wouldn't look too good if the Program's first female Hero got attacked and killed as soon as she went through the portal, and Bastian laughed again. "Definitely not."

So that was all this was, then; he was concerned, first and foremost, about optics.

Sloane stood up abruptly and made her way to the railing to hide the hurt that must have been plain on her face. The sun was sinking faster and faster, nature's mocking commentary on how little time she had left in this century, which was probably just as well if the only reason Bastian had been such a tough coach was not because he cared about her more than the other Heroes, or because he was worried about her safety, but because he was worried about how any success or failure on her part might impact his future prospects with his investors.

"Wait," she heard him say. "Sloane, that came out wrong."

He joined her at the railing, and she steeled herself against the possibility that everything Eleanor had told her about Bastian's romantic interest in her had been fabricated by Bastian himself as part of some manipulative strategy to make her feel special so she'd train harder.

"I don't care how things look to the world," Bastian said, his eyes bright with anxiety. "I know I've been hard on you since I got back, and that's on purpose. It's because I need you to be bulletproof. For the Mission, yes, but mostly because I personally can't bear the thought of something happening to you."

"You…personally?"

He nodded.

"Oh."

He took a step closer. "Sloane…"

"Yes?"

He swallowed, then looked at his shoes.

"What is it?" she asked.

Bastian looked up. "Was there anything else you wanted to ask me?"

She didn't know how to tell him she had a hundred more questions. A thousand. Every question ever uttered by every human being that ever walked the earth, if only she could remember what they were.

"Greenland," she said, somehow. "Before you went to Greenland, why were you always…looking at me…that way?"

"What way?"

"Staring."

"I'm sorry," he said. "I didn't mean to stare."

"You didn't?"

"Okay, fine. I was staring."

"Why."

"Three reasons."

Sloane laughed. "Only three?"

Bastian must have left the bashful child back on the bench because he took her hand, flipped it over, and held it in his. He touched his index finger to the middle of her palm—reason number one.

"I watch you like a hawk because watching you is all I can do. I can't be in there with you, training you myself, because—as you so astutely argued today—interns are just supposed to be observing."

She cringed. "Sorry about that."

"I deserved it."

"So, you're hard on me because you care about me. But you stare at me because you're keeping an eye on your investment."

Bastian sucked in his breath. "I wouldn't have put it that way, but—"

"But you did put it that way. You're very invested in the Program's success."

He narrowed eyes. "That damn memory. Fine. That's the first reason I was staring at you."

"What's the second reason?"

"The second reason," he said, stretching out a second finger, "is because I can't take my eyes off of you."

Her stomach did a flip flop, but she told herself to not. freak. out. She said if he stared at her because he couldn't take his eyes off of her it was circular logic.

"Pardon me," Bastian said. "What I meant was, I can't take my eyes off of you because you're too beautiful for words."

Something in Sloane's vision flickered as if her brain had short-circuited. She started to ask Bastian to repeat what he'd just said, just in case she'd hallucinated it, but she changed her mind—she'd rather remember those words as if he'd actually spoken them, even if he hadn't.

"You don't believe me," Bastian said.

Do.

Not.

Freak.

Out.

She took a deep breath. She let it out. She asked Bastian what the third reason was.

He added a third finger, then pressed their palms together, holding her hand. "I can't tell you that right now," he said. "But I promise that as soon as I can tell you, I will."

He was so close now he could have leaned in to kiss her, and she ached for him to. She'd promise not to freak out if he did.

"More questions?"

"Only like ten thousand more," she said, watching him watching her.

"But I can't remember what they are."

"But you remember everything."

"I'm sure they'll come back to me."

Bastian grinned, let go of her hand, and leaped up the stairs that led to the treehouse, breaking whatever spell he'd just cast. Sloane felt like a song that had been cut off before it reached the final chord. She worried he had to go back to real life, back to work, and that their talk—was it just a talk?—was over.

"While we're waiting for you to remember, want to come inside? It's a bit warmer in there. If you're cold. Of course, if you don't feel comfortable, I understand. But I promise not to, um, attack you."

"You actually live there?"

"You were expecting something…bigger?"

"I was expecting the servant's quarters to be bigger."

Bastian laughed his deep, rich laugh, and Sloane's heart sang at the sound. He was sorry to disappoint her. He liked to keep things simple. He looked worried then, as if she might actually object to being a guest in such a humble abode. "Will you? Come inside? Sorry, I know I just said you don't have to, and you totally don't. It's just that I sort of…attempted to. . ." His blush was back, and he toed the ground, laughing at himself. "I made you dinner."

Well, she supposed she wouldn't need to take the steps up to the treehouse, then.

She would float.

BASTIAN LEFT HER AT THE landing and disappeared into the treehouse's tiny kitchenette, telling Sloane to make herself at home. She stood at the threshold, thrilled to be invited inside, into his house, into his world. And the weird thing was, it did feel like home. She was in a place she had never been before, in a country she could not name, with a man she'd barely spoken to before tonight. But the cooking smells that filled the treehouse were familiar, somehow, and the soft, crackly jazz music reminded her of Simon's collection of old LPs. Large monstera plants and potted palms filled the space, and with a clear view of the tree canopy through the glass dome, the effect was of stepping back outside as much as stepping in—being inside the treehouse reminded her of standing among the trees in Stanley Park as a girl, except here, she could step inside the tree itself. In the dining area off the kitchenette, a small table was set for two, with wooden chopsticks and little ceramic bowls next to the oversized spoons and forks. The rest of the space was furnished with simple, stylish floor mats, a rattan ottoman and loveseat, floating bookshelves—exactly how Sloane might have decorated her own treehouse. Even the bed looked a lot like her futon back in Vancouver. The most powerful man in the world slept on two slim mattress pads propped on a low, bamboo bedframe sans headboard. On top of a thick, down comforter lay a lone pillow, and she let herself hope Bastian wasn't accustomed to sleepover guests. Well, sleepover guests that weren't her. She wondered if making herself at home might involve slipping inside his organic cotton sheets, and just the thought made her body throb with anticipation. If home was the certainty there was nowhere else in the world she'd rather be, then she had never been as certain, never as home, as she was now.

Over the cheerful clanging of pots and pans, Bastian called to her from the kitchenette.

"I hope I got this right," he said.

"It smells amazing," said Sloane, debating which vision to drink in next. A skylight had been cut into the dome roof to offer an even clearer view of the evening's first stars, and she stood beneath it until she'd counted every one—there were sixteen so far, even more than she'd seen the other night. The Western wall of the treehouse was just as thrilling and no less picturesque, every inch filled with framed artwork. There were black brushstrokes on white canvas; colored pencil on architectural tracing paper; floating paper spheres strung together with miniature glass beads. She stepped closer and was surprised to discover the content of each piece was identical—every painting, drawing, and sphere displayed the same hand-drawn symbols rendered in the same pattern, as if Bastian were a collector of some extinct logographic writing system she'd never seen before. She reached out to touch one of the spheres, enthralled. The work was not only visually beautiful but seemed almost alive, with a beckoning, magnetizing power that drew her in and made her want to get closer.

"Something to drink?" asked Bastian.

"Wine?"

Sloane was so mesmerized by the art gallery that it was several moments before she noticed Bastian leaning over the counter, watching her in that evaluative way of his. She straightened up, smoothing the front of her dress, and he chuckled.

"What?" she asked.

"Just wondering if you're nervous. To be here."

She shrugged, and Bastian smiled and disappeared back into the kitchenette.

"Maybe that's why you want wine, but with all the medication in your system right now, you'd have a raging headache after half a glass."

Before she could insist that she was absolutely not nervous, which of course she was, Bastian was back with a pair of ceramic platters on each arm. She watched him arrange them on the table, futzing with the placement and presentation until she cleared her throat, teasing him.

"Sorry," he said, pulling out a cushion and inviting Sloane to sit. When she did, he helped her scoot in closer. "Anyway, you drink, and you forget stuff," he said quietly. "Well, maybe you don't forget stuff, but I do. And tonight, I want to be like you and remember every second." He sat down across from her, smiling at some private thought, as if he knew his words had just sent her heart racing.

"How did you manage all of this?" she asked, gaping at the veritable Thanksgiving feast he'd just set out.

"I cheated," he said, uncovering the platters. "Enkh helped me with the kebabs, but the rest I got to-go."

Stuffed grape leaves, fresh whipped hummus and warm pita, cucumber yogurt, soy chicken kababs. Sloane stared at the familiar feast, the menu prices of each item flashing in her mind.

"Raffi's Place."

Bastian beamed. "I had the Data Science team pull movement stats from a week before and after your birthday over the past few years. Lucky me, they found a pattern. Unless that's creepy, in which case, forget everything I just said, and Raffi's Place was just a lucky guess."

"It's where Simon and I would always go. Our favorite place."

Bastian's face fell. Simon was there, just for tonight, and he'd taken her away from him. Even after Sloane promised him it was fine, Bastian looked doubtful.

"We had time to catch up, and I know he's going to be okay when I'm gone thanks to you. Trust me—he'd want me to be here."

"He would?"

"He's always saying I should get back on the…"

"…horse?"

"Train," she said. "The, um, dinner train."

They both looked down at their plates.

"But how on earth did you…? I mean, this isn't just Raffi's style. This is actually Raffi's. Isn't it?"

"There's a travel tunnel that lets out a few blocks from there," he said, passing the grape leaves. "It's the same one I used when I went to your coffee shop."

"You went to Vancouver yourself? Today?"

He smiled at her, one cheek stuffed, and she could suddenly picture him as a little boy—the kind who knows without a doubt that he's adorable.

"Let me get this straight," she said. "I literally gave you a concussion. I acted like I'm the one in charge of the Program instead of you, dishonored the memory of your dead wife, and then, when you trusted me with the world's biggest secret, I pretty much fled the room like a toddler. And your response to all that assholery was to go pick up my favorite food from the other side of the world?"

Bastian laughed so hard he almost fell off his cushion. Sloane laughed too, and their laughter rang out into the forest and reverberated into the treehouse, surrounding them with the amplified echoes of their own mirth, and making it sound like they were a couple hosting a dinner party for a dozen of their closest friends. She could practically taste it—Sloane and Bastian together in another timeline, another life, where he wasn't Fred and she wasn't a Hero and dinner together wasn't an anomaly but a nightly occurrence. A cherished, comfortable bore.

"How do you know it was the other side of the world?" he asked.

"Because I think we're somewhere in Asia."

Bastian bit into his pita, his eyes sparkling. "Hmm," he said.

Sloane pressed her face into her hands, overwhelmed by the absurdity of being somewhere in freaking Asia eating freaking Raffi's on a dinner date with freaking Fred. It was so much, and when she suddenly said so, Bastian worried it was too much.

"No!" she said. "I just mean you've given me so much. Just getting to come to Basecamp would have been enough to last a lifetime. But then I get to see Simon one last time, and eat Raffi's one last time, and see your house. And everything you're doing for Simon, and that night out there on the tower…"

They looked into each other's eyes.

"You mean the night you were upset, and I..." Bastian trailed off, picking at his plate.

"I want to thank you for that," she heard herself say. "You didn't even know what had happened with Harry, and you—"

Bastian winced.

"Oh," she said, embarrassed "Right. Of course you knew about Harry. Sorry, I keep forgetting that you probably know everything. I just didn't know people like you could be so—"

"People like me?"

"Sorry," she said. "I just meant. Well, you know."

"I don't."

"Um, okay. Rich, powerful, basically in charge of the whole world."

Bastian narrowed his eyes.

"I've never had dinner with a quadrillionnaire world leader before. So I didn't realize people in your position could be so...down to earth."

"Ah," said Bastian. "That's probably because I'm only a *trillionaire* world leader."

Sloane threw a piece of pita at him, and he ducked.

"I've also spent some time with a begging bowl. If that gives me any street cred in the down-to-earth department."

"A begging bowl?"

"Begging for my meals in the street. That's a grounding experience you never forget."

Bastian had lived in Nepal for five years. He told Sloane he went there on a whim after Ashleigh died and stayed in a monastery in Kathmandu with a bunch of Buddhist monks.

"Did you *become* a monk?"

"Not really," he said. "I was just a hurt kid who thought running away would help, but it turns out you can't run away from yourself. So, since I was there anyway, I did what they told me. Meditation, chanting, I went into silence—"

"You stopped talking?"

"That's the easy part. The hard part is silencing the mind. That's what helped me the most, though—the silence. There's peace in it. It helped me accept my parents' deaths, but I still had a hard time letting go of Ashleigh. My teacher would call her my 'earthly anchor'—my last remaining attachment to this world." Bastian smiled, looking wistful. "My teacher is very wise, but you've probably figured that out by now. At least I hope you've noticed him. We've dedicated most of Enkh's time to you since you got here."

"Enkh is your teacher from Nepal?"

Bastian grinned. "He's from Mongolia originally, but he gets invited to teach all over the world."

"How can he teach?" she said. "He never talks."

Bastian laughed appreciatively. He said silence was a powerful teacher.

"But *can* Enkh speak?"

"I've enjoyed a choice word or two over the years."

"Such as?"

Bastian cleared his throat, pointed at her, and adopted a faint accent. "'Clear the warehouse—now!'"

"Why did he say that?"

"Because a couple of guys were on their way to our warehouse to kill me."

"Eleanor told me! She said Enkh saw them coming."

"He did—about eight hours before they got there."

"What?! I thought she meant he saw them when he looked out the window."

Bastian tapped his temple. "Not that kind of seeing."

"Are you saying Enkh is psychic?"

Bastian shrugged. "You don't believe in that stuff."

"After coming here, I honestly don't know what I believe anymore."

"See, to Enkh, that's the beginning of true wisdom—not knowing. That was his teaching when he visited the monastery in Kathmandu. He was only supposed to stay for a week, but he ended up staying six months just to work with me. I always got the feeling that he'd also lost someone he loved—that he knew how hard it was, and that's why he wanted to help me."

"And did it help? I mean, did Enkh teach you how to let go…of the person you couldn't let go of?"

"No," he said, looking into her eyes. "I was stubborn. A slow learner. And just when we were starting to finally make some real progress, I had to leave Nepal to go back to UNNA."

"Monks kicked you out, huh?"

Bastian smiled. "That would have been a lot simpler than what actually happened."

#   #   #

"One day when I was deep in meditation, I had this vision. Not like a psychic vision or anything. But out of nowhere, I saw these images in my mind. They appeared the way I imagine your memories do—in a flash, all at once, fully baked. The images looked like lexigraphs, but they weren't from any language I'd ever seen before. The lexigraphs appeared on a great canvas that filled my inner vision like a painting that fills an entire wall. I could see the symbols in their totality, as this unified shape, and I could see the individual details—the angles of the lines, the spacing between them. I knew the lexigraphs comprised some sort of language, and that the language was important and that I had to remember it. I ran to the temple office shouting, 'Paper! Pen!' in Nepali. The monks sort of freaked because I hadn't broken my silence in three years. They didn't have paper and pen, just a couple of broken pencils and a sharpie. I tore off my robe and sat on the floor and used the sharpie to draw the markings I'd seen in my mind. When I was finished, every inch of my robe was covered."

"Oh my god," she said, looking from him to the gallery wall. "I thought you were the art collector. But you're the artist."

"'Artist' seems overly generous."

"But all those symbols on the wall—are those the lexigraphs you saw in your mind that day?"

They were. It turned out the lexigraphs were part of a language, but nothing used by humans. At least, not before Bastian discovered them. "It's a coding language," he said. "But not like anything you're used to. It's…new. Newer. It's the language we use to write Saffron."

"Saffron."

"The intelligence that opens the time travel portal."

She stared at him, shaking her head in wonder, not even caring if he saw her staring, which he did. "You took this vision you had, invented a new coding language, and then used that coding language to create artificial intelligence that lets people travel back in time."

"I can't say I invented the language. I just copied it down. And it's not accurate to say that Saffron is artificial intelligence. But that *is* what we tell world leaders. And people who give us money. And almost everyone who works for the Program."

"If Saffron's not artificial intelligence, what is it?"

Bastian pressed his lips together the way he did when he'd revealed as much as he could.

"You can't tell me that right now," she said. "But you promise that as soon as you can tell me, you will."

Bastian's eyes lit up. "Speaking of right now, what are you doing?"

"What am I doing?"

"I mean I've taken up a huge chunk of your evening on your one free night. Did you have…other plans tonight? Or can you stay?"

#   #   #

He refused her offer to help clear the table, and insisted she make herself comfortable on the loveseat. Sloane took off her shoes and tucked her legs beneath her, arranging her dress around her like a fan, then undoing her work, then arranging her dress around her like a fan again. When Bastian brought out a tea service, he caught her fiddling with the dress, and she caught him glancing at her chest. He sat down next to her and filled a pair of beautiful ceramic teacups with steaming hot milk-tea. When he noticed her shoes on the floor, he removed his, too. Then, he loosened his bow tie and put his feet up on the ottoman, the vision of his white socks as intimate as if he'd just stripped to his underwear. They sipped in silence for a while, and he dimmed the lights so they could watch the stars dance above the dome. When Sloane glanced at him out of the corner of her eye, he was frowning into his teacup.

He said there was something he'd been meaning to tell her.

"Something other than the fact that you're Fred?"

"Yeah," he said. "Sorry. I hate to ask you to endure one more thing today. But…can I?"

"Wait—I know. This was all a prank, you really are just an intern, and we've broken into Fred's treehouse with a stolen key."

Bastian managed a weak laugh. "That sounds like a fun night."

"Did you kill a puppy?"

"What?

"Are you planning to murder me and collect the insurance money?"

"What?! No."

"Then whatever you have to tell me, it can't be as bad as the look on your face right now."

Bastian waited so long to speak that Sloane could have gone to the bathroom and come back by the time he finally worked up the nerve to open his mouth. When he did, he told her that the day he saw her in the coffee shop in Vancouver was not the first time he'd seen her in person.

She expected him to say more, but he just sat there cringing as if waiting for a bomb he'd just dropped to detonate.

"Okay," she said uncertainly. "Because you guys were staking me out, right? I figured as soon as I became a Candidate, you'd be watching me."

Bastian shook his head. "The first time we met was ten years ago, Sloane."

Never had she ever imagined she would meet Fred, let alone have dinner with him in his treehouse. But she had especially never imagined knowingly giving Fred a command.

"Explain."

"IT TOOK TWO YEARS OF trial and error before I understood what to do with Saffron's code," said Bastian. "After researching all these extinct and dead languages and ruling those out, I tried using the code as a programming language, mapping it to existing computer codes. Nothing worked. Then I met Eleanor, who has a background in mechanical engineering, and she suggested we try building hardware in the shape of the code. We used copper and brass, molding the metals until they were physical representations of the markings I'd seen in my mind. But still, nothing. One day, there was a storm, and the power went out in our warehouse. As I was resetting the circuit breaker, Eleanor and I had the same idea at the same time. Saffron couldn't run on modern computer code, but she couldn't just run on found parts, either. She needed power—electrical power. We wired her up, and she started to glow. But something still wasn't quite right." Bastian grabbed a napkin from the tea service and spread it flat on the ottoman. "Imagine this is one of the drawings of Saffron's code. It's flat. Two-dimensional, right? But when comparing my drawings with what we'd built, I realized the code wasn't meant to be rendered in two dimensions." He wrapped the napkin over his closed fist to form a sphere. "To be functional, the code on one side needs to be able to see the code on the other side. There needs to be a reflection so she can—"

"—see herself," said Sloane, and Bastian stopped short. "So she can see all of herself."

"Exactly," he said. "How did you…?"

"I don't know," she said.

They stared at each other.

"Keep going."

"So, we bent the metal parts to create a spherical frame and connected those parts with glass. That way, every inch of code was visible from every other point on the sphere. When we wired her up again, boom! A portal opened right there in our warehouse. It's sort of like the tunnel you went through in Vancouver, but it's louder, and the wind is faster, and the pressure is more intense. You hear the wind first. Then the air itself sort of cracks apart, and this circular opening materializes. Beyond the opening, you can see this dark tube spinning like one of those vortex tunnels at a carnival. Eleanor was standing too close to the portal when it opened, and the wind was so powerful she got blown back against the wall, so I cut the electricity, but the portal stayed open, and the wind kept coming and coming and it seemed like it would never stop. That's how we first learned it takes a minute or two for the portal to close once the power is cut. It's sort of like when you unplug a fan, but the blades keep spinning? Anyway, I took Eleanor to the hospital, and her neck and shoulder were all messed up. She ended up having to go to physical therapy for months."

"Oh, no!" said Sloane. "That's awful."

"The price we pay for innovation," he said. "The price *she* paid, as she loves to remind me. Daily."

"And this happened in Vancouver?"

He shook his head. "We were still in New York then."

"I was in Vancouver, then. I thought maybe that's where you saw me."

"Ah! I promise I'm getting to that part."

"I'm not in a hurry."

Bastian paused, the thread of his story momentarily lost as he looked into her eyes, making her feel as if no one else existed or ever had. She felt her inhibitions dissolving under his gaze, and as the seconds ticked past, the idea of climbing into his lap seemed less and less ludicrous; if she didn't look away right now, she just knew she would embarrass herself.

"You were saying?" she said, breaking their gaze.

"I was saying," he said, his voice as dulcet as a dream. But in the next breath, he cleared his throat, shifted in his seat, and went on. "I was saying that we wanted to try again. Eleanor was recovering, so I wanted to try and go through the portal myself. But I knew I could get blown back like she did, so I figured we'd better be prepared. You should have seen it, Sloane. We padded up the walls and put crash pads all around the warehouse, and I was wearing this ridiculous marshmallow suit, like a—"

"Like a Sumo wrestler?"

"Yes!" he said. "Just like a Sumo wrestler. I needed padding in case I got blown against the wall, but I also needed supplies just in case I went through the portal. I had everything sewn into the lining of my Sumo suit. Laptop, camelback, protein bars. I don't know where I thought I was going— computer camp?" Sloane touched his arm as they laughed, and he put his hand over hers, holding it against his bicep for a moment before letting go. "So, we booted her up again, the portal opened, and I was swept through."

Sloane's smile faded. "Holy shit."

"I landed in an alleyway in a city by the sea."

"Holy *shit*."

"My thoughts exactly at the time."

"Wait, why could you pass through the portal but Eleanor couldn't?"

"I can't tell you that right now," he said. "But I promise—"

"I don't understand the logic of what you can and can't tell me," she said. "Just tell me everything."

"Sorry. I'm trying not to freak you out."

"Too late."

"Should I stop?"

"No!" she said. "You landed in an alleyway in a city by the sea…"

"And I hid the Sumo suit. I wrapped a blanket around myself to hide my clothes and found myself in this crowded shipyard. Did Eleanor tell you I'd planned on studying history in college?"

"She said you're a history geek.'"

"We prefer the term history buff."

"Nerd."

"Fair. I was such a nerd, that even though I never went to college, I had studied enough on my own to recognize the clothing I saw and the dialects I heard in the shipyard. I knew I had landed in the South of France in the sixteenth century."

"What."

"That's exactly how I felt."

"But the South of France. In the sixteenth *century*?"

"I know."

"But that's where I'm going. That's where my Mission…"

"I know."

"But how are you here? It's not possible to travel to the past and return."

Bastian pulled his feet off the ottoman and clasped his hands between his legs. When he spoke, it was to the floor. "People assume it's not possible because none of our Heroes have returned. Heroes need time to accomplish their Missions, often a lifetime. They stay in the past because we need them to. Not because it's not possible for them to return."

She gaped at him, unbelieving. "It's possible to come back."

He glanced at her and away, looking nervous. "It is possible for you to come back. Yes."

The only reason she was interested in coming back at all was the possibility of coming back to him; the possibility that, when she said goodbye to Bastian in a week, it didn't have to be goodbye forever.

"So, after a few days, I found out I was in Toulon—"

"But I'm going to Toulon," she said. "Toulon, France. 1521!"

"I know," he said. "Now, I know. But when I was there, I didn't know what year it was. Even if I had spoken Provençal, it's not really the kind of thing you can ask someone, you know? And back then, most of the population of France was made up of illiterate peasants, so there weren't exactly stacks of newspapers with that day's date just lying around. But I knew it was Christmastime, sometime in the sixteenth century, and that I had traveled through the portal five centuries into the past. And that's where I first saw you."

Sloane was speechless. Something about the look on her face inspired

Bastian to massage his temples and groan, and she reached for his hand to find it hot to the touch.

"Hey," she said. "It's okay. Whatever it is, whatever happened, it can't be that bad."

He squeezed her hand, then let it go. He stood up and started to pace.

"How much do you know about time progression?" he asked.

"Just what everyone else knows," she said. "When a Hero goes back in time, their actions override the current timeline beginning with the point in time they landed and rippling forward to the moment they departed."

"Exactly. So, Saffron sent me to the year 1521, which is where I first saw you. But it couldn't have been the 1521 from our current timeline because in our current timeline, 1521 has already happened, and you were never there because it's centuries before you were born. In our current timeline, as of this moment, you haven't traveled back in time yet."

"Are you saying…what are you saying?"

"I'm saying Saffron can access any point along our timeline—past, present, and future. When Saffron let me pass through the portal that day, it appeared that she had sent me to the past. Now, I know she actually sent me to the future—a future version of 1521; the version you'll travel to next week."

Sloane stared at him, flashing on the broadcast of the first-ever Hero ceremony ten years ago. She remembered the disbelief she'd felt when she'd first heard about Climate Reversal Technology, and the ongoing mental recalibration of what was and was not possible in technology, physics, the universe itself. And now this. She felt unmoored, the way she imagined people felt when they first learned the Earth was not the center of the universe.

"But…why would Saffron do that?"

"As soon as I stood on the docks in Toulon, I received another vision. Saffron's code was clearly some kind of language, but this vision was different. I saw the ships in the harbor disappear, and the houses on the mountain dissolve. There was this citadel, this military base, and its outlines flickered, coming in and out of focus until it was gone, too. And then suddenly, everything was gone, and I was alone, staring out at the sea, as if I'd gone even further back in time. No people, no harbor, just gorgeous green all around and blue sky above the water. The scene flickered again, and the boats returned, except now they were these enormous tanker ships in this industrial shipyard, and the water reeked with filth, and I could taste the chemicals in the air the way I could in New York. The scene kept flashing like a glitchy simulation, showing me these different versions of Toulon at different points in time. I saw Toulon before humans, Toulon in the Roman Empire, Toulon in an alternate 21st century where cars had never existed. And then I was back in the shipyard in sixteenth-century Toulon, and floating all around me were these intersecting pathways, like a thousand crisscrossing freeways above my head. The pathways were moving and shifting like the lines on a Mind Map, and I had the idea I was seeing inside the mind of the planet. I knew the intersecting pathways were timelines—our own, and an infinite number of others that were possible on Earth. And not just infinite possible timelines, but infinite possibilities for each point along each timeline—as many possible versions of a single moment in time as stars in an infinitely expanding universe."

He stopped pacing and turned to her. "The fact that you and I are in the same timeline sharing the same moment in time is nothing short of a miracle."

It was a miracle. It was a miracle to see his face, to hear his voice, to listen to his astonishing stories and find it within herself to believe them. Every moment with Bastian was a miracle because the man in the dream was never supposed to exist in the first place. And if Bastian had not only experienced time travel but 'seen inside the mind of the planet,' maybe learning he'd been the star of her recurring dream for the past decade wouldn't come as such a shock when she finally told him.

"Back then, you remember—of course you remember—that the world was in crisis. Governments passed laws to try and reverse course, but even if we'd stopped all industry and grounded all airplanes, the deterioration of the planet would still have been irreversible. When I saw those timelines in my mind, I understood we were being given a do-over. The chance to override and rewrite our timeline, to undo the mistakes we had made as a species. By accessing different points in the past, we could prevent our worst environmental mistakes from happening. We could stop destructive corporations from forming and make sure our most harmful inventions never got invented. That was why I'd been given Saffron's code. With it, we had a chance to save ourselves. It was my mission to help humanity take that chance. But then, I had no way to get back here, to the right point in time, to get started."

"Did I help you get back?" she guessed. "Did I tell you about the future, about the Program?"

A shadow fell across his face, and he shook his head. "I didn't give you the chance."

"Because I did something super embarrassing when we first met, didn't I?" she said. "It's okay to tell me. I can take it." Sloane smiled then, but Bastian pursed his lips and resumed his pacing.

"In Toulon, I got an innkeeper to rent me a room in exchange for chopping wood, cleaning dishes, whatever he needed. I worked in the inn all day, and at night, I snuck out to a blacksmith's shop and bribed him with money I stole from the innkeeper. If anyone asked, he'd say he never saw me, that I was never there. The blacksmith let me use his tools and forge, and I figured out how to turn the laptop I'd packed in my Sumo suit into a Saffron. I modified the parts with a bending fork until I fashioned a frame that matched Saffron's code. It took weeks to get enough glass to hold the frame together. As you've learned, glass was very expensive then, and I'm afraid the innkeeper wasn't the only person I had to steal from to get it."

"And then you plugged her in to the sixteenth-century outlet and she started to glow."

Finally, a smile.

"I ended up making these rudimentary solar panels," he said. "It was morning on the day after Christmas, and I was in my bedroom above the inn. I opened the window, held Saffron in the sun, and finally got the portal to open."

"Don't leave yet!" she said. "I haven't made my cameo."

"I didn't," he said. "The portal didn't open in my room—it opened all the way down at the far end of the docks."

"No!"

"In New York, and for the launch of every Hero Mission, Saffron has always opened the portal in the portal room. But when we've done testing off-site, the portal has opened anywhere from five to twenty meters away from the base unit. And in Toulon, it must have been forty meters away. Our

Atmospheric team thinks Saffron is strengthened by fresh air and nature and weakened by being inside. Maybe the air quality in the past improved her reach. I think she just likes to keep us on our toes. Especially that day. I was already being run out of my room, and I nearly got myself killed trying to get to the portal before it closed."

Sloane raised an eyebrow. "You were run out of your room…?"

"I had an encounter with the innkeeper's wife. And he wasn't too happy with me."

Sloane felt a lump at the base of her throat, and she clenched her jaw, ignoring the pang of jealousy she had no right to feel. Except she did feel it—a possessiveness that stretched into Bastian's past before they had even met and claimed him as hers and hers alone. Bastian must have sensed the hitch in her demeanor because he launched into a campaign to defend his innocence.

"I saw the portal open, and I turned to leave, but the innkeeper's wife was blocking the door. And she was naked."

"Naked?"

"Completely naked. I moved for the door because I had to get to the portal. But she thought I was moving toward *her*, so she took a step toward *me*, and when her husband burst into the room behind her—"

"No!"

"She lunged for me, then he lunged for me, so I jumped out the window." Sloane shrieked, and Bastian laughed. "It was probably only ten feet to the ground. But while I was leaping out, the innkeeper was running down the stairs and grabbing an ax. I took off running, and the guy was chasing me through the shipyard while I was weaving in and out of bodies, trying to get to the portal. The wind was getting louder, like a huge wave was about to crash down onto the docks. And then, over the roar of the wind and the shouts of the innkeeper, I heard your voice."

They stared at each other.

"I stopped and turned. I remember that part so vividly because it was death to stop and turn. The guy was gaining on me, and the portal could close at any second. But I heard that voice, your voice, and it was familiar somehow. You were in distress, and the pain in your voice pained me in a way I couldn't explain, like the earth had swallowed my heart. I spotted you in the crowd and you were showing me your chest."

Sloane frowned.

"No!" said Bastian, crossing to join her on the loveseat. "I mean your dress had split open, and you were pulling back the fabric to show me this orange undershirt thing underneath. Like you were using the bright color to help me spot you in the crowd like a flare. And you were screaming my name over and over, and we locked eyes, and I knew that I *knew* you, somehow. You were running after me, trying to reach me, but these men were pulling you away. They had you by the shoulders, and I saw you struggling against them, fighting to escape. Fighting for your life. It was clear you didn't just need my help—you expected it. I had a split second to decide what to do. I could run to you, try to save you. Or I could jump into the portal."

In the dim light of the treehouse, Bastian seemed to shrink, as if the memory was consuming him.

"And I…I left you there."

That sat in silence for a long time.

Sloane pictured herself getting dragged through a crowd and imagined Bastian's torment as he realized he would have to choose—save one woman in the past or save humanity in the future. He'd made the right decision, of course. The Program wouldn't exist if he hadn't turned his back on her, leaped into the portal, and left Sloane to face her fate alone. It wasn't that decision that was weighing on her heart so much as the possibility that Bastian had only invited her here tonight because he wanted to atone for the past. Dance with her, cook for her, pass her romantic messages through Eleanor, all so he could assuage his longstanding guilt for abandoning her in the shipyard.

Bastian was looking at her pleadingly. He asked if she remembered any of that, but of course she wouldn't remember because it hadn't happened to her yet.

"It's my past," he said, "but it's your future."

He said people saw him disappear into the sky, and that some historical accounts mention a series of incidents in Toulon around the time he thought he was there. Women were burned at the stake for witchcraft, and he had always worried he was to blame. He had always worried about her.

"Once I came back, I understood you were from this timeline," he said, turning toward her. "I hadn't used my real name with anyone I met in the past. How else would you have known my name? And then, once we started the Program, I realized you must have been a Hero, and that I'd stood there like a fucking idiot watching one of my Heroes get captured." He smacked his forehead, and she reached out to pull his hand away, tutting. He grabbed her hand and held it, worry overtaking his face. "I didn't know if you were going to be the 5th Hero or the 25th. But I knew that I'd find you, and when I did, I'd do everything in my power to prepare you. To keep you safe."

His hand in hers triggered the memory of his hands around her neck in the corridor. "That's why you attacked me," she realized.

"A dress rehearsal. I needed to know you'll be ready when they come for you."

"That's why Saffron sent you to my drop point—so you could see what was going to happen to me and warn me."

"That's part of the reason she—"

"That's why you stared at me in the coffee shop."

The disappointment in her voice was plain, and Bastian looked more and more anguished. He must have thought she was upset about the way he'd left her in the shipyard. But really, she was replaying the memory from the first time they'd met in the coffee shop, watching the look in his eyes through a different lens. She had wanted it to be a look of longing for her, but maybe, he'd simply longed to warn her and finally clear his conscience.

"When you came up in our system, I noticed the similarities between you and the woman from the shipyard right away. But it wasn't until I saw you in person that I was sure it was really you. And to find you, to finally find you after so many years of searching and waiting…it was a shock, to say the least."

"Right."

Sloane fiddled with her dress until he reached out and took both her hands in his, stilling them on her lap.

"Sloane. I am so, so sorry I left you there. I know I can't ask for your forgiveness, but—"

"There's nothing to forgive."

"Don't do that. Don't just let me off—"

"It hasn't happened yet, right? It's your past, but it's my future. Which means I can still change it. Prevent it from happening."

"That's not the point."

"You did what you had to do," she said.

"Will you stop it? You're allowed to be freaked out I'm telling you this. Angry I left you there. Creeped out."

"Creeped out?"

Bastian shrugged. "Some of the predictive models I ran said you'd be creeped out that a guy you'd never met had been looking for you for a decade."

"Maybe I would be. If you were a guy I'd never met."

"Fine. A guy you've known for two weeks. To me, we have ten years of history, but to you, we're practically strangers. I have to remind myself that you don't know what it's like to have someone living in your head for a decade, and then, WHAM—suddenly they're real."

Sloane burst out laughing. Bastian looked confused, then hurt, and she waved her arms apologetically. "Sorry! It's just that I do know what that's like. I know exactly what it's like to have someone living in your head like that."

"You do?"

Sloane remembered all the times she'd fantasized about telling the man in the dream that he was the man in the dream, and how she'd hoped her confession might result in his; as unlikely as it seemed, she'd held out a thin thread of hope that he'd been dreaming of her, too. That the blue place was the place their souls went to be together when their bodies were apart. But that was before she knew he was Fred and she was the woman from the shipyard. There wasn't much to be gained from telling him about the dreams now—no lingering hope that her confession would inspire Bastian to act out a vignette from her Mind Map. Just the small satisfaction of swapping her secret for his, and the comfort in him finally knowing the truth.

"You're supposed to know everything about me, but obviously you don't know about the dreams."

"What dreams?"

"Technically, it's just one dream," she said. "I've dreamed the same dream basically every night for the past ten years."

"Whoa," he said, his gaze intensifying. "What's the dream?"

"Well…it's this dream where I'm floating in this place that's all blue. There are no ceilings or floors. It's not a room. It's not outside. It's just blue nothing."

"But you're there?"

"Yes. I'm there, and—"

"Are you blue?"

She smiled. "I'm me. Normal me, and there's…a man there. He's lying down, sort of floating, and his eyes are closed. And he's…well, I guess we're one-for-one in this department, because he's totally naked."

"Oh!" said Bastian, raising an eyebrow. "So, the two of you…?"

She blushed. "Not…exactly. When I first see him, I feel this deep longing. I want to touch him, but when I try to touch his face, my fingers pass right through him. I try to embrace him, but it's like I merge with him, like I'm a ghost or he's a ghost. I scream for him to wake up, but no sound comes out of my mouth. But then, after what feels like centuries, he opens his eyes, and like a miracle, he says my name. And when he looks at me, every memory from my whole life materializes around us. They're all there, sort of floating in the air, and I know he can see them. I try to hide the memories, try to hide from him, but I can't, and he knows how my memory works, how my brain is different from everyone else's, and it's actually okay with him. At first, I think 'Wow, he wants me anyway.' Like, he accepts me despite my memory. But then, I understand that my memory makes him love me more; that he loves me because of my memory. He loves me because of the thing I've always hated most about myself. And once I understand that, I feel so safe, and accepted, and wanted. Like unconditional love actually exists, am I making any sense?"

The look in Bastian's eyes was identical to the way he'd always looked at her in the dream—so intent and striking that it almost made her wonder if Bastian's guilt about the shipyard might be tinged with something else, something that was not guilt at all, and she prayed that she hadn't been projecting her longing onto him, and that the look in the dream and the look in real life didn't mean two different things.

"So, that's been the dream, every night, for the past ten years. But then, just a few weeks ago, the ending changed. And now, when the man in the dream opens his eyes and says my name, he reaches out and touches my face. And it's so lucid—in the dream, I can really feel his touch. And his touch is just…it probably sounds so stupid, but I don't know how else to describe it except ecstasy. I could stay there, in that moment with him, forever."

It was a lie. It wasn't the dream she wanted anymore, but this moment—with Bastian, in the treehouse, on the loveseat, with that look in his eyes—that she could stay in forever.

"That's not stupid," he said, taking her hand. "It's beautiful."

"Oh," she said, worried he wasn't getting it, that he thought she was just being allegorical. "I wonder if you'd still feel that way if I told you I sort of think it's a soul mate thing. Like, the blue place is this place where the man in the dream and I get to be together when we can't be together in real life. And that the dream became more real just before he became real, and then it stopped entirely when he walked into my life. It was sort of like foreshocks before an earthquake, and the earthquake was you. Because you are…him. The man in the dream, I mean."

Bastian furrowed his brow, a slight smirk playing at the corner of his lips. He let go of her hands and crossed his arms as if waiting for the punchline to a joke.

"When you came into the coffee shop that day, I stared at you because you were the most beautiful man I had ever seen. But also because I recognized you. Not from the shipyard. From my own dreams. I can't explain it, but that doesn't make me any less sure. The person who's been with me day and night for the past decade—the person I've been dreaming of—is you."

Bastian's mouth hung open, and he scratched the back of his head for a while before putting his hands in his lap. "*I'm* the…?"

She nodded.

"You mean, this whole time I've been waiting for you, you've been dreaming of…me?"

She nodded again. "I didn't understand it until I saw you in real life. But now I think the dreams were a sort of gift. It was a way to be with you until I could be with you for real. The first dream happened ten years ago tonight, and ten years ago was when you first saw me in the shipyard. I think the moment we met was some sort of catalyst. And that even though we were in different timelines on different sides of the planet, a part of me must have known subconsciously that a version of me had met the person I was always meant to meet."

Bastian collapsed against the back of the loveseat, looking dazed. Sloane waited for him to say the words that would send her home: he didn't believe her about the dreams. Or he didn't believe in soul mates. Or he believed in soul mates but she wasn't his—she was just the woman he'd left in the shipyard. The woman he needed forgiveness from, not love.

Bastian's eyes were closed, and he was leaning his head against the wall. "I don't know what to say."

"You don't have to say anything," Sloane said. "I don't expect you to believe what I believe. I just thought, you know, one truth deserves another. And I'm not, like, getting my hopes up. I know that all this was just—"

His eyes snapped open. "All what?"

"Dinner, dancing. Eleanor playing wing woman. I get it now. I'm here tonight because you feel guilty about what happened in the past."

Bastian looked stunned. Called out.

"I'm sorry," she said. "I know it's coming from a good place. And I get why you'd want to, like, make amends. I think the dreams just got me a little confused because the dreams are very romantic. So, I guess I thought…I mean, I had *hoped* that maybe you and I…but that was before I knew you were Fred, and before I knew about the shipyard, and now I feel like an idiot, and I'll just go."

She moved to stand but he stopped her, pulling her down next to him. He took her by the shoulders and gently shook her until she looked into his eyes, which were glistening with tears.

"Sloane Burrows, if you honestly think I asked you here tonight because I feel *guilty*…" He scoffed, his eyes darting between hers, his face so close she could smell the sweet milk tea on his breath. "Am I really that difficult to read? Is it not obvious how nervous I am around you?" He took her hands and placed them on his back so she could feel where he had sweated through his shirt. "I hoped you might forgive me, but I barely let myself hope you

195

would give me a chance to make it up to you. And here you are talking about soul mates—"

"That was a stupid idea," she said. "I don't really—"

"I do," he said, taking her face in his hands. "That is exactly the way I've always thought of you. Of us. So if you still think there is a cell in my body that doesn't want you the way you want me, then yes. I would say yes, you are an idiot."

He kissed her, drawing her in until the soft sweetness of his lips had answered every question, destroyed every doubt, and she was suspended in blissful relief as his mouth held vigil over hers.

Bastian pulled back, watching her, and through her hazy vision she tracked his shoulders rising and falling with his breath.

"So, you *like* me-like me, then?" she said softly. "Like, not just as a friend? Because I don't want some sort of pity kiss—"

He stopped her mouth with his, brushing her lips apart with his tongue. She drank in the wetness of his mouth, milk-tea and mountain air and the nectar of her dream coming true. Their mouths fit together like their hands fit together, like their bodies fit together—parts of a machine with perfectly interlocking components, as if she'd been born kissing him, as if kissing him was her natural state. His hands were everywhere, gripping her back, tangled in her hair, his tenderness rapidly hardening into something more urgent, something that had been gestating for ten years and demanded to be born now, tonight.

And then the insistent ring of an old cell phone cut through the night.

They froze mid-kiss, listening to the tinny music vibrating through the treehouse.

Din-da-din, *din*, din-da-din, *din*, din-da-din, din, *diiiiiiin*!

When the sound continued, Bastian pressed his forehead to hers. "Maybe, if we pretend we're not here, it'll stop."

…din-da-din, din, *diiiiiiin*!

He ordered her not to move a muscle, not even an eyelash, and that *was* a requirement. He jogged to the table to answer the call, removed the ringing phone from his tuxedo jacket, and studied the screen as he made his way back to her. She was out of breath, trembling all over, every inch of her skin tingling from his touch. She wanted to climb him like a tree and wrap her legs around him and never, ever let go, but she told herself she shouldn't be greedy. When he reached the center of the room, he looked up, and she fixed him with her best do-what-you-have-to-do expression.

"Fuck it," he said. Then he whipped the ringing phone out the open skylight. Sloane gasped. They listened to the phone hit the roof, bounce twice, and disappear into the jungle below, the ringtone fading into the night.

"Are you sure that was a good idea?"

"Are you going to let me kiss you again?"

She was.

"Then it was the best idea I've had all year."

"Won't Eleanor—?"

"If it's actually important, she'll parachute in through the skylight."

"Is it actually important?"

He sighed, his hands forming fists at his hips, and she felt she was watching his body slip into Fred-mode and away from her. "If she tries to reach me again, then yeah. We're dealing with this thing with Ghana right now that's…"

"Of course," she said. "I completely understand."

He narrowed his eyes, watching her for a moment. Then his gaze drifted slowly downwards to rest where the fabric split between her breasts, and she watched the heat return to his face.

"I don't understand," he said.

"You don't?"

"I don't understand why I'm acting like I could leave you right now, as if it would be easy. As if it would even be possible."

"But if it's important…?"

"The only thing that's important right now is that you know the truth."

"I thought you told me."

"I haven't, though. Because I haven't told you that I'm in love with you. Except I guess I just did. So, there it was. And, I am."

Sloane froze, clutching the train of her dress like it was a life raft. "You…?"

"It was the third reason," he said, newly apprehensive, as if, after all she had revealed to him, she still might be capable of crushing him like a bug. "The reason I can't be in the same room with you without staring like a fool. The reason I couldn't speak in the coffee shop. The reason I could finally let go of the person I couldn't let go of. You asked why I took off my wedding ring tonight, and it's because I didn't want the woman I love to think I'm still in love with someone else. Because from the moment I saw you in the shipyard, Sloane, it's only been you."

She sat very still, waiting for the moment to reveal itself as a dream within a dream, the word love repeating itself in her mind over and over like a song. Not just *like* or *attraction* or *let's just have fun while we can*. Bastian was as illogical and helpless as she was, his heart as blind to the hopelessness of their circumstances. He loved her like the man in the dream loved her. And she loved him.

An inner wave pushed her into Bastian's arms, and she kissed him until she'd forgotten why they'd ever stopped. His hands in her hair became a hand on her breast, warm and sure as it slipped beneath the fabric of her dress. He sighed with some mix of pleasure and relief, murmuring that he'd been wanting to do that all night, she'd been torturing him all night.

"Blame Kofi," she said, her skin blooming beneath his touch.

"Remind me to fire him in the morning."

He loved her, he loved her, he loved her, and he traced his breathy mantra down her neck and along her collarbone until he could no longer speak because his mouth was filled with her breast. And then his hands were tangling in the knot of her dress, but he couldn't undo it, and now Kofi was double fired. Sloane said Kofi was defending her honor, that it was a chastity knot, and Bastian begged her for the key.

She slipped the knot over her head and pushed the straps down over her breasts and let go. Momentum sent the heavy garment swinging over her hips to rest in a pool around her ankles, the white silk piled like a snowbank in the middle of the treehouse floor. She stood before him in nothing but a thong, the mountain air prickling her skin, and he stepped back to take her in, looking almost pained to trace the curve of her hip with his hand. "Somehow, you've managed to be even more beautiful than I'd imagined," he said. "And you can't imagine how beautiful I'd imagined you to be."

It was worth it.

It was worth being born with this memory if she got to remember this; this consummation of longing, this precious diamond that could only be forged under the pressure of yes, and only if both said yes in equal measure.

She tugged off Bastian's undershirt and flung it to the floor. She traced the indentations that emerged from the top of his trousers, contemplating slipping her hands inside, dizzy with possibility, with wanting all of him immediately and wanting to slow everything down, to freeze frame every caress, preserve every touch in amber.

Bastian asked her if she wanted him. Her tongue felt heavy in her mouth, but she managed to communicate how stupid she found the question.

"Do you want me, yes or no."

"Yes."

"Why?"

"You know that I…"

"I never assume," he said. "I just hope."

"Bastian…"

"It's just that you haven't said the words."

"There aren't words. I don't know how I can possibly—"

"—if you don't feel how I feel, it's okay. I just—"

"Stop it, stop it, I love you."

Bastian touched a finger beneath her chin, tilting her face back so he could study her.

"But in love?" he asked.

"Desperately. Pathetically. All the adverbs."

She watched him swallow, the flesh of his lower lip trembling. "Say it again."

"I am hopelessly in love with you," she said. "I knew I couldn't say it before because I didn't know you so I'm not supposed to love you but I do. I was in love with you before I knew you, and I love you more now that I do."

Bastian lifted her into his arms and pressed his mouth to hers, wetting her face with his tears and laughing because it's not easy to kiss when you're crying. He laid her down on the bed and climbed on top of her, a swift remedy for their tears. When she felt the full weight of his body on hers her breath caught, and he made the softest moan—a sound so helpless in its wanting she thought the sound alone would be enough to make her come.

She unfastened his belt and pushed his trousers over his hips, sighing in astonishment when she saw him. Bastian looked uncertain, as if he had no idea how objectively attractive he was, let alone how attractive he was to her. But seeing his perfect body made her realize it wasn't his body she loved at all. It wasn't even his mind. It was something that lived behind his eyes, something looking out at her from a bottomless depth, something essential that reflected her own heart back to her. She reached for him, but he dodged her hand, pushing her back on the bed and gently pinning her wrists above her head. Her mind protested—she wanted to touch him, taste him, worship him—but her body responded to his swift, assured movements like a flower unfolding to the sun; it yielded to him, softening, opening, blossoming beneath his touch, and she was powerless to resist. His lips traced her shoulders, suckled at her breast. He ran his tongue over her stomach and down her thighs, moving as if they had all the time in the world, as if each kiss would be the only kiss, his only chance.

"Bastian."

"Mm."

"Is this really happening?"

"God, I hope so."

He slipped a finger beneath her thong and pulled it to the side.

"Is this okay?"

When she said it was so much more than okay, he reached for her hand and guided it to the back of his head, as if he wanted her to push him down, as if he longed to suffocate between her legs. She flashed on her Mind Map. With a dizzying mix of mortification, relief, and excitement, she realized he must have seen her Mind Map the night it had been converted to Visual Mode. Maybe he had been logged in to the network from the treehouse. Or he reviewed the recording later. Studied it, even. But Eleanor must have been right when she said Bastian's Mind Map probably looked a lot like Sloane's, because she could tell he was not merely reenacting her fantasy to placate her. His was not a selfless act; not a public service in the style of past lovers, or a chore he only performed long enough to earn reciprocity. Bastian wanted to be where he was. He wanted to eat her alive. To take her. To make her…

Oh, Jesus.

It felt like her elbows were dissolving, and his kiss remained steadfast as her spine unraveled, her toes curled, and a starburst shot through her body like a silent firework. Sloane herself was anything but silent, though, and the siren song that poured from her drew Bastian's body to hers. She was overcome by the sweet, metallic taste of herself on his lips, the weight of his body, the electric heat of his skin against hers—so sublime, so right, it frightened her. She was afraid she wanted this more than he did—whatever this was, whatever it might become—or that he wanted it now but would later change his mind, or that they both wanted it in equal measure, but she would find a way to ruin it.

"I'm…" she said.

"Nervous?"

"Terrified."

"I'm not going to hurt you," he said.

"I'm not talking about the sex part," she said.

"Neither am I."

He was inside her then, all of him, and they both gasped. He stayed there, completely still, as if he had waited so long to be this close that he couldn't bear the thought of separation, not even the negligible distance he'd need to retreat to move inside her again. They lay there, interlocked, kissing so deeply for so long that she nearly forgot he was inside her until the slightest hitch of his hips reminded her. And then he was moving, they were moving, and he was kissing her so hungrily she thought he might devour her, and she discovered she wanted nothing more than to be devoured by him. Every memory she had of Bastian penetrated her mind, jockeying for position in her consciousness, and she said yes to them all. They opened in her mind's eye in hundreds of beautiful, overlaid images, blooming brighter as her insides unraveled. A sound resonated from deep inside Bastian's chest, and it was the sound of the death of their longing, the animal sound of two becoming one. They came together, everything warm and wet and melting and disappearing, but he held her so tightly that even when they lost themselves, they never lost each other. At its peak, the memories fell away, and waves of relief washed over her. Gone were the feelings of longing. The remedy, the sweet relief, was him and her together, where she didn't know where he ended and she began, where she loved what they became together even more than she loved him.

Hours later, they lay on the bed, entangled beneath the skylight, surprised to look up and see they had not blown the dome off the treehouse or caused the stars to burn out in the sky.

WHEN SLOANE OPENED HER EYES, pale morning light had chased the shadows of night from the little treehouse, and Bastian was snuggled against her, warm and asleep, his hand cupping her breast. Between the first bird calls of dawn, she could hear a faint, familiar whirring sound—the sound the floor made in her Basecamp bedroom when it opened to swallow the bed. She sprang up, ready to make a leap for it, but it wasn't the bed that was moving—it was Enkh. The monk was ascending into the room through a hole in the floor as if he were standing on an invisible escalator. His palms were pressed together, and his eyes were closed above a wider-than-usual smile. Embarrassed, Sloane covered herself with the bedsheet and shook Bastian until he'd groaned himself awake.

"Mr. Punctual," he said, squinting at her. He pulled the comforter over their heads and kissed her, whispering that she was the most beautiful sight he'd ever woken up to. When she returned his kiss with a self-conscious peck, he scolded her for denying him her morning breath. He loved her, godammit. He wanted all of her, every smell and taste, and he persisted until he got his way.

Bastian threw back the blanket and leaped from the bed, his naked body gorgeous and lithe, a marble statue come to life. He disappeared into the bathroom, and soon a terrycloth bathrobe was flying through the air. Sloane caught it and slid it on beneath the covers, avoiding Enkh's blind gaze, not to mention his shit-eating grin. When she emerged again, Bastian was on the floor in a pair of silk pajama pants, prostrating before Enkh and touching the monk's feet like he was some kind of god. The ritual complete, Bastian jumped up, grinned at Sloane, and disappeared back into the bathroom.

"Sloane," he called, turning on the tap. "Guess how old Enkh is."

Enkh opened his eyes and smiled at her, bowing to greet her as if he hadn't realized she was there until that moment. Sloane pulled the robe tighter around herself. "Um, twenty? Twenty-five?"

Bastian laughed. "He'll be seventy-four in February."

"Stop it," she said.

Enkh just smiled wider.

On his way from the bathroom to the kitchenette, Bastian pounced on Sloane, wrestling her into a bear hug on the bed. She shrieked and smacked him—we have company—and Bastian released her, raising his arms above his head in victory. "Did you hear that, Enkh?" he said. "*We* have company. We're a *we*." Sloane threw the pillow at him, and Bastian dodged it and disappeared into the kitchenette, laughing like a fool in love. Enkh winked at her before sinking to the floor and resuming his usual meditation, and Sloane collapsed back on the bed, face in the sheets, groaning with the absurdity of her own happiness.

"Forgive me if I have to work a little?" Bastian called. "Just our regular morning meeting. Shouldn't take long."

"Should I leave?"

"No."

"But aren't I supposed to be somewhere?"

"You're supposed to be with me."

"But won't Eleanor wonder why I'm—?"

"She knows. Watch your feet."

The floor of the treehouse spiraled open again, and Eleanor rose into the room with a phone pressed to her ear. Without a glance in her direction, Eleanor shoved a stack of clothing into Sloane's arms and paced around the ottoman, demanding someone get the Prime Minister back on the line for the love of God.

Bastian emerged from the kitchenette with two steaming mugs. He brought one to Sloane and stood there watching her take the first sip as if he wasn't listening to Eleanor's exchange (which she knew he must be), and all that mattered was her. If he had exaggerated his feelings for her last night, she wouldn't have blamed him. They were both love-drunk in the darkness, and she'd braced herself for some diminishing returns in the light of day. But in Bastian's eyes, she saw every moment from last night holding fast this morning, and that if anything, he had even downplayed his love, holding back until he was convinced his feelings were wanted and welcome; by the way his eyes were shining as he looked at her now, he must have been satisfied that they were.

Eleanor ended her call and, as if everyone were fully dressed and the treehouse didn't smell like sex, informed Bastian that Germany and France were demanding deployment in the next forty-five minutes.

"Good morning to you, too," he said. "Since when do we hold our morning meeting in English?"

Sloane had never seen Eleanor at a loss for words before.

"*I* know," said Bastian. "You must be speaking English because you're tired. And you must be tired because you were up. all. night."

"You should talk," said Eleanor, throwing Sloane a glance.

"I slept great," he said, peering at the clothing in Sloane's arms. "Unlike some people. Kofi wasn't up in time to get Sloane's outfit ready, and you're clearly exhausted. It just makes me wonder if anyone else overslept. Anyone like…I don't know…Poppy?"

Eleanor threw her phone at him. Bastian caught it and handed it back to her, grinning like a bratty little brother—the two of them reminded Sloane of her and Simon. She prayed Simon had had the kind of night with Kofi that she'd had with Bastian, and that she might catch him before he left Basecamp so they could mutually dissect and analyze every delectable moment.

Eleanor told Bastian to take it down a notch for the love of God and launched into her morning report. From her iGlass, she projected a color-coded hologram of Planet Earth, where nearly every country in the world was flashing in red. "UNNA and her allies are demanding deployment of our agents and full disclosure of the Mission in the next forty-five minutes," she said. "The countries in red have already signed a disclosure petition, and everyone else is signing at a rate of 0.5 countries per second." She frowned at the floating globe for a moment, then clicked her tongue impatiently. "Make that 1.7 countries per second."

"Stall them," said Bastian, using a voice Sloane had come to think of as his 'Fred voice'; confident, assertive, and in complete control. He had used that voice several times last night, and its effect on her this morning was Pavlovian: she felt the robe dampen between her legs.

"We've been stalling for days," said Eleanor. "We've never waited this long to announce our projections for the outcome of a Mission before. The uncertainty is rocking the markets, and we're minutes away from being shut down."

"Aren't we always minutes away from being shut down?"

The world was still waiting to hear what would happen once Sloane passed through the portal because the Program still hadn't released any data on the likely outcomes of her Mission. Program agents had not yet been deployed to help impacted regions transition to the new timeline, nor had the Program specified exactly what the people in those regions would be transitioning to.

"No announcements and no deployment until we have a reliable confirmation of the Mission's outcomes," said Bastian.

He squatted on the floor next to Enkh and took the monk's hand. Enkh's eyes popped open, and he looked at Bastian as if he were looking right through him, his gaze like burning obsidian. In a reverent voice, Bastian asked if there had been any changes. Enkh's eyes snapped shut, and everyone waited in silence. Sloane realized that by a "reliable confirmation of the outcome," Bastian hadn't been talking about the Program's predictive models or algorithms. He'd been talking about confirmation from Enkh. She wondered if Enkh had 'seen' the outcomes of the past twenty-two Missions the way he'd 'seen' the hit men coming for Bastian in Seattle, and she was filled with sudden trepidation about what Enkh might see when he looked at her Mission and why he hadn't seen anything yet.

After several minutes, the monk opened his eyes and shook his head.

"Still nothing," said Bastian.

"Nothing?" said Sloane, alarmed.

Bastian and Eleanor exchanged looks.

"It's nothing to worry about," said Bastian. "We may be looking at an atypical intervention, that's all."

"That doesn't sound like nothing to worry about," said Sloane.

"I have to tell them something now," said Eleanor. "Nanda's threatening to disclose our location to the North American military."

"That's a bit dramatic," said Bastian.

If engaged, the military would enforce the shutdown of the Program and the commencement of Operation Underground.

"Fine," said Bastian, pacing. "We'll deploy. Without real confirmation, we'll have to base the deployment numbers on our projections alone."

"Thank you," said Eleanor, tapping her earpiece and issuing a series of commands.

"What's the current projection for overall success?" asked Bastian, speaking over her.

"Above average," said Eleanor, whose ability to carry on three simultaneous conversations while manipulating her iGlass at lightning speed never ceased to amaze Sloane. "Projected Mission success rate for the 23rd Hero is…sixty-seven percent."

"Up it to ninety."

Eleanor cried out as if someone had dropped a wine glass. "Since when do we deploy based on a projected success rate of ninety percent?!"

"Since we got the best Hero we've ever had," said Bastian. He looked at Sloane, who was sitting on the bed holding a pile of rumpled clothing to her chest, barely achieving a ninety percent success rate at keeping her robe closed.

"Need I remind you that our best Heroes only achieved seventy percent success on their Missions."

"Need I remind *you* that our best Heroes weren't as good as her."

"But—"

"Ninety percent success," he said. "Deploy based on that."

"You are talking about an additional forty thousand agents in the field," said Eleanor. "Not to mention supplies."

"From what we've seen in training, ninety might be low-balling. I'd rather eat the costs if I'm wrong than have people stranded without aid if I'm right."

"I mean this with all due respect to all parties involved, but you're thinking with your dick."

"If I were thinking with my dick, I'd tell you to do whatever the hell you wanted, and Sloane and I would go back to bed."

Eleanor started to protest, but Bastian cut her off. "Ninety percent success rate. I want the media to have that number, too. Tell them we expect major infrastructure changes in the northeast of North America, especially in and around Nova Scotia and Newfoundland, where the zero-carbon cultures of the Mi'kmaq and Beothuk peoples will have survived over five hundred years. On P-Day, hundreds of thousands of people in the current timeline will return from the Safety Zones to find a sustainable structure where their house used to be. We're looking at trillions in payouts for the losses and substantial training to teach people how to live sustainably in their new homes."

"You want to weigh in on the PR angle for that?"

"Sure," he said. "The campaign slogan is, 'Would you rather live underground?'"

Eleanor rolled her eyes, fighting a smile. "And Europe?"

"Anything Sloane invents for King Francis will be manufactured sustainably, which will change the way industrialization happened in France. Be sure to flag any factories or industrial sites that are still operational, especially anyplace still using fossil fuels, because they're likely to disappear as soon as she goes through the portal. Let's go."

Everyone moved at once. Eleanor was shouting, the floor was opening, Sloane was scrambling into her clothes as fast as she could. She felt a sudden pang of regret that she had never applied to be part of the Basecamp crew; she could have been a part of this, a part of them, and not just for eighteen short days of training. If she had been part of the crew instead of a Hero, she could have stayed here with Bastian forever.

When she looked over at her lover, he was fully dressed, pressing an earpiece into his ear, but all at once his body went rigid and he stopped where he stood. Eleanor noticed the look of agitation on Bastian's face and fell silent, and for a long, tense moment, they stared each other down. Finally, Eleanor told her callers to hold.

"How long?" Bastian asked.

"She's recalibrating," said Eleanor. "We're working on it."

"How long has Saffron been offline?"

The best friends glared at each other, Bastian's jaw clenched, Eleanor's eyebrow twitching with tension. "The team's been working on her remotely all night, but so far, no dice. She's not responding to the electrical current. P-Day timer's down, too. We think it's a hardware issue."

"You're not answering my question."

Eleanor looked at the floor. "Seven."

"Seven minutes?"

"Seven hours."

Bastian's face turned purple.

"It happened after you and Sloane left the party. I tried to call you, but—"

Bastian slapped the treehouse wall, making the paintings of Saffron's code tremble. Enkh sprang up from the ground and placed a hand on Bastian's chest. Sloane watched Bastian take one deep breath, and she could practically see the anger leaving his body. Bastian glanced at Sloane, mouthing an apology, but she could still see the panic behind his eyes.

"I wasn't concerned enough to interrupt you," said Eleanor. "She does this sometimes."

"Never for seven hours."

"If it's a hardware issue, maybe I could fix Saffron," Sloane heard herself say.

The three of them turned in unison to look at her. A zebra dove cooed its morning song from outside, filling the awkward silence until Eleanor said *no* just as Bastian said *yes.*

"No fucking way," said Eleanor. "She's only got six more training days. Her schedule is jam-packed."

"As if she needs more training," said Bastian.

"We just got the horse on-site. Sloane has never ridden before. You're gonna send her back there as a Turkish royal with zero horseback riding experience?"

"She can learn to ride a horse after she fixes Saffron."

"You're not thinking straight, B. No one touches Saffron but you."

"You trust Sloane to save the planet, but not to fix some old scrap metal? She could do it in her sleep." He smiled at Sloane, shrugging, and asked if she'd give it a try.

"I mean, if Eleanor is cool with it."

"Are you cool with it?"

Eleanor sighed at the ceiling. The treehouse floor opened, and she jumped into the pressurized tunnel and disappeared, shouting to get President Nanda on the line. Enkh bowed to Bastian and Sloane in turn before leaping into the air, his blaze-orange robes trailing behind him like fishtails after the rest of him had disappeared.

Sloane stared at Bastian as if they'd both just survived a plane crash. "Just a typical day at the office?" she asked.

"You're such a trooper," he said, pulling her into his arms. "Sorry about all that."

His gaze fell to the orange dress Eleanor had grabbed from Sloane's bedroom, and a strange look flashed across his face.

"What is it?" she asked, looking down at her dress. "Not your style?"

"It's just nice to see your real clothes," he said quickly. "What you'd wear at home."

A pang of sadness made her chest constrict. Bastian would never get to see her in her regular clothes, because soon, he would never see her again. Before, she'd thought of their inevitable separation as the dissolution of a dream, the end of something that was never real to begin with. But last night, through a thousand little intimacies they'd made in the darkness, she and Bastian had bound themselves to each other and made the dream real. Now, separation was no less inevitable, but it would be the physical, painful rift of two who'd become one torn in two again.

"What is it, my love?"

She rested her head on his shoulder so he wouldn't see her face when she lied. "Just a little worried about the Mission. Because of what Enkh said. Or didn't say."

"Nothing to worry about," he said, rubbing her back. "There's just something at work with your Mission that we don't understand yet."

"Maybe because I'm going to ruin everything," she said.

"Maybe it's because you're going to achieve something even better than what the team has planned."

He tapped his earpiece and told Eleanor they were en route, ETA three minutes.

"What's wrong with Saffron?"

"She does this sometimes—shuts herself down to recalibrate. It's not the first time it's happened during training. She's usually back up in a few minutes, and the countdown timer picks up where it left off. But…"

"But what? Why were you so mad?"

"Sorry," he said, pulling her close. "It's just that sometimes a shutdown can alter the training schedule."

"Alter it how?"

Bastian pressed his lips together, making his I've-said-all-I-can-say face.

"Alter it *how*, Bastian?"

"Extend training by a few days."

"We'd get more time together?"

He looked at the floor. "Maybe. Hopefully."

"But does it ever…reduce training time?"

Bastian looked up, his smile not quite reaching his eyes. "It did once. But only by a few days."

There were less than seven days until the portal opened. The possibility of even less time with Bastian than she already had made Sloane feel like she'd been hit by a truck. She couldn't let that happen. She had to fix Saffron so the countdown timer extended her training time, or at the very least, picked up from where it left off.

"We should go," she said. "As soon as you answer one more question."

"Anything," he said.

"When do I get to kiss you again?"

Bastian lifted her into his arms and moved them toward the opening in the floor.

"Now."

Then he launched them into the abyss, making good on his promise as they soared through the darkness together.

212

BASTIAN AND SLOANE APPROACHED THE viewing panel outside the portal room as if it were the window of a hospital nursery. The vision of Saffron behind the glass took Sloane's breath away. A perfect blue sphere the size of a classroom globe, Saffron was suspended inside an air pressure tube, spinning counterclockwise like the Earth, pulsing with a soft blue light like a Wi-Fi router that needed to be reset. Her frame had been sculpted in perfect replication of her code, the swirling lines of copper and brass connecting one glass panel to the next like continents connected over the sea. Beneath her, enormous servers and a computer bay with half a dozen monitors connected Saffron to the Basecamp network, and she stood out against the ugly wiring and hardware like a pearl on a metal grate.

"She's beautiful," said Sloane. Bastian agreed, but when she looked his way, she realized he hadn't been looking at Saffron when he said it. She wanted so much to be the beautiful woman he seemed to see when he looked at her, and when she saw herself reflected in his eyes, she could almost believe she was.

"You won't mind if I reset her to extend my training time, right? I'm hoping to find a way to turn six more days into six more months."

"Six more years," said Bastian, putting his arms around her. "Sixty."

"Or better yet, send somebody else back in time so I can stay here with you."

She'd meant it as a joke, or at least to sound like a joke, but by the way Bastian rested his chin on top of her head and sighed, he seemed to know she wasn't joking at all. She couldn't imagine leaving him now. As soon as she'd found out who Bastian really was, Sloane had assumed he'd chosen her as the 23rd Hero. But now that she knew he loved her, she couldn't understand why he'd want to send her away forever.

"Remind me what I told you last night when you asked about artificial intelligence."

"Um. You said, 'It's not accurate to say that Saffron is artificial intelligence, but that is what we tell world leaders, and people who give us money, and almost everyone who works for the Program.' But what does that have to do with—?"

"Saffron is divine intelligence, my love."

Sloane broke away and gripped the railing, turning her back on Bastian. "If you don't want to talk about the fact that I'm leaving in less than a week, we don't have to."

"I am talking about it," he said. "I would give anything to send someone else back in time so you can stay here, but it's not my decision. Saffron decides the time and place of the Mission. She decides how much training a Hero needs before going through the portal. She even decides who the Hero should be."

Sloane felt as if her blood had halted in her veins. Bastian touched her tentatively on the shoulder and she spun around to scan his face, searching for signs that he was holding back or putting her on, but his expression was somber, and his eyes reflected her own feelings of helplessness.

"As soon as you applied and we inputted your DNA into our system, Saffron chose you. It was Saffron who started the countdown on your training time. That's why we only give the team a few hours to develop a Mission— once that clock starts, we have no control over the countdown. That's how it's worked for the past twenty-two Heroes, and Saffron hasn't been wrong yet. You know how much I believe in you as a Hero, but I'd send someone else in your place in a heartbeat if I could. But I can't. The Hero has to be you because you're the one Saffron chose. There is no one else alive who can do this but you."

Sloane backed away from him, shaking her head. "You said Saffron just opened the portal."

"She does open the portal."

"But that's enough. That's trippy enough. Now you're saying she's sentient?"

"She is sentient, yes. Silent, but conscious. She knows when and where the planet needs the most intervention, which Hero will be the most impactful in a certain time and place. So much of what the world thinks of as the Program's brilliance or Fred's brilliance is really just her."

"But it's impossible."

Bastian reached out and cupped her face. "There was a time, not long ago, when time travel was impossible, too."

"You didn't choose me."

"I *did* choose you," he said. "Just not as the 23rd Hero."

He said he never would have chosen this for them, but it wasn't up to him. It had never been up to him.

"But my assessment…"

"It's all just for show," he said. "The competition, the announcements. Half the teams we employ around the world are just for show. Just so no one knows that the fate of the human race is in the hands of someone who doesn't even have hands."

"But even the Candidates are just for show?" she asked. "Even Debbie?"

Bastian said Debbie was bullshit, and that for the record, he did not find her attractive.

"Hold that thought because I'm going to want you to repeat it later, when I can fully appreciate it."

"Holding," he said with a grin.

"This is why you never chose a woman before."

"Saffron never chose a woman before. We hated it, but there was nothing we could do. We can't modify her. We can power her on and off, open the portal, but that's about it. We can't decide who goes through, or when. Did you ever read *Aladdin and the Cave of Wonders* as a kid? Saffron is just like the cave. She'll open for anyone, but only Aladdin can enter and get the lamp."

"I don't know what to believe anymore," said Sloane. "I don't know what's real and what's not."

Bastian kissed her, and his lips absorbed the shock, and his tongue softened the blow of impossibility, until the only thing that needed to make sense was his mouth with hers.

"That is real," he said.

With all impossibilities momentarily forgotten, Sloane focused on what was still possible: his hands, his lips. She told Bastian he shouldn't start something he wasn't going to finish. Bastian told her not in front of the divine intelligence and pushed away her hand.

"But if you can fix Saffron," he said, whispering in her ear, "I just might have Eleanor insert an extra break into your training schedule today."

"Oh?"

"Unless you think you'll be too sore from horseback riding to take another ride in your room?"

Her groin flooded with heat, and she flung herself against the viewing pane, palms against the glass, let me fix her—now.

Bastian opened the portal room wall. As Sloane passed through, moving toward Saffron, the plexiglass casing that surrounded her ascended into the ceiling. Saffron remained floating on the airstream, but now nothing was separating her from Sloane, who pantomimed to Bastian through the viewing pane—did she need special gloves or something to touch Saffron? She didn't. Sloane reached out and removed Saffron from the pressurized column of air. The metal frame was cool to the touch, the whole apparatus lighter than she'd expected. She still wasn't sure about the whole divine intelligence thing, but Saffron did seem alive somehow, like an egg that could hatch any minute.

Sloane sat on the floor, guarding the orb in her lap, and examined her carefully, looking for signs of damage. Ah ha! A small section of her frame had moved out of place over time, creating a triangular shape that broke the laws of spherical geometry. Sloane used her finger to press the metal back into place, molding it to the code she'd seen on the gallery wall in the treehouse, the code that had been burned into her memory as clearly as

Bastian's face. When she was finished, Saffron stopped blinking and turned solid blue. Sloane waited, but nothing else happened, so she placed Saffron back onto the airstream, surprised at the pang of sadness she felt in having to let her go. Bastian beckoned her outside, and they booked it down the corridor in search of Eleanor and a sign that Sloane's small fix had worked.

A siren wailed throughout the Basecamp compound. It took Sloane a minute to understand that it was celebratory in nature and not an emergency. She heard clapping and whooping sounds echoing through the corridors. Then she saw the familiar flash of the countdown timer floating at the intersection up ahead.

"You did it," said Bastian, beaming at her. "She's back online."

Sloane squinted at the countdown timer as they neared the intersection, hoping six more days of training time had increased to ten, or twelve, or six hundred days more. But before she could make out the numbers, Eleanor careened around the corner, and stopped dead in her tracks when she saw them. Something terrible but definite passed between Bastian and Eleanor, who resumed her march in their direction, dragging the countdown timer along with her until she was close enough to toss it to Sloane.

The portal was set to open in six days and twenty-two hours—one hundred and sixty-six hours in total. But the countdown timer did not display one hundred and sixty-six hours.

The countdown timer displayed fifty-eight minutes, thirty-seven seconds until portal opening.

00:00:58:36.

00:00:58:35.

00:00:58:34.

Bastian grabbed Sloane's arm before the numbers could make sense in her mind. His grip was firm, and she was grateful for it because it was soon the only thing keeping her from sinking to the floor. He swiped the countdown timer away and reached out his hand to Eleanor, who grabbed it and held on tight, the three of them standing together holding hands like children playing Ring Around the Rosey. *Ashes, ashes, we all fall down.* Sloane's shock started to tip toward panic, but Bastian held her up.

"Listen to me, Sloane," he said. "I'm going to speak with Eleanor for exactly one minute. And then you and I are going to go to your room. Right now, I need you to stand up, and wait, and save everything for when we're alone. Can you do that for me, my love?"

Sloane nodded, leaning on the strength of his tone, and his grip, for they contained the only strength she could conceive of when everything else was a weakened plea, a desperate failure, a pathetic mistake. Bastian said Saffron decided when a Hero was ready to go through the portal, but what if Sloane's 'fix' had really been a mistake that made Saffron decide wrong? Sloane could have messed up the angle when she'd pressed Saffron's frame back into place. Her fingerprint could have damaged something in Saffron's code, altered it somehow, cutting her time with Bastian from a hundred and sixty-six hours to mere minutes.

She should have seen this coming. Bastian had first seen her in the shipyard in Toulon at the exact moment she had first dreamed of him back in Vancouver. That moment had taken place ten years ago last night. Midnight on Christmas night in Vancouver was 9am on the day after Christmas in Toulon. Bastian said he had seen her in the shipyard in the morning on the day after Christmas. Which meant she was always going to meet him in Toulon on the day after Christmas, AKA today—not six days from today. How could she not have seen something so obvious?

"Stop it," said Bastian, taking her by the shoulders. "Don't leave me before it's time to leave me." He'd been speaking to Eleanor, but Sloane hadn't tracked what he'd said. Something about Poppy's location, Poppy's iGlass, make sure to grab the iGlass with the projector attachment.

"Initiate worldwide lockdown immediately with the shelter-in-place order," he said. "There won't be time to get everyone to the safety zones, but let's at least get anyone in a multi-story building to the ground floor in case the buildings disappear once she goes through the portal. I want all her gear in the portal room in exactly forty minutes. The place where we'd usually put provisions, only fill it halfway. There's a package in my lockbox in the treehouse—send Enkh for it now. Make sure there's enough room for that package inside her travel cloak. If you have to sacrifice other supplies, do it. That package is the most important thing she needs. Have Poppy set up her injections next to her wardrobe and shut down the feeds. At ten minutes to portal opening, no one is in the room. No one is near the room. No one is watching the room. From anywhere."

Eleanor nodded, snuffing out Sloane's remaining hope that they could somehow reset the timer.

Bastian handed Eleanor his earpiece and told her he wanted her to run point until further notice.

"Without you?"

Bastian's pained silence was the only answer she received. From Eleanor's alarmed expression, Sloane could tell he'd never stepped away from his role at a moment like this, and she realized he was doing it to mentally prepare himself for the outcome of her Mission. Within a few hours of her leaving, Bastian would know whether she'd escaped or succumbed to whoever had dragged her away from him in the shipyard; whether she'd lived a long, happy life at court; whether she'd married and had children with someone else.

"I'm on it, B," said Eleanor. He nodded a silent thank you and started to pull Sloane back down the corridor, but Eleanor threw her arms around Sloane and held her close. In a shaky voice, she told Sloane to say her goodbyes, and for the love of God get her head on straight because training was over and it was fucking go-time.

"I believe in you, Burrows," she said.

Then she turned and sprinted down the corridor with a finger to her ear, shouting commands to parties unseen.

IN THE PORTAL ROOM, SLOANE winced as Bastian slid another needle into her arm. Poppy and the Basecamp doctors had prescribed an injection for the air pressure in the tunnel, another to prevent infection, an appetite suppressant, a urinary suppressant, a hydration shot, and a mammoth dose of LORI. "She should last about six months," Bastian said. "She'll help you speak Provençal when you land in Toulon, and she'll make it easier to onboard at Fontainebleau."

The medicine made Sloane's frontal lobe tingle and buzz, which seemed fitting since the rest of her was already trembling. She and Bastian had spent the past forty-nine minutes in her room, crying and clinging and joining so hard and fast that for a few blissful moments, it seemed possible to fuck away the incomprehensible rift of separation, and she had almost believed their love could turn back the clock. But Saffron would not be swayed—the countdown timer was free-falling toward zero, the floating blue sphere growing brighter with each descending second. This was happening.

"Let's get you dressed," Bastian said, frowning at her orange dress. He chose a blue gown from the hastily set up wardrobe, and Sloane held out her arms, hoping he'd put the gown on over her dress, but Bastian wanted her to remove the dress first. He said that was the dress she'd been wearing when he saw her in the shipyard. That was the dress she'd been wearing when the men dragged her away.

"I promise not to attract attention to myself in the shipyard. Just please let me keep the dress on. It smells of you. It's still wet with your tears." His tears. His sweat. His everything.

Bastian's gaze softened. "If you leave it on, you have to stay away from the shipyard altogether."

"But if you never saw me in the past, you never would have recognized me in the coffee shop. Could that change the way you feel about me?"

Bastian's eyes filled with the old longing. He hoisted the gown over his shoulder and took her face in his hands, tracing his thumb over her lips. And then he kissed her as if the timer were counting down from infinity.

"You know better than anyone that no matter how the timeline changes, we still remember the version of history we lived," he said. "If some past version of me never sees you in the shipyard in Toulon—I'd still know. I promise I'd recognize you anywhere, in any time."

He slipped the blue gown over her orange dress, and over the gown he fastened a travel cloak. The cloak was a modest navy-blue affair meant to downplay her social status while traveling so as not to invite the interest of thieves. The travel cloak was waterproof, fireproof, and tamper-proof with a self-regulating temperature mechanism that would keep her cool in balmy, Mediterranean Toulon and warm in the north. The garment itself was a wearable compass, with built-in magnets whose pull indicated which direction she was facing—she felt a tug inside the fabric over her heart when she faced north, another at her right hip when she faced east. She could even convert the cloak into a small tent. The compartments inside could only be opened with Sloane's fingerprint, and they were packed with everything she would need for her immediate survival: sixteenth-century *denier tournois* coins; weapons; nutrition pods; three bras and a dozen pair of underwear she'd have to conceal lest anyone question her strange, futuristic undergarments; and a waterskin that looked like an animal bladder but had patented Program technology to automatically purify water every time it was filled.

The countdown timer flashed four minutes, thirty-seven seconds. Bastian reached behind her to grab something off the table as if he'd forgotten one last injection. With his free hand, he peeled the Mind Mapping sticker from behind her ear. She thought he meant to throw it away, but he held the tiny black dot on the tip of his finger, considering it. Then, he stuck the Mind Mapping sticker behind his own ear and began swiping his hand over the object he'd grabbed from the table—Poppy's iGlass with the projector attachment that linked to the Mind Mapping room.

All around them in 360 degrees was Bastian's Mind Map converted to Visual Mode.

Sloane was face-to-face with a thousand images of herself. Her stunned expression the first time she'd seen Bastian in the coffee shop. Her anguished face in a crowded French shipyard. The moving image of her glancing at Bastian over her shoulder in the training room and fixing him with a look of such love and longing that it took her breath away. She hadn't known how much she loved him until she'd watched the truth flash across her own face.

Perhaps his fantasies had always been purer than hers. Or perhaps they'd acted out so many of those fantasies last night that a different kind of dream was at the forefront of his mind. Bastian had fantasized about living a quiet, ordinary life, a post-Program life, the life he'd dreamed of living with her. He'd dreamed of Sloane falling asleep with her head on his shoulder while they watched a movie in her apartment. He'd imagined bringing her coffee and a print newspaper in the morning, the two of them lounging in bed while he did the crossword in nothing but a pair of reading glasses. He'd even envisioned Sloane's dark eyes behind a white wedding veil. Sloane gasped, and she covered her mouth with her hand as she watched the two of them exchanging rings. He didn't just love her now—he would have loved her forever. She wasn't just letting go of an affair; she was letting go of an entire life they could have had together.

Bastian sank to the floor and buried his face in her skirts. It was from that place on his knees that he brought forth what must have been his ultimate fantasy, his perfect dream: Sloane's swollen belly, a hospital bed, and a child—their child.

She took his face in her hands, blinking back tears.

"Would you have…" He broke off, choking on the words.

"Yes."

"But if you were staying, do you think we could have…?"

"Yes," she said, holding him as he wept. Yes to all of it. Yes to anything and everything as long as it's with you.

The countdown timer flashed two minutes, seventeen seconds.

Now that she had said yes, Bastian said he would never touch another woman as long as he lived.

"No," she said, when she really meant yes; when she really meant if another woman so much as looks at you, I'll come back through the portal and kill her myself. "It's not right. You shouldn't be alone."

"I won't be," he said, lifting her to her feet. "We won't be alone because you are coming back to me."

Sloane flashed on the previous night in the treehouse when he'd told her it was possible for Heroes to return from the past. Except he hadn't said that, not exactly. He had said it was possible for *her* to come back.

From behind the wardrobe Bastian retrieved a small, spherical case. Shiny and silver, like an oversized Christmas tree ornament, he presented it to her like a precious gift. When Sloane fingered the latch, the case popped open. Inside was a miniature globe, its frame sculpted with swirling lines of copper and brass that connected each glass pane like continents connected over the sea.

"It's...a mini Saffron?"

Bastian smiled. "I made it for you the day I first saw you in the coffee shop."

Sloane balked. "You just assumed I'd fall madly in love with you and want to come back?"

"I never assume," he said. "I just hope." He called it Saffron 2.0, the portable kind, similar to the one he'd made to get back from Toulon. Saffron 2.0 was solar powered, so there was no need for electricity. He revealed a small, hidden compartment at the sphere's base where Saffron 2.0's ON and OFF switches were located. Sloane could power her ON and hold her in the sun for a few seconds to open the portal.

"And you really think she'll let me pass through? I'll be able to get back?"

"As soon as Saffron feels you've accomplished your Mission, I have faith she'll send you back to me."

Sloane imagined what it would be like to return to him, to marry him, to have his child. Would she still be young enough to have children by the time she came back? If she came back? Was it right to ask Bastian to wait? There was a difference between living passionately for a few days and putting a piece of yourself on hold for the slim chance of reunion in a distant future. It would be a sacrifice on both their parts to hang on to that possibility. Something told her it would be easier to let go, easier to mourn what could have been than to hold out hope for what could be. But she'd meant it when she'd said she wanted everything and anything as long as it was with him. The possibility of 'someday' was a burden, but it was also the finest sliver of hope she'd ever held.

The countdown timer flashed and dinged. A siren started to wail in the room, but Bastian made the AI silence it. "You can open the portal any time using the portable Saffron but be gentle with the glass. There's some special glue in the case if you notice any hairline cracks. Worst case, you know the code to build a new one."

Sloane felt a rush of cortisol coursing through her veins. Yes, she knew Saffron's code, but she wasn't sure where she'd start if she had to build a new one from scratch. She straightened up, steeling herself against the insurmountable nature of her Mission; yes, she had trained for this, but she had merely trained for this—there was no way of really knowing what awaited her on the other side of the portal, or whether she'd ever be able to return. All she knew for sure was who she was leaving behind.

She promised she would do everything she could to return to him. He promised to open the portal ever damn day to see if Saffron would let him join her in the past.

"What?!" she said. "But the Program. The world needs you—"

"The world needs the Program," he said. "And Eleanor runs it better than I ever could, anyway." If Bastian couldn't pass through the portal, he'd wait for her here. He'd wait his whole life if he had to. Which was good, because it might take her that long to accomplish her Mission.

"You won't mind if I come back old and gray?"

"I'll only mind if you don't come back at all," he said. "Besides, I want to grow old with you. And if you come back when we're closer to the end than the beginning, it'll be fine. My love for you will be even bigger by then."

Sloane could hear the wind. It was getting closer, growing louder, like a distant wave crashing toward shore.

"You said you'd wait here," she said. "Where is here?"

"You were right when you guessed Asia. We're in the mountains northwest of Chiang Rai in Thailand. If you come back, and things have changed, go to Chiang Rai, and I'll find you."

He slid Saffron 2.0 inside the inner lining of her travel cloak and held her as the wind closed in.

The countdown timer flashed sixty seconds. Fifty-nine. Fifty-eight.

"For the record," she said, "I don't want to go."

"For the record, I don't want you to."

She didn't know what else to say, but she had to say something. Anything. Bastian suggested something stupid. Something he would only know about her if they had moved in together and were living a normal life.

"Um, I love roses. They remind me of my grandmother, my Yeay—she had a rose garden in our backyard when I was a kid. When you guys brought all the roses into my apartment, it just—well, it just made my heart sing. And I'm just now realizing the roses were from you. You knew, somehow, that they were my favorite?"

Bastian hugged her tighter. "Lucky guess."

"Tell me something stupid about you."

"I like my soup lukewarm," he said.

"What?!"

"It's the only way to get all the flavors."

"I'm sorry but I don't love you anymore."

The sound of the wind overpowered the gasping, wet sounds of their laughter, which wasn't laughter so much as intermittent sobs; heaving hiccups of emotion that were as hilarious to them as they were horrible.

She'd think of him every second. She'd dream of him. She'd meet him in the blue place every night until they could be together again in real life. Bastian shook his head. He told her to think of the Mission. Dream of the Mission. "And not because that's all I care about, but because that's what will bring you back to me."

The countdown timer flashed zero seconds, zero seconds, zero seconds.

The air over the computer bay broke apart, and a rush of wind poured into the room, blowing Sloane's travel cloak back from her body. She gawked at the circular opening that had materialized in the air. Beyond it, she could feel a magnetic force drawing her inside a dark, undulating tunnel. She fought against it, kissing Bastian so hard their teeth clashed, unable to recall a single reason why she was leaving the love of her life, probably forever— Saffron 2.0 was a possibility, but Sloane knew she wasn't a certainty.

"I can't do it!" she said, suddenly frantic. Tears pooled in Bastian's eyes, but he pushed her closer to the portal until she could feel Saffron start to suck her inside. "Push me!" she said, pressing her cheek to his. "Please, I can't do it. You have to push me!"

She felt a split second of hesitation before Bastian lifted her up and thrust her toward the portal. The last thing she saw before the wind swallowed her whole was his slate-gray eyes filled with pain.

PART 3

SECONDS AFTER SHE WAS SUCKED inside, Sloane was flung from the portal. For a moment that was both brief and endless, she hung suspended ten feet above the earth, hovering over a narrow alleyway that cut between stone buildings. Before panic from the height could take hold, she plunged toward the ground, tucking and rolling as she made impact with the rough cobblestone.

She pushed herself up, hip and ankle throbbing, inspecting herself. Her travel cloak was secure around her shoulders, with Saffron 2.0's case tucked snugly inside. Behind her, the disembodied wheels of a broken cart had been wedged between the buildings like a barricade. In the other direction, the alleyway opened onto a larger street. She squinted, straining to see past the bright, narrow opening, where she could just make out the silhouettes of passerby, and beyond them, the blur of water. The narrowness of the alley created a tunnel of sound between the buildings, and she could hear the clack of hooves on cobblestone, the dinging of bells, the groans of anchored ships, and the cries of gulls—real seagulls—circling above the water. The murmur of voices strengthened the buzzing sensation in her forehead. LORI pulsed when one voice rang out above the others, but the din was too indistinct to make out the words. She'd have to get closer.

Sloane stood up, and a gust of wind swept her hood off her head, the rush of sea air so fresh it seemed a different element entirely. Her whole life, she'd been breathing a cocktail of ozone and harmful dioxides, the saturation levels of which varied based on how recently the Program had sent a Hero back in time and in which part of the world that Hero had carried out their Mission. But this air. This air! It was warm and wet and without a trace of pollutants. She could detect nothing but a fragrant bouquet of organic compounds; mountain grass and cloud cover, horses and winter blossoms, the pleasant stench of saltwater and fish. And it was the purity of the air— more than the ancient cobblestone beneath her feet, and more than the cries of the gulls—that convinced her this impossible thing had really happened. Like the twenty-two Heroes who had gone before her, Saffron had allowed Sloane into the portal, sucked her through time and space, and spat her out into the past.

She replaced the hood of her travel cloak and made her way to the edge of the alley, inching along in her thermoplastic polyurethane cow-mouth slippers with her back to the stone wall. She peered out onto a wide, crowded thoroughfare that ran the length of a crescent-shaped harbor. Strong men with ruddy faces unloaded stone, lumber, sacks of grain, and crates of wine from anchored rowboats onto horse-drawn carts. Merchants and sailors in tunics and hosen rushed past. Beyond them, Sloane could see warships bobbing on the water, their enormous masts accented with rippling flags, their sails rolled up like giant carpets. Past the ships, in the distance, she spied a stone military fort at the tip of a narrow peninsula. And to the northwest, across the flat, gray bay, rolling brown and green mountains majestically rose, their foothills dotted with brightly colored stone houses stained yellow and rust and pale pink, their pane-less windows like eyes keeping watch over the sea. To the south, row after row of wooden docks hugged the edge of the harbor. To the north, the exposed skeletons of half-built ships jutted into the sky like ribs. Those must be the same docks Bastian had leaped over to get to the portal ten years ago, AKA today. Saffron had dropped her right next to the shipyard she'd sworn to avoid.

Bastian—ten years younger and from a different timeline, but still Bastian—must be here, too. A surge of sorrow bloomed within her at the thought of him. She couldn't bear the thought of running into a past version of him who wouldn't even recognize her. The sight of a Bastian who was not her Bastian would make their separation more real. She conjured the memory of the flesh and blood person she'd touched and kissed and clung to mere seconds ago, but it made her insides twist with grief, and she shut it down. She wasn't ready for him to be just a memory. She'd never be ready to let the real him go.

She had to get away from the shipyard and hire a valet as her bodyguard. Paid with the coins in her travel cloak, the two of them would stay in Toulon until she could figure out why Saffron had selected this town as her location drop. When they were ready to leave the city's relative safety for the dangerous roads outside, the valet would help her arrange passage to Fontainebleau.

From the alleyway, Sloane eyed a pair of handsome hackneys hitched to a post next to a vegetable stall, suddenly worried about traveling on horseback. She could smell the animals from where she stood, sweat and honey and an ancient memory of fresh cut grass mixed with shit. She gulped, imagining how high off the ground she'd be if she were to climb on top of one. Not that she knew *how* to climb on top of a horse—if Saffron hadn't cut her training time short, she'd be at Basecamp right now, learning to ride for the first time.

A group of women were walking toward Sloane's hiding spot. As they neared, she noticed their dresses didn't look like hers. The basic shapes of their garments were the same, but the bodices were cut differently, plunging lower than her high-necked dress, the puffs of their sleeves a decidedly different shape. She rifled through her memories of garments training with Kofi, trying to find matches for this different style of dress, and felt a growing unease in the pit of her stomach when nothing came up. When the women had walked a handful of paces past the alleyway, Sloane slipped out and began walking behind them, hoping any onlooker might think she was part of their group. LORI pulsed in Sloane's head as if she were searching for a nonexistent Wi-Fi signal, and the din of the crowd remained foreign and indistinct.

She followed the women along the covered market that ran parallel to the docks. They stopped at a fruit stall and Sloane stood behind them as if waiting in line. All at once she felt LORI connect, latching onto their conversation and flooding Sloane's mind with meaning. In the Provençal dialect of Occitan, the women were asking the fruit seller whether he was offering discounts on his peaches and plums. Because it was the day after Christmas, he said, he had a surplus that he'd consider selling at a slightly reduced rate. Sloane's comprehension improved as the negotiation continued, LORI growing smarter with every new input she received.

Confident she could converse with the valet now, Sloane peered over her shoulder down the thoroughfare, snapping mental pictures of the infrastructure. Across from the far docks was an iron gate where the crowd bottlenecked, people passing from the harbor into the city and from the city onto the docks. When the women moved on to another market stall, Sloane broke away and headed south toward the city gate. The wind whipped her travel cloak around her, and she held it to her body to make herself less conspicuous. But she was still a woman alone in a shipyard, and through the crowd, a nobleman narrowed his eyes at her as she passed by. From the cassock that sparkled beneath his fur overcoat, Sloane guessed that he was a member of the Catholic clergy. His opulent attire matched the portraits Kofi had shown her of sixteenth-century French bishops. Waxy burn scars covered the left half of his face, the skin raised in plaster-like tufts across his cheek and forehead, and his gaze was unyielding beneath his red skullcap. She looked away and quickened her pace, gooseflesh prickling her skin. When she glanced back, the bishop's stare was boring through her as if he were a corpse or wished for her to be.

She turned, ducking her head, only to stop in her tracks. The air above the farthest dock looked like it was breaking apart. The wind picked up, and she heard the sound of a distant wave crashing toward shore. A circular aperture appeared in the air, and past its opening, a dark, spinning tunnel invited Bastian, wherever he was, to leave this timeline forever. If Bastian was about to leap into the portal, it meant she was about to get captured. She had to get out of the shipyard. She had to—

Thump!

A tall, strapping man jumped out of a second-story window right above her head and fell to the ground not two meters away from her. He tucked and rolled as he made impact with the cobblestone, then sprang to his feet with the grace of an athlete.

It was Bastian.

For a split second, they were paces apart, and every cell in her body cried out at the sight of him. All thoughts of avoiding capture evaporated, as did the promises she'd made not to call to him or show him the orange dress that still smelled of him, the orange dress that, mere minutes ago in the future, he had practically torn as he'd made love to her for the last time.

Bastian took off running, darting through the crowd as angry shouts echoed from inside the inn behind her. She watched, horrified, as a man sprang from the doorway wielding an ax and cursing emphatically in Provençal. It was the innkeeper who thought Bastian had seduced his wife. Sloane sprinted after the innkeeper as he sprinted after Bastian, weaving between the bodies in the crowd. Bastian was nimble and surefooted as he churned toward escape. He leaped from the thoroughfare onto the nearest dock, then began leaping from dock to dock, over rowboats and trunks. The innkeeper was so stunned by this display of athleticism that he stopped in his tracks long enough for a pair of men to wrestle the ax away from him. Sloane continued after Bastian, running along the road as he bounded over the docks toward the portal.

With their mouths agape and their hats blowing into the harbor, a crowd had gathered beneath the opening in the sky as if attracted by the portal's magnetic force. But there was only one person Saffron would allow to pass through the portal today. And Sloane could not let that happen. She could not lose Bastian twice—across two centuries, in two different timelines—in a single day.

When Bastian reached the portal, she shouted his name. People stared at her, but she just kept yelling.

Standing beneath the open portal on the dock, Bastian snapped his head toward her, his eyes scanning the crowd. The vision of him looking for her, of him wanting to find her, obliterated any remaining inhibitions she had. Sloane felt as if they were the only two people in the shipyard, the only two people who had ever existed or would ever exist, and that to come here without him had been the biggest mistake of her life. She yanked back her hood and tore the travel cloak from her body, flinging it off her shoulders into the crowd. She ripped the bodice of her blue gown to expose her modern dress beneath, the bright orange fabric against the muted clothing of the crowd like a flare in the night sky. She called Bastian's name, over and over, until their eyes locked.

"It's me!" she said in English. She tried to take another step toward Bastian, but someone grabbed the neck of her gown and wrenched her backward. She was falling.

"Bastian, please!" she said. She was dragged over the cobblestone, arms flailing, feet pawing the ground. Her eyes remained fixed on Bastian's, which were full of torment and indecision. She reached behind her head and grabbed her captor's wrists, but she could not break free. The men hauled her through the shipyard like a sack of grain as the wind grew stronger, its ferocious rush whistling louder and louder. Bastian tore his gaze from hers and vaulted into the portal. To Sloane's despair, Saffron sucked him inside, ushering him back to his own time, and the dumbstruck, terrified crowd watched the love of her life disappear into the sky.

Sloane writhed and twisted, dragging her heels over the stone. She clawed at the people she passed, reaching for their shoulders, their sleeves, but they only cleared a path for the men to drag her. They pulled her across the thoroughfare, away from the water, and flung her onto the hard ground as the spinning portal began to slow and the sounds of the wind began to fade.

A ring of priests in white robes closed around her. She scrambled to her feet, but they pushed her down, her kneecaps slamming against the cobblestone. Someone grabbed her chin and jerked her head back. Sloane locked eyes with the bishop, the man with the burn scars who'd been staring at her moments before. He turned her head this way and that, as if she were a horse he was considering purchasing. His bulbous eyes shifted from her to the crowd, who had congregated around the farthest dock and were still pointing to the sky. Snippets of their conversations floated on the air, the Provençal words for "witchcraft" and "devilry" ringing in her ears like a death sentence. The white frocks of the priests hung from their bodies like ethereal judge's robes; they looked ready to condemn their prisoner to Hell.

The bishop spoke to them in Middle French, describing in vivid detail how Sloane had just ripped her gown to "expose herself" in public. Sloane ignored the half-dozen rebuttals LORI suggested in response to this blatant exaggeration. She remained silent and still, listening to the men discuss the foreignness of her orange dress, the brazenness of her behavior, and whether she might be responsible for the witchcraft in the sky.

She did a body count. Two priests had her by the shoulders. The bishop made three. In her peripheral vision, she could see three others forming a tight circle around her. As they speculated whether she was a whore, a gypsy, or some sort of witch sent by the Devil to tempt and dazzle good Christians with acts of sorcery, she considered explaining that she was a royal concubine of Suleiman the Magnificent and an expected guest at King Francis's court. But the bishop's declaration of an official charge of public indecency, and his orders to place her in the nearest pillory for public shaming until he could arrange a trial, quickly convinced Sloane that such efforts would be futile.

The priests jerked her to her feet. The bishop put his face close to hers. "Until we meet again, *demoiselle*," he said. "I never forget a face, and it will be a pleasure to remember yours."

Every hair on her body stood on end. Her spine went rigid, the muscles of her pelvic floor engaged, and beneath her skirts, she shifted into a defense stance as if she were back in the training room with Johnny. *Work with what you've got*, he'd say. *These mongrels have you by the shoulders, but your hands are free.*

Sloane reached behind her, grabbed the priest's wrists, and flung her legs up to kick the bishop in the face. She made impact, and the bishop grunted in surprise. She dropped low and dragged the priests down with her, slipping behind them and kneeing them, hard, in the backs of their legs. A third priest lunged for her. He was moving fast, a blur of white robes and red cap above her, and she knew she was ill-positioned to use any of her self-defense moves on him. So she kicked him in the balls instead, bit the hand of the next priest who grabbed her, and escaped, fleeing through the shipyard. Her gown was torn, and her travel cloak, supplies, and Saffron 2.0 were lost—trampled beneath the feet of the crowd.

SLOANE CREPT THROUGH THE DESERTED shipyard toward the harbor, weaving between the bodies of the ships. Her breath was short, and her heart was pounding from her sprint through the city. Throughout the day and deep into the night, she'd been hiding inside an empty whiskey cask behind a pile of firewood at the end of an alleyway. When it had been hours since she'd heard signs of life outside the barrel, she'd emerged, following the path back to the shipyard by memory, terrified she'd run smack into the bishop or his priests. But she'd found the open thoroughfare along the docks without spotting another soul, guided by the light of a star-filled sky, the likes of which she'd never witnessed before.

Now, she crouched inside the half-built hull of a massive ship, hidden in shadow, and surveyed the length of the harbor. She listened for footsteps or hoofbeats, no matter how faint. But the night remained still, the silence broken only by the puttering of a rat along one of the ship's beams, the sea lapping softly against the piers and jetties, and the soft clack-clacking of the moored boats bumping each other as they bobbed in their narrow berths.

She retraced her steps to where she'd thrown the travel cloak off her shoulders. She scoured the ground and saw coils of rope stacked in neat pyramids against the pier. No cloak. Could someone have tossed it into the harbor? Stepping onto the slats of a shallow jetty, she got down on her hands and knees and scanned the dark water. Tangled masses of seaweed floated between the boats. No cloak. She stepped back onto the thoroughfare and combed the area again, running her hands over crates and reaching behind barrels. But no cloak.

Sloane traced the path the priests had dragged her along. No cloak. She moved on to the market, patting down the wooden legs of the covered stalls in the darkness. A crumpled silhouette caught her eye. At first glance, it looked like someone had discarded a tarp next to a pile of horse shit. But when she fingered the crushed velvet, she knew it was hers. She practically tackled the travel cloak, shaking it out and patting the inner compartments to check for damage. It was crunchy with mud and feces, but it was dry inside, and the compartments sealed.

As she swung the cloak behind her to tie it around her shoulders, she heard the distinct, tinkling sounds of shattered glass, and new fear struck her heart. She pressed her finger against the opening mechanism, reached inside, and pulled out Saffron 2.0. When she opened the case, she gasped. The glass that connected the metal parts had shattered. Dozens of razor-sharp shards lay at the bottom of the case, leaving gaping holes in the skeletal frame large enough to stick her fingers through.

There's some special glue inside the case if you notice any cracks, Bastian had said. *Worst case, you know the code to build a new one.*

Build a new one. No big deal.

She swallowed the sob that longed to echo through the night, replaced what remained of Saffron 2.0 in her case, and with the ripe scent of horse shit filling her nostrils, moved swiftly along the market stalls, seeking the cover of the stone and clay cob houses. But a poster plastered to a hitching post caught her eye. By the glow of the moonlight, she gaped at an illustration of a woman with a seductive expression on her face and naked breasts pouring out of her torn dress. Above the woman's head, dancing devils and demons leaped onto her shoulder from an opening in the sky. The woman was her. The bare breasts, a crass exaggeration of the moment she'd torn her gown to get Bastian's attention in the shipyard. The opening in the sky was the portal that no one but Bastian should have seen.

Her hands shook as she reached out to touch her own face. Whoever had drawn this had made Sloane look eerily beautiful. Harry had always said that Thida's beauty had been "diluted" when they'd had children, implying that neither he, nor his children, were as good-looking as his late wife. He wanted to appear charming and self-deprecating, but the subtler message was clear: your mother was the beautiful one, Sloane. Not you. But looking at the poster now, she realized he'd been wrong. Stunned, Sloane traced the dark ink of her hair and the outline of her jaw as a lifetime of memories recalibrated themselves. She could see herself the way Bastian had always seen her, and she marveled at how right he had been. She *was* beautiful. Arresting, just like her mother.

She traced the lines of the illustrated breasts to the text beneath the portrait. There, her finger stopped. The moonlight cast shadows over the elaborate script written in French and Provençal: *Wanted Dead or Alive: Heretic Whore Charged With Public Indecency and Witchcraft. Sightings to Be Reported to His Holiness the Bishop of Toulon. Captors Rewarded With Eternal Life in Heaven in the Holy Presence of Our Lord Jesus Christ.*

Sloane ripped the sign from the post, the sound tearing through the silence of the night. They'd hung replicas of the poster on every market stall, and more were strewn across the ground. Even if she destroyed every last one, who knows how many dozens or hundreds of people had walked by during the previous day and seen her face—the most wanted woman in Toulon.

She wasn't supposed to leave town without a valet, without information, without some sort of crucial insight Saffron meant for her to have. That's why Saffron had dropped her in Toulon in the first place. And yet she fled, racing through the darkened streets, Saffron 2.0's broken pieces clinking softly in her pocket.

At the city gates, she snuck past the sleeping guard and sprinted onto the dirt road in the direction of the next-closest town. She knew from training that the village of Saphir lay some twenty kilometers northwest along this route, which snaked north before cutting a westerly path toward the foothills of the Alps. There, she could find someone to help her get to King Francis. But she dared not take such a well-tread route by herself, let alone at night. She stepped off the road into the virgin wilderness and began elbowing her way through the heavy underbrush toward Saphir, shifting her direction northwest by following the magnetic tugs inside her cloak. She hoped that traveling through the woods would be faster than taking the road. She hoped there wouldn't be bears. She hoped that unlike the roads, the forest would not be under the control of murderous thieves.

239

AFTER SO MANY WEEKS SLEEPING in the forest, it was heavenly to be indoors again, lying on a large, soft bed, tucked snugly inside a warm, woolen blanket.

So nice.

Even if she didn't know who had tucked the blanket around her.

Or whose bed this was.

Or how she'd come to be here.

Wait a second.

Sloane bolted upright in bed and her head spun, stars crackling in her peripheral vision. She blinked them away, taking in the dim, low-ceilinged room, desperate for a sight or a sound or a something that would spark a memory of where she was and how she'd come to be there.

A collection of drying rushes had been strung to the rafters above her head, and above those, a thatch roof. The lone window was shuttered, and next to it, between a fearsome sickle and a weathered ax, hung two dark, heavy-looking garments—her travel cloak and gown. Carefully laid on top of them were her bra and underwear from the future that no one was supposed to see.

She didn't remember hanging the garments there. She didn't remember taking her garments off. She looked down to see she was dressed in a simple, linen chemise, the laces tied to form a dainty eyelet above her breasts.

A rooster crowed, startling her. Between the crowing and the cacophony of clucking hens and bleating sheep in the yard outside, she almost missed the soft shushing of someone sifting grain from chaff in the next room.

There were only a few times in Sloane's life when she hadn't been able to remember something: thrice when she was extremely sleep-deprived, and once when she was fall-down drunk. Neither of those applied now. Was there something wrong with her memory? How could she accomplish her Mission if there was something wrong with her memory?!

Think, think, *think*.

She retraced her steps, scouring her memory for a point in time when things had still made sense.

# # #

The night she'd left Toulon, she'd pushed through the woods for an hour before she'd felt safe enough to stop for a moment and finally do what she'd longed to do in town—stand still and gape at the stars. She'd figured the night sky would be clearer in the past, but she never imagined she'd be able to see the visible galaxy spilling across the sky like salt on black cloth, or that thousands upon thousands of stars would be as silent as falling snow. She hadn't realized the stars would leap and pulse, or that the entire sky would undulate above her like a second sea. She'd stood there among the trees—palm and umbrella pine, fig and olive and oak—and memorized every star, every cluster, every visible constellation, wishing everyone in the future could be swept through the portal into the past, if only for a moment, to view the living night sky from the living earth.

Even when she'd resumed her trek through the woods, she couldn't help but glance skyward every few steps. The forest floor was covered with knotty roots, the trees thick, but she couldn't help herself, and during a particularly ill-timed glimpse upward, she'd tripped hard, rolling the same ankle she'd fractured at Basecamp. A sharp, shooting pain tore up the length of her leg and she collapsed on the forest floor, cursing. She found a stash of hydrocodone in her cloak, swallowed two capsules, and watched her ankle swell to the size of an apple.

She had a few choice words for Saffron, then.

And she would have traded ten billion stars to be back at Basecamp with Bastian instead of alone in the woods in the middle of the night in agony, a wanted fugitive.

Whenever you're tempted to think of me, think of the Mission instead. That's what will bring you back to me.

The following morning, it was clear that her ankle was broken. But the reassuring sound of Bastian's voice in her head had fortified her resolve. She had to get to the next town. In Saphir, she could make a cast for her ankle and hire a valet for the journey north. She just had to get there first.

She'd made a splint for her ankle out of sticks and the space-age Duct tape she found inside her cloak. She'd tied palm fronds around bundles of tree branches to make crutches, which worked well enough, except the tops of the crutches stabbed her armpits with every step she took, and she soon had armpit blisters to add to her list of injuries. After seven days of hobbling through the woods, her ankle had turned a concerning shade of green, and a heavy, seductive fatigue had descended upon her like a blanket. She'd tried to keep going, but she could only limp along for a few minutes before she needed to rest again. By the eleventh day, she'd begun sleeping for fourteen hours at a time, lying unconscious in the belly of the forest beneath her makeshift tent. She'd worried the infection in her ankle had traveled through the rest of her body. She'd grown petrified she had sepsis and needed medical care—even sixteenth-century medical care—but she'd been too weak to move any faster.

Along with the pain and fatigue had come a hunger she'd never known before. She'd burned through the nutrition packets in her cloak in fourteen days—half the time they were supposed to last. Fat figs, purple grapes, and sour apples had been plentiful but burdensome to forage on crutches and hadn't satisfied her unrelenting cravings for something more substantial. Her hunger drove her to try mushrooms that were not on the safe list from wilderness training, and she was soon vomiting as if the shame around her memory had never left her.

After twenty-one days, she'd reached the edge of the forest, emerging at the top of a hill to see a picturesque patchwork of farms, orchards, and vineyards spread across the breadth of a wide valley. A winding river snaked its way across the valley floor, where dozens of sheep milled inside a sizable, fenced-in pasture like tiny, quivering cotton balls. South of the pasture, a stable and a lone, thatched-roof cottage were the only visible structures for kilometer after wild kilometer. To the north, the valley inclined sharply, giving rise to a steep cliff, and at its crest lay the fortified village of Saphir. So close, but still so far; she'd never make it all the way across the valley in her condition, let alone up that cliff.

But maybe someone lived at that lonely little cottage by the river.

Someone who could help…

She'd taken one step.

Then another.

Then a sparkling blackness had overcome her vision, and she'd vomited into the grass before collapsing in a dead faint.

#   #   #

Now, she pulled back the blanket to inspect herself and gasped. Her skin was soft and clean, as if someone had bathed her. A camphorous poultice had been applied to her many cuts and scrapes, and her carefully wrapped ankle was half the size it had been the last time she'd seen it.

The sifting sounds abruptly grew louder, and Sloane drew the blanket over herself just as a petite, dark-eyed peasant woman poked her head into the room. When she saw Sloane awake, she yelped, slamming open the door and trailing a cloud of dust behind her. Powder-white grain was streaked across the woman's tan skin, and the age lines around her eyes and mouth were at odds with her youthful figure. She wore a simple linen veil drawn low on her forehead and knotted at the nape of her neck. When she said something in Provençal, LORI buzzed to life slowly, as if she were just as disoriented as Sloane. The warm, bubbling sensation grew stronger behind her eyes, and after several seconds, the translation came through. Upon seeing Sloane, the woman had said, "finally."

The woman tossed her winnowing fan on the bed and climbed up next to Sloane, pressing the back of her hand to Sloane's forehead. Her touch was gentle but sure, and Sloane leaned into her hand with relief, trusting her instantly.

"How do you feel today, my foal?" she asked, the words translating faster now.

Sloane opened her mouth to reply, and a word tumbled out, its meaning only made clear to her at the precise moment she spoke it.

"B-etter," she said in Provençal.

The woman nodded as if she'd understood perfectly. "Much better than last night. You were delirious. In and out of sleep with much unhappiness, remember? Or did your fever burn up your memories?"

"It is…unclear."

"Do you at least remember me?"

Sloane shook her head.

"Poor dear!" the woman said. "You needn't be frightened, my foal. I am Lady du Merkatoria, but last night you called me by my Christian name, Alona. You are at Merkatoria now, remember? You are here with us at home." Alona hopped off the bed and opened the window with a flourish, revealing a wide expanse of gently sloping pastureland abutting a dense forest.

Sloane must be inside the cottage she'd spotted just before she'd fainted. She couldn't fathom how this tiny woman had managed to bring her here. "How," she said. "How long have I—?"

"You came to us last night, *domaisèla*," said Alona. "Ma-hee-dev-rhan. Mahidevran, yes? Did I say it correctly? It is terribly difficult to say. May I call you Mahid instead, little foal?" Sloane nodded to be polite, inwardly panicking about what else she'd revealed last night. "How strange you are, with your foreign garments and underclothes! Your accent is strange, too. Do you prefer to speak Provençal? Last night you spoke mostly French. Half dead, delirious French. That was quite strange, too!"

"I can speak both languages," Sloane said, anxious to ensure her cover was intact. "But I'm here in France to improve my French. My education is a gift from my sultan, Suleiman the Magnificent."

"Yes, we heard all about this Magnificent last night!" Alona said, hopping back on the bed as if she were at a slumber party. "You told us about the pirates who stormed your ship just before you landed in Toulon, and how your valet drowned, and how you set out for the king's palace on foot when you got lost in the forest and broke your ankle and ate poison mushrooms. A wonderful story, and very entertaining! Even my son laughed several times, and I have not heard Zacarie laugh in years. Ever since his Colette and their baby went to Heaven, the poor man barely speaks. What a blessing to hear his laughter once again!" Alona beamed, revealing charming gaps between her small, white teeth. "Anyway," she said, "we enjoyed hearing your tale of adventure. But tell me the truth, my foal. Has your husband abandoned you, then?"

LORI swelled with three different responses at once, which made Sloane's forehead pulse. "I am from...where I say I am from," Sloane said. "I am not married. I am the second royal concubine of Suleiman the Magnificent. It is my sultan's will that I accept the invitation of the French king to join him at court."

A shadow passed over Alona's face, and she regarded Sloane with sudden seriousness. She started to say something, then pressed her lips together, forcing a smile. "Of course, my foal. Forgive my ignorance. We do not encounter many royal concubines in our little village."

Alona slid off the bed, eyes darting from side to side as if she were thinking of something unpleasant. "You have slept nearly half the day," she said to herself, rubbing her hands over her apron. "It is almost suppertime. Espi must be fed again, and you must try and eat something, too."

Alona moved for the door just as a goat skidded into the room and leaped off the dirt floor, taking Alona's place on the bed. Sloane shrieked, scrambling backward until she hit the wall, and Alona dissolved into a fit of giggles. "Now you are scared of Espi?" she said. "This goat was your bedfellow most of the night, curled up at your feet! It was Espi who woke me when your fever broke." With a snort, Alona disappeared, leaving Sloane alone with her terrifying savior. Espi the goat had black and white coloring and a belly that jutted out sideways as if she'd recently swallowed a tire. The animal stared at Sloane with strange, rectangular pupils slashed sideways across her ice-blue eyes. Alona returned and plunked a basket of hay on the bed between Sloane and the goat. "You have much in common, yes?" She ducked out again, leaving Sloane mystified—what could she and this creature possibly have in common? Besides the horses in Toulon, she'd never even seen a real farm animal until now, let alone been close enough to feed one. Her Grade 4 class trip to the last remaining farm in British Columbia had been canceled when all the animals died from toxins in their water supply.

Sloane held out the basket to Espi, who backed away, her hooves leaving little depressions on the bed as she turned in uncertain circles. Sloane grabbed a fistful of hay, held it on her open palm, and slowly slid the offering across the bed. Espi lowered her head and took the daintiest bite, gumming the hay a bit before drawing it into her mouth and grinding her jaws in slow, contented circles. Espi didn't smell too bad. A bit like old popcorn, the odor mingling with the scent of hay and camphor and smoke wafting into the bedroom through the open door. Sloane laughed when the goat took another bite, then another, munching straight from her hand until she'd polished off the basket. Espi nuzzled Sloane's armpit in thanks, leaped off the bed, then eyed Sloane expectantly. "Maaa," she said, augmenting the bleats of her brethren in the stable and the grunts of the sheep in the pasture beyond. LORI didn't translate Goat, but Espi's meaning was clear: *That basket's not gonna refill itself, lady.*

"Alright, alright, I'm up," said Sloane, enchanted by her new friend. She carefully slid off the bed, grabbed the basket, and limped after Espi into the dim center room of the cottage.

Standing before a banner of thick stone walls, Alona was stirring the contents of a steaming cauldron suspended over an inground fire pit. The room was sweltering—at least ten degrees warmer than the bedroom—and sparsely furnished with a ramshackle table, a collection of wooden stools, and a knotty ladder that led to a sagging hayloft. Off the main area, a small mudroom housed a collection of dirty boots and riding gear and connected the cottage to the stable. The only ventilation was an opening in the stone that served as a front door, and when the full force of the smoke hit her nostrils, Sloane's stomach turned.

"Mother Mary, Mahid!" said Alona when she saw Sloane in the doorway. "What are you doing out of bed? Do you need the chamber pot?"

"Fresh air," she said, hopping toward the door.

"For the love of the Virgin," said Alona, rushing into the mudroom and disappearing from view, "we must dress you before you leave the house! Our village priest is a patient, understanding man, but not everyone in our village has been blessed with Father Pierre's virtues. You must take care not to call attention to yourself, my foal."

She emerged from the mudroom with an armload of skirts, tugging them over Sloane's chemise and tying an apron around her waist. She placed a cut of stiff cloth over Sloane's head, twisting and tying it into a knot at the nape of her neck, and taking care to cover her ears and every last strand of hair.

"There, now" Alona said, adjusting the fabric. "With that wild hair of yours covered, you are a beacon of piety and modesty. You will blend right in with the women in the fields or the town. But do not speak of the sultan or the king—a foreign concubine on her way to the palace is sure to cause a stir. If you stay silent, your skin will make them think you are a sharecropper, like me. Perhaps we will call you our cousin from Basque country, here to help with the spring planting. I hope you do not find this beneath you since in your country, you are a lady of the court. But it is safer for you this way, my foal."

Sloane nodded, desperate to get outside. Alona produced her crutches, now outfitted with thick, folded blankets secured to the tops with twine. They felt like marshmallows under her arms, and she thanked Alona profusely as she scrambled out the door, sucking fresh air beneath a high, noon sun.

The vision of the valley rushed in to greet her, fresh and green and bright. When the nausea had eased, she used her crutches to turn herself in a circle, drinking in the landscape and relishing the feeling of warm soil beneath her unwrapped foot. In the orchards to the west, women in wide-brimmed hats were beating trees with long rods to make apples fall into their baskets. And in the vineyards to the north, she could see peasants tending to the vines on the hillside, shepherding soil into wine. Above them, the wide, thick teeth of the walled city cast shadows on the steep cliffside, and in the distance, green, rolling mountains gave way to sharp, snow-capped peaks. Without the hazy filter of particulate matter and ground-level ozone, the sky was clear save a few wisps of cottony clouds. The same breeze that pushed those clouds across the sky swept down to greet her. Her throat didn't close. Her eyes didn't water. The breeze ballooned her skirts away from her body until she felt like one of the bell-shaped lilies growing in Alona's flower garden in the front yard. She could hear real pigeons cooing in the stable rafters, and the gentle rush of the river that ran behind the cottage, flowing and drinkable and clean.

She had never been so completely immersed in nature before. For weeks she'd been in the forest, but she'd been too miserable to appreciate the stillness of the surrounding trees. And as a child, a visit to Stanley Park had only created the illusion of immersion—she always knew, in the back of her mind, that the city was still right there. But here, she was not only enveloped in the natural world but looking at a picture of her Mission, accomplished; a world where people, plants, and animals lived in harmony; a world where the planet's vast resources were cherished and protected, cultivated and shared. This little patch of paradise in Provence was precisely what she'd been sent back in time to preserve.

A dark shadow caught her eye where it moved against the rolling green backdrop. Beneath the blade of her hand, she spotted a lone horseback rider galloping toward the cottage, the thundering of hoofbeats growing louder as he reached the valley floor. Alona popped outside and spotted the horseman. "It is Zacarie!" she said, waving her apron like a welcome flag. "Come, let us finish preparing the supper for my hungry son. He spent the morning tilling Monsieur du Anouilh's barley fields. The Anouilh farm is up the mountain, an hour's ride north of Saphir, but he pays sharecroppers double what our stingy landlord pays."

She disappeared inside the cottage and Sloane hobbled after her, pausing at the entrance to see if her stomach would acclimate to the smoke. She took shallow, tentative breaths, watching Alona's son as he raced toward the cottage on the back of an ebony hackney. When he reached the sheep enclosure, he swept a leg over the back of the animal, alighting in a single, fluid motion that conjured an old memory of a bird landing on water. He moved to the front of the animal, wiping away the foamy sweat that had collected along her snout. He pressed his forehead to hers, as if in thanks, then released the reigns. The mare moved through an open gate in the fence to the nearest water trough, in which she promptly dunked her head.

As Zacarie made his way toward the cottage, Sloane hypothesized that he was adopted; it was the only way a woman as tiny as Alona could call a man as large as Zacarie her son. He was tall, with broad, muscled shoulders and thick, strong legs, the curve of his quadriceps visible inside his hosen. This was not a body made strong inside a gym, but a body chiseled by day labor. Zacarie was dressed much the same as the peasants in the paintings Kofi had shown her—a linen coif covered his head, and a billowy, belted tunic fell around his hips and split down the middle to reveal his codpiece.

Unsettled, Sloane searched for somewhere else to rest her gaze and ended up fixated on his face.

Bastian's face.

Sweet Mother of Mary. The memory of Bastian's face was superimposed on Zacarie's body, and the effect was like two stars colliding. For a few delicious seconds, she let the timelines blur together, relishing the fantasy of Bastian returning home to her after a hard day's work in the fields. The image successfully burned into her memory; she closed her eyes to reset to the present moment before Zacarie caught her staring. But when she opened her eyes again, it was still Bastian walking toward her. She shook her head. She hugged her crutches to her sides and blinked, willing away the memories. But when she looked at him again, still—*still*, Zacarie wore Bastian's exact face. He had the same angular jawline, the same straight nose, the same full, pillowy lips.

Sloane hobbled toward him, her mind racing with possibilities. Saffron had let Bastian through the portal. He had traveled back in time and found her here, somehow.

But no.

No.

As Zacarie closed the distance between them and removed his coiff, a handful of atomic differences came into focus like the telling freckles of an identical twin. Instead of Bastian's chestnut waves, Zacarie's hair was so black it shone in shades of blue and purple when it caught the sunlight. Instead of eyes like the sea, Zacarie's eyes were as green as the surrounding valley. And instead of the warmth that Bastian inspired in every fiber of her being, Zacarie inspired a surge of heat that was concentrated solely between her legs.

At the entrance to the cottage, Zacarie stopped. He leaned against the stone, considering her, and she was enveloped in a musk of bergamot, sage, and sweat.

"Well then, woman?"

The timbre of his voice sounded just like Bastian's, too.

LORI served up several responses in Provençal, the best of which was "I have a name, and my name is not 'woman.'" Sloane started to repeat the phrase, but she'd barely gotten two words out when a plume of smoke from inside the cottage brought on a coughing fit that made her stomach swim.

"Sorry—" she said, waving him away. "I think I'm going to—"

Zacarie cocked his head to the side, his concerned expression so like Bastian's that a whimper of heartache escaped just before she doubled over and vomited bile onto his enormous boots. Zacarie didn't flinch. He rubbed her back as she retched, and he made comforting sounds—*shh, hush*—until it was over. Then he picked her up and carried her inside, holding her to his chest just as Bastian had the night he'd rocked her on the tower. Too surprised and too weak to protest, she closed her eyes, forgot her mortification, and burrowed into him, pretending she was home.

"Mother Mary!" Alona said when she saw them.

Zacarie carried Sloane into the bedroom and laid her down on the bed. Alona swept in with a basket of supplies and set to work wiping Sloane's face and loosening her apron, shooing Zacarie from the room. "Out!" she said. "Leave women's things to the company of women."

From the other room, Zacarie switched to a language Sloane didn't recognize. "Is she who she says she is?" he asked, his tone casual and light, as if the universal music of nonchalance would convince Mahid they couldn't possibly be talking about her.

"It seems certain," Alona replied, slipping into the same language, the same easy tone, as she wiped soil from Sloane's unwrapped foot.

"And her condition?" said Zacarie. "You are certain of that, too?"

"I have never been wrong about that."

A flood of questions from LORI made Sloane's forehead pulse. The intense pressure would ease if she repeated the questions aloud, but she couldn't think up a believable reason Mahid would understand a language she couldn't even name.

"You'll want me to tell him, then," said Zacarie.

"Ay," said Alona. "Tell him who she is and where she is going."

Zacarie scoffed. "So he can turn her into the next Renée de France? If the inquisitors find her guilty of heresy, Renée could be put to death."

Releasing Sloane's foot, Alona said, "He was thinking of the good of the whole. He did what was best then, and he will do what is best now."

Zacarie leaned into the room to look at Sloane, who hoped the alarm she felt wasn't as plain on her face as it was on Zacarie's. "He should consider her condition," he said.

Alona turned to her son, and in a sharp voice, told Zacarie to eat his supper, and when he was done, to go and tell 'him' everything.

When Zacarie quit the room, Alona smiled at Sloane. "Women's things to the company of women," she said, switching back to Provençal as if the previous exchange hadn't happened. She remarked upon the cold sweat that had broken out on Sloane's brow, attributing it to a resurgence of fever from the previous night.

Fever. Sure.

Sloane asked Alona if it would be alright if she stayed here at Merkatoria for another day or two. She promised that by tomorrow, or the next day, she'd be out of their hair.

"My hair?"

"I won't burden you much longer," Sloane said, hoping to dissuade Alona and Zacarie from telling "him" about Mahid. Whoever he was and whatever he might want with her, Sloane wasn't going to stick around to find out. "I'll be out of here the second I feel well enough. Promise."

"It could be months until you feel well enough, my foal."

"Months?!"

Alona nodded, poking and prodding Sloane's abdomen. "Just thank Mother Mary that Zacarie found you on the field when he did. You would be in Heaven right now if he had not."

A memory from the night before, dim and grainy, swam somewhere beyond Sloane's peripheral vision. The coarse hemp of a soiled tunic, the hard muscle beneath, the jostling motion of her body against Zacarie's as he'd quickened his pace toward the cottage. Zacarie's arms weren't merely Bastian's arms in duplicate; they were the arms that had carried her across the breadth of the valley, the arms that had saved her life.

"But Mother Mary is protecting you because we are better equipped to help you than anyone in the village. I was born in Bayonne, in Basque country—"

Basque country. They had been speaking about her in Basque.

"—moved to Toulouse to escape the plague, but the plague caught up with us anyway. My husband died of it, so I came here, to Saphir, as a young woman. A woman traveling alone, just like you."

"But what is wrong with me?" said Sloane. "I can't imagine the effects of toxic mushrooms would last for months."

"Silly foal," said Alona. "You and me, we are the same. When it happened to me, I was madly in love and dumb as a donkey. But you need not worry because I am the best in the village at treating this condition. To get well, you must stay here and let me care for you. Then we shall see what is to become of you. We will know more by the time of the woad planting in the spring."

"The spring?!" By Sloane's count, it was already the third week of January. Technically, she had three years before Verrazzano petitioned King Francis to invest in his expedition to the New World. Beyond that, she was supposed to spend the next twenty-six years ensuring the king's inventions were manufactured sustainably until his death in 1547. But she refused to be separated from Bastian for decades. She would secure her position as the king's Royal Astrologer, invent a sustainable pencil, and get the right manufacturing in place in the space of a year. Maybe two. But that accelerated timeline would be seriously delayed if she was stuck at Merkatoria until the freaking spring.

"The spring," Alona repeated. "Even longer if you are like me. You could be unwell until the Feast of the Assumption at Midsummer. And if you are extremely unlucky, you could be unwell the entire time!"

"I'm sorry, but what do you mean, 'the entire time'?"

"How long since you have been bled?" asked Alona.

Baffled, Sloane waited for LORI to make the unfamiliar phrase make sense. Was Alona talking about bloodletting? Like, with leeches?

"I have never been bled," said Sloane.

"You have *never* gotten your *flowers*?!"

The phrase took a second to translate, but Alona's meaning was unmistakable this time. She was asking how long it had been since Sloane had gotten her period.

In stunned silence, Sloane flashed on the last time she remembered getting her period. It was the day Bastian had walked into the coffee shop. That was thirty-nine days ago, which meant her period was eleven days late. But surely…surely that was due to stress, fatigue, a broken ankle, dietary changes, food poisoning, and *time freaking travel*. It was impossible for her period to be late for any other reason. Certainly not *that* reason. There was only a 0.000129032258-percent chance of that, which was as good as impossible. Besides, *that* took a certain amount of *time*.

She pulled up a memory from her Human Growth and Development class in Grade 9 and recalled that ovulation typically occurs around the fourteenth day of the menstrual cycle. The fourteenth day of her cycle had been Christmas, the night she and Bastian had…but no. No way. And yet her memory insisted that implantation can occur as early as six days after conception, and that morning sickness can start as early as four weeks from the first day of the last period. But it had been five and a half weeks since the first day of her last period. *She* was five and a half weeks…

What Alona had been trying to tell her finally made sense. Alona was the village's resident midwife—the best in the village at treating this condition, this condition being pregnancy. Mahid and Espi had "much in common" because Espi's belly wasn't ordinarily tire-shaped. Espi was pregnant, too.

Alona rocked her, singing lullabies in her native Basque. Sloane slumped against her, bracing for the panic that was sure to set in at any moment. But verse after verse, the panic lay dormant, and wave after wave of wonder, and even joy, overcame her. The memory of the portal room materialized in her mind, and her consciousness was split between the sixteenth-century cottage and twenty-first century Basecamp, between Alona's arms around her and Bastian's face buried in her skirts, between Alona's insistence that her life was not ruined and Bastian's certainty of the life they could have had, the future he'd imagined on his Mind Map: a hospital bed, Sloane's swollen belly, and a child—their child. And then the memory took her over completely and she was sinking to the floor in the portal room and taking Bastian's face in her hands and telling him yes, she would have. Yes, they could have. Yes to anything, to everything, as long as it's with you.

254

AT MIDNIGHT, SLOANE WAS ALONE in the stable in her travel cloak trying to figure out how to mount Zacarie's horse. She cursed Saffron for sending her through the portal before she'd had a single horseback riding lesson, but she needed to get on the road tonight. Not that she was panicking, but the embryo inside her was probably doubling by the minute, and her identity as Mahidevran would only work if she arrived at Fontainebleau before her pregnancy started to show. So, she'd made a few teensy adjustments to Johnny's strict rules for sixteenth-century travel. Instead of wasting time trying to hire a valet, she'd travel alone. (Could she or could she not defend herself against six grown men? She could, and she had. She'd be fine.) Instead of wasting time sleeping all night, she'd leave as soon as possible, traveling at least fifty kilometers before dawn—even further if she could convince the horse to gallop. And instead of worrying about carts and riverboats, she'd take the most direct route possible, riding north through the Rhône Valley and on to Fontainebleau.

When Alona and Zacarie had been at work that afternoon, Sloane had started preparations for the journey, pocketing a few sad-looking potatoes for the times she could keep food down (and a bucket for the times she couldn't). She'd pieced Saffron 2.0 back together, using the glue designed for "hairline cracks" to adhere thirteen shards of glass. She prayed the patchwork job would be good enough and that she wouldn't have to build a Saffron 3.0 from scratch. While Saffron 2.0 was drying, she'd made a proper cast for her ankle out of clay, flour, and egg white. Now it was near midnight, and while the cast hadn't completely hardened and Saffron 2.0 was still a bit tacky, she couldn't wait another minute. Besides, fleeing through the night on horseback was sure to help wet things dry faster.

The hackney was standing perfectly still with her eyes open, but Sloane couldn't tell if the animal was dozing or staring into space. She grabbed an empty crate and placed it next to the horse as a mounting block. Suddenly concerned about brain injuries, she repurposed her designated puke bucket as a helmet, tucking the handle beneath her chin. The horse was wearing a leather bridle with the reigns slung in a loose loop over her neck, but her back was bare. Sloane worried she'd wake Zacarie and Alona if she tried to lug a cumbersome saddle from the mudroom, so she'd grabbed a blanket to use as a makeshift saddle instead. Unrolling a few inches of fabric at a time, she covered the horse's spine with the blanket. When the mare didn't stir, Sloane hopped onto the crate, swung her broken ankle over the animal, and hoisted herself, Saffron 2.0, a satchel of stolen food, two crutches, and all her skirts onto the horse's back. She held her breath, waiting to see what the animal would do, the bucket-helmet sliding lower and lower until she couldn't see a thing. When she was convinced the horse didn't mind her weight, Sloane pushed the bucket-helmet back into place, dreading the view of the ground far beneath her.

What she saw instead was Zacarie standing at the entrance to the mudroom in nothing but his underwear.

She froze, her eyes darting to his bare chest, the exact duplicate of the chest of the father of her child. Except hairier. And—God, forgive her—even more defined. Half asleep, Zacarie squinted at the bucket on her head and bit his lip. Any attempt at an excuse would have sounded preposterous—'Just going for a midnight pleasure ride on your horse without asking you, back soon!'—so she said nothing, dug a heel into the horse's side, and hoped the animal would pass through the stable gate and race into the night.

The horse did not budge.

Sloane nudged the stubborn thing with a bit more force. When she glanced at Zacarie, he was leaning against the doorway with his arms crossed, fighting a smile. She kicked harder and the horse startled, rearing back with her front legs pawing the air. Sloane shrieked, clinging to the horse's mane as the blanket slid off the back of the animal with her on it. Just before she hit the ground, Zacarie caught her around the waist, his deep voice soothing the mare until he'd steadied her on four legs again.

"Whoa, Flor," he said. "Whoaaaaa."

Zacarie set Sloane down, and with the slightest nod of his head, directed her through the mudroom and back into the cottage, where Alona stirred in the loft.

"Mother Mary," said Alona. "What is all the commotion?"

"Go back to sleep," Zacarie said. "It is nothing." He followed Sloane as she hobbled into the bedroom. When they were both inside, he gestured for her to sit on the bed, then stood over her, glaring. He said in Saphir, the penalty for horse theft was branding. He asked her which part of her body she would like him to burn.

She gulped.

He waited for her answer.

"Technically, I didn't succeed. So shouldn't I be punished for attempted horse theft?"

Zacarie said nothing, tossed a blanket down, and lay on the floor next to the bed.

"What are you doing?"

"Standing guard against attempted horse theft."

"Standing guard? Like I'm your prisoner?"

"Go to sleep."

"You can't sleep in the same room as me."

"I will sleep wherever I please."

"But it's against my religion to sleep in the same room as an unmarried man. At least, I assume you're unmarried, but if you *are* married, all the more reason we shouldn't be—"

"I am a widower," he said.

Bits and pieces of the day rose to the surface of Sloane's mind, and she cursed the stupid morning sickness for dulling her senses and her memory. *Ever since his Colette and their baby went to Heaven,* Alona had said of Zacarie, *the poor man barely speaks.*

"I'm so sorry," Sloane said now. "You take the bed. I can't sleep here tonight, anyway."

Zacarie propped himself up on his elbow, peering at her.

"I'll leave the horse alone, okay? But you have to let me go. I am expected outside Paris. I am already very delayed because of my ankle. If my sultan doesn't get word I have arrived safely, he will send Ottoman soldiers to look for me. He may even send his fiercest warriors, the Janissaries! He is a very jealous lover. Extremely violent. If he discovers I've been delayed because of you, he might even have you killed. So, for your safety, and for your mother's safety, I must leave immediately."

The squares of moonlight that shone in silver patches on Zacarie's chest were not quite bright enough to illuminate his eye color, and without clear assurance that his eyes were green and not gray, he looked so much like Bastian that she found she couldn't look away.

"If you will not let me take your horse," Sloane said, "then take me yourself."

Zacarie's eyebrow twitched in surprise.

"Or make arrangements for me to travel with someone you trust. Get me to the Rhône. I can transfer to the Saône River at Lyon and get as far as *Chalon-sur-Saône* by riverboat. But I must leave for Fontainebleau, and I must leave tonight!"

Zacarie squeezed the bridge of his nose as if her plight had brought on a sudden headache. She waited, but he lay there for so long without speaking that she decided he'd fallen asleep, and she considered her chances if she snuck out now and set out on foot.

"This jealous, violent sultan of yours," Zacarie said, interrupting her thoughts. "Does he know you are with child?"

The question felt like a knife through Sloane's heart. *"Viech d'ase,"* she cursed, repeating one of the colorful phrases she'd learned from Alona during the course of the evening.

Donkey's cock.

"He does not know," said Zacarie. "And is it…his child?"

Insulted, she started to protest, but bit her tongue instead; as a concubine, Mahid may very well have had other lovers if and when the sultan felt like lending her out to his friends.

Zacarie waited, and when she said nothing, concluded, "It is his child, so he sent you away."

"It's not like that," she said.

"You said last night, in your fever, that he sent you away."

"Yes, he sent me away. Well, I sent myself away, sort of, but we didn't know I was—"

"But of course, he knew you could have been," Zacarie said.

"You know, your mother said you didn't speak much."

"I often find there is nothing to say," Zacarie said. "Now, I find it necessary to say what you do not wish to hear but need to. If this sultan laid with you, he knew there was a chance you could be with child."

"You don't know what you're talking about."

"I know I would not send a woman away, alone, to another country, if there was a chance she was carrying my child."

Sloane was mute, her skin crawling with the echo of his words. In the future, hardly anyone got pregnant anymore. But in a time and place without phthalates and endocrine-disrupting chemicals, Sloane's internal environment had begun to reflect the external, the conditions ripe for new life. Parts of Bastian had managed to survive inside of Sloane, but that wasn't Bastian's fault—not even Fred could think of everything.

"If you care for the child," Zacarie said, "and if you care for yourself, you must stay here and rest. At least until the sickness stops."

"Your mother said she was sick her entire pregnancy. The sickness never stopped!"

"Then stay the entire pregnancy."

"I told you, I can't! And why are you suddenly insisting I stay, when two seconds ago you were ready to brand me like some kind of criminal—"

"You were committing a crime."

"God. Okay. I'm sorry, okay? But can't you just help me get out of here?"

"I have already helped you enough for a lifetime," he said. "Twice now have I saved your life—once on the field, and again when you nearly fell to your death trying to steal Flor. Three times, if we consider what a lesser man might have done to a woman attempting horse theft."

Sloane stared at him, dumbstruck, but LORI was quick with a comeback. "All the more reason to send me away, where I won't be so much trouble. Help me get to Paris and you'll never need to help me again."

"Perhaps, after so much lifesaving, it is now you who owes me a favor."

"You're right," she said. "I owe you. I owe you big. And I'm sure I can get you what you want, the second I get to court. It's just that I have to get there first, which is why we should—"

"—why we should wait. For now, you are ill with child. You must rest."

"But—"

"And we must discuss what happened on the field."

"What happened on the field?"

He stared at her, surprised. "You…do not remember?"

"Remember what?"

He studied her for a long moment. "Fine," he said. "If that is what you want, we shall forget it."

"I can't forget something I don't remember."

"I am tired. Let us rest now."

"I *told* you—"

"You are in my home," he said. "You will sleep here tonight, and that is final. If you want to…to just forget the field…well. Very well. Then forget it. Forget your debt to me for your life, thrice saved, and offer yourself instead to the road thieves to appease this tyrant sultan who cares naught for you or your child. But do it far from here, where no one will trace your death to us. And do it tomorrow. No one from this house is going to die tonight."

Long after he'd fallen asleep on the floor, Sloane remained awake in bed, mentally admonishing Zacarie and Saffron and the Program and humanity and agonizing over what could have possibly happened on the field and plucking out the terrible thoughts Zacarie had planted in her mind about Bastian. Had she known the outcome, she still would have invited Bastian inside her, unencumbered. She would have said yes to anything he'd wanted to give her, done anything he'd asked of her, even the most difficult thing—the one thing he hadn't even realized he'd asked.

THE NEXT MORNING, SLOANE HOBBLED through the front door with her veil secured to find Alona gone and Zacarie standing in the field west of the cottage surrounded by men on horseback. Donning the white robes and the red caps of the Toulon clergy, they flanked an ornate carriage that had stopped along the path to Saphir. With his hands clasped deferentially behind him, Zacarie was conversing with the carriage's lone passenger, a man with burn scars across the left side of his face. The nobleman who had captured her in the shipyard. The Bishop of Toulon.

Sloane's crutches fell to the ground with a *tha-thump*, and she dove instinctively into the nearest hiding spot—a covered cart hitched up to Flor in the front yard. She scrambled beneath the tarpaulin to find the cart bed filled with baskets of soaking woad seeds. There was no room for a person, but she squished herself between the baskets anyway until she was lying on her back with her heart set to burst out of her chest. She froze, straining to hear footsteps or voices, but there was only the sheep bleating behind the fence and the pigeons cooing in the stable rafters. She imagined the bishop handing Zacarie one of her Wanted posters from Toulon, and Zacarie—annoyed with her attempted horse theft and whatever had "happened on the field"—happily informing the bishop that yes, he had seen this woman before, and if the bishop would kindly step out of the carriage, Zacarie would arrange a meeting with her. Last night's frenetic confidence crumbled as she pictured herself trying to take on the bishop plus all those priests plus Zacarie. Her self-defense training had accounted for six grown men, but it hadn't accounted for Bastian doppelgangers or broken ankles or freaking pregnancy.

There were footsteps on the grass, and they were coming closer. She braced herself for a fight.

The cart shifted, and she heard Zacarie giving Flor a command as he settled into the driver's seat. He clicked his tongue, and the cart lurched forward with a jolt, rolling in the direction of the hill that led to the village.

"You there!" one of the priests called in French. "Make haste!"

"I follow close behind, Your Grace!" Zacarie replied in French. "Forgive me! I seem to have forgotten how heavy woad seeds can be."

#   #   #

Amidst the clacking and shouting and hammering sounds of the village, Zacarie made one sharp turn, then another, before rolling to a stop. The tarp jerked upward in a blur of color and light. Zacarie stared down at her, his green eyes blazing as he confirmed the source of the cart's mysterious hundred-and-twenty-pound increase.

"You there! Boy!"

Zacarie whipped the tarp back over her and squeezed her calf, imploring her to stay still. "His Holiness's declaration was not a request. He expects prompt delivery of his order to the warehouse."

"Of course, Father," said Zacarie. "I beg your leave to ensure no seeds have spilled on the ride up the hill lest they dry out and ruin His Holiness's woad crop."

The priest told Zacarie to hurry.

"I also beg your leave to await my cousin," said Zacarie. "She is en route from the market now with a special fertilizer for His Holiness's crop. It is the best fertilizer in Saphir, Your Grace, and only the best will do for His Holiness." Sloane held her breath, her fears quickly recalibrating themselves; if Zacarie was going to hand her over the clergy, he would have done it by now.

"Very well," said the priest. "His servants await your arrival."

Zacarie assured the priest he would be quick, then waited five eternal seconds before lifting the tarp again and glaring fiercely at Sloane. "Out," he

262

said, barely moving his lips. "Now."

"I must stay hidden."

"*Out.* Before he returns and makes a more thorough inspection of the cart." He grabbed her legs and tugged her toward the cart's edge, but she resisted, terrified the bishop would spot her the second she emerged. "Wait," Zacarie said. "They're looking." He ducked beneath the tarp and climbed on top of her, his codpiece pressing into her thigh. "If you wanted a ride into town, you could have just asked."

"I wasn't sneaking a ride. I was hiding from the bishop! I thought you were going to—"

"How do you know the bishop?"

"How do *you* know the bishop?" she asked.

"He is our landlord, and the lord of all Saphir. And he will not be pleased if you delay me further in getting this order to his warehouse."

"Is he out there, right now?" she asked.

"He is across the square at the pillory," Zacarie said. "He has come to hear a prisoner's confession."

"Then I must stay hidden."

"Why?"

"The bishop captured me in Toulon, but I escaped. I am a wanted woman there."

Zacarie's eyes widened in surprise. "That is not good."

"You're telling me."

"That is very bad, Mahid."

"I'm *aware*."

"What did you do?"

"It's a long story."

"The clergy know my cart," he said. "If they find you hiding here, they will punish you and me."

"Then I'll hide somewhere else."

"It is safer to hide in plain sight."

"The bishop will recognize me," she said. "He never forgets a face."

Zacarie frowned, considering this. "What were you wearing when he captured you?"

"Um. My travel cloak. My gown."

"But was your head covered as it is now? Or were you as I saw you last night?" The blood rushed to her cheeks, and she became hyper-aware of the many places his body was in contact with hers. "Your hair is unforgettable," he said, gazing at her in the dim light. "If the bishop saw you uncovered, he will be looking for a glimpse of your hair."

"Oh!" she said, blushing harder. "I guess my hood was down. So, he saw my unforgettable. I mean, yes. He saw my hair."

"Then he should not recognize you with your head covered now." Zacarie withdrew. He pulled her from the cart, and she blinked in the harsh daylight, the blood rushing back to her brain. He'd parked off a small village square, which was surrounded by a peculiar collection of homes, their facades a chaotic mix of stone, wood, and thatch, with freshly painted latticework not nearly as common as sagging, decrepit terraces. On the far side of the square lay the village church, a towering gothic structure whose flamboyant turrets and expensive stained glass stood in stark contrast to the obvious poverty of the rest of the town. Foot traffic across the square was light, with men pulling hand-drawn carts and women carrying baskets on their hips and heads. In the center of the square, a young woman stood trapped in a pillory, her head and hands protruding from the holes that had been cut into a wooden plank secured to the top of a post. She was petite and pear-shaped, with porcelain skin and dark brown hair that hung through the hole past her shoulders as she swayed in the confines of her prison. Large, wet milk stains had soaked through her tunic over her swollen breasts. The clergy encouraged passerby to gather around the pillory. The crowd grew thicker and louder, but Sloane could still hear the woman groaning in pain.

The bishop stood behind the pillory in his cassock, adjusting the traditional, beehive-shaped *mitre* hat that towered fourteen inches above his head. His clergy stood around him like bodyguards, and another priest—handsome but shabby in a faded black frock and matching skull cap—attended him like a handmaiden, smoothing and arranging the fabric of his robes.

"Father Pierre," Sloane guessed. "The village priest?"

"Indeed," Zacarie said, rifling in the cart.

"And what of your cousin?"

Zacarie withdrew a noxious sack from the cart and slung it against Sloane's chest. "*You* are the cousin," he said, ignoring her when she gagged. Supporting her weight, he helped her to the front of the cart, instructing her that she was called Amaia, his cousin from Basque country. She only spoke Basque—no Provençal, no French. If anyone spoke to her, she should say she did not understand, and say it in Basque, '*ez dut ulertzen.*' He told her to try and say it now.

"*Ez dut ulertzen,*" she said, her accent perfect.

Zacarie's eyes bulged. "You speak Basque, too?"

"Hardly any."

He lifted her onto the cart and climbed up next to her, nodding to the sack of fertilizer in her arms. Switching to French to imitate a clergyman, Zacarie asked her what was inside the sack she was holding.

"*Ez dut ulertzen,*" she said. I do not understand.

"Good," he said. "Chin up, now, cousin. Basque women hold their heads high."

Zacarie pulled out from the alley and drove the cart toward the square. The bishop made the sign of the cross over Father Pierre, then the two men faced the crowd, whose murmurings quickly subsided. In the sudden silence, Flor's hoofbeats echoed off the cobblestone, and the wheels of the cart creaked so loudly that several villagers turned to look at them. Unperturbed, Zacarie angled the cart toward the high street, driving around the periphery of the crowd. Sloane clasped the cart bench, white-knuckled, as the bishop's gravelly voice boomed across the square.

"Daughter!" he said. "Your husband, one Claude de Tournebeut of Saphir, a landowning Christian and a valued member of Father Pierre's congregation, accuses you, his wife these seven years of heresy. You are charged with being a known Huguenot, a heretic who has defiled marriage, the king, and the law, and thus has defiled the Church Herself, the Bride of Jesus Christ, Our Lord!" The bishop spoke like an actor performing for the crowd. He over-articulated his consonants and drew out the vowel sounds, but his words made no sense to Sloane. Her trainers had taught her that in 1521, Catholic violence against French Huguenots was rare in the north and practically unheard of in Provence. A charge of heresy for being a Huguenot must be religious tensions in an embryonic state; the inaugural splitting of a cell that would not become a tumor for years, and this poor young woman, the first to be split.

Out of the corner of her eye, Sloane saw the bishop turn his back to the audience to face the accused. "Confess to these crimes," he said, "and while your body will face the gallows, your soul will be saved, and you will spend eternity basking in the sweet mercy of our Lord Jesus Christ, who will forgive you." They rounded the square and rode closer to the pillory. A bubble of breastmilk popped through the soaked fabric of the woman's tunic, and she groaned as if in the pangs of childbirth. "Do you confess?" asked the bishop.

"I confess!" she said, throwing her voice to the heavens as if she, too, were acting out a role in some predetermined play. "I confess I am a Huguenot! I confess I am a heretic! I confess I have defiled marriage, the king, and the law! I confess I have defiled the Church Herself!" She repeated the confession, directing her voice toward one corner of the square, then another, as if she had borne witness to this exact scene many times before, only now she was in the starring role. "Mary, forgive me," she said, weeping now. "Holy Mother, Blessed Virgin, Sweet Mother of Mary, forgive me!"

The bishop whispered something in her ear, and she went quiet.

"May our Divine Mother Mary accompany your soul as you fly to Heaven on angel's wings," he said.

The young woman would be put to death. This was what the Church did to women. This was what the bishop, and all those priests, wanted to do to Sloane.

"In the name of Jesus and his mother Mary and all the company of Heaven, may the peace of Jesus Christ be upon us," said the bishop, bowing his head to pray. The clergy and the crowd mimicked him, bowing their heads and praying in lifeless monotone as Father Pierre made the sign of the cross in the air above the woman's head.

As they pulled onto the high street, Sloane glanced over to see Zacarie tilting his head at the strangest angle, ear to shoulder, as if he had a crick in his neck. He was staring past her with an alarming intensity, his eyes never leaving the pillory as he slowly righted his head. With the bishop's head bowed in prayer, Sloane dared to follow his gaze.

Zacarie was staring at the village priest, Father Pierre.

Father Pierre was looking right at Zacarie.

And then the priest's gaze locked on Sloane.

AFTER UNLOADING HIS SEEDS AT the warehouse, Zacarie hid the cart in an alley behind a dye shop. He carried Sloane into a hidden alcove, through a secret opening in the stone, then down a passageway that dead-ended in an ancient, pitch-black tomb hidden beneath the church. Ferrying her through the darkness, he slipped past the threshold of an open door and into the narrow confines of the tomb, the air heavy with the musk of peasants, long dead, who couldn't afford burial in the church graveyard. He set Sloane down, took her hands, and helped her find the wall so she could balance without putting weight on her ankle. The wall felt bumpy, smooth nobs and dull spikes covered in a layer of dust and grime, as if the Church had converted a cave of fossilized seashells into a tomb. Sloane inquired about the texture. "Bones," said Zacarie, and she whipped her hands off the wall as if she'd touched a hot stove, stumbling into him just as a door shut somewhere close by. They both froze, listening to the footsteps coming toward them. The faint glow of candlelight grew brighter in the passageway, illuminating their surroundings. Three of the walls were indeed constructed of human bones—and the odd skull—which were stacked in reticular towers from floor to ceiling. The fourth wall was split by the door and lined with interlocking rows of seated funeral drains—ancient stone toilets used to catch the liquefied tissues that leaked from the bodies placed upon them.

A cloaked figure stepped into the room. He set his candle in the lone wall sconce and closed the door, shutting them in with the bones.

"I saw your signal in the square," said Father Pierre. "You wish to meet with me?"

"We do," said Zacarie.

"Very well. I have naught but five minutes, my son."

The priest's lean frame was swallowed by the folds of his cloak. He had the slumped shoulders of an academic, and when he pushed back his hood, the hair beneath his skull cap was shock white. Father Pierre was decades older than Zacarie or Bastian, but he had the same cheekbones, the same jawline, and the same full lips as the younger men (such a waste on a priest not permitted to kiss anyone). Or maybe she was seeing Bastian's face everywhere she looked because she was one misstep from being put in a pillory herself, and lookalikes might be the closest she'd come to ever seeing the real Bastian again. Zacarie swore Father Pierre was a friend, but Sloane wasn't exactly jazzed about making friends with a man who'd just participated in the ritualized death sentence of a young mother.

"*Demoiselle* Mahidevran," said the priest, dipping his head in greeting. "You have made a fast recovery from your fever."

"Oh," she said with a start. He knew who she was, she realized, because Father Pierre must be the "him" of "go and tell him everything."

"Mahid has returned from the shores of death only to have her life threatened again," said Zacarie. "The bishop seized her in Toulon. She managed to escape, and the rat went and put her face on a poster in the shipyard, wanted, dead or alive. She is in grave danger if he recognizes her."

Father Pierre reached into his robes and withdrew a scroll. He held it in the candlelight, and Sloane's stomach dropped—it was a near-perfect replica of the poster, with the same dancing demons, the same torn dress, the same seductive expression on her face. But this artist had doubled her cup size from the original poster and rendered her nipples as stiff, pointed peaks.

"*Bon diu*," said Zacarie, ogling the drawing. "Mahid, did you really…?"

"No!" she said. "I never—that is *not* what happened."

Pinching one corner of the poster like a dirty sock, Father Pierre said, "The bishop delivered this upon his arrival this morning. He said he will not rest until he finds the woman from the shipyard, for it is God's Will that all witches and foreign heretic whores be eradicated from Provence."

Sloane's throat felt like it was closing up, and she forced some air in through her nose, trying not to panic. "You must understand, Mahid, that while His Holiness has arrested many women, you are the first to escape." But she hadn't escaped. She'd merely enticed the bishop to chase her to the ends of the earth so he didn't sully his perfect arrest record. "If I see this woman," Father Pierre continued, "I have orders to detain her and bring her to His Holiness with haste."

Sloane tensed, paralyzed by the sudden fear that Zacarie had betrayed her and that she would have to make a one-footed run for it. Father Pierre's voice seemed to reach her from across a great distance, as if there were an ocean between them and not a meter of stone floor. He had hoped to have spent the past hour praying for the soul of the condemned, but he'd instead spent it scouring Saphir for the woman from the shipyard, an effort he described as "fruitless." With a disappointed shake of his head, he added, "I have not seen this woman anywhere."

"I told you as much," said Zacarie, loosening Sloane's vice grip around his arm. "Father has not seen the woman from the shipyard anywhere."

Father Pierre studied the poster again. "His Holiness will be disappointed, but I have never seen this woman, and I can predict with absolute certainty that I never will." He held one corner of the poster to the candle flame until it caught fire. They all watched the bishop's wanted heretic whore burn until the poster had curled and collapsed into ash.

"Did the bishop notice her in the square?" asked Zacarie.

"No," said the priest, snuffing out the smoldering remains with his boot. "So let us ensure it stays that way. Take her back to Merkatoria and keep her hidden until the clergy have departed Saphir."

"It is not safe for her there," Zacarie said. "They rode past this morning. They could stop at the cottage upon their return."

"But if I keep my veil on—"

"It is too great a risk," said Zacarie.

"Are you kidding me?" Sloane said. "You just said the bishop wouldn't recognize me if my hair was covered, and that I should 'hide in plain sight.' You just drove me right *past* him—"

"I was a fool."

"No arguments there!"

Father Pierre threw up his hands for silence. "Zacarie did not know about the poster, or the great lengths the bishop has taken—"

"I should have known," Zacarie said. "With or without her veil, she is too beautiful to miss."

Sloane looked at him, surprised. When Zacarie met her gaze, a memory of Bastian rushed in, distorting her view. The tomb dissolved and Sloane was standing with Bastian on the tower in the setting sun as he told her she was too beautiful for words. Bastian, his gray eyes shining in the fading light, was looking at her as if he loved her already because even then, he already did. Even when they'd barely spoken to each other except to fight, he'd known. She leaned in, wanting to change the memory, wanting to kiss him and tell him she loved him too, but the darkness returned, and she was back in the tomb, clinging too tightly to another man's arm. She pushed away from Zacarie, keeping just two fingertips on his forearm, the minimum contact needed to stay balanced on one foot.

"The artist must have made considerable study of his subject to have captured her likeness so perfectly," said the priest. "I should expect that the bishop would recognize Mahid, regardless of her attire."

"Gross," she said. She'd assumed the bishop had commissioned an artist to illustrate the posters, never imagining the artist was the bishop himself. She pictured the old man bent over his worktable in an opulent room, sketching with a piece of charcoal between his fingers, tracing and blending her nipples hour after disgusting hour.

"Praise God he was occupied with Bertrand today and did not notice you," Zacarie said. "If there is a blessing in this tragedy, it is that."

"I'm alive because the bishop, not to mention your 'friend' here, was busy sentencing another woman to death? I'd hardly call that a blessing."

Father Pierre's face fell. "Had I my way, we would never sentence anyone to death," he said quietly. "And never in the name of the Lord."

"Then why did you just stand there?" she asked. "You could have said something. You could have tried—"

Zacarie hissed as if he were silencing a dog, and Father Pierre turned his back to them and leaned into the wall. When he found his voice again, it sounded like someone's hand was around his throat. He said if he'd been able to speak with the bishop sooner, he might have stopped him from condemning Bertrand. He'd stopped the bishop before. With the right timing, the right words, Father Pierre had been able to obtain a prisoner's release. That was how he freed Giselle. And Perrine.

"Do not forget Dauphine," said Zacarie.

"Dauphine. Banished from Saphir, but still alive, I pray. But it was too late for Bertrand. The bishop had already taken her."

"Taken her?"

"As his *amoureux*," said the priest. "There was nothing I could—"

"His…lover?"

"Oh, Mahid," he said, rubbing the heels of his hands into his forehead. "Forgive me, I forget you are a foreigner in this land. Yes, his lover. His Holiness has a habit of taking his…pleasure…with the women he detains."

"*C'est un violeur*," said Zacarie.

He is a rapist.

"The bishop believes that when these women die, his sins die with them."

This is what the Church did to women.

This is what the bishop wanted to do to her.

Sloane remembered the bishop's sour breath when he whispered in her ear: *I never forget a face, and it will be a pleasure to remember yours.* She could feel the bishop touching her, gripping her chin, shaking her shoulders, grabbing her wrists, and she was shouting for him to get off, *get off!*

"Get off!" she said. "Don't touch me."

Father Pierre was holding her by the wrists to stop her arms from flailing. When Sloane told him again not to touch her, the priest said *he will not.*

"He will not touch you, Mahid."

Sloane snapped back to the present, struck by the palpable stillness that radiated from Father Pierre, his regrets about Bertrand replaced by an absolute, steadfast certainty. He was too late to save Bertrand. But he was not too late to save her. The bishop would not come near her again. Father Pierre let go of her wrists and wrapped his arms around her, drawing her into the folds of his robes, his essence of incense and ink. This was the type of protection Father

Pierre offered Sloane—not the swipe of a father's sword raised in her defense, but the whoosh of a mother's skirts shielding her from harm.

A sudden clamor of footsteps echoed into the tomb from above. They all held their breaths as the sounds stopped right above their heads. Sloane craned her neck, staring at the ceiling for seconds that felt like hours. Then the footsteps resumed, moved away, and began to fade. Father Pierre pressed his ear to the door. He drew the candle from its holder. The bishop was taking Bertrand to the gallows now. Sloane said no, please, she's someone's mother. The angle of the candlelight revealed fine lines that fanned out around Father Pierre's eyes, making him look as if he'd aged ten years in a matter of seconds. He said they should take comfort that today Bertrand will be with Mother Mary in Paradise.

"But—"

"Were I to speak out against him, I could no longer help you or anyone else. A priest's robes burn faster than a barley field in famine. But if the bishop continues to trust and confide in me, I can save more lives than he can take. And if we remain patient and steadfast, then one day Zacarie, Alona, and all our people in France and abroad will be free to love God, and each other, without fear."

"All your people?" said Sloane.

"The Huguenot people," said Zacarie. "When he speaks of the Huguenots, Father speaks of himself. And my mother. And me."

Father Pierre drew his hand to his skull cap and tipped it. "Our friends in Geneva fight for change in public," he said. "In France, we have had more success in private."

"Infiltrating the Church from the inside," said Zacarie.

Father Pierre was an ordained member of the clergy, but he was also the undercover leader of the Huguenot movement in Provence. He'd been commissioned by the bishop to hunt Huguenots, putting him in the perfect position to protect the very people he was supposed to be arresting—people like Zacarie and Alona and himself.

"Sometimes it really is safer to hide in plain sight," Zacarie said.

"As long as one is not a great beauty," said the priest.

"Off with you, old man."

"Off with Mahid," said the priest. "You must be off to Paris at once. Zacarie can accompany you on your journey, but in return for your safe passage, we humbly implore your help."

Sloane felt the hairs stand up on the back of her neck. She had the sinking feeling that she'd walked into a trap after all.

"Zacarie tells me your sultan is a close ally of our king," said Father Pierre. "He tells me that upon your arrival at court, you plan to meet with His Majesty privately, at a regular cadence."

"Oh," she said. "I guess? It's hard to say until I actually—"

"You have seen with your own eyes how the king's current policies are encouraging Church-sanctioned murder in our village. Bertrand is not the first in Saphir to be lawfully massacred in the name of God and Crown."

"But the king is a humanist," she said. "The Church may be out for blood, but the king is tolerant of Huguenots." Tolerant, humane, progressive even—at least, he would be until a fateful night in 1534, when anti-Catholic posters would mysteriously appear in cities across France—including a poster tacked to the king's bedchamber door.

Father Pierre's eyes blazed with indignation. "You have been misinformed, *demoiselle*. The king has an insatiable appetite for Huguenot blood. It is with His Majesty's encouragement that men I have called brothers for years have become murderous thugs who feel no guilt taking innocent lives, all the while preaching for the people to love one another as Jesus loves them. But you can put a stop to the hypocrisy, Mahid. Zacarie will teach you what to watch and listen for at court. You will inform us of any meetings that take place between the king and Church officials. You will alert us of planned attacks against the Huguenots so our people can clear the villages before the commissioners arrive. Zacarie will connect you with our people in Paris, whom you can trust. As long as you follow our instructions, no one will ever suspect your relationship to the Huguenot cause, so there is no reason not to help us as we have helped you."

"There is the child to consider," said Zacarie, glancing sideways at Sloane. "We shall hide Mahid from the bishop until she gives birth. Not at the cottage, but close by, so mother can attend her. Then I will accompany Mahid and the child to court, and she can—"

The priest cut him off before Sloane could. "How many innocents will perish in the next three seasons if we wait? Mahid's arrival is a blessing from Mother Mary. We must act now or suffer the losses of a dozen more like Bertrand in Saphir alone."

"Yes," Sloane said.

"Yes, you will help us?"

"Yes, I should leave now. Today."

"You are ill," said Zacarie.

"I'll take a bucket."

Sloane broke away from Zacarie and leaned against the wall of bones, which no longer seemed half as frightening as agreeing to Father Pierre's request to become a freaking spy for the Huguenots—the favor she owed Zacarie for him saving her life. She couldn't do this. She couldn't add another layer of impossibility to an already impossible Mission. But she couldn't get Bertrand's pink, tear-streaked face out of her mind. That could have been her. If Sloane was in a position to help other women, she had to try. But no matter how well she played the part of Mahidevran, Royal Astrologer, her influence with King Francis would have its limits. She might succeed in saving Huguenot lives only to fail at her actual Mission. She might use all her influence protecting people in the past only to abandon people in the future and never get back to Bastian.

"What if it's too dangerous?" she asked. "What if the king won't listen to me, or I just can't do it?"

Father Pierre rubbed his chin. "Cannot do it? Or will not?"

She looked from him to Zacarie, feeling trapped.

"We cannot use the resources needed to protect you on such a long journey unless it is for the cause," said the priest. "If you cannot help us, we will—"

"—deliver me to the bishop?" she said, pressing her back to the wall. "Is this whole thing...Are you blackmailing me?"

Zacarie scoffed. "Is it not obvious that I only wish—that we only wish to protect you?"

"How could we blackmail you?" asked the priest. "You know our secret, too."

Sloane looked at him until his smile faded.

"If you will not be able to help us once you arrive at court, Zacarie must stay here," he said. "We will try our best, of course, to distract the bishop from his hunt for the woman from the shipyard, but your journey north will remain your affair. You will be at the mercy of the road thieves—"

"And anyone who accuses you of being a Huguenot."

"But I am not a Huguenot," said Sloane.

"My child," said the priest, pushing past her through the door. "Neither was Bertrand."

ZACARIE DROVE THE RICKETY OLD cart hard over the untrodden fields, racing east along the base of the mountain ridge away from the village. When the fortified city walls were no more than a white speck on a distant cliff behind them, he slowed Flor to a trot. The smoother ride soon eased Sloane's morning sickness enough for her to ask where they were going. "Somewhere you will be safe," Zacarie said, "until we receive word that the bishop is back in Toulon and our path is clear to go north." When she asked how long that might take, Zacarie rattled off a typical schedule for the bishop's visit as if it were a travel itinerary: Five minutes to parade Bertrand through the streets of the village to the gallows. Another five minutes for the hanging. Ten to fifteen minutes to bury the body, and half a day to attend to his other business in town. That is, if the bishop followed the same agenda he'd used when he'd paraded four other women to the gallows in the past year, each one condemned for practicing the Huguenot faith.

"Father Pierre said Bertrand was not a Huguenot."

"She was not," said Zacarie. "Father smuggled out the last of our kind several years ago, and we are the only ones left."

The real reason Bertrand was put to death, Zacarie explained, was not because she was a Huguenot, but because her husband had fallen in love with another woman. Church law required married men to stay married unless their wives died, at which point, they could take another wife, a circumstance Bertrand's husband was eager to bring about. He'd first appealed to Father

Pierre, who knew the husband's accusations of heresy were baseless. So the husband dictated a letter to the bishop detailing Bertrand's frequent disappearances to secret Huguenot meetings where she would plot the murders of priests and toss crucifixes onto the fire.

"But Bertrand confessed to being a Huguenot," said Sloane. "Why confess in front of everyone if she was innocent?"

"So she might bypass Purgatory and gain swift entry into Heaven," said Zacarie. "If she confessed, her body would be put to death, but her soul would be saved. If she refused to confess, her life might be spared, but she would be cast out of the Church and condemned to an eternity in Hell for dishonoring her husband and the bishop."

Sloane couldn't believe Bertrand was more afraid of the idea of Hell than the reality of death. Zacarie said death visits us but once, but the suffering of Hell was eternal. Sloane couldn't believe people really believed that, and Zacarie said people believed whatever the Church told them to believe. Conveniently, the most important teaching of the Church was that those who question the Church would spend an eternity in Hell, while those who blindly followed Church law would spend eternity in Heaven.

"How can people not see the obvious corruption?"

"If you were told something was true from the time you were a very young child, would you not believe it, too?"

Sloane flashed on her four-year-old sick bed, the Game of Memory, the certainty that her memory meant something was wrong with her, and how Harry's truth had become hers.

"You're right," she said. "Of course I would believe it."

They bumped along over the wide, green expanse that stretched before them. The tall grasses swayed in the wind, the blades reflecting the sunlight. It looked as if Flor was pulling Sloane and Zacarie down a shimmering emerald river on a day far too beautiful to have been contaminated by death. Sloane wondered what would happen if, instead of terrifying the people into submission, the Church used its influence for good. Like if people believed they could get into Heaven by protecting the planet. The thought made her smile. If that belief was passed down through generations, humanity would never create an endangered world like the one she'd come from. The only problem was the promise of Heaven and the threat of Hell would fall flat—people in the future no longer believed in God.

Zacarie said not everyone was blind to the corruption. There was a small but growing number of Huguenots who not only saw the corruption but yearned to expose it. They had formed an underground network of active Huguenot cells in towns from Provence to Paris, risking their lives so everyone could find their own God and create a Heaven on earth—not after death, but here and now.

The underground network was a ray of hope for both the Huguenots and the falsely accused, but hearing about it made Sloane's stomach turn. Just as the Catholics and Huguenots weren't supposed to be fighting yet, the network Zacarie described wasn't supposed to exist yet. Sloane rifled through memories but couldn't recall any of the other Heroes being sent to a time when the history books had been so wrong. The Program didn't make these kinds of mistakes. And Saffron didn't make mistakes, period. Sloane begrudgingly entertained the idea that she might be remembering the history wrong. She worried that some crucial part of her history lessons had been modified in her mind or abandoned to the same blurry No Man's Land where the memories of her first night at Merkatoria had gone. The possibility sent her heart racing just as Zacarie finally pulled the cart to a stop.

"Are you well, Mahid?" he asked. "You look pale."

"Fine," she said. "Just ready for a break."

"We are almost there," he said, coaxing Flor toward a dense thicket. The horse pulled them through the foliage onto a neglected path, where the limbs of ancient oak trees formed a gnarled tunnel above their heads. They rolled over roots and stones toward a clearing in the distance. As they neared it, the underbrush thinned, and Sloane could see a pool of sunlight and pops of bright color through the trees. With a final push through a grove of flowering almond trees, Zacarie pulled Flor to a stop at the edge of a garden. Sloane gasped, stunned to see a wide, meticulously cultivated plot in the middle of the forest in the middle of nowhere, with row after row of rosebushes grown taller than cornstalks in the sunlight, their blossoms bursting in vibrant shades of fuchsia and salmon and coral.

"Bulgarian roses," said Zacarie, helping her down from the cart. "Their oil is the most expensive in the world. We grow them to sell them and donate the profits to the cause."

Zacarie would harvest the roses, and Father Pierre would sell the crop to an oil manufacturer in Toulon. The deal would give Sloane and Zacarie enough money to fund their journey north, where they would make a sizable financial contribution to the Huguenot cause in every town along their route. If Zacarie worked swiftly, and if Father Pierre delivered the roses to his buyer tonight, Sloane could be on the road to the king as early as tomorrow morning.

Zacarie palmed a plump, coral-colored rose, inviting Sloane to sample the mild perfume. The second she inhaled, all the fears and uncertainties about her Mission fell away, and her mind was flooded with memories of Bastian. She was at once standing in the middle of the rose garden with Zacarie and standing in the portal room with Bastian, telling him how roses made her heart sing. The memory shifted, and she was lying on Bastian's bed in the treehouse, feeling as sacred as a rose as he touched her for the first time, transforming her skin into roses, kissing every petal at once. She grew dizzy with ecstasy as the sweet floral scent in the garden was cut with the pear and cedar and salt of Bastian's skin. And another essence—a less familiar base note of earth and sage, mint and sweat. Heat and metal and desire.

Sloane looked up to find Zacarie standing far too close, twirling the stem of a pale pink rose between his fingers. "I could not have harvested the roses before this moment," he said, snapping off the length of the stem. "But now, they are ready." He fixed her with an evaluative gaze, and she felt the blood rush to her cheeks.

"Ready to die for the cause," she said.

"Ready for their beauty to be seen."

Sloane stared at the rose, transfixed by the way Zacarie was caressing the flower with the pad of his thumb, until an un-Bastian-like sprig of chest hair poking out the top of his tunic broke her trance. She limped backward, congratulating Zacarie on the garden, then hopped toward the cart on her good foot, babbling about the importance of staying hydrated during pregnancy and her sudden need to drink water, and lots of it, right now.

Zacarie set to work harvesting the roses, breaking off the blossoms and tossing them into jute sacks. From a blanket spread beneath a band of oak trees, Sloane watched him work, mesmerized by the ease with which he parted the roses from their stems. He alternated between humming a baseline for the Calandra larks trilling in the trees and regaling Sloane with a steady stream of stories, the point of which seemed to be entertaining himself as much as her.

The rose was the most precious flower in the world, Zacarie said, not only because of its monetary value, but because the rose was the flower of Mother Mary. Did Mahid know the story of Mother Mary? Facts about Mother Mary in Catholic France rushed forth from training, but a Muslim concubine like Mahid was unlikely to know as much as Sloane did.

"Mother Mary. I think an angel got her pregnant, right?"

Zacarie laughed freely, as if the sopping weight of the morning's events had evaporated in the sun. "The Immaculate Conception is the least of the miracles God bestowed upon Mary. The greatest miracle happened long after the resurrection of Jesus, when, at the hour of her death, God gave Mary a choice: her body could remain on Earth while her soul flew up to Heaven. Or she could ascend into Heaven, body and soul, her flesh made immortal just like her Son's. Mary chose physical immortality, but she was not content to ascend into Heaven the way Jesus had, with just a handful of disciples to witness the miracle. Mary was like the rose—she wanted to share her beauty with as many people as she could. So, God blessed Mary with angel wings, and she flew up into the sky in front of everyone in Jerusalem!"

"She made a spectacle of herself," Sloane said.

"Yes! A spectacle. Our Divine Mother made such a spectacle that we are still telling her story fifteen hundred years later."

"Divine Mother," Sloane heard herself say. "Like Mother Earth."

"Twice now you have spoken of this mother of the earth. Is she a goddess in your land?"

"'Mother Earth,'" Sloane said with a smile. "And she's more of a myth than a goddess. She doesn't watch over the Earth so much as exist *as* the Earth. I mean, she spins, I guess, but she doesn't fly. And speaking of flying, wasn't everyone scared when Mary flew up to Heaven like that? Didn't they think she was a witch?"

"Witches can fly without wings," Zacarie clarified. "Angels need wings to fly. And it was this angelic assumption that transformed Mary from a mortal woman to a sacred Mother. One day, Mary will fly down from Heaven to prepare the way for the second coming of her Son. Until that day, we celebrate her heavenly flight during the Feast of the Assumption at Midsummer. In every village and town in Provence, the people light thousands of lanterns. They string garlands of roses from every rooftop and light bonfires in the streets, and the smoke from the fires rises into the sky just as Mary rose into Heaven."

Sloane wondered if Mary ascended into a sky as beautiful as this one. It was a pale blueish white, its hue blown out by the brightness of the sun as it reached its zenith. Zacarie peeled his tunic off his body and hoisted another sack of roses onto the growing pile in the cart bed. After rummaging around in his saddlebag, he produced a small, black book, which he delivered to Sloane with a flourish, holding the volume flat on his palm as if offering her a bar of gold.

"Mary embodies the spirit of the earth," he said, "but her story is just one of many that point the way to the truth of God."

"But this is the Bible," Sloane said, thumbing through the tissue-thin pages.

"It is indeed."

"But this is written in French!"

"An illegal copy from Geneva," said Zacarie. "Our people are printing the Holy Bible in the vernacular and teaching peasants how to read. We are giving people the chance to interpret the stories for themselves so they can find a personal, direct connection to God without a priest."

Sloane told Zacarie how noble she found such work, hoping her encouragement might mask her sinking heart. The appearance of Zacarie's Bible meant her trainers had gotten yet another piece of history wrong; they'd taught Sloane that the first French Bible was printed in Belgium in 1530—nine years in the future.

She scanned the pages that weren't supposed to exist yet, taking mental photographs of the words in case she might need them later. The written language looked familiar from training, but she still needed LORI's help to understand the words and phrases she'd never seen before. She read about the promise of Heaven, the threat of Hell, and the certainty that every human being was inherently flawed and therefore destined to drown in a lake of fire and sulfur unless they faithfully confessed their sins and repeated the perfect cocktail of prayers.

"This is just as full of the Heaven and Hell stuff as the bishop," she said, slapping the Bible shut. "It's a collection of all the beliefs you said you were trying to undo."

Zacarie smiled patiently, taking the book from her. "That is true if you interpret each verse literally, as the Church does. They teach people that Heaven and Hell are physical places we go after death, instead of states of mind we experience during life. They teach that God only exists in places that can be seen with the eyes and ignore the unseen places God frequents within the heart."

Zacarie flipped to a passage in the Book of Genesis and set the open book on Sloane's lap. "God is both seen and unseen, and so He exists in the words and the spaces between them—in that which is written and that which is left unwritten. If you pay attention to the deeper meaning beneath the words, you will find so much..." Sloane looked up from the Bible to find Zacarie gazing at her, his lips parted with his unfinished thought. "So much left unsaid." They regarded each other until Sloane looked away, hoping Zacarie couldn't hear her pounding heart. Zacarie cleared his throat and ran his fingers over the print in search of a passage. He flipped to the Book of Genesis 1:26. He said the new religion was born from that still, silent place that can be felt but can never be named, and that silence was the most powerful teacher because what is left unsaid is the breath of God. With that, he returned to his work.

She was back in the treehouse with Bastian, laughing over soy chicken kababs, too enamored with the sound of his voice to register the wisdom of his words. Bastian had said silence was a powerful teacher. He'd said it of Enkh. She wondered if the things Enkh had left unsaid were the breath of God, too. She wondered if Bastian thought Saffron was divine intelligence because of her silence. Saffron could act without speaking, solve without thinking, teach without saying a word. Bastian had often been silent around Sloane, as if he thought no words were better than the wrong words. Maybe he'd been reaching for that same breath, learning from that same teacher. If she could learn what he knew, maybe what was waiting for her in the silence, in the spaces between the words, was him.

All at once, the Bible was no longer a tome, or a collection of stuffy religious aphorisms, but the key to those shadowy places in Bastian's heart he'd kept hinting at, but that she hadn't wanted to see. Until now. Now, every word was beautiful, every blank space rife with meaning, every page a goblet of nectar she would have poured down her throat if she could have. For the first time since she'd first learned to read, Sloane didn't speed-read. She read slowly, meticulously, letting LORI's translation rise and fall like the tide, then sitting in silent contemplation, waiting for some subtextual, subterranean meaning to rise to the surface, waiting for Bastian, for Saffron, for the silent breath of God.

She read, "Let us make mankind in our image, in our likeness, so that they may rule over the fish in the sea and the birds in the sky, over the livestock and all the wild animals, and over all the creatures that move along the ground." What rose from the silent spaces between the words was not a thought, or a bundle of thoughts, but something LORI could never have translated. It appeared inside Sloane as a deep knowing, an irrefutable truth, fully formed and foreign to anything she'd ever thought before, and just as she knew it was true, she knew it was something she never would have conceived of on her own. The passage said God had created humanity for the sole purpose of *caring for the Earth*. Let us make humankind in our image so that they may rule over every living thing that crawls upon the ground (but also the ground itself); every creature that takes flight through the air (but also the air itself); every fish that swims in the sea (but also the sea itself). The passage meant that people were created to rule the Earth as God ruled over them—not as fearsome tyrants, but as protective parents, created for the sole, divine purpose of being *stewards of the Earth*.

To her utter amazement, the Bible was packed with passages about the Earth. In Psalms, Isaiah, Matthew, and Revelations, the subtext of each passage made plain the divine connection between people, their planet, and their God. The deeper meaning that was lost on LORI became clearer to Sloane the more she read: as people tended to the needs of the Earth and its creatures, they tended to their relationship with the divine. As they cultivated the soil, they cultivated their holy covenant with God, fulfilling their God-given purpose to be stewards of the Earth.

In the future, the planet and its people were perishing because no one remembered their purpose. And here in the past, people were perishing because they'd misunderstood their purpose; they thought they were born to follow Church law when they were made to be the guardians of the planet, connected to their home down to the bedrock. If every human being in every timeline understood their true purpose and protected the Earth accordingly, the beliefs of the past would dissolve, the violence against women like Bertrand would stop, and the Earth would thrive in perfect homeostasis under the care of Her stewards, who would sustain the planet in perpetuity until the sun burnt out in the sky.

That sky.

Sloane looked up from the Bible to find the garden transformed into a swaying sea of greenery backlit by the rapidly sinking sun. The horizon was streaked pink and peach, as if the artist who'd painted the roses had used the same palette to paint the sky. She felt as if she were more than a hub for the elements of the Earth, or even a steward of the Earth; she was part of the Earth, as intrinsic and connected to the planet as an infant to its mother, protected and nourished by a life source whose generosity knew no bounds. The Earth was the mother who would never leave her. Unlike Thida, Mother Earth could still be saved.

Zacarie joined Sloane on the blanket, startling her back into the world of time. From his pocket, he produced the pale pink rose he'd plucked when they'd first arrived at the garden. "I have harvested every rose," he said, "but this one, we shall not sell." He pushed back her veil to tuck the flower behind her ear, but the fabric gave way and the veil ended up halfway back on her head.

He tried to tug the veil back in place.

Sloane reached up to help him and their hands touched. She pulled her hand away and felt him hesitate, reverse course, and slide the veil backward until it dropped to the blanket behind her. The motion of his hands and the movement of the veil made her feel as if she were back in the treehouse, her dress tumbling to the floor.

Zacarie tucked the rose behind Sloane's left ear, making careful adjustments to her hair to hold the flower in place. When he was finished, he hovered with his cheek inches from hers, as if waiting to see if the rose would stay in place. Seconds ticked by, and the rose stayed put, but so did Zacarie. Sloane thanked him for the flower. Asked how it looked. He said it looked beautiful, and she said you're too close to see, and he said, "I see." They sat there, breathing together on the blanket, until the slightest tilt of his head spooked her, and she flinched.

"What are you doing?"

"I…just thought we might practice again."

"Practice?"

"The sign."

"Oh," she said. "The sign."

The weird head tilt she'd caught Zacarie making at the pillory was the secret sign of the Huguenots—a discreet signal they used to identify and communicate with each other in public. Huguenot leaders in Paris often changed the sign so the Catholics didn't catch on, but Father Pierre had just received word that the head tilt was still current. During breaks from harvesting, Zacarie had coached Sloane until she'd gotten the move just right: tilt the head to the right, ear to shoulder, then lift the head to a count of five as if stretching the neck.

She tried it now, tilting her head away from Zacarie, who was so close she could feel his breath pulsing against her skin as she moved.

"Slowly," he said, and she felt the faintest flutter on her skin, as if he was tracing her collarbone with the tip of his nose.

"You said…lift…to a count of five."

"When you practice, you must go slower."

By the time she had righted her head, Zacarie's lips were waiting, parted and ready, to meet hers.

She could pretend.

It wouldn't hurt anything or anyone if she could feel Bastian's lips on hers, just for a moment, as long as it was Bastian's lips she wanted and no one else's.

Zacarie leaned closer, and Sloane's eyelids fluttered closed. But the second before his lips brushed hers, the memory of her last moments in the portal room swept in, flashing the tortured look in Bastian's eyes in painful close-up, and she gasped, pushing Zacarie away.

"I can't."

Zacarie stared at her, stupefied.

"We can't."

"But—"

"I shouldn't be here. I shouldn't be…"

Zacarie leaned back, studying her. "You said you wished to forget, but I must confess I did not believe you. Or perhaps I did not want to believe you because I, myself, did not want to forget. *Do* not want to forget."

"Forget what?"

He narrowed his eyes in disbelief. "Christ, Mahid. Do you truly not remember what happened the night I found you?"

"Ahem," said a voice.

Zacarie spun around just as Sloane sprang to her knees, bracing to flee if the voice belonged to the bishop. But it was Father Pierre clearing his throat from across the garden. The priest was mounted on a handsome rouncy, looking surprised to have found Zacarie and Sloane on the cusp of a kiss. Alona sat in the saddle behind the priest. She laughed and clapped her hands, and Zacarie cursed under his breath, leaping to his feet to block Sloane from their view.

"Quickly," he said, "your veil."

Sloane turned her back to the unexpected audience and tied the thing, assaulted by the playback of every word she'd uttered about her "sultan" over the past few days. What a hypocrite to have waxed poetic about her undying love for the father of her child, only to be caught bare headed like a hussy with the first handsome man she'd met. When Zacarie offered his hand to help her up, she refused it. Everyone could just relax. Nothing *happened*. And it wasn't like Father Pierre was a real priest, anyway. "It's not like you've never seen me without my veil before, so it's really not that big of a deal.

"When I saw you without your veil before, Mother was in the next room!" Zacarie said. "I would never be alone with you when you were *uncovered* unless we were—"

"Married?" said Alona, bounding up to them like a happy Labrador. She flung an arm around Sloane's shoulder and another around Zacarie's neck, kissing each of them in turn. "And why not?" she wanted to know. "Father tells me Mahid is going to help the cause. You are one of us now, Mahid! And with Zacarie a widower and you already with child, the two of you make a perfect pair. No one need pretend to be a virgin!"

Appearing nothing short of mortified, Zacarie shrugged his mother off, wiping away her kiss as he stalked toward the cart without another word.

Unruffled, Alona smiled at Sloane and tucked the pale pink rose back in its place.

#   #   #

Alona, the priest, the rouncy, the cart, and all the roses were gone. Alona had to get home to attend Espi, whom she predicted would go into labor sometime tonight, and Father Pierre had to race to Toulon, sell the roses, and return with the proceeds before dawn. Zacarie was saddling up Flor for the ride back, and Sloane was fretting over the conundrum of two bodies, one horse; no matter where she sat when she climbed onto Flor, either her arms would be around Zacarie, or Zacarie's arms would be around her, and she didn't even want to think about what their hips would be doing. But she had no choice. Even though Father Pierre had escorted the bishop out of the village and onto the road to Toulon, the bishop could have shown Sloane's Wanted poster to others in Saphir. She couldn't risk being spotted by anyone, so she couldn't return to the cottage until well after dark. That left Sloane alone with Zacarie again, except now she was ten times more aware of the inherent risk of the two of them being alone together, under the stars, with only her veil for a chastity belt.

At least he'd put his shirt back on.

A gibbous moon hung low in the eastern sky, while the last rays of sunlight slipped beyond the trees that lined the garden's western edge. The racket of the cicadas surged as if to herald the night, or perhaps to fill the silence between Sloane and Zacarie. He'd barely spoken since Alona and the priest had left, giving only the briefest instructions for Sloane to use Flor as a crutch while he finished adjusting the saddle. As tempted as she was to pretend the almost-kiss hadn't happened, Sloane had to find out what *had* happened the night Zacarie had found her unconscious on the field. If she could recover her memories from that night, maybe she could find other rogue memories, too—memories that would resolve the alarming discrepancies between the tolerant King Francis she'd learned about in training, and a King Francis whose kingdom was already stained with Huguenot blood.

"So, that was awkward," she said.

In the low light, she could just make out Zacarie's eyebrows twitch upward in agreement. "Guess they thought we pretty much got engaged, huh?"

Zacarie said never mind them, they were old-fashioned.

"That damn veil."

He smiled. "Had your veil been in place with a thousand yards between us, still, they would have speculated."

"Seriously?" she said.

"'Lovebirds sing only love songs,' or so they say."

"Which means...?"

"Lovebirds are foolish enough to assume the rest of the world is in love, too."

"Wait, who's the lovebird in this scenario?"

"Come now, Mahid," said Zacarie, tying Flor's reigns into a knot so he'd have a knot to untie. "You are an intelligent woman. Surely you can see obvious things when they are obvious. And mother and Father are very obvious."

"Mother and... Father?" Sloane hadn't paid much attention to Alona and the priest because she'd been too embarrassed about getting 'caught' with Zacarie. But when she played back her memories, the priest's hand had lingered on the small of Alona's back for several seconds after he'd helped her down from the horse. And when Father Pierre had teased Mahid about being alone with Zacarie without her veil, he and Alona had both burst into laughter, speculating about what might happen when Zacarie and Mahid had been on the road together for many long, lonely nights. "It will get colder the farther north you go," the priest had said. "You must keep warm somehow." Alona had smacked him in mock outrage, and he'd grinned at her, a smile that reminded Sloane of the way Bastian looked at her in the treehouse the morning after they'd made love.

"When you say mother and Father, you mean your mother and your father."

She waited.

Zacarie stroked Flor's snout.

But she thought priests had to take a vow of celibacy. She thought Alona's husband, Zacarie's father, had died of the plague in Toulouse.

Zacarie looked up at the first smattering of stars that peppered the sky. "Yes, priests take a vow of celibacy. No, my father did not die in Toulouse. Alona has told that story for so many years, I think she has forgotten it is a lie."

"What's the truth?"

"My mother has never been married. She left no husband when she left Toulouse."

"If she had no husband, and if Father Pierre took a vow of celibacy, then how are you…here?"

Zacarie tightened the straps around Flor's belly and moved to help Sloane onto the horse. "I assume I do not have to explain the mechanics of such a phenomenon to a woman who is pregnant."

"I just wondered if your real father cut and run, and Father Pierre adopted you. Raised you as his own."

Zacarie grabbed Sloane around the waist and hoisted her onto the animal. Flor's muscles twitched beneath her, and Sloane tensed as the memory of falling off the horse in the stable rushed in.

"Easy, there," he said in the same soothing voice he used with Flor. He said she was alright, that he would not let her fall. His hands felt strong and certain as he guided her legs into the stirrups, and surer still when he began lightly slapping her calves, her thighs, her biceps. He said she was tense and worked his way down her arm like a masseur. If she was tense, the horse would be tense.

"The horse is what's *making* me tense," she said. "Distract me. One of your stories, maybe."

Massaging her hand now, Zacarie appeased her. "When Alona was younger than I am now, she was traveling in Toulon with her father. Every day she went to Mass and listened to Father Pierre give the homily. After a week of attending Mass every day, she went to Confession, timing her trip so Father Pierre would be in the confessional when she arrived. And what she confessed and asked forgiveness for was falling in love with him."

Sloane made a scandalized gasp. "And what did he say to that?"

"I am grateful they have spared me the details of that part of the story because whatever he said, she was pregnant with me soon after. Her father insisted she return to Toulouse and marry immediately; no one would be the wiser. But she refused, and her family disowned her. She has been in Saphir with Pierre, together but not together, ever since."

"Does everyone in the village know?"

He gestured to his face, as if the resemblance were too obvious to miss.

"You're both handsome, but I didn't know he was your father until you told me."

Zacarie crossed his arms. "You did not know I am a bastard."

"You're not a—

"I *am* a bastard. That is why you are ashamed of me."

"I'm not ashamed of anything. Where I come from, that's not even a thing."

"The money, then. You are used to a sultan's wealth, and you are ashamed that I am poor."

"Poor?" she said, laughing. "Have you looked at those stars? Those are yours to look at, every single night. And this air. You just breathe this air like it's nothing, like it's not fresh to the point of intoxicating, but the air is yours, too. Your mother and father are alive. They actually love each other. They love you. God, you have so much more than I've ever had. You have more than my sultan. He's one of the richest men in the world, but he doesn't breathe this air. He doesn't see these stars every night. He doesn't have his parents anymore. You, Zacarie du Merkatoria, are the richest man I've ever met."

Zacarie was quiet for several moments. "If you are not ashamed, why choose to forget what happened?"

"For the zillionth time, I didn't 'forget' anything. How could I forget what I don't remember?"

"But how can one not remember such a thing?"

"Do you typically remember things when you're unconscious?"

"You were perfectly conscicus," he snapped. "What do you take me for?"

"Conscious for what, then? Will you please just tell me what—?"

"You practically made love to me!"

Flor startled, stumbling backward, and Sloane slammed her chest against the horse's neck, gripping the animal for dear life. Zacarie grabbed Flor's bridle and steadied her, cooing to her in Basque until the horse, unlike Sloane, was calm. She took her time righting herself in the saddle, avoiding Zacarie's eyes and mentally directing LORI to repeat the preposterous phrase he'd just uttered, convinced she'd heard wrong.

You practically made love to me.

Bastian's face floated into the foreground, and she could taste his kiss, feel his hands cupping her face, hear his voice telling her he would never touch another woman as long as he lived. She imagined Bastian confirming how faithful he'd been within moments of her return to the future. She imagined having to tell Bastian about what she'd done with Zacarie mere weeks after leaving him. What she'd done with Zacarie while she was pregnant with Bastian's child. Christ, what had she done?

"The night I found you, I nearly ran you over with my horse. You were filthy and you smelled of vomit. I thought you were a prostitute. But then, as I was carrying you home, you reached for me. I do not know why. You took my face in your hands, and you kissed me." Sloane glared at him in the darkness, and Zacarie threw up his hands. "I did not want this!" he said. "Mother Mary, your breath was worse than Flor's."

She glared harder.

"But when your lips met mine, it was as if something that had been dead and buried inside me came to life again. For the first time in years, I remembered what it was to feel wanted. To feel loved. And I felt this love emanating from you, coming into me, and it was deeper than anything I had ever experienced before, even with my wife. You cannot kiss a man like that, give him all of yourself, and ask him to forget it ever happened. You cannot awaken him, only to tell him to go back to sleep."

It all came back to her in a rush. The night Sloane had come to

Merkatoria, she'd awoken in his arms, his profile backlit by the rising moon. She'd lifted her head and rested it against his shoulder as he carried her home. He'd peered at her with concern, his eyes greener than gray in the moonlight, but oh, how she'd missed them, and him. She knew that she had died, and that he was Bastian, and that he was taking her to the blue place so they could be together forever. She'd pressed her lips to his, longing for the tender warmth of his kiss, but he'd pulled away from her, recoiling, and she'd felt her heart splinter inside her chest. After several more kisses landed on his cheek, he had slowly met her lips with his, and she'd melted into the wetness of his mouth with relief. The last thing she remembered before the darkness called to her again was the warmth of his tongue inside her mouth, its essence of mint and earth. Foreign soil.

"Oh shit," she said in English. And then, in Provençal: "I'm so sorry. I…"

Zacarie grabbed her hand, looking up at her in earnest. "Do not be sorry for being the cause of a miracle."

She hung her head. A miracle? She was pretty sure Bastian would have some other choice words for what she'd done. Her throat clenched as she imagined achieving her Mission and passing back through the portal only for Bastian to learn the truth and want nothing to do with her.

"When I lost my wife and son in the same hour, it was as if they took God with them when they died. But then there you were to bring Him back from the dead. When I am near you, I can once again feel God's benevolence. When I see your face, I can forget my wife's."

A cloud passed over the moon, obliterating any semblance of a difference between Zacarie and Bastian, and she felt like she was in some sort of alternate reality where Bastian was begging for her love, and for reasons she couldn't fathom, she was denying him.

"My face makes you forget," she said, "but your face makes me remember."

"Makes you remember what?"

"My sultan," she said, reaching out to touch Zacarie's cheek. "You are his very likeness."

"I am?"

He pressed her hand to his face. She could feel the beginnings of stubble beneath his skin, the callouses on his hand from today's work and all the days that had come before. "Then let me be the sultan. Call me by whatever name you like."

She could topple off the horse and onto him and finish what they'd started on the blanket. He would feel like Bastian. He would have the same look of hunger in his eyes when he nestled himself between her legs. She could love him tonight, and on the road north, and for years to come, but she would always taste sage when she wanted salt, soil when she needed the sea.

She pulled away. She told Zacarie he should keep his own name, save it for someone who'd never want him to change it the way she did. She said it had nothing to do with who his father was or how much money he did or didn't have. It was just…just that…

"It is because I am not him."

She blinked back tears to look at him, this Bastian who was not Bastian saying he was not Bastian. And yet she still felt, somehow, that it was Bastian's heart she was breaking when she promised him he would find someone else.

"Ha!" he said, looking at the stars as if they might confirm the ridiculousness of the idea. "You'll find someone else. You'll have another child. Where do women learn these empty comforts? You expect a man to replace the object of his affection with another when you, yourself, refuse to consider anyone but the object of yours!"

"I'm not the object. I'm just a reminder. A friendly reminder that you are capable of love. And now that you know that, you can find the real object—person—you're meant to be with."

Zacarie turned his back to her and toed the dirt. "Were that even possible, you forget that I am a landless bastard. No woman will have me, Mahid."

"Colette would have you."

"The one woman who would have me is gone."

"I would have you, okay? I would, if I could, but I can't."

"Christ, woman!" he said, spinning around to glare at her. "Take pity on a man."

"What now?"

"Tell me you feel nothing," he said, pacing now. "Tell me I repulse you, that you'd rather make love with the bishop than with me. Do not be so cruel as to tell me you *would* if you *could*, for the love of Christ."

Sloane sputtered, searching for the right words, the right lie, but she'd used them all up. Zacarie made a frustrated growl and strode away in the darkness.

She called out, tracking his silhouette as he neared the garden's edge. He couldn't leave her alone up there on the horse. She'd fall! She watched the outline of his figure stop moving. She begged him to come back, growing petrified Flor would startle again. She knew he was angry, but she needed him!

Sloane heard two loud clicking sounds and felt Flor's muscles tense beneath her. Zacarie's shadowy figure grew rapidly larger, and she realized he was sprinting at full speed toward the horse. A scream caught in Sloane's throat as Zacarie leaped off the ground and vaulted onto the animal's shoulders, nearly knocking Sloane out of the saddle. In a single, graceful motion, Zacarie caught her by the arms, pulled her close, and pressed his mouth to hers in a ferocious, possessive kiss. She tried pushing him away, but it only made him kiss her more desperately. She reached around and grabbed his hair and pulled, hard. He released her, panting, and she slapped his beautiful face.

SLOANE AWOKE BEFORE DAWN, HER eyes burning from too little sleep. She listened to Alona slamming things in the mudroom and Zacarie out in the yard, loading last night's contraband onto the cart bed. To camouflage the profits from the rose sale—several thousand *denier tournois*—Zacarie and Father Pierre had dumped the coins into the bottoms of two-dozen baskets, filling each with fresh topsoil so it would look like they were carting a load of woad seeds. Sloane had waited up for Zacarie as long as she could, but he never came to sleep beside her on the floor, choosing instead to extend the painful silence that had accompanied them the entire ride back from the garden. Well, silent apart from the buzzing cicadas and LORI, who knew fourteen ways to say "I'm sorry" in Provençal, none of which Sloane repeated out loud.

When Sloane finally slept, she'd dreamed of Bastian for the first time since meeting him in real life, the blue place an unwelcome confirmation of their separation. They fought in the dream, Bastian accusing her of having feelings for Zacarie, Sloane accusing Bastian of sending her on an impossible Mission. Bastian said she'd better figure something out, and fast, because if she gave birth in the past, she would never risk bringing the baby back through the portal; if Sloane gave birth in the past, they would never see each other again.

Sloane limped into the main room dressed for the road, her travel cloak around her shoulders, her veil tossed haphazardly over her head. Alona fluttered about, chirping orders to no one in particular—find the scissors! Gather more blankets! Do not crowd her! Sloane stood groggy and confused until she noticed Espi pacing in the middle of the floor, pawing the ground, and whimpering with the early pains of labor. Midwife Alona insisted Zacarie and Mahid postpone their journey to help with the birth, but Zacarie refused. If he was going to get Mahid out of Saphir while it was still dark, they had to leave now—dawn was almost upon them.

"King Henry can wait one more day," said Alona. "Our poor, dear Espi cannot."

Sloane's palms went suddenly damp.

"Mahid!" said Alona, clapping her hands. "Quickly now! More water! More blankets! And where are those scissors you made for me?"

Alona hadn't stoked the fire yet, but all at once the room was sweltering. Sloane's cloak and gown felt heavy, her half-tied veil cutting off blood flow to her head. Either that, or LORI was malfunctioning long before her six-month expiration date. LORI seemed to have difficulty translating proper nouns, switching around Bastian's name with Zacarie's in Sloane's mind, conflating the names of kings. When Sloane thought about it, it was really LORI's fault she had almost kissed Zacarie, and LORI's fault that Zacarie had kissed her. Sloane would tell Bastian as much the second she got back to Basecamp.

"We're off to the palace," Sloane said, her mouth tasting faintly of metal. "The king…King Francis…is expecting me."

Alona jerked her chin in confusion. "King Henry, my foal. King Francis, Henry's father, passed away last spring, God rest his murderous Catholic soul."

Sloane froze where she stood, her fingers tangled in the slapdash knot of her veil.

"What is it, child?" asked Alona. "You look as though you've seen a ghost."

"I must be tired," Sloane said. "Just now, it sounded like you said King Francis passed away last spring."

"I did indeed."

Sloane stared at her. "Metaphorically, you mean?"

Alona looked confused.

"You mean, 'The king is dead to me.' As in, he's dead to all Huguenots because Huguenots no longer recognize Francis as king. That's what you meant to say. Right, Alona?"

"The heart and entrails of King Francis are ashes in the royal urn," Alona said, spinning Sloane around to fix her veil. "His son, King Henry, has reigned for nearly a year now. Did you not know?" She poked her head over Sloane's shoulder, using the veil like a pair of reigns and forcing Sloane to turn her head. When Alona saw the look in Sloane's eyes, she speculated that perhaps word of the king's death had not yet reached Mahid's country by the time she'd sailed for France. Alona finished tightening the veil and bustled toward the stable to tell Zacarie that Mahid thought she was going to King Francis's court. She bustled back, shaking out a blanket, saying they'd had high hopes when Francis died. Father Pierre thought an ember of humanity— or at least youthful rebelliousness—might have still been burning in young Henry's heart. But thus far, the son had all but upheld his father's policies. Zacarie said no, King Henry was worse than his father because he cut out Huguenot tongues. "If only the king would listen to his queen," said Alona. "She is far more tolerant of religious dissent than he. The Italian woman, what's-her-name, something Medici."

Sloane couldn't speak. She couldn't breathe.

"My foal, if you are not the palest I have ever seen you! Is it the nausea? The more nauseous you are, the more beautiful the child will be. Why do you think Zacarie is so handsome? Come and attend Espi. It will soothe you both."

Alona sped off to her next task, and Sloane sank to the floor where she stood, calling after her. She had a question she had not thought to ask Alona until now.

Alona flew back to Sloane's side, her dark eyes bright, and said yes— she did think Zacarie was in love with Mahid. Meeting her had finally healed his heart. And if she felt the same for him, then—

"N-no," Sloane said. "I need to know the year."

"The what?"

"The year, Alona. What is the year?"

Espi whined, and Alona leaped up to fetch water, glancing back at

Sloane as if the pregnancy hormones had shaken her sanity. Scrambling to cover herself, Sloane said according to the calendar in her country, the year was 1521. Silly her, she had just assumed the year was the same in France. But perhaps she was mistaken. Perhaps they counted the days according to a different system.

"Ah!" Alona said, perking up. "Pierre has told me about this. In some lands, people count the days according to the cycles of the moon!" She scuttled back with a bowl, the water sloshing over the sides and staining the dirt floor a darker shade of brown. "This is the last of the fresh water. We will need more from the river." She held the bowl to Espi's mouth, and the goat lapped at the liquid, her dark, purplish tongue sending water onto the floor.

"What is the year, Alona?"

"Yes! We are different from you. In France, it is the Year of Our Lord 1548."

"Of course," Sloane said, her stomach churning. "Because King Francis died March 31, 1547."

Alona creased her brows. "I do not recall the exact date of the king's passing. Around planting time last spring, I suppose."

Every red flag that had been staring Sloane in the face for weeks came sharply into focus. The women in the shipyard in Toulon had been dressed differently from her because they'd been wearing fashions of a different decade. Zacarie's Bible was written in French because they'd been printing Bibles in French for the past eighteen years. When Sloane had discussed "His Majesty" with Father Pierre and Zacarie, *she'd* been talking about King Francis, but *they'd* been talking about King Henry. Bertrand was murdered because King Henry and his father before him had been persecuting Huguenots by the thousands for the past fourteen years.

Her trainers hadn't gotten the history wrong.

Sloane was just in the wrong year.

Which meant it had been twenty-five years since Verrazzano petitioned King Francis to fund the explorer's expedition to North America. Twenty-five years since the king had made the investment. *Twenty-five years* since Verrazzano had sailed for North America, claimed indigenous lands for France, and set a precedent for French colonization throughout the New World.

The ship had already sailed.

Literally.

But this couldn't be 1548—Bastian had first seen her in this timeline, in 1521 Toulon. Hadn't he?

When I was there, I didn't know what year it was. There weren't exactly stacks of newspapers with that day's date just lying around.

Shit.

Shit, shit, shit, shit, shit.

Maybe she could stop Jacques Cartier from—

No. If it was 1548, it had been fourteen years since Jacques Cartier first set foot in Newfoundland. It was too late for that, too.

But what about Francis's son Henry, the new king? Sloane could go to court and convince him to—

To what? Travel back in time and undo what his father had already done or manufacture inventions that had already been invented?

It was too late. Period. Her Mission was officially impossible.

"It is growing light," Zacarie said, pacing at the entrance to the mudroom. "I know you have grown fond of Espi, Mahid, but we must go. Worry not about the birth. Under Mother's care, all will be well."

When Sloane didn't respond, Zacarie tried to help her up, but stopped short when he saw her face.

"What is it, Mahid?"

She lifted her head as if she were underwater. "I'm fine," she said. "Are you…?" She gestured to a spot of blood that had dried around his nostril where she'd slapped him.

"Fine," he said. "But we must away."

"I can't go."

"Dear Mahid, if you are ill, you can be ill in the cart." He hoisted her to her feet, and she clung to him, swaying a bit.

She said her sultan's alliance was with King Francis. She wasn't sure if King Henry would even receive her. She must write to her sultan to inquire how to proceed.

"Oh my!" Alona said, her arms filled with hay. "We must speak with Pierre at once. If Mahid will not be received by His Majesty, then our arrangement…" She trailed off, muttering about all those *roses*, all that *livre*. Zacarie led his mother into the mudroom, and the two of them conversed in Basque. If Mahid could not help the cause, they could not help her. But perhaps she could still help the cause if she writes to her sultan and he writes to King Henry. But how would they keep Mahid safe from the bishop while she awaits the sultan's reply?

"We must attend Espi now," Alona said. "Then we will send for Father, who will advise us."

Alona brought Sloane one of her crutches and an empty pail. "Zacarie will hide the cart until we can speak with Father. For now, go to the river and fetch water for Espi. Quickly now, my foal."

#   #   #

Sloane stood in the tall grasses, watching the uncaring sky blot out the stars. The river meandered around reeds, delaying its inevitable death upon reaching the sea. The buzzing of night insects began to fade just as the birds began to stir, the overlapping sounds dissonant and unfriendly. The whole world unfriendly.

Sloane sat on the bank, hiked up her skirts, and submerged one leg in the cold water. It was a good meter and a half to the bottom, with a riverbed of soft, downy sediment. She considered the bucket. She was supposed to fill it and go back inside, but she sat there instead, thinking about her old job in Vancouver and waiting for the sun to rise.

Whenever a booth had seemed unfixable, she'd go back to the beginning and start over. The gnarlier a problem became, the more likely she was to perform a factory reset because it was faster and easier to start from scratch than find the mistake. That's why her relationship with Harry had always been unfixable—there was no reset button. No way to go back, undo, start over. Her Mission was different, though. An unfixable Mission could be fixed if she could just get back to where she'd started from. Back to the beginning. Back to Basecamp.

The sun broke over the trees to the east, a single, golden ray stretching across the river and landing in her lap. She touched the fingerprint pad inside her travel cloak, withdrew Saffron 2.0, and opened the case. Tiny cracks covered her exterior, the layer of glue thick as icing in some spots. She looked more like a child's ceramics project than a mechanism to manipulate space-time. Sloane toggled her switch ON, positioned Saffron 2.0 in the sunlight, and held her breath.

Nothing happened.

Seconds ticked by. Sloane held absolutely still, listening for the sound of a distant wave crashing toward shore, but she couldn't hear anything beyond the rolling, white noise of the river and the shrill chirping of the birds.

The sky remained unbroken, but Saffron 2.0 grew warmer in the sunlight, pulsing bluer and brighter until the orb was hot to the touch. Sloane set Saffron 2.0 on the riverbank so she'd catch the light. She closed her eyes and finally heard it. The roar of the portal grew closer, and the tall grasses along the riverbank began to tremble as if signaling an oncoming storm. Sloane squinted into the rising sun, watching for the sky to break apart, calling on every god she didn't believe in to intervene on her behalf. There! In the air above the river, a circular opening was spinning into view. The wind burst from the portal, bending the grasses in half and making the trees quiver. Beyond the opening spun a dark, undulating tunnel, the umbilical cord of Mother Earth. The way home.

Sloane backed up to give herself a running start. Putting as much weight on her ankle as she dared, she ran toward the water and leaped into the air, eager for the magnetic pull of the portal to draw her inside. Instead, she was propelled away from the portal with the force of an explosion. She flipped backward mid-air, legs to the sky, the earth spinning somewhere beneath her. She covered her head and braced for impact the way Johnny had taught her, certain she was about to lose the baby.

Sloane hit the water with a loud, stinging slap. She was sucked under, the force from the portal so strong that she must have hit bottom, but all she felt was the gentle tug of the current. She pushed to the surface, gasping, and pulled herself onto the bank. She examined her limbs, wondering why there was no pain. She must be in shock, and yet every part of her seemed to be intact. She pinched herself to see if there was feeling in her body and was surprised to find there was. She tried standing and found that she could.

Sloane glared at Saffron 2.0, who sat there glowing on the riverbank as if all was right with the world. She glared at the portal and at the wind making waves on the surface of the river. She untied her sopping travel cloak and tossed it to the ground. "Let me through!" She ran and leaped toward the opening and was smacked away, splashing into the water again. She climbed out, wriggled out of her sopping gown, and jumped toward the opening in her chemise. Again, she soared through the air, and again she was blown back, landing in the water. The fifth time, she fell to her knees and screamed, not caring if Alona and Zacarie heard.

"You won't let me through until I've accomplished my Mission? THERE IS NO MISSION TO ACCOMPLISH because YOU sent me to the wrong FUCKING YEAR! There is NOTHING for me here!"

The portal's only answer was the sound of rushing wind.

Sloane tried once more, and when the portal slapped her away like a housefly, she stayed underwater and let the waves rock her body downstream. It wouldn't be hard. She would ride the current until there was nothing left that she could ruin, no more Mission, no more future, no more her. But just when her lungs were set to burst, her loathsome, infuriating memory recalled Bastian's Mind Map from the portal room. It was Bastian's vision of a child—their child—that forced Sloane to the surface, gasping and cursing and fighting for the safety of shore.

She crawled her way back to Saffron 2.0, resisting the urge to smash her to pieces if only because it had taken so many hours to fix her. Instead, Sloane toggled the power switch to OFF and collapsed on the bank, her filthy, sopping chemise clinging to her like a second skin. The wind began to wane, and the portal started to dissolve along with her hopes of ever passing through it. It was only when the portal closed completely that she heard Alona's hysterical voice calling her from the cottage.

#   #   #

By the time Sloane got there Espi was already dead. Alona held the newborn goat in a bloody cloth, wiping away the afterbirth. Zacarie was scooping blood-soaked hay into a small wagon. They both stared at Sloane, the pain of Colette's death alive in their eyes, a fresh scab ripped off an old wound. The baby goat tottered on wobbly legs, sniffing for Espi's teat. She found it and began to suckle, not realizing there would never be milk.

"Where were you, Mahid?" Alona said. "We needed you."

Zacarie lifted Espi's corpse onto a blanket. He started to roll her up like a carpet, but a shrill, livid voice shrieked in protest. Zacarie flinched and looked up, his eyes growing wider when the shrieking continued. It was only when Alona shook Sloane by the shoulders that Sloane realized the shrieking was coming from her.

"You destroyed her," Sloane told the baby goat.

Just like Sloane had destroyed Thida.

And her Mission.

And her chances of ever seeing Bastian again.

You destroyed her. You destroy everything. You destroy everything in your path!

Sloane pushed past Alona and lunged for the baby goat. Zacarie intercepted her and got Sloane up against the wall, sending a stack of bowls crashing to the ground around them. He put his arms around her and held her as if she were a bomb he could prevent from detonating. Sloane struggled at first, then slumped against his chest, trembling. Zacarie stroked her back over her wet chemise, murmuring some passage from the Bible in a futile attempt to comfort her.

"Precious in the sight of the Lord is the death of his saints," he said.

It was Psalm 116:15. She remembered. But she found no comfort in Zacarie's words because they were uttered with a stolen voice—a voice Sloane would never again hear coming from its rightful owner.

When Zacarie finally released her, Sloane went into the bedroom, shut the door, and bolted the lock. She pulled the sickle from the wall and slung the blade through the shutter handles, bolting the window from the inside.

She lay down on the bed and wept.

SLOANE DID NOT LEAVE THE room for days. Alona begged her to come out, sliding offerings under the door as if placating an indifferent goddess: baked bread and saucers of milk; Sloane's travel cloak and gown, retrieved from the river and cleaned; comforting assurances that Espi had lived a good life and Mahid was not to blame for the goat's death. Zacarie knocked on the door when he came and went from the cottage, joking that he missed sleeping on the floor. Father Pierre stopped by several times, arguing that the sultan's alliance was with the Crown, not the monarch. Surely King Henry would receive Mahid just as readily as his father would have, so why not proceed to Fontainebleau as planned? When all these efforts were met with silence, the family warned her to think of the bishop. It was dangerous for her to stay at the cottage. Dangerous for all of them.

Still, she scarcely left the bed. She ate the bread and drank the milk to placate Alona and Zacarie, whose threats to break down the door would quiet for a time after she slid the empty dishes back. Twice a day, she'd use the chamber pot, withdrawing the sickle from between the shutters and tossing the contents onto the grass. Then she'd lay back down in bed, her body sinking into the mattress like a corpse into the earth.

Twenty-two Heroes before Sloane had accomplished their Missions as planned. None of them had failed. None of them had ended up in the wrong year. None of them had let everyone down because none of them were walking tornadoes that destroyed everything in their paths. That was the real reason she'd always felt so connected to nature. It wasn't because the trees were kindred spirits. It was because just like Mother Earth, Sloane was a destructress. The same destructive force that had taken Thida and Colette and Espi was alive inside of Sloane—it was the force that had destroyed her Mission.

And the Program.

And quite possibly the human race.

Sloane imagined the moment Bastian first learned of her failure, his gray eyes glazing with shock. She could feel the throbbing pain that must have bloomed across his forehead, could picture the way he would have pinched the bridge of his nose as the inconceivable ramifications piled up, one disaster after another. The love of his life had destroyed his life's work. The Program would be shut down. Operation Underground would commence. And the planet…

Bastian wouldn't have been angry with her. He would have forgiven her instantly, defending her to everyone, which only compounded her guilt. She felt so ashamed, it was almost a relief to think she'd never see him again.

Sloane sprang up in bed in a fresh fit of panic.

She'd never see Bastian again.

She'd ruined their future together. She'd ruined his Mind Map! Coffee in bed, gone. Movies on the couch, gone. Reading glasses, wedding, maternity ward, gone, gone, gone. And if she was lucky enough to survive sixteenth-century childbirth, Sloane would be raising a child in a time and place where their lives would always be at risk. There would be famine in France, and pockets of plague. The Wars of Religion were imminent, and she was a foreign, mixed-race woman in white, Catholic France, with the Bishop of Toulon still hunting her.

If only she had listened to Bastian. He told her not to think of him. He told her to stay away from the shipyard. He told her not to wear the orange dress. Everything might have been different if she wasn't on the run from the bishop from the start. There could have been signs from Saffron that she'd missed because she'd fled Toulon too soon, critical signs that she needed to complete her real Mission, whatever that was, and now she'd never see them because she just had to scream Bastian's name. She just had to flash her orange dress. She just had to make herself a wanted heretic whore within seconds of arriving in Toulon.

That goddamn dress.

Sloane peeled herself from the bed and fished the offending garment out of her travel cloak. She despised the stupid bright color, the stupid pockets, the stupid plunging neckline that had surely contributed to the bishop's conclusion that she was a whore. The dress that had ruined her Mission, her future, her life. The dress that had ruined everything!

She ripped the hem and bit the fabric, tearing the garment until it lay in tatters on the floor. A folded paper square lay amongst the wreckage. She stopped short, her memory skipping like a scratched record. It was the letter she'd tucked inside the pocket of her dress the night she'd left for Basecamp.

The letter she'd found in Harry's attic.

The letter Thida had written to her and Simon before they were born.

Sloane picked it up, unfolded it, and scanned the strings of Khmer to find that LORI could understand every word.

She sank to the floor, the paper trembling in her hands, and began to read.

Dear Simon and Sloane,

You are twenty weeks old inside me now, my dears. Today the doctor told us we will have a boy and a girl, so we have chosen your English names. Harold insists on English names.

I hope you never read this letter. If you never read it, it means what I'm about to tell you doesn't matter anymore because everything has worked out as I'd hoped. But if life has other plans for us, I wanted to put the truth somewhere. I hope you will not judge me too harshly for it. I hope that, when you are older, you will understand.

I did not know what love was when I married Harold. But I am grateful to him because he brought me to the place I met my true love—your real father.

With Harold, love has always been a slippery fish forever wriggling out of my grasp. As soon as I think I have it, he finds another flaw I must fix, another feat I must accomplish before I can earn his love.

With your father, there is nothing I can do to make him love me more than he already does. And there is nothing he could do to change the way I feel for him. Sometimes, afterwards, I am so overcome with gratitude—with the miracle of loving him—that it is more than I can bear to look into his eyes. At first, I thought he had cast a spell on me because I felt so drunk with love in his presence. But then I began to feel this way whether we were together or not. I realized the love I felt was not something he'd given me, or something I had earned—it was inside me all along.

I will try to tell you of the quality of this love. It is the river that flows into the darkest corners of the deepest valley. There is nowhere it will not go, no imperfection that could deviate its route. The love I feel for you both has this quality, too. No matter who you are, or how you are, or what you may become when you grow up, there is nothing that could make me turn away from you. There is nothing you need to do to earn my love because you have it already.

The visa will expire soon, and your father will get on the airplane. A giant flying machine brought me to him, and a giant flying machine will take him away from me. We do not know how we can be together, though he says we are always together, even when our bodies are apart. We hope the flying machine will bring him back to me, or me to him, someday.

My dears. My darlings. I do not know what the future holds, or whether you will ever meet your father. But if he never holds you in his arms, let his teaching embrace you and offer you comfort: love is not something we need to get from someone else. It is inside us already. It is the stuff we're made of. The love inside me and the love inside you is what binds us together, always. It the only thing in this world that can never be destroyed.

Sometimes it takes a very special person to awaken this love—to show you who you really are and what you're made of. But if that person goes away, the love remains.

Love,

Your Mak

P.S. I will teach you Khmer so you can read this yourselves because I think something will get lost in translation. Harold doesn't want me to teach you, but I will try anyway, when he is at work, okay?

Sloane held the letter to her chest and sobbed. She felt her heart cracking open, her bones opening up, and Thida's words penetrating the very marrow.

There is nothing that could make me turn away from you.

Every memory that was tainted with shame, with failure, with not good enough clambered to the surface of her being as if summoned for a final reckoning. In the light of her mother's love, the collective shame of a lifetime crumbled to dust, and the dust dissolved to nothing, as if it had never been. What was left in its wake was a sensation so subtle and fine, Sloane had never noticed it before. And yet it was familiar, too, like a statue she'd passed hundreds of times without ever stopping to really look. She felt herself pulsing with a depthless, timeless, relentless love; a love that relied on nothing outside itself; a love that had been inside her all along. There was nothing this love did not include. It was a healing love, like her mother's. A redemptive love, like Mother Mary's. A regenerative love, like Mother Earth's. Still and silent like the coming spring, this invisible benevolence rolled back dead underbrush, revived rotting limbs, and restored parched earth so something new could take root. There was no separation between the love that made roses bloom, the love that opened portals, and the love that lifted Sloane to her feet now. It had been trying to express itself through her all her life. All she had to do now was let it.

Sloane slid the sickle from the shutters and threw open the window, welcoming a potpourri of alfalfa and fresh manure into the room. The sun was nearly overhead, but she felt as if it were dawn, and she was greeting the world for the first time. A heron swept across the sky, pumping its massive wings as it cut a path toward the river, nature's own flying machine soaring just like her heart. She flew around the room, grabbing discarded items off the floor and tossing them over her shoulder in search of her clothes, determined to be fully dressed and in possession of a nicely articulated apology by the time Alona and Zacarie returned to the cottage for supper. She managed to tug a skirt and an apron over her chemise, but when she tried to cobble together the right words to explain her attempted goatricide and subsequent nervous breakdown, she couldn't concentrate—her thoughts kept drifting, inexplicably, back to Basecamp, to the day she'd made the miniature flying machine during training.

On that day, Sloane had pulled apart wispy bands of cotton and stretched them over a tiny wooden frame, creating a model hang glider to impress the king. Eleanor—Bastian, really—had scolded her for inventing something so technologically outlandish for the time, even in miniature.

She tried to will the memory away, but the scene only grew sharper in her mind, the details more vivid, until she was reliving the memory as if it were happening again right now. Sloane found herself bent over the worktable in the training room, putting the finishing touches on the little cotton sail. As she picked up the flying machine to show Eleanor what she'd made, she noticed beads of color and light shimmering in the air above the worktable, which was weird because Poppy hadn't been projecting Sloane's Mind Map during this session. Sloane watched, mesmerized, as the beads fused together to form some kind of document. Not just any document. A blueprint. A big, floating blueprint that grew until it stretched the length of the worktable and filled the training room halfway to the ceiling. Sloane paused the memory, baffled—there had been no Mind Map, no projections, no simulation of any sort during this training session. There had been no giant floating blueprint. She would have remembered. She scanned the training room to see if anyone else noticed the blueprint that had materialized out of thin air, but the rest of the memory seemed intact. The crew were leaning against the walls, Eleanor was frowning at the flying machine, Poppy was peering at her iGlass, and Enkh was sitting on the floor with his eyes closed.

Wait a second.

At this point in the training session, Enkh *had* been sitting on the floor with his eyes closed. But when she looked at the monk now, his eyes were open, and his gaze was fixed on Sloane.

She asked what he was doing, and her voice rang out in the bedroom. She told Enkh his eyes were supposed to be closed. He couldn't just change her memory!

Enkh smiled. He raised his index finger and pointed to the blueprint, jabbing the air until Sloane looked again. On closer inspection, she realized she was looking at a blueprint of a flying machine—a near exact replica of her miniature flying machine, except with dimensions big enough to fit a person. Sloane looked at Enkh. He held her gaze for a moment, then with the slightest nod of his head, closed his eyes and resumed his original position in her memory. Enkh's hands, which had been palm-down on his knees, were now cradling a pale pink rose.

Sloane's eyes popped open in the bedroom. Images began to flash through her mind at warp speed, as if she were a computer and her programming was being overridden. Flash, flash, flash. Her training memories were copied, then modified and reconfigured. Flash, flash, flash. A Mission bloomed in her mind, every detail of its ascent, its apex, and its aftermath contained in a single, coherent moment of understanding.

She knew why Saffron had sent her to 1548 instead of 1521.

She knew what she had to build.

And she knew her real Mission had nothing to do with King Francis or his son.

She couldn't stop laughing about that part, and she doubled over, wiping her eyes with the hem of her apron. When the rooster crowed, she leaned out the window and crowed back at him.

"This Mission's going to work," she said in English, startling the hens in the yard. "This one's just crazy enough to work!"

The heron appeared again, arcing out over the valley to survey its domain, soaring with enviable ease over a place that was still pristine, a place where stewards of the Earth didn't realize they were fulfilling their purpose with every seed they sowed. Sloane's true Mission was to make them understand. She would awaken the people to their purpose so they could sustain that divine assignment into the future, and in doing so, protect and sustain the future of the planet, where herons would not only exist, but soar ever higher into skies that would never be cloaked in smog.

Watching the bird and considering the blueprint, Sloane thought now might be a good time to finally conquer her fear of heights.

FIVE MONTHS LATER, ON THE first night of the Feast of the Assumption of Mary, Sloane was standing on the edge of a cliff in the middle of the forest, ready to jump. She secured her grip around the triangular base of her flying machine, which she'd made out of hollowed-out tree branches. The wings of the frame stretched thirty feet wide and were wrapped in an enormous silk sail, to which she'd glued hundreds of feathers. She'd outfitted the edges of the sail with a border of carefully secured roses and added additional panels of silk to hide the base where it connected to the frame. A sapphire silk dress hung from the sail like a shimmering tail, its sleeves sewn into the panels that hid the base. When she pushed her arms through the sleeves, Sloane could grip the bottom of the base to steer the machine midair without her efforts being seen. When she landed, she could balance the narrow point of the base over her shoulders, slip her arms through slits in the silk panels, and stand upright with her hands free, creating an optical illusion: the wings of the sail would appear to onlookers to grow directly out of her back like a pair of angel's wings.

As proud as Sloane was of these 'wings,' the most important feature of the flying machine was its homemade megaphone. She'd carved the megaphone in the shape of an ear trumpet and fastened it to the base of the flying machine so it, too, was hidden from view. The megaphone had a small mouthpiece that snaked up through her dress and curved within inches of her lips, allowing her to amplify her voice without turning her head.

She performed a quick microphone check by clearing her throat into the mouthpiece and felt a thrill of excitement when her voice reverberated over the cliff. She'd prepared speeches for each of the three nights of the Feast, and tonight everyone in Toulon would hear her opening act. She hoped that, since she planned to speak in French, the learned men in the crowd would write down what she said verbatim. That way, nothing would get lost in translation when they shared her words throughout France.

A warm breeze tussled the sail, bringing with it the scent of the bonfires burning in nearby Saphir. Zacarie and Alona would be in the village by now, setting up their stall to sell Alona's medicinal oils to the revelers. They would stay in Saphir late into the night and never know she had left her new home in the rose garden—her sanctuary these past months, ever since she discovered her true Mission.

When Sloane had emerged from the bedroom that day (to the profound relief of Zacarie and Alona), she'd put her new Mission into motion, making an elaborate production of writing a letter to Suleiman the Magnificent. In the letter, she'd reported the death of King Francis and asked for the sultan's direction—should she continue on to King Henry's court, or return home to Constantinople at once? There would be no reply to her letter—the "Turkish" script was nothing but a nonsensical transcription of Saffron's code—but she'd insisted on waiting at Merkatoria until the nonexistent reply arrived. It would take time to build a flying machine, just as it would take time for her pregnancy to show. By the Feast of the Assumption in June, she'd be six months pregnant, and able to convincingly portray her part as Mother Mary, pregnant with the Christ child, descending from Heaven on angel's wings to deliver news of the Second Coming of the Lord.

But it wasn't safe for Sloane to stay at the cottage indefinitely—not with the Bishop of Toulon still hunting her. She'd convinced the family to let her reside in the rose garden, touting its cloistered location and proximity to Merkatoria. She didn't mention that the surrounding forest would make a convenient, incognito construction site for her flying machine.

With the caveat that he might visit her daily, Zacarie had agreed to this arrangement, constructing a little hut for her at the garden's edge. Some nights, Sloane would sleep inside the hut, her travel cloak spread over a pile of hay. But most nights she slept outside, among the roses, beneath the stars. Zacarie and Alona visited often, bringing food and water, and helping her pull weeds from between the rose bushes, which Sloane tended with rapt devotion. Between their visits, she'd spent her time in a clearing in the forest near the edge of a cliff, carving, sanding, hammering, and whittling according to the specifications on the blueprint she'd envisioned. At the end of the day, she'd hide her work beneath a tarp she'd woven out of palm fronds.

As soon as she could put weight on her ankle again, Sloane had begun making practice flights to Toulon, using the cliff as a launchpad, and riding the current of a high-altitude airstream down the mountain toward the sea. Once she reached Toulon, the airstream would propel her, boomerang-like, out over the bay then back up the mountain toward Saphir. On each of these trips, Sloane had flown far above the town, but tonight, she would fly to be seen. With her head uncovered and her hair loose, she would swoop down and make a spectacle of herself, just like Mother Mary. She only prayed that the bonfires burning in Toulon would be as big as Zacarie said. Sloane would need the hot airstreams created by the fires to buoy her back up the mountain once she was spotted.

She tugged at the harness beneath her dress, triple-checking that the rope connecting the harness to the sail was secure. She smoothed the fabric of the harness over her belly, sighing with relief to feel the baby shift inside her. "Ready to go for a ride, little one?" Sloane looped the pulley of her parachute around her wrist, praying she wouldn't have to use it, then drew back from the cliff's edge to give herself a running start. Her stomach jumped, and a burst of cortisol flooded her limbs. No matter how many times she'd leaped off this cliff, Sloane was still afraid of heights. But like the pistil hidden inside the petals of a rose, she sensed a core of love inside her that was ever-present and unshakable, even when shrouded in fear. She felt her connection to the Earth and to herself, and though she was afraid, she knew nature would not let her fail—not her nature, not Mother Earth, and not Saffron, whom Sloane now saw as the bridge between the two.

She closed her eyes and listened for a sign that it was time. The breeze was quiet in the trees, and she felt the soil beneath her feet, still warm from the midsummer sun. The hoot of an owl cut through the fading twilight, its call so close, it could have come from inside her. Sloane opened her eyes and sprinted as fast as she could toward the cliff's edge, gripping fifty pounds of homemade hang glider. She pushed off the edge and jumped into the air. The silk sail caught the breeze, and she swung her legs out behind her until she was holding onto the base in push-up position, the wind suctioning her dress to her body, her hair flying out behind her like a cape. She steered southeast over the treetops toward the distant glow of the bonfires raging in the streets of Toulon.

Sloane wouldn't be soaring five thousand feet above the earth right now if it weren't for Zacarie, who'd been an unknowing pawn in her preparations for tonight. Since the moment she received the vision of the flying machine, Sloane knew Zacarie would be the one to help her build it. She also knew that Zacarie's heart would become a necessary casualty of the Mission.

After she'd finished writing a letter to the sultan, Zacarie had driven Sloane back to the rose garden, trying to sound nonchalant when he asked how long she planned to wait for a reply. Sloane paused as if she hadn't anticipated the question, then told Zacarie she'd wait a minimum of five months to hear back. After all, Ottoman messengers were notoriously slow.

"And if there is still no word from him after five months?"

Zacarie had expected the same old song from Mahid—that she'd wait for her sultan forever. Sloane had remained silent, offering a look of encouragement in its place. "Might you consider yourself…in need of a husband?" he'd asked, taking the bait. "And your child, in need of a father?" When she'd admitted that she might, Zacarie had tried to look solemn, but a smile kept breaking over his face. If the sultan did not write her, he was a greater fool than Zacarie had suspected. And she should not marry a fool unless he was a fool in love.

Each day that passed without a letter from the sultan had strengthened Zacarie's hopes for their future. When Sloane had begun making unusual requests (a hammer, an ax, a saw), Zacarie had raised an eyebrow, but he hadn't probed—especially once he understood that the procurement of a hammer would be rewarded with a kiss on the cheek, or that an ax could buy him an afternoon walk in the woods. Under the pretense of making him "something special" for the Feast of the Assumption, Sloane had sent him to Toulon to buy three dozen nails, four reams of silk, two coils of sailor's rope, and several yards of Chinese sandpaper. When he'd returned with the supplies, she'd received him in the garden without her veil, and Zacarie asked what more he might bring her, and what other articles of clothing she might remove when he did.

Whenever she felt guilty for deceiving him, Sloane reminded herself that when the Mission was over, Zacarie wouldn't want her anymore. He'd be too furious with her for lying to him and disappearing without a trace. She only hoped that, between Colette's death and Mahid's deception, Zacarie would learn that heartbreak could never take away the love inside of him, the stuff he was made of. If Sloane couldn't help him understand that, she prayed he'd find someone loving enough to show him he didn't need their love.

As the twinkling lights of Toulon grew brighter, Sloane wondered if Zacarie's person was down there right now, dancing between the bonfires that lined the town square. The biggest bonfire burned in front of the church, where a three-story wooden frame was engulfed in flames that leaped higher than the arcade arch. On her descent, she compared ground-level memories of the city's architecture and layout with this new view from above. Tonight was just a fly-over, the opening overture to her three-act performance, but she'd set aside five seconds to identify a landing pad for tomorrow night's flight, when Mother Mary would speak at length from the safety of the tallest building she could find. Behind the spires of the church, next to the bell tower, she noticed a flat section of rooftop about fifteen meters wide by ten meters deep—not as big as she would have liked for a landing pad, but it would have to do. She had two seconds left to identify a backup option. She eyed the buildings surrounding the church, but their rooftops were too steeply angled to land the flying machine. The first shouts went up from the crowd. Time was up.

Sloane steered the flying machine downward, searching for the hot airstream from the fires but struggling to find it. The machine dipped sharply, and a gasp went up from the crowd. She started to free fall. Straining as she gripped the base, Sloane steered toward the church bonfire until she felt a warm pop beneath her and soared skyward, plumes of warm air buoying the machine up and over the crowd.

"My children!" Sloane shouted into the mouthpiece, her voice exploding from the wide end of the megaphone and echoing across the square. "You who celebrate the Feast of Mother Mary! Look upon your Mother, the Blessed Virgin, who has descended from Heaven and come back to life!"

Sloane followed the airstream's circular path out over the bay. She looked back, wondering if the crowd had not only heard but understood her, and saw hundreds of people standing awestruck in the square as she circled around for a second lap.

"Like Saint John before me, I prepare the way for the coming of the Lord," she said, zooming above the crowd. "Look upon my womb, swollen with life! The Christ Child grows inside me. He will be born again into this world! My Son has a message for you. Our Father has sent me down from Heaven to deliver it to you! If you have ears to hear, return to this place tomorrow night. Light more fires, the biggest you can make! I will come to you again with a message from my Son!"

A murmur spread through the crowd. "*Bruèissa!*" they said in Provençal. "*Sorcière!*" they said in French.

"Listen not to those who would deny me!" Sloane said. "And let not the Devil tempt you with doubt. For some will say that I am a witch. Others will say I have tricked you with bad magic. But witches fly without wings, and I fly with the wings of an angel! I speak to you with the voice of God, for I am the Mother of God, and none other! Be ye Catholic or Huguenot, French or foreigner, gather here tomorrow night to hear the word of your Lord!"

Sloane swept toward the church bonfire, angling the flying machine toward the sky. The billowing heat pushed the silk sail up, catapulting her back onto the upper airstream she had ridden in on. She was trailed by a cacophony of clapping and a crying out of voices, though she could not make out the words. The machine dipped once when it reached the edge of town, but a gust of wind buoyed her upward again, and she rode it to the cliff's edge in the forest.

Sloane angled the flying machine toward the ground, and when she got close enough to the earth, she dragged her feet along the clearing floor until she'd come to a full stop. Gripping the base, she walked the flying machine back to its hiding place, eyeing the surrounding woods with a mixture of trepidation and relief. She slipped out of her silk dress, threw on her chemise, and secured the palm tarp over the flying machine before jogging back through the woods toward the rose garden. At the crest of an embankment she stopped, peering out through the trees over the moonlit valley, where she saw a rider on horseback racing down the hill from Saphir in the direction of the garden.

Sloane sprinted toward her hut as fast as her pregnant belly would allow, racing against the rumble of nearing hoofbeats. She slipped inside the structure, lay down on her makeshift bed, and covered herself with a blanket just seconds before Zacarie entered the enclosure. He'd never come to the rose garden in the middle of the night before. Sloane thought he must be drunk from the Feast, the clear boundaries between them blurred in his mind. She wondered what he might try, not that she'd let him. But the thought aroused her anyway, the old temptation crawling under the blanket and slipping inside her chemise. Zacarie stood there for several moments as Sloane lay still, trying to match her breathing to the rhythm of someone who'd been asleep for hours. He moved closer, pulled back the blanket. Sloane kept her eyes squeezed shut as Zacarie's lips grazed her temple. He kissed her there, close-mouthed and chaste, before standing and quitting the hut. Sloane waited for Flor's hoofbeats to fade before conjuring the memory of Bastian on top of her in the tree house. She acted out the memory as best she could on her own, driving away the lingering traces of mint and sage with the memories of cedar and salt.

"PSSSST."

"Mahid."

"Dear Mahid, wake up!"

Sloane blinked, squinting at the figure standing in the doorway of the hut, his body blocking most of the mid-morning sunlight save the bright beam that spilled between his legs and shone directly in her eyes. And then he was at her side, shaking her.

"Wake up!" said Zacarie. "There has been a miracle in Toulon!"

Sloane sprang to a sitting position, wide awake now. Zacarie's face was flushed, his expression so replete with joy that Sloane thought he might still be drunk from last night. She asked LORI to confirm what Zacarie just said, but LORI had grown sluggish as she neared the end of her six-month lifespan, and all she could muster by way of translation was a single word: miracle.

Trying to look the right combination of surprised and skeptical, Sloane inquired about the miracle in Toulon, but Zacarie was distracted by the laces of Sloane's chemise come undone in the night. She cleared her throat and his cheeks pinkened. He turned his back so she could dress, the words pouring from him like water as she did.

"Last night, the Blessed Virgin Mary appeared in the sky over the town square. Those who were there say Mother Mary flew with the wings of an angel and spoke with a voice of thunder. She is carrying the Christ child in her belly! We have always known that one day, Mother Mary would descend from Heaven to prepare the way for the second coming of her Son, and that day has finally come. Mother Mary will return to Toulon tonight to deliver an important message from the Lord!"

Sloane's hands shook as she tied her apron around her waist. Zacarie was saying the exact words she'd hoped he'd say as if she had written the script herself. And yet she teased him—he must have had too much ale last night. She finished securing her veil and tapped Zacarie on the shoulder. He managed to look both relieved and disappointed that she was fully dressed.

"It is true I drank too much. But I speak the truth, all the same."

"The truth according to people who also had too much to drink."

"The entire town saw her, Mahid," he said. "That's hundreds of people! A messenger arrived in Saphir with the news at dawn. When I left the cottage just now, every soul in Saphir was making the journey to Toulon along the road that cuts across our land. The bishop and his men are claiming the miracle in the name of the Church. They have sent messengers to all the neighboring towns, inviting priests and their parishioners to journey to Toulon by nightfall. But Father says this is the sign our people have been waiting for. Mother Mary called upon foreigners and Huguenots by name. Huguenots. By *name*, Mahid! She has come to bless the Huguenot cause! My whole life, father has been saying 'Someday, our time will come.' That day is finally here. Our time has come, Mahid!"

Zacarie sealed his belief in her manufactured miracle with a kiss on both her cheeks, infecting Sloane with his excitement. People in Toulon, people in Saphir, even the freaking clergy believed the woman flying in the sky last night was truly Mother Mary. Sloane threw her arms around Zacarie's neck, and he laughed and lifted her off her feet in an embrace.

Alona and Father Pierre were already on the road to Toulon. They wanted Zacarie to follow them presently, but Alona did not think Mahid should make a half day's journey in her condition. Zacarie argued that the journey to Toulon was a half day walking, but merely an hour's ride on horseback, but Sloane said Alona was right, and she shouldn't go. Of course, she'd *love* to go, but it was probably safer for her to stay in the garden. Zacarie should go, though. He should definitely, definitely go. (He had to go. If Zacarie was anywhere in the vicinity of the rose garden at any point tonight, it would put a serious wrench in Sloane's plans.) But Zacarie didn't want to leave Mahid alone overnight because he wouldn't be nearby if she needed him.

"It's one night."

"Suppose the baby—"

"The baby is fine."

"Suppose the bishop—"

"The bishop will be in Toulon with the rest of Provence, which makes tonight the safest night I've spent here."

"But all alone—"

"I will have the stars to watch over me."

"I could watch over you."

"And miss the miracle?"

She raised an eyebrow in triumph, and Zacarie threw up his hands. "I will go to Toulon if you will it," he said. "I will always do whatever you ask of me, for when I look upon your face, the only word I can remember is 'yes.'" He held her gaze in an unapologetic way, as if news of the miracle had emboldened him; if Mother Mary could descend from Heaven during the Feast of the Assumption, maybe a miracle between Zacarie and Mahid was just as possible. If only Zacarie knew that by tomorrow night, there would be words other than 'yes' that came to mind when he thought of her. Words like *liar* or *traitor*. Or maybe just *gone*—disappeared forever without even saying goodbye.

Sloane pushed past him into the morning, gravitating toward her favorite rose bush, and ignoring the heat of Zacarie's stare on her back.

"It has been nearly five months since you wrote to the sultan," Zacarie said. "I wondered if you recalled our…agreement, Mahid."

"Of course I do," she said, tugging at a patch of weeds between the bushes.

"And?"

"And I said I'd wait until after the Feast of the Assumption. The sultan has two more days to write me back."

She reached to pull another weed, but Zacarie's boot blocked her way.

"And if the outcome is not as you'd hoped?" he said, touching her arm.

"What then?"

"Do you think these need more water?" she asked, fretting over a perfectly hydrated bush. "I think these need more water. I should go get some—"

"Please, Mahid. I have been patient."

She couldn't look at him, but she said if she hadn't received a letter from the sultan by the Feast's end, she would consider her relationship with him to be over.

"And you will not return to your country."

"I would have no reason to."

"You will give birth here. Then, the three of us will go somewhere the bishop will never find you, somewhere our people can protect you."

"Yes. If he doesn't write, I will—"

"Marry me?"

She held up a finger and shut her eyes as if she felt a sneeze coming on. In those few seconds, she conjured Bastian's face. She knew the outcome of this new Mission would be different than what he'd hoped she'd achieve. She hadn't stopped French colonization of the Americas, so she probably wouldn't reverse the glacial melt around Greenland or pull sinking Florida from the sea. At the very least, she hoped her success would keep the Program going until they could find the next Hero, and the next. In that way, her Mission could save millions of lives in the future, which had to be worth more than one man's heart.

"Yes," she said. "If he doesn't write to me, I'll marry you."

Zacarie tried to look serious, but his happiness overcame him, and he threw his arms over his head and shouted, making Sloane laugh. But she couldn't leave him like this, so full of hope. It would hurt more later if he was this happy now.

She moved down the row, checking her roses, trying not to see the smile that kept breaking over Zacarie's face. "On the slim chance the sultan's letter arrives in the next two days, what would you do? Hypothetically."

"What would I do?"

"I mean if the sultan sent me to King Henry's court after all, or if he called me home to Constantinople, you would find someone else. Right?"

"I do not want someone else."

"I'm talking worst-case scenario."

Zacarie repeated the phrase and said he didn't like it.

"I know. Just promise me. Worst-case scenario, if the sultan writes to me, or if something else happens and we can't be together, you won't live out your days alone. Hate me all you want but keep your heart open. Choose someone else and have children and be happy."

"Mahid—"

"Promise me, Zacarie."

"I do not want—"

"Promise me."

He shook his head, his eyes glazing as he reviewed some private memory. She'd forgotten that no woman would have him.

"Colette would have you. I would have you. I'd bet all the coins you have stashed in the stable that pretty much any woman who's laid eyes on you would have you, too. Now promise me."

"I hate this promise."

"Say it anyway."

"I promise to keep my heart open, to find someone else and be happy."

"And have children."

"And have children."

"Good," she said. "Now go. Before you miss your miracle."

Zacarie studied her for a moment. He leaned in, and Sloane offered him her cheek. Instead of kissing her, he cupped the back of her head, pressing their cheeks together, his lips at her ear. "Forgive me, Mahid. But when I see Mother Mary tonight, I shall repeat the same prayer she has heard from me these past five months: that your letter from the sultan never arrives, that nothing would keep us apart, and that I might be the one to make you happy all your days."

Sloane watched him walk to the shady spot beneath the giant oaks where he'd left Flor grazing. 'All her days' was just two more days—if everything went according to plan, she had less than forty-eight hours left in this century. After tonight, Sloane would never see Zacarie, Alona, or Father Pierre again because she didn't want to put the family at risk. Last night,

Mother Mary was a miracle. But after she spoke tonight, she'd become a heretic in the eyes of the Catholic Church. When Sloane returned to the rose garden after her second flight as Mary, she would collect Saffron and her travel cloak and hide out for a night, sleeping in a cave she'd found deep in the forest. The family might search for her when they returned from Toulon, but they would not find her. She hoped her disappearance would protect them if anyone ever made the connection between Mother Mary, the woman from the shipyard, and Zacarie's mysterious cousin from Basque country, who had appeared in Saphir the day Bertrand died never to be heard from again.

It was only when Zacarie mounted Flor that Sloane realized she hadn't even said goodbye. She took off across the garden, weaving through the rose bushes, the memory of saying goodbye to Bastian swooping in to cloud her vision. She saw the anguish in Bastian's eyes, a reflection of her own sorrow, and she felt that sorrow again now, all her love for Bastian conflating with the loss of Zacarie and driving her to his side before it was too late. She called his name. She tore around the end of a row and saw him snap his head in her direction. He yanked the horse's reigns to turn the animal around, his face filled with the old fear that there was something wrong with the baby.

"I'm alright," Sloane said, jogging toward him.

"Is the child…?"

"Fine. We're fine, I just…"

She stopped and looked up at him, memorizing Zacarie's face, especially the features that made him different from Bastian. His green eyes. His jet-black hair shining blue and purple in the sunlight.

"Why do you cry, woman?"

"I just wanted you to know…"

Zacarie's expression softened. He reached out his hand and looked surprised when Sloane pressed it to her cheek.

She told him that she loved him.

Zacarie stared at her, astounded.

"And I, you, Mahid."

Sloane watched him and Flor disappear through the trees. Then she stood in the garden with her eyes closed, listening to Zacarie gallop toward the road that led to Toulon until the sounds had faded to silence. Alone in the garden without him, without Bastian, without anyone but the wind and the roses and herself, Sloane felt Thida's living wisdom permeate her every breath, and she felt it as the silent breath of God; when people went away, the love remained.

AS SOON AS SLOANE BEGAN her descent to Toulon, she could see that something was wrong.

The crowd was astonishing. There must have been thousands of people packed into the town square, their congregation making a low, humming sound she could hear from five thousand feet above the earth. Bonfires raged in the streets, and thousands of twinkling lanterns had been lit for the Mother of God. But her landing pad, the church rooftop, had been overrun. Dozens of priests were sitting in rows of high-backed stalls, offering them a superior view of the miracle in the sky, and leaving Sloane without an inch of space to land her flying machine.

Her heart hammered as she flew toward the church. Of all the possibilities and contingencies she had imagined, she had not imagined anyone sitting on her landing pad, let alone the clergy. She had no choice but to fly straight toward them, breaking the optical illusion she'd worked so hard to create. Her angel wings only looked like angel wings from a safe distance, but she needed the heat of the church bonfire to propel her over the crowd, buying her time to find somewhere else to land.

The priests stared, jaws dropped, as Sloane closed in. She spotted Father Pierre sitting in the first row, and when their eyes met, absolute shock rippled across his face. Her eyes fluttered in their sockets in search of anywhere else to look, as if looking away could somehow make Father Pierre un-see her. Not because she feared discovery, but because she didn't want to take away his miracle so soon. Not like this. Her gaze landed on the man to his left, whose look of surprise was quickly replaced by a smug smile of recognition; at long last, the Bishop of Toulon had found his wanted heretic whore.

Sloane cleared the fire, and a pop of warm air sent her soaring upward. She steered the flying machine out over the water, away from the deafening roar of the crowd, rifling through mental snapshots of the town's architecture to identify an alternate landing pad. She started to panic. Every option was either too low to the ground or slanted at an impossible angle. Looping back around, she zeroed in on the cathedral across the square from the church. The tops of each tower were flat, but landing there would be like trying to land an airplane on a helicopter pad. A sudden gust of wind buoyed her toward the cathedral's left tower, and she tried to swerve away in protest. She needed more space, a runway, a margin for error! But the wind was dead set on the tower, as if Mother Earth Herself was sure of Sloane's next move.

"My children!" she said, yielding to the wind. "If you wish to receive the Mother of God, shut your mouths, close your eyes, and say a silent prayer of thanks for the gift of my Son!" Thousands of people hushed at once. Sloane soared toward the tower, swinging her body off the machine until she was hanging beneath it in pull-up position. She chopped the air with her legs, trying to slow her descent, but the tower was rising beneath her far too fast. She scraped her foot along the stone molding, thrashing in search of a hold. There! Her left foot hooked the ledge, and she hung suspended above the tower, layers of silk and feathers billowing in the night air, tugging her back toward the sky. The wind reversed, the silk exhaled, and she landed on her feet with her back to the crowd. She adjusted her grip on the base, allowed herself one deep breath, and turned to face the masses, rotating the machine like a ship changing direction on the sea.

Far above the peasants and merchants, Sloane had a clear view of the clergy on the church rooftop. She could see the bishop's *mitre* tilting and bobbing as he conferred with Father Pierre, probably telling the priest that 'Mother Mary' and the woman from the shipyard were one and the same. Sloane wondered if Father Pierre would try, once again, to protect her, and what would happen if he didn't. She wondered whether there was a staircase that led to the top of this tower, and how long it would take a man—or dozens of men—to climb it.

She commanded the people to open their eyes and look upon her, and they obeyed. She said everything they had been taught about God, and about themselves, was wrong. Thousands of souls seemed to hold their collective breath. "It has been fifteen hundred years since my Son last walked this earth, and for fifteen hundred years, men have twisted his words to suit their own agendas. You have been taught that you are sinners. That your purpose is to obey Church law, follow the rules of men, and live in fear. That you should sacrifice joy right now for the hope of Heaven later. You have been taught to believe in right and wrong ways to live, to love, and to die, and you kill each other and yourselves to uphold these beliefs in the name of my Son. But my Son cares naught for your beliefs. He cares naught for your religions, and He is deaf to the empty prayers of your priests. My Son cares only that you would know your true selves, for just like Him, you have been made in my Father's image—perfect children, begotten by God, forever bound to Him and to each other by His holy purpose in creating you."

Across the square, the clergy were on their feet, vacating their thrones to converge in the center of the rooftop. Sloane spoke faster.

"God did not make you to tremble before Him or to cower before a priest. He did not make you to make war with each other—not over religion or anything else. God made you to watch over every living thing in this world as He watches over you. He created you in His image so you could care for the fish and the sea, the birds and the sky, the creatures that move along the ground, and the ground—the very earth—itself."

She could feel the audience's rapt attention, their stillness accentuating the clergy's sudden movement on the church rooftop. Like a flock of migratory birds, the priests moved as a unit, their robes swishing in perfect formation as they flew toward the exit.

They were coming for her.

"You are the protectors," she said. "The shepherds of life. The chosen ones who keep the rivers and oceans clean. The blessed ones who use the sun, wind, and water to power your ships and heat your homes. The holy ones who find a purpose for every scrap of cloth just as God has found a purpose for you. You are the ones who light lamps for my Feast alone, and throughout the rest of the year, you marry yourselves to the rhythms of the sun and moon, never dampening the night sky with artificial light. For to see the stars is to see the light of God, which illuminates nightly your holy purpose.

"Until now, you have not understood that purpose. You have punished yourselves and each other, not realizing your true connection to God. He is not pleased when you pay the priest benefices, but when you grow your barley and care for your sheep. He is not pleased when you accuse your neighbor of heresy, but when you walk in His forests and swim in His streams. He is not pleased when you slaughter the lamb in His name, but when you protect your animals as you do your children."

Sloane spotted the bishop's *mitre* bobbing its way through the masses below with half a dozen clergy following in his wake. She calculated how long it would take them to elbow their way through the crowd, reach the cathedral, reach her. Father Pierre wasn't among them—he wasn't coming for her, but he wasn't coming to help her, either.

"Abandon your religions, for they do not gain you entry into Heaven! Relinquish violence against the land, against each other, against the beasts in the forest and field. Eat not of animal flesh, for God has given you every seed-bearing plant and every tree that has fruit with seed in it, that you would nourish your bodies as you nourish the body of the land. Know that you are stewards of the Earth and that your purpose is already fulfilled. All you need do now is sustain it. Continue in your purpose always, even when men come to destroy your Heaven on Earth. And come they will."

The priests pushed past people in the crowd, knocking some to the ground when they didn't move fast enough. A fight broke out, and Sloane raised her voice to be heard over the commotion.

"My Son sends you a prophecy: everyone who hears these words but does not heed them will create Hell on Earth. A race of men who care only for profit and progress will be born into this world. They will come to cut down your trees, drive your animals to extinction, swaddle your land in stone until all the world is paved and your farms barren. These men will make horseless carriages that will poison the sky and blot out the sun. Children will grow up not knowing the scent of a rose or the shade of an oak tree. Women will no longer bear children, their wombs poisoned by the greed of these men. The seas will rise and swallow towns whole, all the Earth consumed by a curse for which you will bear the guilt. Every inhabitant throughout every land will perish for breaking the everlasting covenant to be God's stewards of the Earth."

The priests had disappeared, and the crowd cowered in silence. Sloane waited for the poison of her prophecy to infect every heart—the greater their fear, the more effective her antidote.

"Everyone who hears these words but does not heed them will create Hell on Earth," she said again. "But everyone who hears these words and heeds them will create Heaven on Earth! You will make a world fit for my Son's return, a world that will endure for your children's children and beyond. On this new Earth, every human being will know their purpose and rejoice in fulfilling it. You will no longer live in fear, for you will feel your connectedness to yourselves and to each other, to God and all living things. And when some forget their purpose, threatening the good of the whole with the greed of the few, you will not let them succeed. You will strike down their ideas as you would flint upon a stone. You will show them that harming the Earth for any reason—for *any* reason—is the road to Hell. You will remind them that failing to honor God's gift of this world is humanity's guaranteed end, and that nothing matters more than their God-given purpose to be stewards of the Earth."

A gust of wind overtook the sail, tugging Sloane toward the edge of the tower as if Mother Earth were telling her she must fly, and *now*. She tightened her grip around the base of the flying machine, preparing to flee, eyeing the shallow runway that ended in a meter-high balcony. "Remember me! Remember every word I have spoken here tonight! The learned among you shall write down these words and share them with your children's children. And every year at Midsummer, during my sacred Feast, you shall read these words to remind yourself of God's gift to you—the Earth—and His purpose in creating you—to protect it."

An ancient door creaked open nearby. Sloane turned the machine and came face-to-face with a half dozen red caps and white robes. One of the priests lunged for the sail, and she leaped off the balcony to the sound of tearing silk in a snowstorm of disembodied feathers. The crowd gasped as she plummeted toward the church bonfire, the tear in the silk causing the flying machine to bob and shudder. Just when she felt the heat of the fire starting to singe her skin, a burst of hot air filled her wings and propelled her skyward for a final lap around the square.

She said if the people did not heed these words, they would perish in the flames of Hell, but if they heeded these words, they would live forever in Heaven. She instructed them to come again, once more, tomorrow night. She used the airstream to propel herself up the mountain, the deafening roar of the crowd ringing in her ears, the left wing of her sail trembling like an injured bird's wing.

As she neared the cliff in the forest, she sunk lower and lower until she was flying a few feet above the treetops. She aimed the flying machine toward an opening in a fig grove, swinging her legs out beneath her. She descended through the tree canopy and felt herself lurched upwards, a shooting pain slicing through her neck. There she hung, bobbing in space, her wings caught on the treetops, her hands losing their grip on the base. She kicked her legs and tugged the flying machine toward the cliff face, reaching for the safety of the ground. There was a loud tearing sound, and she bounced a meter closer to the earth. She pulled again, this time wrapping her foot around a root. Another tug and the whole apparatus came scraping through the trees, and she fell on her side with the flying machine on top of her. She pushed the thing off of her and saw the fabric of the entire left wing flapping in the night air with the frame completely exposed and the right wing torn in three places. Sloane slipped out of her dress so she didn't tear that, too, and secured the base over her hips so her hands were free. With her belly suspended above the ground, she began to climb.

It felt like several hours had passed by the time she reached the top of the cliff. She pushed the shredded machine over the edge and pulled herself up, allowing herself two full seconds to recover on her back in the grass. She sprang up, pulled the tattered flying machine into its hiding spot, and secured the palm tarp. Then she grabbed her chemise from where she'd stashed it and headed in the direction of the rose garden to retrieve Saffron and her travel cloak from the hut. She'd sleep for a few hours in the hidden cave she'd found, then get started on repairs—she'd need every second if she was going to fix the broken wings in time for her final flight tomorrow night.

Sloane reached the open embankment in the forest in record time and slowed to a walk. She pushed her head through the neck of her crumpled chemise, slid her arms through the sleeves, and tugged the nightdress over her pregnant belly. She started to move again, and a tree at the edge of the clearing began to move, too. She gasped, straining to see in the dark. Not a tree. A man.

A man who was staring straight at her.

"MAHID?"

It was Father Pierre's voice that floated to her across the clearing, her name foreign on his lips, as if he were meeting her in another lifetime and wasn't entirely sure who she was.

"Father—"

"Shh!"

He was at her side in a flash, grabbing her hand and pulling her into the thicket where the moonlight was not so bright.

"I fear I may have been followed," he whispered.

"Followed?"

"We must be quick," he said. "I saw you tonight. I know your secret. It was not the miracle I was expecting, but—"

"I'm sorry. I—"

"Sorry?" He peered at her in the darkness, looking surprised. "You do not know what you have done."

"Believe me, I know," she said. "I knew they would come for me. They're after me now, I'm sure of it."

"You do not know what you have done for the *people*," said Father Pierre. "What you have done for me, Mahid."

The priest dropped to his knees and drew Sloane's hand to his cheek. His face was wet with tears.

"Mother," he said.

"I'm not—"

"Not what I expected. But when is a miracle exactly what we expect?"

"You know I'm not actually Mary, right?"

"Are you not blessed?" he said. "You have come to point the way back to God. I cannot say I was not shocked by your duplicity, Mahid. But when I heard you speak, my heart sang with recognition of the truth. I had thought the people needed a direct connection to God through His Word. But words are merely signposts pointing to a deeper truth. Our connection to God is more direct. When we fulfill our purpose to care for the earth and all living things, we become the hands of God made manifest in this world. We become the living, breathing body of God. Have I understood you correctly?"

Sloane regarded him in the dim light. She caught a tear with the pad of her thumb and wiped it across his cheek until it had disappeared. She told Father Pierre she'd hoped the teaching might resonate with him, but it seemed that he had understood her words better than she had.

"Resonate?!" he said, taking her hands in his. "Mahid. I wish to be your disciple. I wish to follow you and spread your message throughout France, throughout the world! I wish to call you Mother if only you would accept me."

"Oh! Um, sure. I mean, I would. But—"

A branch snapped somewhere nearby, and the priest clutched Sloane's hands more tightly. "We must go," said Father Pierre, drawing himself to his feet. "We must get you out of Provence before they—"

The words seemed to catch in his throat, and then the darkness went pitch black. Sloane gasped, her breath stifled, her nostrils filling with the familiar scent of jute. Someone tried to pull her arms behind her back, but Father Pierre was pulling her in the opposite direction. She screamed, trying to free herself, and Father Pierre lost his grip. A half dozen others barked at her, and at each other, in a language she didn't understand. Even Father Pierre, whose calm, deferential voice was all but drowned out by the racket, was speaking in the strange tongue.

"*Claude os tuum!*" said a voice.

Claude os tuum, Sloane thought. Was that Latin? It sounded like Latin. LORI?

Come on, LORI.

Come on, LORI, *claude os tuum*!

But LORI was silent because LORI was gone. The Language Open Receptor Injection had worn off completely. There was no one to translate the Latin, no telling who was forcing her arms behind her back, no way of knowing who was tying her wrists with rope or what they were planning to do to her.

Thwump. Sloane heard the sound of a fist hitting flesh, and then Father Pierre was silent, too.

She felt herself being passed from one pair of hands to another. She was lifted up and hoisted onto a horse, landing hard on the pommel. Someone grabbed her hips, sliding her into position in front of him in the saddle. He wrapped his arms around her, adjusted the reigns, and helped himself to a handful of her left breast.

The horse took off through the forest, the quickening thuds of hoofbeats amplifying her pounding heart. With her eyes open inside the sack, Sloane wondered if Zacarie would keep his promise to find someone else and be happy; blind, bound, LORI-less and alone, this definitely seemed like the worst-case scenario.

·

WHEN THEY FINALLY YANKED THE sack off her head, Sloane was inside the church sanctuary back in Toulon, kneeling before the altar on a cold, stone floor with her hands still bound behind her back. She squinted in the dim light, her eyes adjusting after a disorienting hour's ride in pitch blackness. Now, she saw only white. She blinked, trying to bring her vision into focus, and realized she was looking at the flowing white silk of a clergyman's robes. She looked up. The Bishop of Toulon was smiling down at her.

"*Est eius*," said a nervous voice behind her. "*Estne, dominus meus?*"

The bishop nodded to whoever had spoken, closed his eyes, and tilted his head back as if basking in some private moment of deep satisfaction. Sloane broke into a sweat, her palms slick behind her back, her heart racing faster as the seconds ticked by. She dared a glance behind her to see the sanctuary filled with dozens of clergy in white robes. They were packed into the front pews and pouring out into the center aisle, every one of them silent and staring. Her stomach jumped, limbs flooding with a fear so acute it would have been paralyzing had she not had so much practice flying in the face of her fear.

Escape was unlikely, but trying to talk her way out of this seemed downright impossible, so she scanned the sanctuary looking for exits. The narthex at the far end of the church was out—there was no way she could make it past all those men. But the South Transept should have an exit. Her hands were bound, but her legs were free. If she could just—

Slap!

Sloane flinched and ducked her head, a stinging pain blooming across her left cheek.

"*Vide sanctitatem eius,*" said the man who'd struck her. Goddamn it, what had he said? She couldn't understand the content, but she recognized the voice. It was the breast grabber who'd pressed his erection into her tailbone the whole ride here from Saphir. Now he grabbed her by the hair and wrenched her head back, sending a spasm of pain through her neck.

"Dearest Father Gideon," said the bishop in French. "If you must instruct our guest, pray do so in a language she understands. Perhaps the language she uses for oration would be most familiar to her."

Switching to French, Father Gideon told Sloane to "face forward" and keep her eyes upon "His Most Holy Holiness." When she complied, he let go of her hair with a firm push to the back of her head, and she fell forward into the bishop, her face in his crotch. The bishop caught Sloane by the shoulders and steadied her on her knees, his robes emitting a stale bouquet of incense and mildew. She stifled a gag.

"Where did you find her?" asked the bishop.

"In the forest outside Saphir, Your Most Excellent Excellency," said Gideon. "We followed the village priest, and he led us right to her."

The bishop stared at Gideon, unblinking. He reached into his robes and withdrew a white silk handkerchief, which he dabbed along his hairline beneath the red skull cap he now wore in place of his *mitre*.

"Pierre knew where to find this woman and led you there?"

"No, Your Most Gracious Grace. Father Pierre was supposed to be guarding the church while the others stormed the cathedral, but I saw him slip away toward the city gate. We followed him northwest along the road to Saphir then tracked him into the forest. Thus we found him on foot in the woods, except he was not on foot so much as on his knees with his face buried between the bitch's legs."

The bishop stared at Gideon in disbelief.

"That man was on his knees in supplication," Sloane heard herself say.

Gideon drew back to strike her again, but the bishop stopped him with the slightest movement of his index finger. He said they would discuss her relationship with Father Pierre, among other things, when their ceremony here was complete.

"I have no relationship with this 'Father Pierre,'" said Sloane. "If he is the man in the forest, I have never seen him before tonight."

The bishop studied Sloane for a few beats. Then he turned, ascended the altar, and took his place behind the lectern to address the assembled crowd.

"For many months now, the Holy Spirit has called me to pursue this escaped criminal across Provence. After much arduous searching, I have finally found her. God told me she was not just a common whore but a Huguenot conspirator, a radical heretic, and a salacious mimic of our Divine Mother. I only regret not having found her before she could pollute the minds and hearts of our most vulnerable flock." Gesturing toward the stained-glass windows that faced the town square, the bishop bemoaned the poor people sleeping in the streets throughout the city, lying like sacrificial lambs to offer their souls to this fraudulent impersonator. But he said his brothers should not fear, for on the morrow they would reclaim the hearts of the people. They would show them 'Mother Mary' without her wings—show the people this heretic for the imposter that she was. When her sentence was carried out, the people's hearts would rejoice to know they were protected by the Church, who annihilates all evil from the world in the name of Christ Jesus. They should rejoice! For in a few short hours, the woman they saw before them now would be hanging from the gallows.

Sloane sweated through her chemise, the bishop's death sentence ringing in her ears. She pictured her face superimposed over Bertrand's and watched herself writhe in the pillory. She saw herself swinging from the gallows and imagined flames licking her bare feet. And then, with a sickening whoosh, she saw the fire swallowing her and the baby whole.

The bishop held the tip of a lit candle inside a golden incense burner, sending a spiral of fragrant smoke curling into the air. He moved toward Sloane, swinging the smoking burner on its chain, making small circles at first, then launching the thing wider and wider, as if he were manipulating a medieval flail. Sloane held her breath, bracing for impact. But when the bishop reached her side, he swung the burner around her body, bathing her in the smoke as if trying to neutralize a bad odor. Her relief was short-lived when she realized it wasn't compassion that prevented the bishop from harming her, but showmanship—hanging a bruised, beaten woman already halfway in the grave would not be nearly as crowd-pleasing as watching the swift, stunning descent of a perfectly intact, glowingly pregnant beauty.

"Make your confession," said the bishop, "and though we cannot prevent the death of the body, we can forgive and bless the soul so you do not spend eternity in Hell. For the wages of sin without confession is death, and those who sin without confessing will suffer the punishment of eternal destruction."

The bishop was the one speaking, but the voice of condemnation in Sloane's head belonged to the man formally known as her dad. If Harry Burrows were here, his response to her death sentence would be something along the lines of "Well, what did you expect?" He'd say this whole 'punishment of eternal destruction' thing was apt. In typical Sloanie fashion, she'd not only made things worse for herself, but for everyone else. *Lotta good your freak memory did you in the end*, Harry would say, and she had to admit he had a point. It occurred to Sloane that she could just confess. Condemn herself, get it over with. You know what? She *should* confess. She should confess that she was a walking tornado that destroyed everything in its path.

"Such sacred words will not be familiar to a woman like you," the bishop was saying, "but that verse is from the Book of Romans, chapter six, verse twenty-three. Unlike your blasphemous statements from the rooftop tonight, the words I speak are the words of God, who offers you the gift of eternal life in Christ Jesus our Lord. Confess your sins before these witnesses, and though you have destroyed your own life through sin and heresy and attempted to destroy the Church through conspiracy and lies, still God gives the sinner the chance to redeem her soul."

If the bishop was going to use the Bible to justify Sloane's death sentence, he could at least get the goddamn verse right. Those "sacred words" were not from Romans 6:23, but some confluence of Romans 6:23 and Thessalonians 1:9, as if the bishop had jammed the two passages together and made some heavy edits while he was at it. Almost as if he were mucking up the verse on purpose to coerce her confession.

Holy shit.

The bishop probably used that phony verse to coerce a lot of confessions. She bet he'd whispered it to Bertrand just before the young woman had condemned herself to death, using that bullshit verse to convince her that self-annihilation was her only hope for salvation. And come to think of it, wasn't that exactly what Harry had done to Sloane? From the earliest age, he'd convinced her that the way to get love and acceptance was by hating her memory, which meant hating herself. Sloane had held up her end of the bargain, but no matter how good she got at suppressing her gift, Harry still resented her; he could never forgive the unforgivable crime of being born extraordinary.

But Sloane didn't need Harry's acceptance anymore. She didn't need his love. Because she remembered something Bertrand never had the chance to learn.

She remembered what she was made of.

She was not a walking tornado that destroyed everything in its path. She was *not*. She was the coming spring. The invisible benevolence that rolled back dead underbrush, revived rotting limbs, and restored parched earth so something new could take root. She was a savior born to prevent the past from creating a toxic future. A Hero sent to transform this timeline and give birth to something new. Such sacred words *were* familiar to a woman like her because she remembered the real verse from reading Zacarie's Bible in the rose garden. She remembered other things, too. Like the rules of confession from the day Bertrand had died: if she confessed like the bishop wanted, she would automatically be put to death, but if she refused to confess, her life might be spared. She remembered she hadn't been the miracle Father Pierre had been expecting, but he'd still wanted to call her Mother. But mostly she remembered the reason she'd been chosen as the 23rd Hero in the first place: because she remembered everything.

"Repeat after me," said the bishop. "'Bless me, Father, for I have sinned…'"

"I have not sinned," she said. "The Mother of God has nothing to confess."

The bishop stared at her, his eyes shifting to the crowd and back, as if he couldn't quite believe what he'd just heard and was waiting for corroboration from the audience. "Do you mean to tell me that even now, bereft of your 'wings,' with nothing standing between you and the fires of Hell but a single directive from me, that you still purport to be Mary, the Mother of God?"

"I am bereft of nothing. I will fly again when God wills it."

The bishop sounded like a honking goose when he laughed. Gideon laughed, too, but only a few of the other priests joined in.

"But *demoiselle*," said the bishop. "How will you accomplish such a flight without your wings?"

"I will be swept up into the sky on the breath of the wind, propelled by the will of God," she said. "I tell you truthfully that I am the one guided by the divine to destroy the old ways. I am here to bring about a new Earth." It was the truth. She felt it in every fiber of her being.

"If you are the Mother of God, free yourself. Unbind your hands and fly back up to Heaven right now."

"It is my Father's will that you be shown mercy. He is giving you the chance to free me of your own volition so you can be forgiven."

"So that *I* can be forgiven?"

"Yes. So that you can be forgiven for the ill treatment of your Divine Mother. Among other things."

The bishop went pale. Gideon asked for permission to "silence the whore," but the bishop suggested Gideon silence himself. Dabbing his brow with his handkerchief, the bishop again demanded her confession, for the wages of sin without confession was death, and those who sinned without confessing would suffer the punishment of eternal destruction.

"You might also seek forgiveness for your ill treatment of the Word of God," Sloane said.

"*Demoiselle?*"

"My name is Mary," she said, "and that was not Romans 6:23. You said, 'For the wages of sin without confession is death—'"

"So I did—"

"—but the verse reads, 'For the wages of sin is death, but the free gift of God is eternal life in Christ Jesus our Lord.' You have confused Romans 6:23 with Thessalonians 1:9. You have mixed them together."

The bishop turned white, but his burn scars retained their purplish hue, his face like spoiled fruit dropped in the snow.

"I implore His Most Gracious Graciousness to let me teach this cunt a lesson," said Gideon.

"Out," said the bishop, his voice echoing through the sanctuary. The whole congregation seemed to freeze, and in the ensuing silence Sloane heard Gideon shuffling dejectedly down the center aisle toward the narthex.

"To what, *demoiselle*, might we attribute this intimate knowledge you hold of the Word of God? Have you found such passages useful in your plotting against the Church?"

"I know every word uttered by my Son," Sloane heard herself say. "I know who has recorded my Son's teachings in good faith, and who has altered His teachings to serve their own purpose. Your holy book is rife with both, for I know every word of that, too."

The bishop was the only one who laughed this time. "She claims to have memorized the Holy Bible," he told the audience. "A feat the Pope himself could not hope to accomplish in a lifetime!"

"A divine being has no need to memorize. The Word of God is accessible to me at any time."

"I see," said the bishop. "So, if I were to select a verse—any verse—from the thirty-one *thousand* verses that make up the Holy Bible, you would be so kind as to recite it back to me?"

Despite the enormity of the number, the impossibility of the task, Sloane found herself fighting a smile. The Bishop of Toulon wanted to play the Game of Memory.

"I can recite any verse of your choosing," she said. "And once I have proven my divinity, you may redeem yourself in our Father's eyes by releasing me."

"But of course, *demoiselle*. Prove you are divine, and you will not only be free to go—I will get down on my knees and worship you myself."

"Give me the verse."

He regarded her coolly for several moments. "The Book of Luke. Chapter One, verse forty-eight."

The church fell away, and Sloane was back in the rose garden, sitting beneath the oak trees, the midday sun warming her skin. Zacarie placed the open Bible in her lap. She could see the Book of Luke in her mind's eye, though she hadn't even skimmed verse forty-eight in chapter one. But she had turned the page the verse was printed on, and it was enough. She froze the memory, zoomed in on the words, and made them hers.

"And Mary said, 'My soul magnifies the Lord, and my spirit rejoices in God my Savior, for he has looked on the humble estate of his servant. For behold, from now on, all generations will call me blessed.'"

Several priests in the first pew fact-checked her reading, the speediest among them nodding to the bishop—every word was perfect.

The bishop was silent for several moments before congratulating Sloane on her lucky guess. He wondered if her luck would hold for the Song of Songs, chapter eight, verses six and seven.

"Set me as a seal on your heart, as a seal on your arm; for stern as death is love, relentless as the nether world is devotion; its flames are a blazing fire. Deep waters cannot quench love, nor floods sweep it away."

The bishop looked at the floor. The verse checkers looked at each other. Right again.

"Psalm nineteen," said the bishop. "Chapter one."

She hadn't even skimmed the Psalms. She'd skipped ahead from Esther to Proverbs. But she opened her mouth and said, "The heavens declare the glory of God, and the sky above proclaims His handiwork." She knew it was perfect. She knew it even before a fact checker confirmed it, before all the priests began murmuring at once, before they spilled from the pews and gathered around her, calling out verse after verse, their excitement and anxiety mounting.

"First Corinthians," said one man, "14:33."

"For God is not the author of confusion but of—"

"John 18:36," said another.

"My kingdom is not of this world—"

"Leviticus 24:16," said a third.

"Whoever utters the name of the Lord—"

Panicked protests began to drown out the requests. She is a witch. She is Mary. Kill her now. Let her go. A terrible mistake! Think of your Holy

Father's wrath if we burn the Mother of God! We must release her at once!

The bishop pushed through the crowd. Someone was helping her, he said.

"Not I!" said a priest.

"Nor I!" said another.

"It could not be me," said a third. "I have not read Leviticus *or* Corinthians."

"She is cheating," said the bishop. "Someone is feeding her the answers, or she has written down the verses somewhere hidden, so she can read them."

"Read them?"

"But a woman!"

"Check for paper on her person. Ink on her skin."

"But Your Grace—"

"*Check her.*"

There were hands everywhere. They slipped inside her chemise, cupped her ass, swept beneath the band of her underwear. The priests performed this task in near silence save the few who dared whisper in her ear. "Pardon us, Mother," said one. "Forgive us," said another. When the pat down was over and the search fruitless, the bishop grabbed Sloane by the arm and wrenched her to her feet, ignoring the protests of the few who dared question him.

"Thessalonians 1:6," he said, droplets of spittle landing on her lips and cheek.

"God considers it just to repay with affliction those who afflict you," she said.

"That is right," he said, tightening his grip. "And you, *demoiselle*, have afflicted us greatly."

"That is what the book says, but those are not my Father's words."

The bishop slapped her face. The others scattered as if he'd slapped them.

"Make your confession!"

Sloane felt blood pooling at the corner of her mouth. She looked into his eyes. She said, "I confess I am the woman clothed with the sun, with the moon under my feet and my head crowned with twelve stars. The great sign that appeared in Heaven was me."

"Silence!"

The bishop pulled Sloane across the pulpit to the confessional, setting off another round of quarrelling among the priests. Some thought she should be released immediately, while others thought she should be put to death immediately, but they all agreed that putting her in the confessional achieved neither objective. The bishop seemed deaf to their protests. He opened the little closet and pushed Sloane inside, slamming the door and bolting it from the outside. The confessional was cramped and stuffy and smelled like a men's locker room, with a small bench and a sliding window that separated the priest's side of the confessional from the sinner's. Sloane kicked the door. She shoved it with her shoulder, then her hip, but it wouldn't budge. She looked for something sharp that might fray the rope around her wrists, but there was nothing.

Out in the sanctuary, the bishop was ordering the priests to vacate the church and prepare the gallows for morning.

"But she has proven herself!" one man said. "She is divine!"

"She is a witch!" said another.

"The Devil Himself," said a third.

"But if you are wrong, you risk burning the Mother of God!"

"Not to mention the Christ child inside her!"

"Christ child or not, she is *with child*. The law demands we delay her sentencing until the child comes."

The argument culminated in a loud crash, metal against stone, the final symbol of a symphony. There was another crash, then another, and she pictured the bishop throwing the incense burner and sacrificial goblets to the stone floor until every man had rushed from the sanctuary.

Every man but him.

The bishop flung open the confessional door and pushed inside, pinning Sloane against the wall.

"Confess," he said.

"I confess that I am Mary, Mother of God."

"You dare to impersonate the Holy Mother, defiling her with your witchcraft and sorcery. I do not know how you know those passages, but it is the Devil's work, and I shall not stand for it in my Church."

Sloane pumped her knee into his groin, but he was standing too close, and she only succeeded in lodging her thigh between his. The bishop shoved her hard against the wall, holding her by the shoulders. He told her to look upon him. When she didn't, he grabbed her chin and forced her head back until she did. "You recoil at the sight of me as all women do. But I was not born with these scars, *demoiselle*. They were left behind by another beauty who had succumbed to the temptations of the Devil. Through heresy and witchcraft, she sentenced herself to death by hanging and fire. I saved her soul as I will save yours, but I was standing too close to the gallows when I blessed her. As the flames consumed her body, she tore off a piece of her own flesh and threw it in my face."

His grip softened around her chin. The rest of him grew hard.

"There was a time, before then, when you might have looked upon me as a man."

The bishop stroked her cheek and traced her lip with his thumb. He said he knew she would not be cruel to him, for her beauty negated all cruelty. He pressed his thumb inside her mouth, and she tasted metal and tobacco and thought she might vomit. Fighting every natural instinct she had, Sloane closed her lips around his thumb and sucked. The bishop's eyes went wide, and a gasp of pleasure caught in the back of his throat. "Good girl," he said. "I knew you would be a very good girl." Sloane waited until his eyes had fluttered closed to bite down as hard as she could.

He cried out, whipping his hand away, and she pushed past him, ducking beneath his arm and slamming the door open.

"Cunt!"

He caught her around the belly and pulled her back inside, slamming her against the wall and holding her there. She felt him behind her, fumbling with his robes, drawing them to the side. She tried to scream, but she couldn't scream, she couldn't breathe, she was suffocating.

"Like you, that whore was reluctant to confess her sins to the Lord. But when I injected her with the Holy Spirit the night before her death, she gave her confession to me. Just as you will give it to me."

Sloane kicked her leg out behind her and made contact with the bishop's thigh. He slammed her against the wall, knocking her head into the wood so hard she saw stars. His hand was around her throat. He said he would have her confession one way or another. She could feel his erection against the back of her thigh, then a rush of air as he lifted the hem of her chemise. He yanked her underwear down just as the door to the confessional swung open. The bishop flew off her back and landed hard on the chancel, rolling down the steps to the stone floor beneath.

Gasping for breath, Sloane emerged from the confessional to see a small man crouched over the bishop with his ear to the old man's heart. His robes weren't white like the other priests. He wore no skull cap over his shaved head. And when he looked up, his dark eyes were like burning obsidian. But more startling than the intensity of his gaze was the familiarity of his face; even without his brilliant smile, Sloane would have recognized Enkh anywhere.

The monk flew to her side. He touched her head, checking for blood. Enkh pulled off the outer layer of his saffron robes and placed the shell over Sloane's head, pulling the robes down to cover her. Then, he drew her into his arms and held her. Sloane clung to him, her teeth chattering, her whole body shaking with adrenaline as she said his name over and over again, and how was he here, and had Saffron let him through the portal?

Enkh started to reply, but a sharp thwack rocked his body before he could make a sound, and he collapsed against Sloane with a grunt. The bishop was standing behind Enkh, his head bloodied, his arm suspended in the air as if he'd just thrown a javelin.

Enkh spun around to face the bishop, seemingly oblivious to the golden dagger now sticking out of his kidney. Sloane shrieked. The bishop lunged for Enkh again, but the monk leaped into the air as if he'd launched himself off a trampoline. In one fluid motion, Enkh wrapped his legs around the bishop's shoulders, grabbed his head, and with an elegant snap, broke the old man's neck. Enkh landed on his feet. The bishop slumped to the floor beneath the altar, dead.

Sloane screamed, and Enkh covered her mouth. "The others are coming," he said in English. "Now, you take the knife out of my back."

"No!" said Sloane. "You need a doctor, I can't—"

"Take the knife out now," said Enkh, positioning himself so the dagger lined up with Sloane's hands. She gripped the handle, and a rush of blood accompanied the blade as it exited Enkh's flesh. He took the dagger from her and cut the rope that bound her wrists. Then he told her to sit on top of the communion table, shoving the dagger and pieces of rope into her hands.

"Enkh, you're hurt. We have to—"

"Put your hands behind your back and pretend they are still bound. Hide the dagger at your breast."

"What?"

"Make them think you killed the bishop," he said. "Make them think you killed me. If they believe you overpowered two men while your hands were still bound, they will believe you have the power to kill them, too. It will keep them away from you until morning."

"What do you mean, until morning? What am I supposed to—?"

Enkh's eyes rolled back in his head, and he collapsed to the floor next to the bishop.

"Enkh!"

Sloane knelt beside him, shaking him. A dark pool of blood was seeping through his underrobes. His eyes fluttered open. He said when dawn broke, she could use the gift he'd brought her. Look in your pocket, he said.

Sloane slipped her hand inside the left pocket of the monk robes and felt a smooth, spherical case. She pulled it out by the handle, the silver orb gleaming in the candlelight like an oversized Christmas tree ornament.

"Saffron," she said. "Saffron 3.0?"

"He thought you might need it," said Enkh. "Third generation."

"He thought…Bastian thought?! Is he okay? Does he know that I'm—?"

"Make your final speech to the people in the square," Enkh said. "It does not matter what the priests believe. But the people must believe you are Mary. Speak to them in Provençal. *Make* them believe, Sloane. When the sun comes out, you use Saffron. You go home."

"But—"

"They come now."

"But—"

"I will leave this body now."

"No!"

Sloane heard the priests outside the nape, the doors opening and shutting.

"Sit on the table now."

Sloane climbed on top of the communion table. She removed Saffron 3.0 from her case and tucked the glass sphere inside her robes. She slid the bishop's dagger blade-down inside her bra, the strap holding it in place. Then she put her hands behind her back, twisting the broken pieces of rope to make it look like her hands were still bound.

"I'm sorry," she said.

"No sorry," said Enkh, looking up at her. "Seventy-four years in this body. Even before you were born, it was always my Mission…to help you."

He closed his eyes.

"Enkh…"

He smiled. "Such a disrespectful daughter to call your father by his given name." He opened his eyes and looked at her, smiling wider. "Do not be so shocked. Be happy, as I am happy."

"You…"

"So happy to return to your mother. My love. My Thida."

The priests poured down the center aisle like the tide rushing in. By the time they reached the front pews, Enkh—Sloane's real father—had breathed his last breath of God.

The priests stumbled to a stop before the altar, gaping at the bodies sprawled beneath it, and at Sloane, bound and triumphant on top of the table. From the group burst incoherent fits of sound, as if they couldn't decide whether to scream or weep. Some did weep. Some fell to their knees. Others backed away as if they would bolt from the church and never return.

"Look upon those who would defile their Holy Mother," said Sloane, nodding to the bodies on the floor. "And so death spread to all men because all sinned."

The priest who was crawling up the steps to lie prostrate at her feet was Father Gideon. He said she was the Mother of God, and that he'd believed in her all along—he'd just been too afraid of His Most Holy Holiness to say so.

"I believe!" said another, joining Father Gideon on the ground.

"And I!" said a third.

"Fools!" said a fourth. "Here you see His Holiness murdered in cold blood! What further proof need you of Satan?"

The majority remained unconvinced of her divinity but convinced of her terrible powers. They agreed she should be locked in the confessional until morning so no one else ended up dead. But when she refused to follow their commands to get down from the table and enter the confessional, they were at a loss to enforce this plan; those willing to touch her refused to lock her up, and those who wanted to lock her up refused to touch her.

Recalling Enkh's instructions, Sloane told them to abandon their pointless debates, for God's Will was already decided: they would take her to the gallows at dawn and she would go willingly. To the small but vocal minority who protested this plan, she said be of glad heart, for it was her Father's will that she be returned to Him the way her Son had. She let the intensity of her gaze penetrate their hearts with fear, her eyes like burning obsidian—her father's eyes. "If any of you dare to come near me before I step inside the hangman's noose—if any of you are foolish enough to touch me—I promise you will end up dead like them."

The priests backed out of the church, tripping over their robes and dragging Father Gideon and the other believers from the sanctuary kicking and screaming. When they were gone, Sloane untwisted the rope from around her wrists and set the pieces on the table. She lay down beside Enkh, holding him until his body cooled, recalibrating every precious memory she had of her father. She remembered the first night she'd seen him standing outside her apartment building, his bright smile a beacon in the darkness, his deep-set eyes so like hers. Sloane's skin was lighter than Thida's not because of Harry, but because of Enkh. She remembered the way he'd opened her bedroom door at Basecamp and sent her up the tower into the arms of the one who would comfort her. She remembered the way he'd hugged her and Simon a little too long at the Christmas party, and how, for a single, fleeting moment in time, the three of them had been together as a family.

When Sloane had run out of tears, she slid the monk robes to her waist and unfastened her bra. Holding the dagger in her right hand, she reached over her shoulder and pressed the tip of the blade into her skin, carving a half moon over her left shoulder blade. It took several tries, but she finally felt blood trickling down her back. When she was finished with the left side, she started on the right, trying to make the cuts even. She hoped the wounds were big enough to be visible all the way across the square. When the blood had dried, she covered herself and waited, with the bodies, for the dawn.

HEAVY RAIN PELTED THE CHURCH rooftop, dulling the roar of the crowd from outside. Inside the church, Sloane could hear a priest's booming voice cut through the din, silencing the people gathered in the square. For the third time that morning, she listened to a sharp snapping sound, followed by a collective gasp, followed by the monotonous drone of the priest. When he was finished, the doors of the church opened, and a group of priests peered into the sanctuary. With Saffron 3.0 and the dagger tucked inside her robes, and her hands 'bound' behind her back, Sloane made her way down the aisle like a bride marching away from her groom, a woman choosing death over love. It was time.

She approached the open doorway. Throngs of people stood in the rain, their hands shielding their eyes from the mist. The cloud cover was dark and opaque, without a single ray of sunlight to charge Saffron 3.0. Across the square, a stone fountain was framed by a backdrop of wooden gallows, which looked like long-beaked birds around a watering hole. On the first gallows hung Father Gideon. Next to him, the wet bodies of the two other priests who had believed in Mother Mary spun in slow circles above the crowd. On the last gallows was an empty noose waiting to be filled.

Sloane stepped through the doorway and the people spotted her. A roar rippled across the crowd. She was pummeled in the chest with something hard and wet. Raw egg and remnants of shell slid down her robes, and she ducked and covered, dodging the projectile turnips that followed. The priests pushed into the crowd, trying to clear a path toward the gallows, but the square was packed and their progress slow. Sloane was jostled and shoved, and in the chaos, she became separated from the priests and passed down a gauntlet of limbs straight toward the gallows. Twice she was lifted clear off the ground as if she were body surfing at a concert, and with her hands 'bound' behind her back, she had no way to shield herself from the stinging rain and warm spit that splattered against her skin the whole way.

Filthy and short of breath, Sloane reached the fountain and climbed onto the ledge, the empty gallows looming above her. She spotted the priests near the church, making little headway against a crowd that kept churning ever forward, endlessly seeking a better view of her. She scanned the crowd for a glimpse of Father Pierre, of Zacarie or Alona, but every face she saw was the face of a stranger.

Over the din of booing and heckling, Sloane shouted in Provençal, the peasant tongue: "Listen not to those who deny me! I have flown on the wings of the Holy Spirit! I speak to you with the voice of God, for I am the Mother of God, and none other!" The crowd jeered, and the priests pushed their way through it, shoving forward to silence her.

She said only the faithless need proof, but if they were faithless, they would have their proof now. Angling her back to the crowd, she showed the people how the clergy had bound her hands. Then, she wrenched her hands apart, threw the pieces of rope to the ground, and swept her arms skyward as if she'd unbound her hands through divine will. At precisely that moment, the dark clouds rolled eastward across the bay and the pelting rain lightened to a mist, giving the awestruck crowd the impression that Sloane's powers could not only be used to untie knots with her mind, but to control the weather as well.

"They tell you my wings are fake, and thus I am a fake!" she said, pointing to the clergy. "I tell you they have ripped the wings from my body, raping me and defiling me! See here where they have torn your Mother's flesh!" She turned her back to the crowd and pulled her robes to her waist, revealing the bloodied dagger wounds she'd given herself in the church. The people cried out in horror. "See where they have cut off her wings!" they said. "Her wings were real!"

Sloane pulled up her robes. She reminded the people she was there to point the way back to God. What she offered was a direct connection to their own divinity, here and now. When they fulfilled their purpose to care for the Earth and all living things, they became the hands of God made manifest in this world—the living, breathing body of God here on Earth. Do not be tempted by any other purpose than this one, she said, for their one and only purpose, now and forevermore, was to be stewards of the Earth.

The rain stopped altogether, and a single ray of morning sunlight broke through the clouds. Sloane withdrew Saffron 3.0, flipped her switch to ON, and held her in the light.

"Back away!" shouted a priest.

"It is Satan's evil eye!"

People backed away from the fountain, sending worried murmurs rippling across the crowd. Two of the priests were making headway now, still halfway across the square but moving faster through a newly pliant crowd. Sloane's heart pounded as she willed Saffron 3.0 to hurry up and open the freaking portal already. Against the stillness of the crowd, she noticed movement in her peripheral vision. Three heads were tipping to the side in unison. When ears met shoulders, the progression reversed, three heads lifting slowly, synchronously, as if each person was counting to the same beat. As if these three people had been trying to get her attention.

Father Pierre looked bruised and bloodied, but he was alive, his head bare without his priest's cap, his arms around Alona for anyone to see. Alona clung to him, her mouth frozen in a silent cry. Zacarie stood next to his parents, and when his eyes met Sloane's, his face split into a mask of pain.

"To you who have loved me well, know that I return your love, and that I will never forget you."

Zacarie's hand flew to his mouth, but if it was to hold back a sob or touch the lips that would never again meet hers, she couldn't be sure. In his eyes, she saw the rose garden and the little hut he'd made her, a practice structure for the real home he'd hoped to build. Now, as the priests advanced, and Saffron 3.0 grew brighter in her hand, Sloane remembered Saffron 2.0 still tucked inside her travel cloak back in the hut. Her failure to retrieve Saffron before she'd been captured had not been a failure at all. Zacarie would know where to find her. His father would know how to use her.

"There is a man among you today who will lead you back to my Son by leading you back to the Earth. You will know this man because he will carry an orb like this one, which I gifted to him inside a holy cloak hidden in a garden of roses. He cut open the cloak and found a glowing reminder of God, who shines His light upon His people as the sun shines upon the Earth. This man understands his purpose and yours. Listen to him, and heed him, and you will always be connected to God. The stewards of the Earth who follow the man with the orb will never go to Hell but live in Heaven on Earth."

Father Pierre did not tilt his head to the side this time. He tilted his head forward in a nod of assent, ending one world and starting another. The resistance was over. Sloane was passing Father Pierre the torch of a new cause, and Father Pierre was reaching out to take it.

Sloane heard the sound of a distant wave crashing toward shore, and she lifted Saffron 3.0 above her head. "My children! If I die on the gallows today, you may call me *sorcière*. But if I disappear into the sky, have faith that I am Mother Mary, carried back to my Father on the invisible wings of the Holy Spirit! Save yourselves from Hell and spend your lives in Heaven, being stewards of the Earth!"

She'd sort of hoped the people would cheer, or if not cheer, at least get down on their knees and pray or something. But the crowd remained silent and still, and she couldn't tell if it was because they were unmoved by her words, still unsure of who she really was, or simply spellbound by the glowing orb that was quickly becoming hot to the touch. She scanned the air above the crowd, watching for the sky to break apart, willing the portal to open and let her through. Several more seconds ticked by, and she grew uneasy with the alien feeling that she had forgotten something.

Zacarie's voice rang out across the square, confirming her suspicion.

"Mahid! Look out!"

A priest ambushed Sloane and pulled her backward into the fountain. Saffron 3.0 flew out of her hand just as the sky broke open above the crowd, sending a rush of wind tearing across the square. Saffron 3.0 smashed against the lip of the fountain, the glass shattering with the impact, giving Sloane less than a minute before the portal would close. She grabbed her assailant by the wrists and squatted low, maneuvering her left leg behind his right. She slipped and slid around the fountain's slick bottom until the hem of the priest's robe gave her a foothold. Letting go of his wrists, she grabbed the priest behind the knees and toppled him into the water with a splash. She scrambled over the priest and onto the lip of the fountain and leaped into the sky.

PART 4

SECONDS LATER, SAFFRON SPAT HER into the air above a lush, tropical lagoon, slowed her descent mid-air, and lowered her into the crystalline water with a gentle splash. Sloane wriggled out of Enkh's robes, overcome with a ferocious thirst, and gulped the purest water she had ever tasted—fresher than the forest streams in sixteenth-century France. She bathed herself as best she could, scrubbing away the saliva, raw egg, and blood with the sleeves of Enkh's robes. Then she scrubbed her chin, her neck, every godforsaken place on her body the bishop had touched or almost touched, wishing it was possible to wash away every memory of him, too.

Sloane spread the sopping monk robes out on the grassy bank and lay down on top of them, the sun beating down with a delicious heat. She felt the baby move, and she wept with relief. To the comforting din of buzzing insects and jungle birdsong, she fell into a deep sleep.

#   #   #

When she woke, Sloane didn't know what day or time it was any more than she knew where in the world Saffron had dropped her. From her hunger and thirst, she guessed she'd slept for several days. She dressed, drank, and ate her fill of ripe durian fruit before moving west through the jungle. Soon, she came to a clearing. Across it, a curious structure stood among the trees. It wasn't a building, exactly, but as she moved closer, she could tell it was human-made. A monument of some sort. Every square inch of the structure—the base, the legs, the spiraling staircase—was covered in decorative roses.

It was the tower. Except the door she'd walked through when she'd first climbed the tower was gone. It seemed Basecamp itself was gone, though Sloane had never gotten a clear view of what the compound looked like from the outside.

Sloane stepped onto the winding, wooden staircase, tiptoeing over a tapestry of fresh, pink-and-yellow rose petals that had been sprinkled across the steps. Garlands of roses hung from the railings and rafters of each landing, and someone had arranged bouquets in blown glass vases on every flight. She skipped steps, her heart thumping with excitement, stopping only once to arrange a bright, fuchsia rose behind her ear. Then she smoothed Enkh's robes over her pregnant belly and climbed the final flight to the top of the tower.

A sea of limestone karsts reached toward the horizon like frozen waves, every facet of every peak clear and sharp in the pristine mountain air. It was ten degrees cooler up here, and a refreshing breeze set to work drying her sweat-dampened robes. Across the viewing platform, a staircase wound its way into a little blue treehouse that looked exactly as she remembered it. And on the bench, sitting in Bastian's spot, was a young man. He was tall and lean, but he was sitting hunched over with his hands tucked oddly beneath his legs as if trying to make himself smaller. From the angle of the sun, it couldn't be later than 6 p.m., but he was already dressed for sleep. Above his silk pajama pants, a white, sleeveless T-shirt revealed protruding collarbones and wiry arms. He had a thick beard, and his hair hung in long, tangled clumps around his shoulders. A pair of dark, purplish circles beneath his eyes enhanced the impression of a man who was not a resident of the tower, but a prisoner condemned to some terrible fate Sloane couldn't fathom. And yet…

It was him.

There were as many versions of each moment in time as there were stars in the sky, but Saffron had brought them together again, in the same timeline, and it was nothing short of a miracle. It took less than a second of looking at him—even a hopeless him—for Sloane's heart to concede the contest that had never been a contest at all; every moment of confused temptation with

Zacarie, and even the honest love she'd grown to feel for Zacarie, retreated into the folds of her memory, never to confuse her again. Here was her man. It had always been, would always be, Bastian.

Sloane took a step forward, and Bastian looked up, startled.

Since the moment she'd left him in the portal room, she'd longed for those eyes, for perfect slate gray instead of green. But when Bastian's eyes met hers, Sloane saw that all the light and longing had gone out of them. Only the pain remained, his hard stare like a seawall he'd built to contain the storm raging inside.

Bastian stared at Sloane for a long moment. Then, with a sigh so heavy it caught on his vocal cords, he fixed his gaze back on the sunset.

Sloane stood there in Enkh's robes, dumbstruck. In her frequent fantasies of their reunion, this was the only reaction of Bastian's she had not imagined. The evensong of the insects filled the painful silence that followed, until it occurred to Sloane that she should say something. Anything. If only she could think of something to say, other than "I'm-here-I'm-back-I-love-you-I'm-pregnant-take-me-to-bed-right-now-and-make-love-to-me-like-you-want-to-get-me-pregnant-again," which sort of seemed like overkill in response to *nothing at all.*

When she took another step toward Bastian, he scoffed.

"You're in rare form today," he said.

Glaring at her robes, he said he *knew*, okay? Enkh told Bastian he wasn't coming back, and Bastian was well aware he'd sent Enkh to his death for nothing—she didn't have to rub it in.

Bastian stood up, and Sloane gasped at the full view of his shrunken figure. He made his way toward the balcony railing, limping on his right side, muttering that she should quit griping about his appetite or lack thereof. He said if she really wanted him to start eating again, she should stop coming here and leave him the fuck alone. He said appearing in Enkh's robes was bad enough, but the pregnancy, Jesus—he hadn't thought it was possible, but she was still finding new ways to torture him. He laughed, and it was the sound of a bell that had cracked.

Sloane sat on the bench, trying to slow her pounding heart. "I'm...I'm not trying to torture you, Bastian."

"No? If we had gotten pregnant before she left, that's exactly how pregnant she'd be right now, so tell me again you're not trying to torture me."

Sloane stared at him, stupefied. He was talking to her as if the woman right in front of him was a ghost and the woman he loved was lost in the past.

Bastian squeezed the bridge of his nose. Eleanor and Poppy said he had to let her go. When he kept trying to go through the portal, they started to think he'd lost his mind. Saffron kept blowing him back against the wall, but he'd kept trying. The whole time she was gone, he'd kept trying to get to her. Sloane gave his leg a mournful glance, and he followed her gaze. Couple of broken bones, he said. He bent and straightened his leg a few times, sucking his breath through his teeth. The knee was still giving him trouble.

"But you've stopped trying to go through now. Right?"

"It's done now," he said. "When Saffron let Enkh pass through the portal, Eleanor made me promise to stop trying to go through myself. We all hoped Saffron was sending Enkh to a point in time before the anniversary of Sloane's death. We had zero intel on the drop point, no idea of the exact date he'd be going back to. We just knew that Enkh had to locate Sloane in the past before the Feast of the Assumption. June 23, 1548. If he couldn't find her, or if he was too late, it was over. She was never coming back, and I had to accept that. I had to let her go. And now…"

He trailed off, leaving Sloane's head spinning. What was he talking about, the anniversary of her death? For a moment, she wondered if he wasn't right, and she wasn't actually dead. Maybe the portal back to the future had really been the portal to some kind of afterlife, and this place, where Bastian didn't even realize she was real, was Hell. But when she pinched herself, it hurt. And as she sat there on the bench, the baby rewarded her with a strong, irrefutable kick to the bladder. Zacarie said that Heaven and Hell weren't physical places we go after death, but states of mind we experience during life. Which meant that Sloane wasn't in Hell—Bastian was.

He limped back to the bench and sat as far away from Sloane as possible. He said now that it was too late, he had to let Sloane go. And he had to call the doctor. Eleanor had made him promise to call the doctor if Sloane appeared to him again. He told Eleanor she'd stopped appearing, and for a while, she had. But happy deathiversary, he guessed, because three days after the anniversary of Sloane's death—after he'd finally given up hope of her ever coming back to him—here she was again.

Sloane watched him watch the setting sun, her heart aching. She could see past the blank expression and sunken cheeks, and what she saw still took her breath away. The vision of him in the twilight made her realize how imperfect her 'perfect' memory really was. Her mind had only approximated Bastian's beauty, creating a shadow-Bastian that, though still exquisite, was muted and two-dimensional compared to the living, breathing being sitting next to her now. Even at his worst, he was her dream come true. If she could just get closer to him, if she could touch him, she could pull him out of this delusion that she had died in the past and he was talking to some kind of ghost.

"Can I…talk to Eleanor?" she asked, inching closer to him on the bench.

"Be my guest," Bastian said. "You can start haunting her, too, and we can all go crazy together."

"Where is she?"

"With Poppy. On their honeymoon."

"Eleanor wouldn't leave you here alone…?"

"I'm not alone. I have you."

"But where is everyone else? The crew?"

"Gone."

"No."

"Dispersed."

"Since when?"

"Since the 23rd Hero made the Program obsolete."

There was no way the Program could be made obsolete. If she'd failed her Mission, the Program could have been shut down. The Nations could have rerouted all Program funding to the Hidden Valley tech companies, giving them a chance to save the planet where the Program had failed. But Saffron wouldn't have let Sloane back through the portal if she'd failed. And because she hadn't failed, the Program should still be operating. She'd expected to return to stories about the 24th Hero, and the 25th.

"How could they shut down the Program?"

"I didn't say they shut it down. I said it's obsolete."

"That's not possible."

Bastian glanced her way, looking suspicious—she'd never asked about this before.

Sloane held his gaze, waiting for his hard stare to soften into a look of realization, but when it didn't, she said she guessed it was about time she asked.

He shrugged. There were no more environmental problems to solve. They were continuing transition efforts, of course. But the 23rd Hero was the last Hero the Program sent back in time. Earth had reached 93% homeostasis.

Sloane swallowed hard, but the lump in her throat seemed fully entrenched. Not only did Bastian think she was a figment of his imagination; he'd grown completely delusional about the state of the world. She told Bastian he must be talking about France. Right? They no longer had to send Heroes back to France because *France* had reached a state of 93% homeostasis.

He was not talking about France. He insisted the 23rd Hero had rehabilitated the whole planet.

Sloane waited for the punchline, but it never came. She wiped her eyes, wishing she could wipe away the sinking feeling that Bastian had lost his mind.

"You know I can't bear it when you cry," he said.

"It's just that what you're saying is a little hard to believe. I mean, the air quality in and around France, I could see that. But she did nothing to stop arctic ice melt around Greenland. I'm sure she didn't solve the Florida problem. Not to mention droughts, forest fires, flooding, plastic—"

"Plastic was never invented."

Sloane stared at him. Blinked. "But surely fossil fuels are—"

"Are deep in the earth where they belong with no existing technology to extract them—"

"But—"

"—and laws in place to prevent the invention of that technology in the future."

"But…but landfills?"

"The only materials that exist now are biodegradable," he said. "Everything gets reused. The few things we can't reuse break down and turn to soil within a year."

"But…but everywhere?"

He nodded.

"But I didn't—" Bastian visibly stiffened at her poor choice of pronoun. "But *she* was only in Southern France. In the sixteenth century. Before internet, before anything. How could she have possibly impacted the whole world?"

He asked if she'd leave if he told her the rest.

No, Sloane thought. Never again. But she'd promise anything to keep him talking.

"I sent her to a completely different year than the year we'd trained her for," said Bastian. "I didn't realize it until after she'd gone through the portal. None of us did. When Saffron chooses a Hero, she reveals the starting year of the Mission inside a string of code that appears on the display of one of our servers. When that happened for the 23rd time, the year according to the code was 1521, so I figured it must have been 1521 when I first saw Sloane in the shipyard. The day she left, we were so focused on getting Saffron back online and getting Sloane ready for launch that we missed the change in the year completely. When the results of her Mission started coming in, they were light years beyond anything we'd predicted, and we knew something had to be off. The team ran diagnostics on Saffron and retrieved the code from the moment she came back online. That's when we discovered the change in the year. I missed it. I cared more about fucking her one last time than I did about—"

"Don't you dare put it that way—'"

"—and I sent her back there blind. And she was so good, so fucking brilliant, that she created her own Mission. And that Mission was exponentially more impactful than the one we trained her for."

She was back inside the treehouse for a moment, on the morning after their one night together, worrying that Enkh had not predicted the outcome of her Mission like he had for every other Hero. *There's something at work with your Mission that we don't understand yet,* Bastian had said. *Maybe you're going to achieve something even better than what the team has planned.* She wanted it to be true more than anything. Not just for the sake of the planet, but because it would mean Bastian wasn't completely lost to the world. And if a part of him was still hanging on, even by a thread, she would locate the thread and follow it until she found him again. She would bring him back to her.

"On the nights she flew over Toulon, most of the people in the crowd were French peasants. But Toulon was a port city and a military stronghold. There were foreigners in the crowd, too—Spanish and Moroccan merchants, Italian craftsmen, soldiers from the Ottoman army. When they returned to their countries, news of the miracle in Toulon spread across Europe and the Middle East. Mother Mary had descended from Heaven and called everyone to be stewards of the Earth. Over the next several decades, movements sprang up in Spain, Morocco, and across the Ottoman Empire. Her teachings spread across Europe, Africa, Asia, and eventually the Americas."

Sloane gripped the bench, shaking her head in disbelief. "I never thought…I mean, she thought the change would happen in France. *Maybe* it would spread throughout Europe, but only if Father Pierre—"

"Pierre du Saphir?"

Sloane's eyes bulged. "You…know about him?"

"Of course. He was the leader of the French Huguenots in Provence. Or he was until 1548. After that, the Huguenots became the staunchest supporters of her cause. In the previous timeline, the Wars of Religion in France were fought between Catholics and Huguenots. But in the new timeline, the conflict was between the Catholic Church and the Marymakers."

"The who?"

"The Marymakers. They won the conflict, which never escalated to war, and they did it with far less bloodshed than in the previous timeline. It was the Marymaker movement that spread across the world in the decades and centuries after her flights. It wasn't a religion, exactly, but that was what people who followed her teachings called themselves."

Sloane laughed. Somehow, she knew that the merriest woman she'd ever met, Alona du Merkatoria, had come up with that name. She longed to tell Bastian about her surrogate family, but he was wincing as if the sound of her laughter pained him, so she converted her laugh into a cough, gesturing for him to go on.

"In the days and weeks after she went through the portal, there were protests everywhere. Riots in some places. It was chaos here. For the first time in Program history, everyone in the world needed help transitioning to the new timeline at once. Investment bankers suddenly had farms to take care of. Pilots didn't know how to fly solar-powered airplanes. We had to give top security clearance to every agent we had so they could use the travel tunnels to reach every country on Earth. It was all hands on deck for months. A lot of the crew quit. But now…"

Like the sighting of a rare comet, a smile flickered across Bastian's face, appearing for half a miraculous second before vanishing beneath his beard.

"But now?"

"Now that the shock is over, people have really come around. It's like a different planet. When Mother Earth doesn't have to defend herself constantly, she operates the way nature, I mean she, intended. The flooding and fires aren't so extreme, now. They follow natural, ancient cycles that keep ecosystems balanced. And without all the asphalt and human-made materials creating a barrier between people and the natural world, people can feel their connection to the Earth and to the divine. It's not just an idea or a concept to believe in. It's visceral, in their faces and lungs every moment of the day. They can smell it in the air and taste it in the water. They can see it every night when they look at the stars. And from that connected state, people no longer have to be mandated to protect the Earth. They actually want to. It's easy for people to take pride in the preservation of their planet when there's so much we've gained and so little we've had to give up."

"Like what?"

"Well, we don't have cars anymore. But solar-powered trains and trolleys are everywhere, and they're super-fast—zero-carbon and free in most places. The internet is free, too, and available everywhere. It runs on wind energy and self-regulates, constantly deleting unnecessary data so we don't waste energy powering storage servers. Oh, and the whole thing shuts itself down at dusk. Most electricity shuts itself off at dusk, everywhere in the world, so people can see the night sky. Pregnancy rates are climbing, but people are getting pregnant slowly, sustainably, following Marymaker policies put in place in the nineteenth century to prevent overpopulation. Oh, and because of what she said about animal flesh, they've—"

"What did she say? About animal flesh?"

Bastian glanced at her. In a tone that was quietly reverent, he said, "Eat not of animal flesh, for God has given you every seed-bearing plant and every tree that has fruit with seed in it, that you would nourish your bodies as you nourish the body of the land."

It was perfect. The fact that five hundred years of historical telephone had not bastardized her words was no less amazing than the way those words sounded on Bastian's lips—like they'd written the speeches together and he'd signed off on every word.

"They've had five hundred years to perfect the veggie burger," Bastian said suddenly.

"And?"

"And it's fucking delicious."

She laughed again. Her hand flew to her mouth to muffle the sound, but this time, Bastian smiled.

"Stanley Park," she said. "In Vancouver. Is it…?"

"Vancouver was her hometown."

"I know. Is the park back? The trees, the seagulls?"

Bastian shook his head, and her heart sank. Stanley Park was no more. "There's a marker for where the entrance used to be. But you can't really call it a 'park' when all of Metro Vancouver is now a protected sanctuary."

Sloane put her face in her hands, overcome. He said it was all just as she'd seemed to hope. She said it was more than she could have hoped. There was a flicker of recognition in his eyes, and for a moment, he looked at her with what appeared to be total lucidity, and in that lucidity, the old longing.

It didn't last. Bastian's vision clouded over, and he looked away. "Don't go thinking everything's perfect or that there aren't threats to the new timeline. People think her father is the problem because he's so vocal, but he's the least of my worries."

"Her father…"

"Not her biological father," he said off her look. "I mean Harry Burrows. In the new timeline, the Marymaker movement became the primary belief system in Southeast Asia. The Khmer Rouge never came to power, and the

Cambodian Genocide never happened. So, the guy has nothing to talk about now. He tries, but his knowledge is irrelevant."

Sloane pictured Harry pacing around the house in a fury as all his talks got canceled. She felt a strange mix of pity and delight that only Simon would understand. Shit—did Simon think she was dead, too? Bastian must have a phone. If Sloane asked Bastian to call Simon, and if Bastian heard Simon talking to Sloane, maybe Bastian would believe Sloane was real.

"Burrows is one of the most vocal on the extremist talk shows. But there are others. A group that calls themselves the Un-Makers. They want to go back in time and undo what Sloane did."

"How could they 'undo' what she did?"

"Discover Fred's identity, find me, and hold me hostage or torture me unless I send them back in time to before she flew over Toulon."

"Saffron wouldn't let—"

"They don't know that. They think Saffron is AI that I control."

"—and even if they could go back, what are they going to do? Try and stop her from flying?"

"They don't just want to stop her. They want to kill her. Which would change the outcome of the Mission, but not the outcome for Sloane. Whether it's the Unmakers or the Catholic Church, she still ends up dead."

"She's not dead. She was Mary, and Mary is immortal. Mary disappeared into the sky and went back to Heaven."

"No, she didn't."

"Yes, I did!"

Bastian glared at her. He said he'd read everything, and there was nothing in any of the history books about Mary disappearing into the sky. Every single account from France to the Ottoman Empire contained the same story: the Catholic Church had Mary, who was pregnant with the Christ child, hung and burned on the gallows in Toulon. Just like the Romans fifteen hundred years prior, the Catholic Church was responsible for the death of Christ.

Sloane's head started to pound. She stood up, massaging her temples as she paced along the platform. If Mother Mary had disappeared into the sky, the Church could have perpetuated its claim that she was not Mother Mary at all but an evil *sorcière*. But if Mother Mary was burned on the gallows after having her angel wings brutally torn from her body, the Church had not only murdered the Mother of God—they'd killed the Christ child growing inside her. The martyrdom of Mary would have convinced people in the past to condemn the Catholic Church and support the Marymaker cause. But it had also convinced everyone in the future, including Bastian, that the 23rd Hero was dead.

Bastian said historical accounts were consistent on the details of her death, but there was divergence on the pregnancy. She stopped pacing and looked at him. He looked at his hands. The believers said that when they ripped her wings from her body and murdered her, she was six months pregnant with the Christ Child. Other accounts said the belly was a prosthetic.

Sloane pulled her robes taut to enhance the outline of her bump. "Do you think the pregnant belly was a prosthetic?"

Bastian's face darkened. He shook his head no.

Sloane moved closer. He flinched, but she stood her ground.

"How long has she been gone?"

"A long time."

"How long?"

"Six months, three weeks, four days, and eleven hours," he said.

She stifled a sob to learn he had counted the hours. "Six months doesn't seem very—"

"Six months, *three weeks*, four days—"

"—still not a very long time if you promised to wait for someone forever."

"It's an eternity living in a time when you don't exist."

She got down on her knees in front of him. She said this wasn't a time when she didn't exist. He said she only existed in the past now, and no matter how many times he opened the portal, Saffron wouldn't let him go to her.

"I'm not in the past. I'm here now."

Bastian must have noticed her tears because he slammed his eyes shut as if fighting back his own. He said no. He said she was dead. The words sounded like he'd been coached to say them, over and over again, by the people who cared about him most. Sloane was dead, and so was Enkh, and it was his fault, and he would never forgive himself.

He stood and limped toward the treehouse.

"Wait."

He stopped at the base of the steps and peered down the mountain toward the great metropolis, which used to glow with millions of twinkling lanterns. Now, the city was cast in shadow, and the only lights that blinked on were the evening's first stars in the darkening sky. Halfway up the stairs to the treehouse, Bastian turned, his movements stiff as he lowered himself onto a step. Sloane said she had one more question. When he finally looked at her, she asked if she could give him a hug. Or, if that was too much, maybe just hold his hand.

He said no. They'd tried that before, and it never worked.

Conjuring the strong, firm voice she'd used as Mary, she told Bastian that this time would be different. This time would work because this time, she was real.

He placed his hands beneath his legs. "If you touch me again and I don't feel anything, I'll. . ."

"Let me try. If it doesn't work, I promise not to haunt you anymore. I promise to leave you in peace."

Bastian started taking long, deep breaths. Sloane remembered the day she'd accused him of cheating on his wife with Debbie, and how he'd stormed out of the examination room. With a few deep breaths, his anger had dissipated like incense in the wind. What she had seen in him was a man who had complete agency over his body, his emotions, his spirit; a man who had mastered himself. What she saw now was a man without agency. No matter how many times he exhaled, he couldn't stop trembling.

"If you really mean it, then fine," he said. "One more time. I'll feel nothing, and you'll leave me alone."

"Deal."

She sat on the step beside him, leaving a few inches of space between them. Through the scent of his unwashed skin, she could still detect his essence of pear, cedar, and salt. A whisper of the sea. She said she wanted to put her hand on his. After a long pause, Bastian removed his hand from beneath his legs. He gripped the step between them as if bracing himself for the devastation of nothing. Sloane placed her hand next to his on the step, sliding it over the weathered teak until their fingers touched.

A shock passed between them. They both flinched, but Sloane was quick to press her hand on top of his and hold it there. She asked if he could feel that, suddenly terrified he'd say no.

Bastian cried out. His head fell onto his chest, and he wept. Sloane embraced him with all her strength, squeezing and rocking him so he could be sure she was there in the flesh. When his sobs had subsided, she cupped his face and waited for him to open his eyes. Finally, he did. "It's really you," he said, touching her like she was a wax figure in a museum come to life. "I'm sorry. God, I'm so sorry, I thought..."

"It's okay," she said, sobbing so loudly they both laughed.

"It's really you."

"Me, but not just me."

"You, but not you?"

"Me, but not *just* me."

She pressed his hand to her belly. When he felt the baby kick, he pulled away.

"He's saying hi," she said. "He's happy to finally meet his father."

Bastian covered his face with his hands, and she held him again as he keened.

THE TREEHOUSE WAS FILLED WITH history books and sixteenth-century documents that Bastian had scoured obsessively in Sloane's absence. He cleared a path to the bed, swept a stack of musty manuscripts off the mattress, and bid Sloane lie down. He sat on the floor and waited for her to fall asleep, ignoring Sloane's pleas to join her on the bed. Throughout the night, she woke and begged Bastian to get some sleep, but he refused; he was afraid that if he fell asleep, he'd wake up and she'd be gone, and her return would have been nothing but a dream.

The next day, Sloane convinced Bastian to eat some soup, and he finally fell asleep on the loveseat. After an hour, he awoke in a panic, screaming her name, and she held him and rocked him until he fell asleep in the fetal position with his head in her lap. Through the scent of his unwashed skin, Sloane could detect blood, incense, and the bishop's breath, as if she'd brought the church through the portal with her. She stroked Bastian's tangled hair, batting away memories of the bishop's painful grip around her chin, his hand at her throat, the thin, hard stub of his penis against the back of her thigh. When she managed to shove those memories into the closet of her mind, visions of Enkh spilled out in their place; the handle of the bishop's dagger sticking out of his back, the crimson blood seeping through his white undershirt, the inexplicable peace behind his eyes just before he closed them for the last time. If only he'd told her sooner. If only they'd had more time! But just like her mother, the father she'd never known had revealed himself in the same breath he'd been lost to her forever.

On the third day, Sloane sat Bastian on a stool in the shower, trying not to stare at his unrecognizable body. She washed his hair, applying half a bottle of conditioner to the tangled, knotted mass. She washed his chest and arms and back, scrubbing as vigorously as she dared, afraid she might break him. Soon, the only place she hadn't washed was the part of him she'd been dreaming of since she'd left, but she hesitated, afraid of what it would do to him—or to her—if he wasn't aroused by her touch. She moved his hand between his legs and turned away so he could wash himself, feeling farther away from him now than she had from five hundred years in the past.

After the shower, she sat him on top of the toilet and shaved off his beard, trying not to cry as he looked more and more like the lover she remembered. Next, she set about the monumental task of picking out the tangles in his wet hair. While she worked, she talked, telling him everything that had happened to her from the moment she'd landed in the alleyway in Toulon. If Bastian knew where she'd been and what she'd been doing every minute she was away, he could make her memories his own and forget the pain of thinking he'd lost her for good. When she got to the part where she met Zacarie, she ignored the knot in her stomach and recounted the awkward circumstances under which she and Zacarie had kissed (or nearly kissed), categorizing each encounter as intentional or unintentional, welcome or unwelcome, initiated by Zacarie or initiated by her.

"How mad are you?" she asked, setting the comb on the sink.

Bastian stood up and stretched his leg, massaging his bad knee. When they caught eyes in the bathroom mirror, he shrugged. "You had to do an impossible thing. If you were lonely. . .if you wanted to be touched—"

"I was lonely for you," she said. "I wanted to be touched by you."

He leaned against the bathroom door, sighing. "Jesus, Sloane," he said. "Yeah, I'm mad, especially that this guy would force himself on you—"

"Just a kiss and he stopped right away. Well, I sort of had to push him off me, which is harder than it sounds when you're on top of a horse, but—"

"But you wanted him?

"No!"

"No?"

"I mean, if I did, it was only because—"

"I wasn't there."

"—he reminded me of you."

Bastian's face flushed a concerning shade of pink. They stood there in the bathroom in silence, and Sloane felt she might suffocate under the weight of each heavy, strangling second.

"I wasn't there," he said again. "I got you pregnant and pushed you through the portal into the wrong year. I put the whole world—literally the whole world!—on your shoulders. I sent you off alone to face challenges no other Hero has had to face in the history of the Program. If I'd done that to anyone else, I would have fired me. But I did it to you—the person I swore I'd protect. So no, I'm not surprised you found someone else or wanted someone else. I told you I loved you, but I fucked you over. I promised you I'd never hurt you, but I did."

"You didn't—"

"I failed you, Sloane. It's okay if you think that because that's what I think. And I'm so fucking sorry for that. I'm so sorry."

Sloane hadn't realized she'd been harboring any resentments, let alone those exact resentments, until Bastian said them out loud. At the same time, the act of his acknowledging them made every resentment dissolve. As quickly as she accepted his apology, she found it ludicrous for him to apologize at all.

"You tried to get to me. You tried so hard you broke your bones!"

"But I didn't."

His certainty and command had been one of the things she'd loved about him. Now he had turned that certainty on himself, absolutely certain he was to blame for everything. The memory of the person she'd loved in a previous timeline was as vivid as the stubborn, immoveable person standing before her now; they were two men stranded on opposite sides of a vast, impassable gorge, and she had no tools to build a bridge between them.

"I don't see it that way at all," she said. "And over time, I didn't feel so alone. I wasn't alone. I was connected to—"

"To 'Zacarie.'"

"I wasn't talking about him. And it's not his fault. He was…good."

"Oh?"

"I mean, he was good to me."

"I bet he was."

"Bastian—"

"Is there anything else you want to tell me, Sloane?"

"Like...?"

"Like while we're on the topic of who you did and did not fuck while you were in France. And pregnant with my child."

"My child," she said. "My child, too."

"And mine? Or are we not sure?"

"I told you everything that happened with Zacarie. There's nothing more."

"Everything that happened 'with Zacarie.' So there were others?"

Sloane wanted to slap him, but memories of the 'others' overcame her with such potency that she sank to the wet floor, paralyzed. Bastian stood there, his gaze like ice, waiting for a confession of further guilt. Fine, then. She'd give him what he wanted. She'd tell him exactly how many men had had their hands on her. How they'd dragged her in the shipyard, captured her in the forest, molested her on the horse. She tried, but she could barely get the words out.

"My breasts," she said. "He grabbed me. The whole way there. And the bishop. In the church. He told them to. All of them. Their hands, their hands were everywhere. Inside me. Inside the confessional. Around my throat and he shut the door. I couldn't breathe. They left me there with him. They knew what he would do! My chemise. I felt him. He was going to. He would have. Enkh. If Enkh hadn't been there. My father. Did you know? My real father. And the blood. So much blood."

Bastian was on the floor with her, holding her, his injured leg splayed out to the side like a broken kickstand. She clung to him, crushing his body to hers like she could crush the memories to dust. He tried to rock her, but after a few moments, he pushed away, struggled to his feet, and limped out of the bathroom without a word. Sloane leaped up and followed him out, incredulous. He couldn't be so broken that he would blame her for what happened with the bishop. He *couldn't* be.

She found him next to the bed, commanding the treehouse's AI. The bed disappeared into the floor. In its place emerged a rectangular lockbox the size of a suitcase. A holographic retina scanner materialized in front of the lockbox and scanned Bastian's eyes. There was a soft clicking sound. He opened the lockbox to reveal a row of portable silver Saffron cases lined up like miniature bowling balls. Saffron 4.0, Saffron 5.0, Saffron 6.0…

"What are you doing?"

He chose a case from the center row, removed the glass sphere, and switched it to ON.

"Bastian—"

"I'm going back," he said, heading for the door.

"What? But why?"

"I'm gonna kill him."

"The bishop has been dead for five hundred years."

"I'm going back in time to before he died so I can kill him myself."

"Saffron won't let you."

"She has to!"

Sloane tried to grab the Saffron, but Bastian yanked it back and it fell to the floor, the glass shattering into hundreds of pieces around their bare feet. Bastian glared at Sloane, then stepped over the glass to grab another Saffron from the collection he must have made in her absence.

"Bastian, please!" she said, tiptoeing over the glass to grab his arm. "*Please* stop."

"Let me be!" he said, wrenching his arm away so violently that she stumbled backward, falling on her butt on the loveseat. She instinctively crossed her arms over her belly, afraid of him for the first time. Bastian spun around to find her cowering, and his expression crumbled. "That's right," he said. "You should be scared of me. I did this to you." He threw his arms out, pantomiming the causal link between himself and the terrified pregnant woman on the couch and accidentally knocked over a stack of books piled near the foot of the bed. They tumbled to the floor, tha-rump, tha-rump, tharump. When the last few books in the stack didn't fall, Bastian kicked them to finish the job. Tha…rump.

"You were almost raped. You were seconds away from being hung and *burned* to death, and I—"

"But I wasn't," she said. "I wasn't."

"—and it's my fault! I pushed you into the portal into the wrong goddamn year. If one of my crew had been that sloppy, I would have fired them on the spot."

"I asked you to push me. I asked you because you were strong enough to do it when I wasn't. And will you stop saying it was the wrong year? It was the perfect year—we just didn't know it at the time."

He scoffed and turned away, the muscles in his back twitching with tension.

"Everything's okay now," she said. "It's over now. It's all going to be okay."

"How can you possibly say that? I won't ever be able to touch you again. You're alive, you're actually here, you're actually real, and I can't even touch you."

"You *can* touch me. Jesus, I've been waiting three days for you to—"

"Not without giving you flashbacks about the bishop. About that monster."

"That's exactly why I want you to…"

"To what, Sloane."

"I just need the last person to have touched me to be you."

That was it. She knew it as deeply as she'd known she was meant to build the flying machine. Since the moment Sloane was dragged away from Bastian in the shipyard, the hands that had grabbed or restrained or caressed her had been the bishop's, or Zacarie's, or a priest's, but never Bastian's. She felt tainted by all the touch, by all the skin on her skin that hadn't been his. She needed Bastian's hands, Bastian's mouth, Bastian inside her. It was the only way they could find each other again, remember each other, remember how, when they were together, the body became a portal to the soul.

Bastian issued a command to the AI. The lockbox flipped back into the floor, and the bed rose silently in its place. Sloane scooted to the edge of the loveseat, hoping he'd invite her to join him on the bed, but he sat down and stretched out his injured leg without so much as a glance her way. She slumped back on the loveseat, defeated.

He said she was assaulted. Almost raped. She needed time.

"Fuck time. I don't want time. I'm so sick of past and future and years and months and waiting. You, waiting for me to come back. Me, waiting to return. All the years and centuries between us. I don't want time. I want you. Right now."

When he was quiet, she asked him, begged him, to make love to her. He shook his head, every *no* a splinter in her heart. He laughed suddenly, a sad, breathless thing that burst past his lips, surprising them both. From the bewildered look on his face, Sloane concluded that the real reason Bastian had been pushing her away since she'd returned had finally become apparent to him, and it had nothing to do with what had happened to her in the church. "I can't make love to you," he said. "I don't remember how."

It was an opening. A fault line that ran along his heart, begging to be cracked open so the light could be let in. "I remember," she said. "I can remember for both of us."

"You remember everything." He said it as if recalling some passage he'd read in one of the history books spilled across the floor.

#   #   #

"The first night we were together," said Sloane, "you kissed me. Right here on the loveseat. The phone rang, and you threw it out the skylight and said it was the best idea you'd had all year. You said you hadn't yet told me the truth because the truth was you were in love with me. You undressed me, and you looked at me—no one had ever looked at me that way before. You said that somehow, I'd managed to be even more beautiful than you'd imagined."

Sloane slid off the loveseat, knelt at Bastian's feet, and put a hand on his leg. He didn't look at her, but he put his hand on top of hers and left it there.

"You made me feel like I belonged with you because I was just as beautiful as you. You, who could have had anyone in the world, and you chose me. You were too brilliant to choose wrong, so I must have been good enough for you. I must have been. And I was so surprised I could believe that about myself, that I actually deserved the most wonderful person I could imagine. Just to touch you would have been enough for me. But to have you touch me, and to believe I was worthy of your touch? It was everything. More than everything because it was just the beginning. I had no idea who I was yet or what I was capable of. But because of you, I had a starting point. I realized that what I'd believed about myself my whole life had been wrong."

Bastian lifted his eyes to meet hers. In them, she saw the slightest flicker of recognition—the possibility that an ember somewhere deep inside him had been left burning. Just the possibility was enough to stop her breath. *Oh, please*, she thought. *Please come back to me.* "When you were inside me, it felt so good it hurt. And at first, you just stayed there. Remember? And I wasn't sure why, but I thought it was because you had waited so long to be inside me you couldn't bear to pull away. Not even an inch."

The corner of Bastian's mouth twitched in recognition. He closed his eyes and opened them again, tipping his head in a barely perceptible approximation of a nod, as if to say, *that's exactly why I didn't pull away.*

"And you made love to me, and you knew exactly how to touch me, like my body was made for you, and yours was made for me. We came together. The way you sounded when you came…I remember thinking I wanted to hear that sound every day for the rest of my life."

She asked him if he remembered, but she knew it didn't matter if he remembered or not. It didn't matter if he was broken, or if she was, or if they were different versions of who they used to be. It didn't matter because her love was a wellspring bubbling up from inside her, bottomless and infinite, washing over him, both hims, every version of him. She was made of love, and it would always be enough.

For the first time since she'd returned, Bastian seemed to notice her lips. "I remember," he said, his gaze falling to her chest. Encouraged, Sloane lifted her T-shirt over her head and tossed it onto the floor. "I remem—" Bastian stopped, narrowing his eyes. Sloane glanced at her breasts, which had swollen two cup sizes with the pregnancy.

"You wouldn't remember these," she said. "They're…new."

"Huh."

She noticed the crotch of his pajamas grown taut, and he followed her gaze. Sloane worried he would try to cover himself, but Bastian merely stared into his lap for a moment, as if he wasn't entirely sure what was happening down there.

"There are as many possible versions of a single moment in time as there are stars in the sky," she said. "Remember? It's as true now as it was then. The fact that you and I are in the same timeline, sharing the same moment in time, is nothing short of a miracle." Bastian's eyes lit up like there was a flame he'd forgotten he'd left burning—a flame that had always been lit for her. She pressed her lips to his. She kissed his cheeks, his jaw, his neck, his mouth again, tracing his lips with the tip of her tongue. He opened his mouth, shyly responding to her tongue with his, and in the next breath he was gasping as if he was drowning and only her mouth could save him. "My love, my love, my love." He said it over and over, pulling her into his lap and holding her so tightly she had to remind him to be careful of the baby. Bastian pulled back, alarmed, and she promised him she was okay, that everything was fine. And it was, until they started kissing again, and in a moment of passion, Bastian dug his nails into the raw, open flesh on Sloane's back.

She yelped. He let go, wide-eyed, and she told him she had a sunburn from the jungle. Then she shoved her breasts in his face, hoping to distract him; if he saw the wounds she'd given herself in the church, he'd want to stop, and if they stopped, they might never start again. But he lifted her off his lap and discovered the markings from the bishop's blade.

He gasped. She said it was nothing.

He bent her over the bed to inspect her back, gingerly touching the skin around the gashes. "Jesus," he said. "Your wings." He started kissing his way down her back, charting the outline of the wounds. He said she was the most beautiful woman in the world. His voice broke, and Sloane felt hot tears dripping onto her back, the salt stinging her raw skin.

"It's okay," she said, pushing her shorts off her hips. "Everything's going to be okay once we—"

"Sloane, we don't have to—"

"Can you just…?"

Bastian resisted. She pleaded, and he finally helped her slide the shorts down. But when the air hit her naked backside, she tensed, flooded by the memory of the bishop lifting her chemise in the confessional. Bastian paused mid-tug, sighed, then started pulling the shorts back on, saying it didn't have to be now. It was obviously too soon for her, and maybe it wasn't good for the baby, anyway. Sloane said the baby was protected by the uterine wall and even *he* couldn't break through that. She said she hadn't saved the freaking world and traveled five centuries back to him to have to beg for it.

"Sloane—"

She massaged him over his pajamas, and his protests were soon replaced by the soft, breathy sounds of acquiescence. When they were both naked, Bastian kneeled behind her as best he could, and Sloane drew him between her legs. God, he was big. Bigger than the bishop for sure, but longer and thicker, too. The bishop had poked her in the thigh like his dick was a pencil tip and he was trying to puncture her.

No.

No, no, no.

She tried to stuff the memories down, but the church swept over her again like a wave that had retreated only to gather its strength and crash harder onto the shore. She drew Bastian against her, but he must have sensed her terror because he kept pulling away. The anticipation had been the most terrifying part—the emptiness whose inherent threat was being filled with something, and that something was the bishop; at any moment, he would enter her. Bastian had to get there first, to take up space, to fill her completely so the memories couldn't. "Please do it now."

He bent over and kissed her. Told her he loved her. Pressed himself inside until he could go no further. There he stayed, pulsing but still, filling her completely, pushing the memories of the bishop away and banishing them to a dark closet in the deepest recesses of her memory to which she'd throw away the key. He kissed her again and told her she was safe. She would always be safe now. He said it was him. It would always be him, it would never be anyone else, and he was sorry, so sorry, for not being there to protect her.

She kissed him back, moving against him, and he responded in kind, turning every cell in her body into a womb, every womb into a rose blossoming to receive him. His breath quickened, and the moans that resonated in his chest echoed through the treehouse. They were the sounds of losing her and finding her again, the sounds of the death of her death. All the memories of all the nights of wanting Bastian, or Zacarie, or Zacarie to be Bastian swept over her. They had come to serve as midwives, to guide Sloane and Bastian through their chance to be reborn, together. She felt as if her bones were melting. She was catapulted upward and out of herself until she was suspended in ecstasy, everything falling away except the sensation that seemed to be the truth of her reality, and anything outside of that sensation, merely a dream. At the height of the peak, she waited for a descent that, second after glorious second, refused to come. There was only her and him, and then there was only her, and then even Sloane fell away and there was only Mother; the never-ending, nameless love.

There were aftershocks. Sloane came to lying on her side with Bastian's arm draped protectively over her belly. Their bodies twitched and shook, and it made them laugh. When she gazed into his eyes, she felt the familiar satisfaction of fixing a broken thing. They dozed for a few dreamy minutes until she realized what she'd forgotten to tell him. He asked if Zacarie was the real father of her child. Sloane almost cried with relief to see he was joking.

"When I first came to Basecamp, I brought this letter my mom had written to me and Simon before we were born. I couldn't understand it because she wrote it in Khmer, but I brought it anyway. And a few days after I found out I was in the wrong year, I found the letter again, tucked inside the orange dress, the one you didn't want me to wear in the shipyard, remember? Because of LORI, I could read it."

"What did it say?"

"It basically said, I am love. And so are you. And if either of us goes away, the love remains."

Bastian smiled. "If either of us goes away the love remains."

They lay with their foreheads pressed together, hands on her belly, waiting to feel the baby move.

WHEN SLOANE AWOKE HOURS LATER, Bastian was gone. She blinked in the twilight, her eyes searching for his form on the bed next to her, but all she saw was the empty mattress and treehouse wall. She peered around the room, from Saffron's gallery to the kitchenette. Books, books, and more books. No Bastian. Her heart started to race.

"I'm here."

She sprang up in bed and saw him sitting on the floor with his injured leg propped on a cushion. He was dressed in an embroidered, cream-colored kurta and matching silk trousers—formalwear that was far too exquisite for the treehouse. On the floor beside him was a small, silver case. When Sloane spotted it, she frowned. Bastian said even if he wasn't there, she would be okay. He said if either of them went away, the love remained.

"But that doesn't mean either of us *has* to go away," she said.

"My thoughts exactly."

His face was pink and flushed, his skin luminous, his eyes cutting through the weariness of the past months to sparkle with new life—life, but also longing. "In fact, I've been thinking about this for a long time, and I sort of think neither of us should go away ever again. From each other, I mean." Bastian scooted toward the bed until he was down on one knee in front of her. Sloane stared at him, suddenly very aware that he was immaculately dressed, and she was completely naked. He unlatched the case he was holding, and the lid popped open. There, set in a soft pile of pink rose petals, was a blue sapphire engagement ring.

Sloane looked from the ring, to him, to the ring.

He said there was something he'd been meaning to ask her, but he'd forgotten until she'd helped him remember. He plucked the ring from the case, and a few rose petals floated to the treehouse floor. He asked if she remembered when he'd told her about the day he'd built her Saffron 2.0. He blushed. Of course she remembered.

"You said you made it for me the day you first saw me in the coffee shop."

He nodded, frowning at the ring as he twirled it between his thumb and forefinger. "What I didn't get the chance to tell you was that after I left the coffee shop that day, but before I made Saffron 2.0, I ran an errand. Picked this up at Cavalier a few blocks away."

Sloane let the memory of the first day they'd met sweep over her. Through the coffee shop window, she watched Bastian turn to her, remembering the defeated way he'd shaken his head—as if he had something important to tell her but couldn't. Until now. She said she knew he'd made Saffron 2.0, but she hadn't realized the other assumptions he'd made that day.

"I didn't assume," he said. "But I hoped."

When she looked at him, Sloane could see the exquisite, unsolvable mystery of their connection, but she could also see herself—she was the silent spring reflected in his eyes.

"I'm yours," he said. "Whether you're Sloane, Mahid, Mother Mary, or someone else. Whoever you are, and whenever you are, I want to be yours, forever—in this timeline, in death, in whatever time we have." Bastian waited, not seeming to realize he was hoping for an answer to a question he hadn't actually asked. Sloane made a 'keep going' gesture, and Bastian blushed a deeper shade of pink. "Sorry! Sorry. Um, Sloane Sophea Burrows. The 23rd Hero. My hero. My love. Will you marry me?"

She remembered the monologue that had gone through her head when she'd first found out Bastian was Fred. How jealous she'd been of the woman she imagined he was married to, never guessing in a million years that that woman could ever be her.

"You're not gonna make me get butt implants, are you?"

Bastian laughed. He reached around and cupped her ass. He said no, they were good there.

"You know, I don't even know your birthday," she said.

"September 7th. Is this a horoscope thing—?"

"We've only been together for six months. And for 5.999 of those months, we weren't even together."

"It's been ten years—"

"Thirteen days, if we want to get technical."

"Who wants to get technical?"

"I don't even know your last name."

Bastian's smiled vanished. "You don't have to take my name if you don't—"

"But what is it?"

With a sigh, he climbed up next to her on the bed and sat down, holding the ring between them. But after stumbling over an amalgamation of excuses and disclaimers, he still hadn't told her his surname.

"Don't tell me you're afraid of revealing your true identity to me."

"It's not that. It's just kind of a weird name. I got made fun of when I was a kid."

"What is it?"

"Oh. Um, it's Merkatoria."

"Sebastian…Merkatoria?"

"Sebastian James du Merkatoria," he said. "My family only uses the *du* on legal documents, but technically it's—anyway, never mind. Like I said, you don't have to take it if you—"

"Is it French?"

"Kind of," he said, giving her a strange look. "It's actually Basque. On my mother's side. We can trace our ancestors all the way back to—"

"—to the sixteenth century," she said.

They stared at each other.

"What?"

"Nothing," she said. "It's just that I think I may have been… acquainted…with your great, great, great, great, great, great, grandfather."

Zacarie must have found love. Zacarie must have had children, and those children had had children, and their lineage had survived across the centuries until this moment, when the latest descendent in the patrilineal line was kneeling before her, asking her to be his wife. No wonder she'd been so attracted to Zacarie. He hadn't just looked like Bastian; he'd been carrying the seed that would beget the seed that would someday beget her love.

Bastian cleared his throat. "I would love to learn everything there is to know about my great-great-great-great grandfather."

"Great-great-great-great-great-*great*—"

"*After* you answer my question."

"Sorry! I just want to make sure I'm getting all this straight."

"If you say yes, we'll have the rest of our lives to get it all straight."

She was the spring. It would remain true whether Bastian was her husband or not. Whether he was in the same century or not. Even whether he was in love with her or not. She didn't need him. But sweet Mother of Mary, how she wanted him.

"I think my answer is pretty obvious."

"I didn't want to assume," he said. "But I hoped."

She said yes.

Bastian slid the ring onto her finger. Sloane reached for him, and her lips met his in a kiss that felt like the last kiss between the last two humans at the end of the world.

But it wasn't the end. It was the beginning of a new world. A world worth remembering.

Epilogue

SLOANE DU MERKATORIA WAS STANDING on the rooftop terrace of a tropical island villa watching the sun sink over a calm, cerulean sea. Vast sheets of water migrated toward shore and broke over the sand, foaming around the feet of the figure on the beach far below. Eleanor paced along the waterline, satellite phone to her ear, kicking at the surf. When she reached the far edge of the sand, she turned toward the house and scanned the terrace until she spotted Sloane. She gave a quick wave, too distracted by the phone call to bother with the exaggerated military salute she typically made during these regularly scheduled security checks.

At Poppy's urging, Eleanor had been trying harder to make the 23rd Hero feel more like their guest and less like a captive under house arrest for her own safety. When Sloane grew tired of eating homegrown taro and sugarcane, Eleanor had stuffed grape leaves and soy chicken kababs flown in on solar-powered drones. She gifted Sloane a dedicated plot to plant a rose garden, and when the time spent outdoors failed to result in the 23rd Hero's kidnapping, Eleanor let her wander past the property line and lose herself in the lush jungle for hours at a time. Sloane still preferred the treehouse, the mountains. But she had to admit that being under house arrest on a tropical island had its perks—Eleanor had even allowed her to keep a lover.

As she leaned out over the balcony, sipping the sea air, Sloane felt an electric presence behind her, moving across the terrace in her direction and making her spine tingle with anticipation. The presence drew steadily closer, a magnet seeking its opposing pole, finding it, latching on. A pair of arms found their way around her waist. Familiar lips grazed her neck. Eleanor paused her call long enough to pantomime sticking her finger down her throat to induce vomiting. A tanned, muscled arm reached over Sloane's shoulder and swirled one finger in the air, gesturing for Eleanor to turn around. Eleanor rolled her eyes at the newlyweds and resumed her call, the sound of her voice swallowed by the sea.

"Is Roz asleep?" asked Sloane.

Her husband began fastening the hooks on the harness Sloane was wearing, moving slowly and carefully up her back. "Alona Rose is out like a light," said Bastian, pronouncing their daughter's name with a French accent.

"Where's Poppy?"

"Out by the pool. She has the baby monitor."

"Okay. Hopefully, she'll sleep."

Bastian spun her around to finish fastening her up, his gaze falling to her swollen breasts. "I thought you fed her before I put her down."

"I did."

"It looks like all the milk is still in there."

Sloane grabbed a matching harness for Bastian and slapped it against his chest. "We can't all have rock-hard pecs like you."

Grinning, he shrugged the thing over his toned shoulders, which, like the rest of him, had been restored within a few months of moving to the island. He spent his mornings clearing the land around the house, tending to the yam vines and breadfruit trees he'd planted, feeding the chickens, and milking their goat, Espi 2.0. He was eating again, his appetite for Poppy's cooking rivaled only by Sloane's, who was always ravenous from breastfeeding. Their appetites for each other had also been insatiable—right up until the week before the baby came. It was the time spent together in their marriage bed, along with the farming and the food, that had restored Bastian to his former glory, body and soul.

"Ready to go?" he asked.

"Ready," she said. "Right after you tell me what's wrong."

Surprise flashed across his face and froze into the guilty look she knew so well; it was the look he got whenever she caught him rocking Roz to sleep in his arms instead of letting her fall asleep in her crib like he was supposed to. He forced a smile, his attempt to charm her until she'd forgotten why she'd ever been anything but perfectly pleased with him. "What could possibly be wrong?" he said, gesturing to the idyllic panorama that surrounded them. With its westward-facing glass façade and modern teak design, Eleanor and Poppy's home was surrounded by pristine ocean for hundreds of kilometers in every direction. The temperature here was so perfect they never felt hot or cold but part of the ether, like ectotherms auto-tuning their body temperatures to the balmy days and cool nights. Eleanor had married Poppy, Bastian had married Sloane, the quartet of lovers so blissed out on oxytocin and dopamine it felt as if they might never come down. Baby and mother had not only survived childbirth but were thriving, Sloane's breasts swelling with enough milk to feed triplets, and Roz growing rolls of pinchable fat along her tiny arms and legs. Sloane could feel her connection to Mother Earth more strongly here than she could in the past, perhaps because now she was a mother, too. She finally felt recovered enough from childbirth to have sex again. And tonight, there'd be a bonfire on the beach, husband and wife side by side, dear friends reunited, everyone sharing the same miraculous moment in time under a blanket of stars so bright it put the sixteenth-century sky to shame. And don't forget the veggie burgers.

"I saw you talking to Eleanor on the beach," said Sloane. "That's a lot of sand kicking for someone who claims nothing is wrong."

He eyed her for a moment, deliberating, his reluctance sparking a surge of irritation within her. Ever since Roz had been born, Bastian had hesitated to tell her the things he and Eleanor whispered about in remote corners of the villa or at the far end of the beach. He said the 23rd Hero had worried enough for one lifetime, and that it was his turn to worry, now—his chance to protect his new family and the new timeline. Bastian wanted his wife to relax, to rest, to enjoy this time with the baby without the weight of the world on her shoulders. "Besides," he was fond of saying, "if you worry too much, the cortisol will contaminate your breastmilk, and Roz will grow up with crippling anxiety."

Why couldn't he understand that this timeline was *her* timeline, and that turning her back on the new world she'd created felt as impossible as turning her back on Roz? If there were threats to the new timeline, Sloane had a right to know. Hadn't the 23rd Hero proven herself worthy of Bastian and Eleanor's elite, top-secret circle? Wasn't she an insider by now? How could she have proven herself so irrefutably only to get relegated to the world of breast pumps and teething toys while Bastian got to raise his daughter *and* make decisions about the future of the planet? Besides, the secrecy was getting old. When he'd first revealed himself as Fred, she'd been excited to feed on a steady diet of his secrets. But now that they were married, any secret between them felt like a wall she had to knock down and pray he wouldn't rebuild.

They'd cycled through this conversation—argument—*conversation*—so often in recent weeks that their silent standoff had barely begun before she knew she'd won. Bastian's placid expression vanished, and the truth, whatever it was, settled into the lines around his mouth, aging him a decade in the space of a breath and filling Sloane with regret—why did she insist on giving him such a hard time when he was always just trying to protect her?

"They found the treehouse," he said, sending a prickle of fear up the back of her neck.

"Who's 'they'?"

Bastian leaned over the railing, peering at Eleanor as if he could read her lips. "We don't know, exactly. Someone looking for Saffron."

The Un-Makers want to go back in time and undo what Sloane did. That's what he'd told her the day she'd returned from the past: the Un-Makers wanted to discover Fred's identity, find him, and hold him hostage unless he sent them back in time to before she'd flown over Toulon. They didn't just want to stop her—they wanted to kill her.

Bastian withdrew his iGlass from his pocket and projected footage from inside the treehouse. Sloane watched, aghast, as her favorite place on earth was torn apart. Half a dozen figures moved about the space with robotic precision, flipping over the mattress where they'd first made love, shaking out the pages of the books she and Bastian had left behind.

"When was this?" she whispered.

"A few hours ago," he said.

They smashed floorboards and spelunked down the secret air tunnel that had connected the treehouse to Basecamp in the previous timeline. They discovered Saffron's lockbox beneath the bed and opened it in seconds using unidentifiable tools that appeared to be made of pure light. Finding the lockbox empty, they hurled it across the room, where it smashed against the wall that used to display Saffron's gallery.

"I don't understand," said Sloane, trying to keep her voice from trembling. "I know that after I went back, satellites changed, and the netting no longer worked to hide your location. But you said the engineers had the Shield ready as a backup. The Shield blocked the treehouse from view the same way it hides us here. Anyone flying past or sailing by or looking at satellite footage sees nothing but ocean. To anyone looking, there *is* no island, no villa, no us."

Bastian stopped projecting but kept his gaze trained on the rattan rug beneath their feet. "It was chaos after you left," he said, more to himself than her. "Must have been a good twelve hours before we noticed the glitch with the netting. Another eighteen before we got the Shield up and running."

"So, during that window of time you were exposed, satellites captured footage of the treehouse, and these guys found the footage?"

"That's what Eleanor thinks," said Bastian. "I think we should consider an explanation that's…closer to home."

Her memory surged with snippets from their first night in the treehouse, when Bastian had first ushered her into his world of secret identifies and blown covers. "What about the people who know you're Fred?" she asked. "The people you paid off to keep quiet?"

"They're under surveillance," he said. "We monitor every call they make, every message they send. They're incentivized to keep quiet because if they don't, we take away their cash flow. I think it's more likely that someone from the crew led these people to the treehouse through the tunnels."

"What?! Why?"

Bastian shrugged. "People's reactions were mixed when the Program shut down. Astounded by your performance. Relieved for the planet. But nobody thought you'd perform them right out of a job." Sloane reached for his hand, and he looked up, his gaze heavy with hurt. "Or maybe it all started before the shutdown," he said, "and we had a double agent in our ranks all along." Bastian said jealousy was the main reason he hadn't wanted Sloane playing poker with Johnny that night—but not the only reason. "He was clean before we hired him during the 3rd Hero's training, but he made some questionable acquaintances after he joined the crew. We had an eye on him."

Memories of Johnny rushed forth, and she scanned every frame, searching for signs of betrayal. But all she saw was a buff Australian bro who hadn't been quite as professional as she'd thought. "Oh, my God," she said, slowing down a memory from the training room. She watched Johnny scan her body with a gaze that, at the time, she had interpreted as clinical. "He *did* want to get in my pants."

Bastian smirked. "Everybody did."

She rolled her eyes but couldn't help blushing. "Everybody else kind of faded into the background," she said. "All I could see was you."

Bastian drew her into his arms and rested his chin on top of her head. "I'm so fucking lucky," he said.

"We're lucky," she amended. "Whether it was Johnny or someone else, they didn't find anything in the treehouse, right? All the Saffron units are locked up here, and the only copy of her code exists in my memory. And even if they got their hands on a Saffron, she'd never let them pass through the portal—not if they wanted to undo everything she's done to save us."

"You're right," he said. "As long as no one develops their own time travel technology to sabotage your Mission in the past, we'll be fine."

Sloane's body went rigid.

"Forget I said that."

"But is that possible?"

The bamboo chimes strung across the terrace plinked in the wind.

"*Bastian,*" she said, pulling back to look at him. "Is it possible?"

"Only Enkh knows," he said, flooding her mind with memories of her father. She pictured him on the floor in the church, embracing his grim fate with all the grace and acceptance of the enlightened master he was.

"I miss him," she said.

"I do, too."

"And Simon. Are you sure I can't call him? I hate that he thinks I'm dead. Especially if there's a chance I might actually be dead soon."

"That's not funny," said Bastian. "And no, I'm sorry. Not until we're a hundred percent sure it's safe for him and us. The agents protecting him think you're dead, too. We have to make sure they're on our side."

"There are sides now?"

Bastian hesitated, biting his lip. A gust of wind rushed in from the east, urging them toward to the edge of the roof, where the open sky and endless sea beckoned. It was her Mother calling her back from the unknowable future into the knowable now. Sloane was with Bastian in the same timeline, sharing the same moment in time, and it was nothing short of a miracle. She was suddenly filled with the deep certitude she'd felt the first time she'd leaped off a cliff in Provence in a pair of homemade wings—Saffron *had* her. Mother Earth would not let her fail. And neither would her father, who hovered around her sometimes, an invisible wave of peace that swept through her, cleansing away fear, leaving pure love in its place. If Enkh could confront his violent end with perfect grace, surely his daughter could face the intangible future with the same.

"Whatever happens," she said, "the love remains."

Bastian squeezed her in agreement, mashing her sore breasts to his chest until she yelped with discomfort. "Sorry!" he said, cupping her over her harness. Despite the tenderness from the recent feeding and subsequent pumping session—not to mention the possible threat on her life—warmth flooded her womb, and she wanted him as badly as she had when she thought she'd never have him.

"That was nothing," she said. "Yesterday, Roz clamped down on my nipple so hard I thought I'd need a crowbar to get her to let go."

"The things moms have to put up with," he said, caressing her. "A baby who treats you like a chew toy." He slid a finger into her cleavage. "A lazy husband." Her traced his thumb across the rise of her breast.

"Lazy?"

"I've only made love to you *once* today. It's pitiful."

"You were up all night with Roz!"

He groaned, admitting he was exhausted.

"You hide it well," she said, eyeing the bulge in his shorts. "I would have guessed you got a full night's sleep."

"I can compartmentalize my exhaustion," he said. "It's a talent of mine."

"One of your many, many talents."

He pressed himself into her, and she could feel the heat and strength of his desire as he kissed the tops of her breasts. "Sorry," he said. "I know these are for the baby."

"The *milk* is for the baby."

"And these are for me?" She sighed as he worked his way up her neck to her lips, kissing her as if they were back in the portal room saying goodbye forever.

Sloane pushed him away, breathing hard. "If we don't go right now, the baby's going to wake up, and Poppy's going to call for me."

Bastian laughed, releasing her. "Just give me a second to deal with this," he said, glancing at his erection. He got down in push-up position and started to pump. She watched him for a moment, mesmerized, flashing on the memory of him doing one-handed push-ups in the training room, back when she wouldn't even let herself hope he might be showing off for her. She shook the memory away, searching for some distraction so she didn't tackle him and rip off his clothes and ruin the proper date they'd been planning for weeks. She grabbed the base of her hang glider, marveling at its weightlessness, the sleek design, the nylon wings that would never tear. A different kind of excitement gripped her, and she lifted the contraption over her shoulders, readying herself for launch, debating leaving Bastian behind, on the ground, breaking a sweat.

"Let's *go*," she said.

"One…more…set," he said, huffing.

"You're already bigger than you were before I left."

"When we're cleared to go back—"

"*If* we're ever cleared to go back to civilization," she said. "And by 'we,' I mean the most wanted man in the world and the most famous woman in history."

"We will be," he said. "Maybe with different identities."

"Maybe with different faces."

"When we go, I don't want any *Zacarie* types walking around with bigger muscles than me."

"Please. We both know you just want to look good if you ever run into Debbie Allen again."

Bastian hopped up and grabbed his hang glider. He gazed at Sloane with a look of such longing and love that for a moment, she forgot to breathe. "Debbie who?" he said. Everything he did every day was for Sloane, for Roz, for their family; every moment of every day was his Mind Map come to life. In the light of the setting sun, his face looked entirely familiar, as if she'd known him across a thousand lifetimes. At the same time, he was new to her in each moment, revealing himself to her, letting her solve the unsolvable mystery of Fred, the man who had kept the Earth alive long enough for her to save it; the hero who'd made Sloane believe she could be a Hero. Nothing surpassed his beauty except the way Sloane felt when he looked at her. And, if she was honest, the way she felt whether he was looking her way or not. Accepted. Loved. At home in the world and in herself.

"How many times have I told you I love you today?" he asked.

"Only seven."

He clicked his tongue. "I'm taking you for granted already."

"I can think of a few ways you can make it up to me."

His eyebrows shot up. "Now?"

She hesitated, letting her gaze linger between his legs, a mischievous grin on her face. Then she jumped off the roof and flew toward the setting sun, soaring over Eleanor as she negotiated with powerful people on the other side of the planet. The beautiful, blue planet that would remain. Eleanor looked up and waved when she saw Sloane, not bothering to cover her tense expression. Sloane looked to her left. Bastian was flying alongside her, and she knew there was nowhere she could fly that he would not come. She looked out over the sea toward the horizon.

She flew on.

Author's Note

THE 23RD HERO IS A work of fiction. I've always thought of this story as a fantasy in the strictest sense of the word, in that it relishes the improbable and the impossible. As the writer of such a story, I was more concerned with plausibility than factual accuracy, though I welcomed accuracy whenever it served the story. And while I was content to build a world that was merely plausible if not perfectly accurate, it was important to me to be aware of the facts I was fictionalizing. To that end, *A History of France* by Joseph Bergin was an invaluable resource. Alice Chen, my tireless fact checker, primarily consulted *France in the Sixteenth Century* by Frederic J. Baumgartner and *A History of Sixteenth-Century France, 1483–1598* by Janine Garrisson. My own travels were also influential to the world of the story. My imaginings of a future Vancouver are based on my trip to that beautiful city in the spring of 2012 and my consultations with colleagues who live there now. Khmer cultural details are likewise based on the time I spent in Cambodia in 2014 and the ensuing conversations and interviews I conducted with Cambodian friends who remain in Siem Reap.

While much of the history in the book is accurate (Verrazzano led France's first expedition to the New World in 1524; King Francis I died in 1547), certain historical facts are fabricated—sometimes partially, sometimes entirely. I played freely with the timing of events, often moving late-sixteenth-century milestones earlier in time to meet Sloane where she landed: the presence of a shipyard in Toulon; the inventions that comprise the 'B objective' of Sloane's Mission; the confessional box Sloane gets trapped in; the use of the term "Huguenots;" all of these appeared closer to the end of the sixteenth century than they do in the story. I fictionalized the Feast of the Assumption, drawing heavily on the English St. John's Feast rather than the French Assumption Day (I needed the bonfires!). I gave the Merkatoria family an unlikely reverence for Mother Mary—as Calvinist Protestants, they probably would have rejected the Catholic devotion to the Sacred Mother altogether. I color-corrected the robes of holy men to enhance the story's themes, turning Enkh's robes from likely burgundy (Vajrayana Buddhism) to less likely orange (Theraveda Buddhism) to match Sloane's fateful dress. I turned the black robes of the Catholic clergy white; throughout so much of Western history, it was the white guys who were the bad guys. The village of Saphir is also fictional and based only loosely on the real French town of Le Castellet. The language spoken by the Merkatoria family is overly simplified so as not to bog down the reader with linguistic complexities, of which there are many: at that time, in Toulon, the Merkatoria family would have probably spoken Maritim, a subdialect of Provençal, which is itself a dialect of Occitan.

Some fictionalized aspects of the story are closer to fact than not. Mahidevran was a real person—a concubine in Suleiman's court who bore him a son and enjoyed his favor for a time. Unlike Sloane's alter ego, Mahid, the real Mahidevran was likely an enslaved Christian who left the sultan's harem when her son was awarded a governorship in another province. The Bible verses in the book are mostly real, though I made some minor edits and selected translations from whichever passages served my purposes best, with Biblehub.com as a primary source.

I hope this mix of fact and fiction enhances the fantasy world of my imagination, and that no one makes the mistake of using this book as historical or cultural reference material.

Oh, and all that stuff about the nature of love? That part's all true.

Acknowledgements

I AM DEEPLY GRATEFUL TO the dozens of wonderful human beings who have helped me bring this story to life. Jason Henderson and In Churl Yo said YES when so many others said no; I am forever grateful. Rebecca Amrhein, Heather Bailey, and Krissy Hien were gentle, encouraging first readers. Mandy Berman dove deep into early drafts and guided me from the fifth dimension back to Earth. Courtney Maum and Megan Records provided superb feedback and ideas on character and story. Erich Maas offered a much-needed reality check on the nature of holograms. Hannah Tinti, Dani Shapiro, and Michael Maren changed my life forever when they brought me to Sirenland, and Team Tinti 2022 offered invaluable feedback and enthusiasm for this story—thank you. My wonderful writing group and dear friends Meg Vorm, Jessica Pearce Rotondi, Veronica Sucholdolski, Samantha Silva, and Karen Masuda all contributed their time, creativity, and feedback on so many parts of this and other stories—you are all my Heroes. Lauren DePino and Alan Caudillo believed in this story before I did, and Elodie Yung helped me imagine it on the big screen. Thank you for your passion and positivity—it's infectious!

Deepest thanks to my dear friend Ratha Suon and his colleague Thoun Siev Thean who helped me with the Khmer language in the book and audiobook. Ratha also fact-checked my memories of my time in

Cambodia and clarified various Khmer cultural nuances—any errors are my own. Thanks to Alice Chen for fact-checking everything from Vancouver infrastructure to sixteenth-century cod pieces. Again, historical inaccuracies and errors are mine.

Susan Choi, Courtney Maum, Samantha Silva, Elan Masti, Mandy Berman, Melodie Winawer, and Jessica Pearce Rotondi agreed to set aside their own writing to read mine—THANK YOU. Hannah Tinti, Susan Choi, Giles Anderson, Samantha Silva, and the good people at The Author's Guild all gave sound advice and guidance when I needed it most. Thank you to *Wintermute Lit* and *The Write Launch* for publishing early excerpts from the novel. Thank you, Daniel Ladinsky, for permission to use your gorgeous Hafiz poetry in the book, and thanks to Melissa LaScaleia for facilitating. Thank you, Sharon Bially, Camile Sardina, and the team at BookSavvy for your tireless work connecting this story with its readers. Thank you to Trish Sheppard, Steve Kultgen, and the team at Independent Studios in Milwaukee for your efforts bringing the audiobook to life. Erik Singer, thank you for your kind and expert help with accents and dialects (and for making my French accent sound less like Pepé Le Pew.)

Thank you to my parents, Pat and Margie Voss, for creating the time and space for me to do what I love. Thank you to Emily Hawkins and Sydney Meinholz for looking after my children so I can write. Thank you to the Lovato family for champagne and chocolate. Thanks to Tom and Rebecca for moral support, perspective, and memes. Patrick, Aden, and Prema, thank you for keeping me grounded in what really matters (Legos and Godzilla, obviously.) And finally, thank you to Sloane and Bastian for letting me play puppeteer with your lives—I hope your happy ending makes it all worth it.

About the Author

Rebecca Anne Nguyen (she/her/hers) is a Milwaukee-based writer, playwright, and co-author of the award-winning memoir, *Where War Ends*. Her writing has appeared in the *New York Times, Insider,* and *Slackjaw*, among others. *The 23rd Hero* is her first novel. rebeccanwrites.com.

CASTLE BRIDGE MEDIA RECOMMENDS...

If you liked this book, you might also enjoy reading the following titles from Castle Bridge Media available on Amazon or by order at your favorite book store:

Animal Charmer
By Rain Nox

Austinites
By In Churl Yo

Bloodsucker City
By Jim Towns

The Burning Gem
By Don Sawyer

THE CASTLE OF HORROR ANTHOLOGY SERIES
Volume 1
Volume 2: *Holiday Horrors*
Volume 3: *Scary Summer Stories*
Volume 4: *Women Running From Houses*
Volume 5: *Thinly Veiled: The 70s*
Volume 6: *Femme Fatales**
Volume 7: *Love Gone Wrong*
Volume 8: *Thinly Veiled: The 80s*
Volume 9: *Young Adult*
Volume 10: *Thinly Veiled: Saturday Mournings*
Volume 11: *Revenge*
Edited By Jason Henderson
and In Churl Yo
*Edited By P.J. Hoover

Castle of Horror Podcast Book of Great Horror: Our Favorites, Top Tens and Bizarre Pleasures
Edited By Jason Henderson

Cherry Dark
By R.L. Wilburn

Dream State
By Martin Ott

Dominic
By Lee Guzman

FRENCH DECEPTION
A Forgery in Paris
By Janice Naçourney
A Forgery in Lyon
By Janice Naçourney

FuturePast Sci-Fi Anthology
Edited by In Churl Yo

GLAZIER'S GAP
Ghosts of the Forbidden
By Leanna Renee Hieber

Hellfall
By Jay Gould

Isonation
By In Churl Yo

JAYU CITY CHRONICLES
The Hermes Protocol
By Chris M. Arnone
Necropolis Alpha
By Chris M. Arnone

Junk Film: Why Bad Movies Matter
By Katharine Coldiron

MID-LIFE CRISIS THRILLERS
18 Miles From Town
By Jason Henderson
Lost Angel
By Sam Knight
Ties That Kill
By Deven Greene

Nightwalkers: Gothic Horror Movies
By Bruce Lanier Wright

THE PATH
The Blue-Spangled Blue
By David Bowles
The Deepest Green
By David Bowles

SURF MYSTIC
Night of the Book Man
By Peyton Douglas
Dark of the Curl
By Peyton Douglas

The 23rd Hero
By Rebecca Anne Nguyen

Vinyl Wonderland
By Mark Rigney

Yesterday's Tomorrows: The Golden Age of Science Fiction Movies
By Bruce Lanier Wright

Please remember to leave us your reviews on Amazon and Goodreads!

THANK YOU FOR SUPPORTING INDEPENDENT PUBLISHERS AND AUTHORS!

castlebridgemedia.com